The Rufford Rose

Margaret Lambert

London | New York

Published by Clink Street Publishing 2018

First edition.

ISBN:
978-1-912562-61-9 - paperback
978-1-912562-62-6 - ebook

To my husband and sons Alastair, Matthew and Simon, for their support throughout the creation of this work.

To Joan Tyson and Jo Hudson from Rufford Old Hall who have read every version of the story and lived it with me and without whose knowledge of the house, their encouragement and support my work would have been much harder.

I would also like to include my sincere thanks to all involved at Authoright , to Gareth, Hayley and Faye without whose expert help and guidance this book would still be just a dream.

CHAPTER ONE
Great Harwood
1523

'Where is my brother?' demanded the grim looking woman as she swept in through the main entrance door of the hall, ignoring the small servant boy who was staggering past with an armful of logs.

'My lord is in his private chamber,' replied an older man, hurrying forward.

'Inform him that I am here,' the lady said, drawing off thick leather gloves and thrusting them into the hands of the man.

'I understand that he does not wish to be disturbed.' The steward of the household, for that is who the man was, knew that his lord would not welcome an intrusion at this time, especially from this lady.

She drew herself up to her full height, which was not very much, even in the thick soled boots that she always wore when travelling in winter, and looked at him with steely eyes.

'Do you know who I am?' she demanded.

'Of course, my Lady Kighley, and he will see you I am sure, when he has completed the business he is engaged in. May I offer you refreshment whilst you wait?' He bowed and indicated the entrance to the Great Hall of the house.

'What 'business' can be more important than receiving his sister, his eldest sister?'

The steward coughed nervously, smiled and went on, 'He has his priest with him.'

'Why should that be an impediment? I can wait in another room until his prayers are finished, unless the priest is taking his confession. Come, take me to him.'

'I really must insist …'

'Insist? Insist! How dare you? I will see my brother now. You forget yourself, John Assheton. I could have you thrown out for this, this … insolence.' She made as though to sweep past him but he stood in her way again and she raised an imperious eyebrow at his temerity.

'They are not alone,' persevered the steward. She looked suspiciously at him.

'What are you hiding? Who is with my brother and the priest that I cannot go to them?'

John looked decidedly uncomfortable.

'It is a young … gentleman.'

'What gentleman? Out with it, man.'

'It is his … his son, my lady.'

'His son! He has no son.'

'It is his son, Robert.'

The lady went so red in the face that John feared she would have a fit. She spluttered and fumed, unable for the moment to speak, then her hand flew out and caught John a resounding smack across his left cheek and ear that made him stagger back.

'How dare you call that bastard my brother's son?' she hissed through clenched teeth. 'How dare you? His name is never to be mentioned in this house. Do you hear? Do you?'

'Yes, my lady,' replied the steward, holding a hand to his stinging face.

'I will go to my brother's chamber and I will see him … alone, and that … imposter will be thrown from the house, never to be permitted entrance again. Is that understood?'

'If my lord wishes to see …' began the poor man.

'Is that understood or do you wish me to speak to my brother about your further employment here?'

'No, my lady, I mean, yes.'

With a snort of annoyance she swept past him and across the entrance hall to the private chambers of the family. The steward followed, wishing he could warn his master of his unwelcome visitor. Lady Margery was a fierce opponent, used to getting her own way and a mere steward was not going to stop her now. There was going to be trouble and he wished he could spare his master at a time like this. He was far from well and the physician did not expect him to recover from his malady. Having his domineering sister descend on him in a temper was not going to be at all welcome but there was nothing that poor John could do.

Lady Kighley burst into her brother's private rooms and stood in the doorway glaring across the room at the three men there. All three were looking at her with surprise at the sudden intrusion. The priest was the first to recover and came across the room towards her with the benign smile on his face that he habitually wore when faced with possible trouble. He may be as tall and thin as a reed but he had a core as strong as oak and would not be cowed by this fearsome woman with her mean face and sharp eyes. He sensed a smouldering anger that would burst into full fury if provoked.

'Lady Kighley,' he began, but got no further. She swept past him and made straight for the chair where her brother was sitting, smothered in fur rugs and covers, his feet raised on a stool, his thin hands plucking at the blanket across his lap. Even she could not fail to be moved at the sight of him. She had not seen him since the Christmas celebrations and a distinct change had come over him. He had been ill then with a racking cough but he had still been the devastatingly handsome man he had always been. Now here was an old, old man, thin and wasted, his skin grey and wrinkled as though all the life was being sucked out of him. His eyes were bloodshot and sunken into his skull with dark shadows beneath. His glorious head of hair was thin and straggled across his cheeks from beneath the cap he wore on his head. What she could see of his neck was scrawny, like a chicken's, looking hardly strong enough to hold that once noble head upright. He looked ancient, yet he was not yet even sixty.

'Thomas,' she said, bending down to look into those blue eyes now dulled with pain and weariness. 'What is this? You, ill and no word to me? Who is caring for you?'

'Margery,' he said, his voice thin and rasping from a throat sore from coughing. 'I am well enough. I have faithful retainers. I lack for nothing.' He began to cough and his frail body shook with the effort, a cloth held to his mouth as he tried to clear the irritation that plagued him constantly. When, at last, it ceased, he was gasping for breath, one hand to his chest as though by sheer effort he could still his racing heart. His brow was wet with fever.

'You should be in your bed,' said Margery, taking the thin hand in her own. It was cold as ice. 'Have you seen the physician? He should bleed you immediately. I will send for my own physician. He can treat you better than this.'

'I have been bled regularly but it has no effect. I have had leeches applied, I have been purged and taken draughts and potions until I am sick with them. I have nothing left to fight with, nothing left that can be taken out of me for the curing. I am dying and there is an end to it, Margery. I have made all arrangements necessary and you will comply with them.'

'At least go to your bed. You will be more comfortable.'

'No, no. I cannot breathe unless I sit upright. I live here in this chair now that the coughing is worse. I do well enough though I know my days are numbered.'

'Nonsense,' said Margery, conveying a cheerfulness she did not feel. 'With proper care you will soon be back to your old self, riding out to the hunt, visiting your tenants and dear, dear family.' She put special emphasis on the last word. 'Why, I came to invite you to come to stay awhile with Henry and me. It is long since we spent time together.'

'It was the Festive Season,' replied Thomas, 'and you and that husband of yours could not wait to get away from here. Your attempts to match me up to some woman young enough to be my granddaughter did not go well with me, sister dear.

No, do not deny it. Ever since Grace died thirteen years ago, you have been trying to marry me to someone or other. I tell you, I am happy with my Alice.'

'Then why do you not marry her?' blazed his sister, all pretence of concern gone.

'We are happy as we are. We have three fine children who are strong and healthy.'

'Unlike that weakly son your Grace managed to bear you, I suppose. Hardly surprising he died.'

'Yes,' persisted Thomas, 'strong and healthy, and the eldest stands there beside the fire.'

He pointed to the youth watching this domestic scene from the far side of the great fire.

Margery ignored him.

'You have no *legitimate* heir,' she shouted. 'No one who can take the title when you are gone. No son to bear you sons.'

'I have declared Robert my heir,' Thomas said quietly, a new strength flooding through him as he tackled his sister. 'Father Egbert here has drawn up the necessary papers and it is all recorded legally and rightly. Copies have been made and the papers will be lodged with my Lord Derby. When the time comes they will be read and accepted and there is nothing you can do to change that. Robert will inherit everything, he will be the next Lord Hesketh.'

'Never! Never, never, never! As long as there is breath in my body I will defy your ridiculous claim. That … that *boy* will not inherit something he has no right to, no right to whatsoever. You have nephews who have precedence over a, a … *bastard*.'

'Bastard he may be but he is a far better man than any of your sons or those of your sisters will ever be. I have watched them all grow and I do not like what I see. I would not entrust the Hesketh name and fortune to any of them. Your husbands are all wealthy men. They can provide for their sons and *I will provide for mine,* no matter which side of the blanket they were begot. Now, leave me sister, you tire me with your incessant arguing and pleading. Robert is my heir and nothing will change that.'

'I will say that you were out of your mind when you drew up those papers, that you were mad. I will have what is rightly mine and my family's.'

'You will not. There are witnesses who will swear that I was of sound mind when the papers were written. Desist from this and leave me. I am weary.'

Thomas glared at his sister with all the venom he could muster and with an impatient hiss of rage she swept from the room, knocking a servant boy out of her way as he carried a tray of food to tempt his master. The tray flew into the air and crashed to the ground, spilling food and wine across the floor. Lady Kighley struck out at the innocent youth and sent him to the floor amidst the mess with a hearty smack across his face then marched out of the house, snatching her gloves from the steward who was standing by the main door. In a welter of hooves and flying mud she tore down the drive, her manservant following in bewilderment.

Back in Thomas's room the priest was gently settling Thomas back against the cushions of his chair. The mess outside the door was being cleaned up and Thomas called the servant to his side.

'Did she hurt you, boy?' he asked kindly. The boy, a child of twelve years stood before his beloved master, his face scarlet from the blow and tears threatening in his huge dark eyes.

'Not much,' muttered the boy, his ears ringing.

'Good boy.' Thomas smiled weakly at him. 'My sister has a temper. I have felt her anger more than once as a child, and she was younger than me. The hurt will go and I doubt she will be back. Go back to your work and put it behind you.'

'Thank you,' whispered the boy. He had had worse beatings from his drunken father before he had come to work for Lord Hesketh. Now he had a safe home, good food, a roof over his head and clothes on his back, more than his father had ever given him. He was devoted to his master and would do anything for him, even take a beating from his mad sister.

As soon as the boy had gone Thomas leant back against the cushions and closed his eyes. Father Egbert gestured to

Robert to follow him out of the room but Thomas heard the movement and without opening his eyes, called,

'Robert, stay a moment.'

Father Egbert left them alone. Robert went to his father's side and sat on the low stool at his knee, waiting. Thomas opened his eyes and looked at this fine son of his. So young to leave to face the world, a world that would not accept him readily.

'I know that you will have a struggle to claim what I say is yours but be strong. Names she may have called you but you *are* my recognised heir, you *are* the one I know will do this family proud, not those mealy-mouthed nephews of mine. It is all in writing, as I told her. With Lord Derby's protection you *will* inherit. Make me proud of you Robert. If you have any trouble, go to my Lord Derby. His family have been good friends to this family and I have no reason to doubt that he will champion your cause. I talked to him about it before I had the documents drawn up. There is nothing any of my sisters can do about it.'

'Thank you father, but surely, there will be years before …'

'Robert, I am a sick man, a dying man. I know it and I believe, in your heart, that you know it too. When I am gone you must take your place in the world. It is time, I think, that we had a house that we can be proud of, somewhere where you can build a place that is yours, all yours, not something that you inherit and make do with. Build one to impress all these doubters who would deny you what I say is yours. Do not skimp on size or design. Find the best craftsmen you can, build something to be remembered by. Stamp your presence on our estates. But remember, treat well those who work for you and they will work the better. Always be fair and just. Live your life as well as you can for it is by our deeds in this life that we are judged in the next. I know that I have not perhaps treated your mother as well as I should by not marrying her but we loved each other and we were happy. Take care of her when I am gone. You and your brother and sister have never wanted for anything, have you?'

'No, father. We were well loved always, but father, how can I build such a place. It will take a great deal of money, will it not? Do we have that much?'

Thomas laughed and started another coughing bout but when he had recovered he smiled fondly at this beloved son of his, so young in some ways but so wise in others.

'There will be money enough.' He pointed at the strongbox on the table in the corner where Robert had seen the copies of the will deposited by Father Egbert. 'In there, there is a paper which you must take to Father Abbot at the Abbey of Whalley. Father Egbert will advise you. I have put a little money away for you which will help you realise your house. Do not fear. All will be taken care of.' He laid his thin hand on Robert's head. 'My son,' he murmured. 'I give you my blessing. I love you so much. Remember me when I am gone.'

He felt a tremor pass through the boy.

'Leave me now and send Father Egbert to me. Do not fear, I will see you again nearer the time. Go to your room and pray for my soul.' He lifted Robert's face to him and saw the tears lingering on the lashes. 'Shed no tears. Not yet.' Then he kissed the top of his head and lay back on the cushions, closing his eyes as Robert stumbled from the room.

CHAPTER TWO

Chester 1528

Nobody saw him fall. There was no cry of alarm, no scream of fear, no sound at all until the body landed with a heavy thud on the stone floor of the hall in the middle of the morning on a June day in 1528.

For a moment there was a silence that was palpable, then everyone moved at once, as they converged on the distorted figure in their midst. It was obvious from the impossible angle of limbs and neck, the wide open but unseeing eyes and the growing halo of blood that was spreading about his head that Jethro Milton was dead. Even so, one man knelt by his body and laid his ear to Jethro's chest, listening for sounds of life. Eventually he sat up.

'He's dead,' he announced. 'Couldn't be deader, poor bugger. Neck's broke, I reckon.'

'That and every other bone in his body,' said another. Several heads nodded in agreement. Accidents on a new building were common, especially on such a big building with its towering walls and huge wooden beams high up in the roof. Jethro wasn't the first to die in the building of this Great Hall, nor would he be the last.

'Best fetch the priest,' someone suggested, and ran off, out into the sunlight, heading for the church.

'Who'll tell his wife?' asked another.

'Where's Cuthbert? He should tell her,' said a third.

'Went to fetch a ladder. Said they needed a longer one.'

'I'll go and fetch him.' A youth who was standing near one of the pillars turned towards the door. At the same moment a tall young man entered backwards carrying one end of a long wooden ladder. He was talking to someone outside.

'Mind that pile of wood there. What fool left it in the doorway?' He turned back as he manoeuvred the unwieldy ladder through the doorway and suddenly became aware of the group of people standing in the centre of the Hall. 'What has happened here?' he asked, for everyone was looking at him and there was a strange tension in the air. 'What is it? What are you hiding?' He lowered the ladder to the stone floor and stepped tentatively toward them.

The group parted as Cuthbert approached and he saw the crumpled and broken body on the floor behind them. He instantly recognised the bloodstained tunic of his master.

'No!' he cried in a strangled voice, and flung himself down on his knees beside him. He made as though to touch him then drew back and looked into the face of the man he regarded as close as a father, as well as his master, the man who had taken him in, a bewildered child of eleven and raised him as his own after Cuthbert's parents died. Tears stung his eyes and his face paled as he noted the blood and the awkward angle of the man, the ultimate stillness of death already on him. With a trembling hand he felt for the beat of his heart, held a finger to his lips to feel a breath that would not come. Only then did he put his hand over the face and gently close the eyes for the last time, eyes which had seen and recorded so much in his life, eyes which had watched him as a child and seen the potential in him then nurtured that skill to make him the man he was, the respected worker in wood that he now was. The finality of it all hit like a blow to the heart. Never again would they work together, plan and discuss what they were doing, laugh and joke and be together every day in their work and in the home they shared.

Cuthbert looked up at the faces around him.

'What happened? How did he fall?' he demanded.

'No one saw,' said one of the group. 'We heard the thud as he landed, nothing more.'

'What was he doing?' asked another, and a cold hand gripped Cuthbert's heart.

'It's my fault,' he whispered. 'It's all my fault. We were fixing the carvings in place at the top of the wall and we couldn't quite reach. I told him to wait while I fetched a longer ladder but I met Thomas and talked to him instead of coming straight back. He must have got tired of waiting for me and tried to do it himself. If I had come he would not have fallen. It's my fault he's dead, all my fault.'

'Nay, lad,' said Ned, the old man who had first pronounced Jethro dead. 'I saw you go and it's not above a few minutes since. Jethro was not one to try to do something like that himself; he'd have waited for you. How do you think he reached the age he has if he took risks like that? He was always known for being careful particularly when he was working up high. What did he always teach you, lad? Be careful, especially up them ladders. No, summat else caused him to fall and we may never know what it was. All I can say is he died doing what he loved above all else. He said he'd work until his dying day and he's got his wish. You must never take the blame on your shoulders, lad.'

There was a murmur of agreement from those gathered round but Cuthbert still felt the loss like a physical pain.

'There is summat he would have wanted you to do though,' went on Ned, quietly. 'Go and tell his Mildred what's happened. He'd have wanted her to hear from your lips alone.'

Cuthbert looked at him, horrified.

'No! What do I say?' he said. 'I cannot find the words.'

'You will, lad, you will, but you must go now before someone breaks the news to her sudden like.'

Cuthbert got shakily to his feet. All he wanted to do was get away from this dreadful scene of death, somewhere where he would not see that broken body, the blood, the waste that was imprinted on his eye for ever. But Ned was right. He had to go. He had to be the one to tell her. It was what Jethro would have expected of him.

He turned away, brushing his rough sleeve across his eyes. He would not cry. He was a man, not a child. He had cried bitter tears when his parents died and had vowed he would not do so again, but it was so hard. He went out into the sunlight, stepping over the fallen ladder which he had dropped when he entered just minutes ago. To his surprise the sun was still shining, people were walking about in the street, talking and laughing, unaware of the tragedy that had just occurred only yards away from them. A huge lump grew in his throat, threatening to choke him but he swallowed it down. He would not cry, he would not cry. He must be strong. He must be brave and go and do the hardest thing in his life so far. He had lost one set of parents; was he losing another couple who had become their substitute and whom he loved with all his heart?

Cuthbert made his way with heavy footsteps and a heavier heart to the modest house just off the main street of the town of Chester that had been his home since Jethro and Mildred had taken him in. How was he to tell the woman who had been like a second mother to him that her husband was dead? How was she going to survive now? He knew a little of their personal affairs and he knew that Jethro worked hard and was well respected. They lived a comfortable life with few luxuries. They were never hungry or cold in the winter, their clothing, though plain was of good quality and Mildred kept it in good condition. The house was well furnished because he and Jethro made whatever was needed themselves, but could he and Mildred live on what he could earn? He had completed his apprenticeship but there was still so much to learn. The thought never crossed his mind that he may have to leave Mildred alone whilst he sought work.

He turned the corner by the church and stopped to look across the street, unwilling to take the few steps across to the house and break the dreadful news. He imagined Mildred in the house, working with the young girl, Nell, who was her maid but was treated more like a granddaughter by the couple. What would happen to her now the master was dead? Was another life to be blighted by the tragedy?

Cuthbert took a deep breath, wiped his sleeve across his eyes again, squared his shoulders and crossed the broad street, his heart pounding in his chest. He pushed open the heavy street door which he and Jethro had made together and only hung last winter to replace the old, broken one. It fitted snugly in its frame and swung open on well-oiled hinges. In the narrow passageway beyond he paused again until he heard the murmur of voices coming from the kitchen at the back of the house. Mildred was instructing Nell in the making of pastry, passing on her culinary skills to the girl and for some strange reason he envisaged them standing behind a market stall selling pies and bread to make a living. Jethro would never have permitted it but it may be a course she would have to take.

He stood in the kitchen doorway for several minutes watching the two females. Mildred, a short, well-built woman in her late fifties, her thick grey hair pulled back into a coiled plait on the back of her head, and Nell, the slim thirteen-year-old girl with raven black hair that hung in a thick plait down her back. Mildred was showing the girl how to shape the pastry for the pies, how to put the meat and rich gravy into the shells and cap them before transferring them to the bread oven to bake. A domestic scene he had witnessed many times and which he loved for its peaceful tranquillity, something he was about to shatter for ever.

Mildred suddenly became aware of his presence and turned with a beaming smile on her face, wiping her hands down the piece of sacking she wore about her ample waist to serve as an apron.

'Cuthbert! What a surprise! I did not expect to see you at this hour. Have you forgotten something? A tool or a piece of timber?'

Then she saw Cuthbert's stricken face and paled, clutching the edge of the wooden table with one hand, the other going to her heart, as though the action itself would stop the sudden fear that clutched at it.

'What has happened?' she whispered. 'It's Jethro, isn't it? What's happened?'

Cuthbert moved to her side and held her arms firmly.

'Sit down, Mildred, here, on this stool,' he said, pulling one out from under the table with his foot. 'Nell, a cup of water for your mistress. Quickly!' The white faced girl snatched a wooden cup from the shelf and ran to the bucket of water in the corner. Her hands were shaking as she carried it carefully back to Cuthbert.

'It's bad news, isn't it?' said Mildred. 'Tell me, my boy, tell me quickly. Best that way. Say it quickly.'

Cuthbert knelt on the hard floor and took both her gnarled hands in his and forced the words out through trembling lips.

'There was an accident,' he said. 'Jethro was up the ladder fixing the carving at the top of the wall. He couldn't quite reach so I said I'd fetch the big ladder and help him. I told him to come down, to wait until I came back, but he didn't. He must have tried to do it on his own again and … and … he fell. I don't know how it happened. I wasn't there. Nobody saw. He didn't cry out, the ladder must have shifted or … or he leaned too far, and … he fell. There was nothing anyone could do.'

He felt a wetness on their joined hands and realised that tears were falling unbidden from his eyes. Mildred released one of her hands and laid it on his cheek, wiping the tears away with her thumb with a gentleness he had experienced once before, on the night his father died.

'Don't blame yourself,' she said, gently. 'You know Jethro, always feels he can do a job better himself. He wouldn't blame you, it's not your fault.'

'But … he's dead,' stuttered Cuthbert, fighting for control. There was a tightening of the hand still holding his and a long pause before Mildred said,

'I thought as much. You wouldn't be so upset if he was only hurt. It is God's will, hard though that is to understand. It was his time, he would have said.' She smiled. 'It's the way he would have wanted it. Quickly, no suffering, doing the job he loved. It *was* quick, wasn't it?'

'Yes,' gulped Cuthbert. 'Old Ned was there, said he broke his neck in the fall, it would have been quick.'

'It wasn't the fall that killed him,' said Mildred, unexpectedly, and Cuthbert looked up in surprise. 'No, lad. My Jethro knew he hadn't got long for this world. It was the pains, you see, the pains in his chest. They had been getting much worse recently and he said to me only last week, 'I'm not long for this world, my love. Soon it will be over.''

'He never said anything to me.'

'No, he wouldn't. You see, he didn't want you to worry, to fuss over him. He wanted to carry on as usual for as long as he could. His old father died the same way, pains in the chest for months beforehand, gradually getting worse and more frequent until one day he dropped down dead in the street. Jethro has been having the same pains for nearly a year now, but he hid them from everyone but me, I knew. He had a bad one last night, in bed, and he said he couldn't take many more like it. Well, it seems he didn't have to. It was his heart that killed him, not the fall. I reckon he was probably dead before he fell.'

'That's why he didn't cry out!' Cuthbert had wondered how that could be. It was the natural thing to do for a man in peril, to shout out. Knowing that was what had happened did not help the pain of grief though and he bowed his head over Mildred's hand as the tears came again. Nell was standing by the table still, sobbing quietly and it was Mildred who seemed the strongest of them all. She laid her hand on Cuthbert's head and stroked his hair as he wept, murmuring soft, comforting words.

When his first grief was spent Cuthbert pulled himself upright and looked up at her as she sat quietly and calmly on the stool.

'I am sorry,' he whispered, not trusting his voice to speak clearly. 'If there was anything I could have done, anything …'

'There was nothing you could have done to save him but there is plenty to do now,' said Mildred. 'We must send for the priest and arrange for Jethro to be laid to his rest. The monks will prepare his body.'

'Somebody went to fetch him,' said Cuthbert, 'before I came here. He will be with him now.'

'Then come with me now, Cuthbert.'

Mildred pushed herself to her feet and took off the sacking apron. She reached for the shawl on the peg behind the door and threw it around her shoulders before going to Nell and taking the child in her arms and comforting her. 'Now, come on lass. No need to take on so. You stay here and mind the pies. Don't let them burn, will you? We won't be long. Meanwhile, you clear up all these things, make all nice and tidy, just the way we like it, right? That's it, wipe your eyes. Good girl. We'll talk when I come back.' With a motherly squeeze she left the girl and followed Cuthbert out of the house, closing the door quietly behind her.

They reached the hall just as Jethro's body was about to be laid on a board to be carried to the church. The priest had brought four of the lay brothers with him to carry him and he told them to wait when he saw Mildred and Cuthbert enter. He rose from his knees beside the body and went immediately to Mildred.

'What happened here was a terrible accident,' the priest said.

'Aye, an accident,' repeated Ned, 'nowt more. An accident.'

'It was his heart,' said Mildred, quietly. 'Just like his father. He knew it was bad. Pains, bad pains, but only I knew of them. He must have had them again up the ladder. No one's to blame.'

The priest took Mildred's hands in his and bowed his head to utter a quiet prayer. All those standing by crossed themselves at the familiar words, their heads also bared and bowed in respect.

'Have no fear for him, mistress. We will bear his body to the abbey and prepare him for burial. I will send for you when all is ready and he is fit for you to see again.'

Mildred nodded her head in thanks, unable to speak as she watched the lay brothers gently lift the twisted and broken body of her husband onto the board they had brought with them. Slowly they carried him away and Mildred turned to Ned, whom she had known all her life.

'He was a good man,' he muttered, 'a good man.'

'As you are, Ned. At least he was among friends at the end. He would have liked that.' She turned to Cuthbert. 'Come back to the house when you are ready. You must finish the tasks Jethro was doing. He would not like any job to be unfinished because of him. No, lad,' she hurried on when she saw him about to protest, 'you must do it. For Jethro.' She squeezed his arm and smiled encouragingly at him, then turned to leave. Cuthbert watched her walk firmly out of the hall, back straight, head up, proudly, he felt, for proud of her husband and his work she had been all the time he had known her. She would grieve in private, as was her way.

Completing the work they had been engaged in was the hardest task Cuthbert had ever been asked to do. Jethro had been a perfectionist never satisfied until the last piece of work was in place and of the highest quality he could produce. It was something that he had always instilled in Cuthbert. 'Never accept shoddy work,' he used to say. 'If it is not of your best, you are letting yourself down above anything else. Only the best should ever be allowed for we work to God's glory and praise. Even a simple wooden peg must be worked to perfection for the whole piece could rely on it in the end, just as God relies on every one of us and our place in His great plan. Who knows what the consequences might be if a peg should fail and the joint it holds fall apart. So must we live our lives for we are all part of the lives of those around us and if one fails, we all suffer. No, lad, never ever accept second best, even if it means starting again to get it right.'

As Cuthbert worked with a heavy heart over the following days, those words echoed in his mind time and again. They had worked together for so long now that he knew exactly what Jethro would be saying to him as he completed the carved frieze they had made for the upper walls. Even though it was barely visible from the floor of the hall Jethro would say 'God knows it's here,' and would treat it in the same way he did every job. Somehow Cuthbert got through those difficult early days, the work filling his mind and his time but the day after Jethro was laid to rest he realised he finally had to face up to his future.

CHAPTER THREE

'You must go,' said Mildred, emphatically. 'I will be perfectly all right. Jethro had plenty of money put aside for just such a time as this. Nell will stay with me and we will manage well enough. I have my health, this house and many friends. No, you must think of yourself now. You are young and have your future before you. You must not feel tied to me or to this place. It is time for you to set out on your journey and make your own way in life, but always remember this. If things do not work out there will always be a place for you here.'

It was the same argument that Mildred had been putting forward for several days now, trying to persuade Cuthbert to go and seek work on his own, but she knew that he was torn between leaving her and staying. He felt a strong responsibility for this simple woman who had brought him up and meant so much to him. On the other hand he had heard that woodcarvers were being sought for new buildings being constructed in many parts of neighbouring shires and he was tempted. He was a craftsman after all.

'One more thing,' she said. 'It was always Jethro's intention that you should have his tools. I have no use for them and other craftsmen have their own. You must take what you will need. If there are more than you can carry, then leave them here, they will be perfectly safe until you either return for them, or send for them to be sent on to you, wherever you are.'

Cuthbert was overwhelmed at this generosity. He knew that many of the best tools had belonged to Jethro's father before him and were of the finest quality, as befitted a master craftsman.

There was no great monetary value to them but there was incalculable sentimental value for both Jethro and for him. Just handling the fine wooden handles and imagining the hands that had held and worked them gave Cuthbert the greatest pleasure and he was eternally grateful to Jethro for his generosity.

'I don't know how to thank you,' he said, shaking his head.

'Tools are made to be used, not stored away in old boxes. Jethro recognised that you had a great talent. He said that one day you would make great things with them, you have a gift that must not be wasted, so take them. We had no son to follow in Jethro's place but you are like a son to us and always will be. Take them. They are yours.'

Cuthbert accepted the generous gift gratefully but was still undecided as to where he was going to go when two days later some visitors brought an offer that seemed too good to refuse. The year before Jethro had been asked to make a chest for the Abbey at Chester in which they could store certain precious relics. It had not been very large but he had lavished all his usual care to its making and had asked Cuthbert to decorate it, the wood carving being his special talent. Cuthbert had spent many hours at the work, carving the date onto the front along with the name of the saint in whose church it would be used, then covering the lid and sides with wonderful crisp images of trees and flowers intertwined with small animals and insects, the things of nature that he loved to observe whenever he could. Even Jethro had agreed that it was the best work he had ever done and people who saw it agreed.

'It is truly a thing of beauty,' Jethro had said. 'This is where your future must lie. I have seen few who could better this. It is a rare talent but not always appreciated. People think that just because I can make a door or a window shutter or a milking stool I can also carve the wood like this. I can but not as well as this. You have a special talent, an eye for the detail that brings everything alive. Look at that butterfly. I can imagine it flying away any moment. I only hope that Father Anselm also appreciates it.'

It was Father Anselm who came to them now with another monk who Cuthbert did not recognise. The distinguished looking monk greeted Mildred kindly and accepted refreshment from her on behalf of himself and his visitor. Cuthbert greeted them and then turned to leave them, thinking that it was Mildred that they had come to see.

'Wait, Cuthbert,' said Father Anselm, gently. 'It is you that we have come to see.'

Surprised, Cuthbert turned back to the group.

'Cuthbert, this is one of our brothers from the Abbey at Whalley in the valley of the Ribble.'

'I have heard of your house,' said Cuthbert, wondering what they could possibly want with him.

'My name is Brother John,' said the second monk, so quietly that Cuthbert had to strain to catch the name. 'I have been visiting our Benedictine brothers here at Chester and during that time I could not fail to notice a chest in the Abbey library, a chest so beautiful that it seems to be made from the living creatures which adorn it. The relics within are truly held in a thing of great beauty. Father Anselm tells me that it is you who created such a wondrous piece.'

'I carved the decoration, yes, but my late master built the chest itself. I only adorned it in a way I felt fitting for its place in the Abbey's great library.' Cuthbert found himself speaking as quietly as Brother John. 'I am glad that it gives you such pleasure.'

'It does indeed,' nodded Brother John. 'Father Anselm also tells me that your master departed this life only recently and that you are now seeking your future. I may be able to help you. At Whalley we try to create works of great beauty with which to adorn our Holy church. Would you be willing to travel to our Cistercian house at Whalley with me and meet Abbot Paslew, our Holy Father, for whom we seek out only the best of craftsmen to work to the Glory of God? When I tell him of your work here I am sure he will be eager to employ your great skill in our Abbey.'

Cuthbert was taken aback. Was this meant to be? Could this be the beginning of his work and life away from the town of Chester? It would certainly be the answer to his problem of where to go to seek work and if the life suited him and his work was accepted, it could lead to even greater things. He looked across at Mildred who was smiling broadly at him, her eyes alight and eager. She gave him a quiet nod.

'I thank you, Brother John,' he said, smiling. 'It would give me great pleasure to accompany you.'

When the brothers had departed Cuthbert sought out Old Ned, his father's and Jethro's most trusted fellow carpenter. He knew that the older man had worked at Whalley many years ago before coming to Chester and he was eager to hear what he knew of the Abbey at Whalley.

'Whalley?' said the old man, rubbing his bristly chin. 'A fine place, by the river, a Cistercian house if I remember correctly. Abbot Paslew keeps a good house there, renowned for its wealth. There were many craftsmen of note employed in the great buildings and none more so than in the Church. I never saw such stone carving and woodwork, the floor tiles themselves must have cost a pretty penny, and the screen and altars, why, they were beautiful. There seemed to be no expense spared for the beautification of the whole building. It was a joy to behold, that it was.'

'Do you think there would be work there for me?' asked Cuthbert.

'Why yes, there would. But why do you think of there? There are many other places where your work would be valued. Under this king there are many of the noble families who look to better themselves, and one way is to build finer and finer houses. There is plenty of work if you know where to look for it.'

'I have been asked to go with one of the brothers to meet this Abbot Paslew. He thinks there may be work for me there, in the Abbey church. It could be a new start for me, a chance to visit other places. I have never travelled far from Chester. Perhaps it is time to widen my horizons, see more of the world.'

'Then seize the opportunity,' said Ned. 'Perhaps it is a sign that God's will is for you to serve Him in His place at Whalley.'

So it was that a few days later, his work completed in this great town of Chester, Cuthbert set out with the gentle monk, carrying a few of the tools he now owned in a stout leather satchel. There were too many to carry them all but at least the basic few would help him in his new work, that and the fact that he had been apprentice to Jethro Milton. There were tearful farewells from Mildred and Nell and wishes of good luck from the men he had worked with under Jethro's eye, and as he passed the graveyard where Jethro rested, he said a silent prayer of thanks for all the old man had done for him. He turned his face to the north, taking the road to the river and his future.

Cuthbert was a fine looking young man. Twenty-three years of age, tall and lean, but strong. As a child he had often accompanied his father to the various buildings where he was a master carver, one of the best in the country. At his father's side he had learned the basic skills of the trade he was to follow. By the time he was ten it was recognised that the boy had a real feel for the wood; he could see the finished piece in his head when he looked at a piece of rough timber, imagining the curves and shapes as he carved it. He was a quick learner too; his mother had taught him to read his letters from an early age for unlike most people of the time, she saw the value of it. Her mother had been a maid to a rich widow who had encouraged her servants to read, recognising it as an advantage to them and not a threat to their masters as many saw it. It was not unknown for a master to flog a servant he discovered could read, or dismiss them to find other work. His father had shown him how to measure and calculate for the work he was doing. Accuracy was needed to construct the framework of the wooden buildings he helped to design and build. Only by measuring to the tiniest quarter inch could a strong building be built that would last for generations. Cuthbert used to make little models of the buildings they worked on, using discarded odds and ends he found. That way he had learned what his father was always telling him, only perfection will last.

Then tragedy struck. His mother fell ill with a fever and died within a few days. Cuthbert was just short of his twelfth birthday. His father had been devastated, distraught over the loss of his only love and his work began to suffer. He made mistakes, he could not concentrate, he neglected himself and his son, until one day he walked under a beam that was being hoisted into position, something he was always telling Cuthbert he must never do. The ropes slipped and the beam fell, pinning his father to the ground. When the men lifted it from him it was found his back was broken and he was paralysed from the chest down. He lived a mere three weeks, dying slowly and leaving a bewildered child without a home or means of support. If it hadn't been for Jethro Milton taking him in he would have been destitute. Jethro and his wife, Mildred, had no family of their own and they had been close friends of Cuthbert's parents. Jethro also saw the huge potential in the boy so he apprenticed him as soon as he was able and taught him everything he knew. It was to be a legacy he would value for the rest of his life and something he must draw on now as he set out alone.

As he walked north he at first enjoyed his freedom but he soon realised that work was what he needed to sustain the basic essentials of life. Even the simplest of food cost money and he did not want to have to beg for it. The few coins he carried at his belt would not last for ever.

He and Brother John were sitting in a roadside tavern enjoying a meal of fresh baked bread and a wedge of cheese when the landlord started to chat to them. The tavern was quiet and the man was of a garrulous nature so he was soon questioning Cuthbert about his work and where he was travelling from and why. Cuthbert gave him the bare essentials, not wishing to divulge personal matters.

'A worker in wood, eh?' said the landlord, scratching his beard as if in thought. 'The blacksmith was looking for a bit of an 'and with some of his work. He might be able to put a bit of work your way. Why don't you go and ask him?'

'I am travelling with Brother John here to Whalley Abbey where work awaits me,' explained Cuthbert.

'It would only take a day or two to do what the blacksmith needs,' said the landlord. 'Surely Brother John, and God, could spare you for that to help a good Christian man.'

Cuthbert looked at the monk who nodded slowly and smiled.

'There is no reason for us to hasten. I have been many days on my journey already. A few more will not matter and the Good Book tells us to help those who need our aid.' Brother John put the last of the cheese into his mouth. 'Besides,' he said round the mouthful, 'with victuals as good as this it will be no hardship.'

Cuthbert laughed. In the few days he had known Brother John he had noticed how much he appreciated the simple but good food they had found along the way. His gentle manner endeared the monk to those they met and he had carried out several simple tasks for fellow travellers or those in the humble lodgings they had used. There was something very endearing about the man that made people like him instantly. He finished his own meal before standing up and asking,

'Which way?'

'Carry on the way you were going. The forge is at the end of the village. Can't miss it. P'raps I'll see you back here later.'

'Maybe,' said Cuthbert, 'and thank you.'

'I shall visit the church over there and say a prayer for both of us,' said Brother John.

The village street ran in a slight curve down the gently sloping hill to the stream at the bottom. Just before the ford a low building on the left came into view, a plume of smoke drifting from the chimney at one side. The sound of hammering on metal could be clearly heard as he approached and the distinct smell of hot metal and burning hoof could be detected. To one side of the building was an open-sided shelter with a thatched roof, under which stood a patient horse. A man emerged from the inner building holding a horseshoe in tongs. He went to the animal and lifted a rear leg, holding it between his knees as he fitted the shoe to the hoof. Noting adjustments he let go of the leg again, patted the horse and disappeared inside once more. Cuthbert followed him and watched as the smith thrust the shoe into the fire again, sparks flying. A boy stood to one side working the bellows.

'What do you want?' shouted the smith above the roar of the fire.

'The landlord at the inn said you were in need of a worker of wood. I am a carpenter and carver.'

The smith drew out the glowing horseshoe and laid it on his anvil, took up his hammer and began to beat the hot metal. Cuthbert wondered whether he had heard his answer and was about to repeat it when the smith plunged the horseshoe into a bucket of water and above the sizzle and steam replied,

'Worker in wood, eh? Can tha make wood handles?'

'Yes,' said Cuthbert, following him out to the horse again. The smith lifted the animal's foot again and held it between his knees.

'Nails,' he shouted and the boy came running with a handful of nails. The smith selected what he needed and put them between his lips as he adjusted the shoe to fit the hoof.

'Village woodman broke 'is leg a while back,' he said through his lips. 'I got more shovels and ploughs as I knows what to do with there in back o' forge. People's waiting for them tools and needs 'em. If tha can fettle 'em I'd be grateful.'

Cuthbert translated the mumbled words with relief. It was a simple enough job and would only take a short while. He did not want to impose on Brother John's generosity too much.

The smith let the horse's foot down and the beast stamped it, feeling the new weight on his hoof as strange and heavy, then shook his mane and nuzzled the man.

'Get away with you!' he exclaimed. 'Don't you go casting another shoe so quick.' He slapped the horse on its rump and untied the halter, leading it back outside. A man was walking down the hill from the inn, took the rope from the smith and with a gruff nod of thanks led it away. 'In here,' said the smith, and took Cuthbert into the forge. In a dark corner was a heap of perhaps half a dozen spades of various sizes waiting for handles to be fitted. Some were clearly old ones repaired but at least two were newly made. Next to them was a small simple plough that a man would use on his strip of land. The smith pointed to a stack of wood in another corner. 'Can you do 'em?' he asked.

'Certainly,' replied Cuthbert picking up a spade and feeling the weight of it in his hands. It was a strong sturdy tool and would need a strong handle. He turned to the wood stacked in another part of the building, looking for exactly the right piece. It needed to be long and straight, without any knots or splits that may weaken it, not too light either as it would be needed to work the ground whether it was wet and heavy, or dry and hard. At last he found a suitable piece and took it outside to work on it. Sitting in the sun he turned the wood over again and again as he examined it more closely then measured it against his own height. Too long and it would be unwieldy, too short and the user would have to bend over and gain an aching back if he worked for long. Cuthbert reached into his leather bag and brought out the tools he needed, then started to shape the handle, smoothing it so that there would be no splinters to catch in the hands, shaping one end to fit the spade blade and the other to accept a handle. When he was satisfied he took it back into the forge.

The blacksmith put his hammer down and took the wood from him turning it over and over in his big hands. He took the spade from Cuthbert's hand and fitted the handle to it.

'Well, I'll be ...!' he exclaimed. 'I've never seen a better fit, and it's just right length for Jacob. He's about your height and you've got it perfect. Now, I just need to fix it in firmly.' He turned to a box on the bench nearby, selected a nail and banged it in to hold the handle in place. Holding the finished tool up he grinned at Cuthbert. 'Tha's done a grand job, a grand job, lad. As good a job as ever I saw.' He clapped Cuthbert on the back. 'Will tha do them others for me?'

'Willingly,' said a relieved Cuthbert, 'but can you tell me something about their owners, so as I'll get them right too?'

'Of course. I can see tha's done this work afore,' said the blacksmith, selecting a smaller spade from the pile. 'Now, this 'un belongs to William down at the end cottage. He's only short is William so he don't need a long handle.' He handed the spade to Cuthbert, nodded and went back to his work.

Over the next two days Cuthbert continued working for the blacksmith, fitting new handles to the spades in the corner, mending or replacing damaged ones, repairing a good wooden stool with a new leg, fixing a squeaky door into the smith's house. Seeing him working outside, farmers who brought their horses in for shoeing watched him at his work and suggested other small jobs they needed doing. Cuthbert was worried that he was taking work away from the injured woodsman but the smith assured him that was not the case.

'There's always work to be done around the village,' he said. 'When he gets back to working he'll be glad to see there ain't more work than he can cope with. He'll be able to start afresh. Don't you worry you're taking his job. He knows abaht it any road. I told him what you was doing and 'e thanks yer.'

Cuthbert was glad to be earning a few coins for his work. At least he could pay for his food and a decent bed at the end of the day, but at last it was time to be moving on and he and Brother John carried on their northward journey towards Whalley.

CHAPTER FOUR
Great Harwood
1523

The funeral was over. Thomas Hesketh had been laid to rest and money had been given to the monks to say masses for his soul. His family had gathered, sung his praises, uttered the words expected of them, smiled at Thomas's tenants, and looked hungrily over the belongings in the Hesketh family home. With no surviving legitimate children, his three sisters and their families had come to look over the spoils. Margery, Dowsabel and Maud had all married well and could look forward to comfortable lives with their respective husbands, apart from Maud whose husband had left her a widow three years before. The three women couldn't wait for the funeral party to depart so that they could divide up the Hesketh fortune between them.

At the back of the church had sat Thomas's mistress, Alice Haward with their three children, Robert, Charles and Ellen. She dared not sit in a more prominent position as she knew of the animosity towards her from the Hesketh. But she also knew that her eldest son, Robert was Thomas's heir. Thomas had explained it all to her in the months before he died. He felt no duty to his sisters, his two wives had produced no legitimate heirs and he felt no ties to their wider families. His first wife, Elizabeth, had been married to him when he was six years old, a convenient alliance arranged between the two families which neither of the young people wanted when they grew to adulthood and their divorce sixteen years later was amicable, Elizabeth already about to bear the child of another man. His second wife, whom he married in 1492, was a great heiress, Grace, the daughter of Sir Richard Towneley of Towneley, not far from the Hesketh manor at Great Harwood. Their one and only child, William, had died in infancy and Grace herself had died after eighteen years of marriage. He had therefore felt no guilt when he took a mistress, Alice, whom he loved dearly, especially when she gave him the longed for sons. He had raised Robert to be his heir and taken care that Alice and her other two children would want for nothing. But Alice knew that Robert would not have an easy time of it.

As people drifted away from the gathering Alice hung back hoping to see at least one of the sisters privately. Margery saw her lurking, as she thought, and marched over to her.

'Why are you and your bastard children here?' she said, haughtily. 'You have no business here. Be off.'

'I have every right,' replied Alice, 'as my son is Thomas's heir.'

'More fool you if you believe that,' sneered Margery. 'Where's your proof? See, you have nothing, have you?'

'The papers, drawn up legally and witnessed by my Lord Derby, are in his care. He will show them to you and you will have to accept his word.'

'Have to? Have to? Who are you to tell me what I believe or not? The Derby's are old and trusted friends of the family. The likes of you cannot hope to have their support. It was all a tale Thomas spun you when he was weak and ill.'

'What is this woman doing here?' demanded Maud, joining her sister. 'Out to cause trouble, I'll be bound. Away with you and take your children with you. They are not fit to be in such company. Away I say.'

'I will go,' said Alice calmly, 'but this is not the last you will hear of this. Thomas loved me as I loved him. We bore our children in love, we cherish them and will see that right is done for them. Thomas may have died but I know I am in the right and we will prove it to you. I will not just go and leave you to pick over what rightfully belongs to our son.'

Before either woman could reply Alice turned away and strode out of the Hall, her children following in her wake.

'Well, really!' exclaimed Maud. 'How dare she?'

'How indeed, but I swear I will beat her down to the lowly position she came from, and her bastards too. To think that people like them could aspire to be our equals! We will see her in court if we have to,' replied Margery, flouncing away to follow her family out.

'Do you believe that tale about Lord Derby?' asked Maud, almost tripping in her haste to catch up.

'Something was said about it last time I saw dear Thomas, but he was ill, rambling, he didn't know what he was saying. I'll soon put it straight. Just you see if I don't.

Three days later Margery travelled to Lathom House, the home of the earls of Derby and asked to see the master. Certain in the rightness of her action she had no doubt that she would have the support of Lord Derby over the matter of the Hesketh inheritance so she smiled broadly when she was shown into his presence. He was not alone, there were several members of the household present including his wife.

'Lady Kighley,' exclaimed his lordship. 'I was saddened to hear of the death of your brother, Lord Hesketh. He was a good man, very honest and true, a good servant to this household in the past. We had many a convivial conversation over a meal over the years. Please accept my condolences.'

'Thank you, my Lord, we feel our loss most deeply but there are certain matters I need to discuss with you. Thomas always said that I could turn to you for advice should the need arise and, I fear, the need has arisen.'

Lord Derby looked at her earnest expression then dismissed the rest of his household with a gesture. When they had all filed out he gestured her to sit on one of the cushioned stools at his side.

'May I offer you refreshment?' he asked.

'Thank you, the journey was difficult over rough roads.'

He poured a cup of wine and handed it to her.

'Now, what is this advice that you need?'

Maud sipped her wine then cleared her throat.

'It concerns the Hesketh inheritance. As you know my brother has no legitimate heirs, neither of his wives producing a surviving son. It is therefore right, is it not, that we as his surviving sisters should share his inheritance between us? After all, there are several nephews of his who have a close claim to it if not we, his sisters, ourselves.' She smiled sweetly. 'The problem is that we can find no will setting down this obvious arrangement so we wondered what we can do to make things right.'

Lord Derby looked at her for a long uncomfortable moment.

'You will find no will to that effect,' he said, at last. 'There is a will and I have a copy of it. The other is held elsewhere. For safekeeping,' he added.

Maud gave a nervous laugh.

'No wonder we could not find it and his man of business refused to say where it was. Why all the mystery? Surely it is quite straightforward in its wording, surely there can be no dispute over its content?'

'Oh, there is no dispute, none at all,' replied the Lord Derby. 'Thomas consulted me many months ago about the question of inheritance and I advised him on the best way to deal with it. I had the papers drawn up, witnessed and signed. Everything was done according to his wishes, it is legal and correct, as verified by all the other witnesses to the document.'

'Oh, I see. I wonder why Thomas wanted it all to be done so secretly. Surely there was nothing difficult about remembering his own family in his will, after all, who else could possibly be involved?'

'Who indeed?' The older man looked at her from piercing eyes. He took a long drink from his goblet before continuing. 'You see, Lady Kighley, Thomas feared there would be trouble on his death and that his wishes would not be adhered to by his family. That is why he came to me for advice, advice I was willing to give, I may add. Remember I knew your brother well, we grew up together, have spent much time in each other's company. He was accountant to both myself and my grandfather, he knew how to look after his own financial affairs but sought my advice over his inheritance. I guessed his wishes before he told me and it was clear to me that his will would prove, shall we say, unacceptable, to you and your sisters. He did not want there to be argument about it so it was set down in such a manner that it is indisputable. There is no way that you can change what has been set down in law.' As he spoke his voice had changed from friendly to stern and Maud flinched at what he was saying.

'So, why can we not see this 'indisputable' will of his?' she demanded, rising to her feet. 'When were we going to be told of its contents? Am I not to know now that I may report to my sisters?'

'Certainly you may know,' replied Lord Derby, 'but, pray, be seated.'

Meekly, Maud sat.

'I will have a copy of the will sent to you as you request to see it but, briefly, it states that, after certain bequests have been made to chantries and alms houses, and certain good works done in the district, Thomas recognises his son, Robert, as his legitimate heir and all his wealth, property, goods and chattels are to be his as of the date of Thomas's death.'

Maud flushed red, then the colour drained from her face. Through gritted teeth she said, 'That *bastard*? He recognises a *bastard* begot upon a *whore* to be his heir?'

'Yes, and there is absolutely nothing you can do about it. A legal document is a legal document and no court in the land will say otherwise.'

'We shall see about that,' hissed Maud, getting to her feet. 'We will go to court and prove that Thomas was insane when he made the will, we will disinherit that *bastard* and see that the rightful heirs receive their rightful inheritance. This is not the end. Thomas has three sisters and their families *will* inherit what is theirs.'

'If that is your wish you may try,' said Lord Derby, 'but I warn you, you will not win, the will is legal and you will have to accept it.'

'We'll see about that!' spat Maud, and swept from the room.

'You can try, dear Lady, you can try,' muttered Lord Derby to her departing figure. 'Thomas said you would be trouble and he was right. May his soul rest in peace for that lady's will not. There is trouble ahead.'

CHAPTER FIVE
Whalley Abbey
1528

Cuthbert and Brother John eventually reached the tiny village of Whalley one afternoon on a glorious autumn day. Their journey had not been long but it was certainly leisurely. Brother John was in no hurry to complete his mission and Cuthbert wondered whether he perhaps enjoyed these forays into the outer world, a welcome change to the disciplined life within the Abbey. During their many conversations Cuthbert had been surprised to learn that Brother John had come late to the cloister having spent many years as a merchant travelling far and wide in England and abroad buying and selling fine fabrics and materials, wool and silk, dyes and fastenings from far flung places in many of the great cities Cuthbert had only heard about. Perhaps this wandering occupation he undertook now kept him in touch with people and places he once knew well. He certainly knew where the best taverns were, where they would be able to find a decent meal and a night's lodging, who would welcome them and places that were best avoided for various reasons which he chose not to enlarge upon.

Long before they reached the village itself they had seen the towering walls of the Abbey of Whalley, set in the valley of the River Calder.

'Is it a large abbey?' Cuthbert had asked.

'Yes, though not as large as some of the others in the country but it is a wealthy place, with many benefactors willing to pay for the enhancement of our church and buildings in return for a place in our churchyard and prayers for their souls. Father Abbot is a strong and holy man, a good leader to his flock and well liked by the people of the village. He has much influence in the area and cares for all who come to him. We have extensive buildings as well as many farms under our care. The wool is profitable in a good year as is the timber from our forests, as well as the stone from our quarries. We have much arable land, tenanted of course, and we take fish from the river too. Yes, it is a rich living. You may find him stern at first but he has a good heart and rewards those who work for the greater glory of God in our Abbey Church.'

They grew nearer and Cuthbert could see a great gatehouse in the stone wall, a building large enough to be a dwelling in any other setting.

'Is this just the entrance?' he marvelled, looking up at the great arches high above the path. They passed through one arch, walked through a lofty passageway and out through another arch into a courtyard. Brother John was smiling at the expression on the young man's face.

'Yes, *just* the entrance,' he said, 'and not the only one. The other is even bigger.'

'Bigger!' gasped Cuthbert, jumping out of the way of a cart being driven out of the courtyard. He stopped and stared about him, trying to take in the size of the buildings around him. The Abbey church was on his right. The arched windows and lofty walls towered higher than any building he had seen, even those he had known in Chester. He walked to the end of the wall and looked round the corner, along the side of the church.

'That's the chapterhouse over to the left,' said Brother John, 'and behind it is the east cloister with the monk's dormitory above it.' All around were great buildings, many of which he had never seen the like of. The stone work was spectacular, great arches leading into doorways or through into further open spaces. Carving of the stonework was crisper, cleaner, somehow greater than that he knew from Chester. Clearly a great deal of time and money had been spent here.

Brother John was smiling at the boy's awed expression.

'I said that Abbot Paslew had rule over a fine house, a rich house. That's his lodging over there, showing above that other building. But come, we are just in time for the evening meal. I will take you to meet the Abbot afterwards.'

Trust Brother John to arrive in time for a meal, thought Cuthbert as he followed his friend along a paved path and down steps into an open cloister with arcades round all four sides. They walked to the end and paused at the lavatorium, the stone trough under a great arch where the monks washed their hands before going into the refectory.

Cuthbert paused in the doorway and looked about him. The lofty roof soared above him, great oak beams supporting it. The windows were set high so that no distracting views would disturb the monks at their meal but each was arched, the tracery delicate and the glass clear to let in as much light as possible. At one end there were steps up to a projecting balcony from where one of the monks would read from Holy Scripture or some other religious text whilst the monks ate. The room was laid out with oak trestle tables lined with wooden benches where the men sat to eat.

As they entered all eyes turned to see who the visitors were and, recognising Brother John, they were beckoned over to a table where there was room for them to sit. A stillness settled over the whole assembly as Grace was intoned in Latin and once the meal started the lay servants carried in the food from the kitchen next door. The meal was taken in silence apart from the voice of the reader on the balcony. Bowls of a healthy looking pottage were laid before each man and once all were served, they took up their wooden spoons and ate. Cuthbert was pleased to find it was very tasty, a mixture of vegetables and oatmeal, cooked slowly over the fire, with hunks of freshly baked bread on a central platter which was handed round. As silence was the rule the monks had developed a sign language whereby they could ask for something along the table and Cuthbert watched as water jugs or bread were passed from person to person.

When Cuthbert had wiped the last of the pottage out of his bowl with his bread he sat back and listened to the reading. It was a new experience to eat in silence, there had always been lively conversation round the table at mealtimes with Mildred and Jethro, discussing the work they had been doing, gossip Mildred had picked up at the market, news of weddings and burials, of new babies and christenings, life in the city. It had been a favourite time, a relaxed and easy end to a busy day. He was not sure whether he could face a lifetime of silent meals.

At last the meal was finished and the reader came to the end of his appointed text. Another lengthy grace followed then, as one, everyone stood up, scraping their benches back on the stone floor, and filed out to whatever task they now had to perform.

'Follow me,' whispered Brother John as they walked out into the cloisters again. 'I will take you to see Abbot Paslew then show you where you will sleep. Come on.'

Compared to the rest of the monastery Abbot Paslew's private quarters were luxurious, for an Abbey that preached poverty, chastity and obedience. Immediately Cuthbert was aware of a richness unseen elsewhere in the abbey. A large fireplace graced one wall, though unlit at this time of year. Rugs were spread on the stone floor, there were tapestries on the wall, the furniture was far from the basic quality seen so far and Abbot Paslew was dressed in a habit of the finest wool with a colourful silken sash about his waist. Behind him Cuthbert could see several dishes left from his meal with the remains of meat and fish, rich sauces and sweet dishes upon them. No pottage for Father Abbot.

Brother John bowed to his Superior.

'Father, I have returned from my journey and have brought with me Cuthbert Watts, a craftsman in wood. Father I have seen his work at the Abbey Church of St Werburgh in Chester and feel sure that he will only enhance our work here with his undoubted skill.'

Cuthbert looked at the man before him. He was of middle age, tall with greying hair around his tonsure. His face was long with a narrow nose, thin lips and piercing dark eyes which were observing Cuthbert with a steely stare. Cuthbert imagined he would be a strict leader who would deal sternly with whoever came before him, whether a monk or a merchant, a farmer or a tradesman. He was not a man to get on the wrong side of. He was beginning to feel uncomfortable under this unblinking stare.

'So,' said the Abbot at last. 'You are from Chester. A fine city with a faithful congregation. Do you attend the Abbey Church regularly?'

'Yes, Father,' replied Cuthbert, feeling as he had when standing before the priest after he had been caught laughing with some other boys during the Easter Mass. Hopefully there would not be a beating to follow.

'A carpenter and woodcarver? Are you apprenticed?

'I was apprenticed to Jethro Milton, master carver in Chester for seven years. I completed my time with him but was working under him until he died. I learned all I know from him, he took me into his home when my parents died and has treated me as a son ever since. I must make my own way now.'

'Very commendable. You are a fine carver, according to Brother John here. What work has he seen of yours?'

Cuthbert looked to Brother John for help.

'I saw much of the work Jethro and Cuthbert had been working on, both in construction and decoration of several buildings in the city but my attention was particularly drawn to a marvellous chest which he had decorated for the Abbey library. Father, the carving upon it was the finest I think I have ever seen. Crisp and clean, beautifully worked with flowers and creatures, all in exquisite detail down to the eyes of the birds and mice upon the chest.'

'A ringing account to be sure,' said Father Paslew, and a slight smile split his lips, then was gone. Cuthbert felt it was a rare occurrence for him to lighten his expression. 'Young man, only the finest of work is seen in our Abbey. I do not allow shoddy or lazy work. We have much wealth from generous benefactors so I can afford the best to work to the greater glory of our Abbey. Do you think you could achieve such high standards?'

Cuthbert squared his shoulders and looked him in the eye.

'Yes, Father. I too believe only the best work should be created, be it a humble door latch or a great carving. Jethro taught me thus and I will continue to do so myself.'

He held his breath and waited for a reply.

'Then we shall see. Tomorrow I shall allot you a task to be completed by the end of the day. Then we shall see if you are worthy to work here.'

He turned away and Cuthbert took this as their dismissal. He followed Brother John out of the room.

'I think he approves of you,' said Brother John.

'Really? He seemed very … very …'

'Severe? Yes, he can be but I think he liked what he saw and what you said. Tomorrow will be a test. If you please him with whatever he asks you to do, you will be safe.'

Brother John led Cuthbert round the cloister pointing out the arched doorway leading to the chapter house, the recessed cupboards where the precious books were kept and the stone seat where the monks sat while they worked on copying and illuminating the manuscripts. The whole way round was covered, allowing their work to continue whatever the weather, but the central square was open to the sky and, at this time of day a welcome sunny spot for prayer or private contemplation.

They were approaching the door into the church but Brother John turned away.

'We will have more time tomorrow for you to see the work being done in there,' he said. 'For now I had better show you to the lay brothers dormitory where a bed will be found for you while you are working here. It is this way, above the west cloister.' They entered through a door in the corner and mounted the flight of stone stairs, ending in a long room that ran the whole length of the building. The roof above was of bare timbers but, to Cuthbert's trained eye, very well constructed. Brother John noticed the direction of his gaze and smiled.

'Already looking at the building I see,' he said.

'Sorry, I can't help it. It's what Jethro always did when we went into an unknown building. He could often tell exactly who had designed and built it, just by looking at it and I have caught the habit.'

'Does it meet with your approval? Is it safe? Will it fall upon you in the night?'

'No. No, no, it is good. Well built.' Cuthbert was feeling embarrassed now.

'Come, I will introduce you to Stephen, he is in charge of the lay brothers and will show you where you may lay your head, for I am sure you are weary after our long journey.'

Stephen was at the far end of the room talking to one of the lay brothers. He turned as he heard their approach and came forward in greeting.

'Brother John. I had heard you had returned from your travels. All went well I trust?'

'Very well,' replied Brother John. 'I visited several of our granges as instructed and all are expecting a good harvest this year so our store barns will be full, thank the Lord.'

'Thank the Lord, indeed. Now who have we here? Not a new brother, I think. You have the look of a craftsman.'

'This is Cuthbert, a woodcarver and craftsman, come to enhance our Abbey I hope. Father Abbot will give him a task tomorrow to see whether he is up to our standards,'

Stephen laughed.

'He will be, if he has had your recommendation already. You know Father Abbot trusts your judgement implicitly. See how many fine craftsmen you have already brought to us from your travels.' He looked sideways at Cuthbert. 'If Brother John likes your work that is all we need to know. Now come, you will be needing a bed whilst you are with us. Let me see, there is one at the end of this row. There are blankets on the shelf over there.

Some of the lay brothers will rise for the services during the night but you do not need to join them in the Abbey Church for every service, only the monks have to do that. Our main purpose is to do all the work so that they can spend their time in prayer and contemplation, that is our service to God. We rise early so try to get a good night's sleep. You will meet the brothers as they come in.'

Cuthbert found it strange to go to bed in a room with so many other people. He had had a tiny room of his own, above the porch, in the house in Chester, and after he had settled down for the night in this long dormitory it took a while to go to sleep with the sounds of other people breathing, someone snoring, others moving restlessly on their hard bed despite the straw mattress. Eventually he drifted off, wondering what the morrow would bring.

CHAPTER SIX
Great Harwood
1529

'That is it, then. He has won. All is lost. The Hesketh name will be borne by a bastard, we will be disgraced, scorned, demeaned.' Dowsabel sighed deeply and sank back on the cushions of her chair. 'All those years of appealing to every court in the land, all that money paid to lawyers and lords and judges and it has all been wasted. Nothing. We have nothing.'

'Oh, come, sister,' said Margery. 'We may have lost the inheritance which should have been ours and our children's but we can still punish Thomas for what he has done to us.'

'How? Lord Derby himself came to tell us of the final ruling. There is nothing more we can do. We have to face it, we have lost.'

'Don't be such a defeatist. We can revile the boy, ignore him and his children, refuse to receive any of them, speak only ill of them all. The county families will be on our side.'

'Don't be too sure,' said Maud from her seat by the fire. She put down the piece of embroidery she had been working on, listening all the while to her two sisters. 'Remember who his chief supporter was. Lord Derby has stood by the man from the very beginning. We cannot forget what high regard he had for our brother, high enough to trust him with the care of the Derby fortune all those years. People will have more regard for the Derby family than for us. Who are we in the pecking order of the nobility?'

'The Hesketh family have been one of the prominent families of the north for generations. Look at all the land we have acquired, the properties, the honours that have been bestowed upon our ancestors by kings, the important families we have married into. We are not minor beings to be ignored,' argued Dowsabel. 'We all have prominent husbands. Or had.'

'As widows that is all the more reason why we should have had the Hesketh fortune,' cried Margery through gritted teeth. 'Our husbands are all dead, all three of our brothers are dead, we only have ourselves to look out for now.'

'That is unfortunate,' agreed Maud, 'but the Hesketh name rose high even in these times. Was not Hugh the Bishop of Man? Was not Richard Attorney-General to His Majesty the King?' The Hesketh name will rise again, I am sure. There is no point fighting against what cannot be changed.'

'Do you not care?' said Margery.

'Yes, of course I care but we are all well provided for by our late husbands, we have our own families and households to care for. Yes, I am bitterly disappointed that our eldest brother could not look to his sisters but it was his fortune to dispose of as he saw fit and I suppose he must have cared for that woman a great deal to do what he has done. We have to take counsel of what Lord Derby said. That is the end of the matter and no amount of money or time will change it. Bitter as it is we have got to accept it. Speaking ill of his heir and trying to disclaim him will do us no good, no good at all, so we may as well accept it.'

'I agree with Maud,' said Dowsabel. 'It is over, we lost. Accept it. But I will never set eyes upon that man again as long as I live.'

'You may be prepared to accept defeat but I most certainly will not.' With a swirl of skirts Margery flounced out of the room, closing the door very firmly behind her.

'Oh dear, poor Margery,' said Dowsabel, going to the window to look out over the garden. 'She always had a sharp tongue and a quick temper. I knew she would never accept the court's ruling. Father always indulged her rather than face one of her tantrums. Well this is one time when she will never get what she wants.'

Maud joined her sister at the window. They linked arms as they watched one of the gardeners gathering flowers for the house.

'Why does life have to be so complicated?' mused Maud, 'I think I will return home. There are so many tasks I need to be attending to.'

'Oh Maud, ever the peacemaker.' Dowsabel kissed her sister on the brow. 'Why are you so calm?'

'Because there is no point getting upset about something we can't do anything about. When we were all young, growing up together, I used to watch you two, listen to your arguments and disputes and wonder why you could get so upset over such trivial things: the colour of a hair ribbon, the name for a new puppy, who was going to sit on father's knee. There was only ever room for two anyway,' she smiled. 'I suppose I was one of life's observers, learning from my elder's mistakes and deciding not to go that way. Hugh left me well provided for, I am happy and content with my life. You would do well to look to your own family. Margery will calm down when she lets her anger cool. All this arguing has tired me. I am going home.'

The three sisters departed for their own homes the next day. Widowhood was something they all settled into easily, it was to be expected in these troubled times and their lives returned to peaceful routine in their respective homes. But not for long.

It was late in 1529 when Maud invited her two sisters to her home at North Meols. Intrigued by the unexpected letters they came with all haste. Barely had they got through the door than Maud stood before them in her private solar with an indecipherable expression upon her face.

'You will never guess what rumours I have heard,' she started. 'Yesterday I was invited to view Alice Greystones new herb garden and knottery.'

'That must have been exciting for you,' replied Dowsabel sarcastically. 'A new herb garden! Since when have you been interested in herbs?'

'It wasn't the garden that excited me but one of her other friends. Lady Astley was there.'

Her sisters looked expectantly at her waiting for the revelation which had drawn them both here. Maud continued.

'Lady Astley is a great friend of Lady Derby, you know, and she says that her husband, Lord Derby has been advising our brother's boy.'

'Advising?' said Margery cautiously.

'Yes, advising. It seems the boy is going to build a new house worthy of the Hesketh name, he says, and he went to Lord Derby to ask about funds to do so and where he thought might be a suitable site for the undertaking.'

'The impertinence!' cried Dowsabel. 'I knew there would be trouble there.'

'What did Lord Derby tell him? Do you know?' asked Margery.

Maud looked from Margery to Dowsabel and back.

'Oh, yes! It seems that our dear brother, Thomas, has been squirreling money away for years and there is a substantial sum in safe keeping for the boy. That can now be returned to the boy for whatever purpose he wants to use it and he has plans for a grand house.'

'Where might this "grand house" be? Not near me, I hope. I could not stand to have him crowing over us,' said Margery.

'Rufford!' exclaimed Maud triumphantly.

The three sisters looked at each other, none of them wanting to admit that they weren't quite sure where this was.

'I believe it is a little place to the west somewhere. We visited once, didn't we?' asked Dowsabel. 'There's a small draughty place beside a lake, very damp and dismal if I remember. Father said it was one of our older houses. We didn't use it much, preferring our home at Great Harwood.'

'Yes, I remember. Didn't father say that way back it belonged to one of our ancestors, that's why his title was Lord of Rufford?' asked Margery.

'So he did,' agreed Maud. 'Well, he's welcome to it. Cold, damp, miles from anywhere important, let him build his grand house in the back of beyond. We don't have to pass it or even go near it. I wouldn't set foot in it anyway and I hope you two agree.' Her sisters nodded in agreement.

'I do wonder though, just how much money Thomas has set aside for him,' queried Margery. 'Still we will never know now though I wish he had made an equal gift for each of us. It is not fair.'

'Don't start worrying about it, Margery,' cautioned Dowsabel. 'You made yourself ill over the court case. Don't do that again.'

'I won't,' said Margery, 'but I can't help wondering, can I?'

CHAPTER SEVEN
1528

Cuthbert rose early, as was his custom and made his way to the church along with many of the lay brothers. It was not expected that all the lay brothers would attend all the services during the day but they were expected to attend once, at least. Their presence in the Abbey did not require them to be able to read or write either as most of them had no need to, their work was the manual labour required to keep the Abbey running smoothly. Cuthbert was unusual in that he could both read and write, it had been necessary when working with Jethro. He did, however, appreciate the beauty of all he saw around him when he entered the great church.

His eyes immediately rose to the soaring roof high above the nave. Eight great pillars marched down each side of the full length of the building, reaching high to support the span of the roof way above his head. Great windows down each side flooded the building with light, their tracery both delicate and decorative, supporting beautifully coloured glass that splashed bright patches of vivid colour across the walls and floor. The floor tiles were highly decorative, arranged in intricate patterns. Everywhere he looked there was carving, in wood and stone. Faces peered down from dark corners, angels supported roofbeams, patterns in the arches of doorways and windows were richly decorated, many in designs he knew from other buildings, but some in patterns he had never before witnessed. A great screen divided the choir from the presbytery, the bell tower soaring above at the crossing point of the transepts, supported on four more mighty pillars. Figures of saints looked down from the walls, side chapels held ornate altars and memorials. The choir stalls were exceptional, richly carved, ornate and beautiful but he could not see them closely during the service for they were filled with the monks who raised their voices in worship.

Cuthbert remembered little of that first service in the church, so taken up was he with looking in awe at the splendour around him and wondering what he could do that would be worthy of this place. Where was there room for more decoration, more space for glorification of this building? As the service ended he stumbled out into the cloister, his mind full of what he had seen, and he sat down on one of the stone seats along the side wall whilst he gathered his thoughts.

'Ah, I saw you in the church,' said Brother John, sitting down beside him. 'What do you think of our splendid building?'

'Magnificent. I do not know how I can do anything worthy of it.'

'Oh, you will, you will. Now, have you broken your fast?'

'No, I went straight to the church, I could not wait to see it.'

'Then I had better take you to the kitchens, see if I can beg some bread for you as the rest of the brothers have already eaten.'

A bowl of gruel was found for their guest when Brother John explained that he was a great woodcarver come to enhance their Abbey. Cuthbert wasn't so sure about the ringing recommendation but he was grateful for the food and ate it quickly.

'Abbot Paslew will send for you after Chapter. If you would like to look round the rest of the Abbey you are very welcome. I will come and find you.'

Cuthbert walked right round the outside of the Abbey Church. The warm stone was perfect for such a beautiful building. Many arched windows with buttresses between and flying buttresses above to support the towering walls, were all decorated with tracery and finials and statues. The doors were solid oak. Everything was built to last, as it had done for the last two centuries. Succeeding generations of monks had worked and worshipped here, every generation adding to its glory and he was in awe of their skill and craftsmanship. Even the buildings housing all the domestic offices, the refectory, the dormitories, the infirmary, the Chapter house and the reredorter were built on the same grand scale and everywhere he looked the lay brothers were busy about their duties, in the kitchen, in the cloister, tending the animals in the stables and pig sties, in the herb garden and in the fields beyond. Yet there was an order and peacefulness about the place, no raised voices, no people running from place to place. Cuthbert felt the calm order of the life they lived here.

He was standing near the great arched gateway he had entered by when Brother John found him.

'Father Abbot will see you now,' he said, and led the way through the grounds to the Abbot's lodging where they had made their first visit yesterday. This time they were shown into a different room which looked more like a place of business. There were tables piled with scrolls and documents waiting to be dealt with, two standing desks where two of the brothers were busy writing. The number of candlesticks arrayed around the room showed that work clearly continued into the night and a great fireplace, although cold and empty now, would make this a very warm room to work in in the cold weather. The monks only had their one warming room where a fire was allowed but the Abbot liked his comforts.

Abbot Paslew was standing by one of the desks talking to the brother. He turned to greet Brother John and Cuthbert.

'I trust you had a restful night,' he said and went to sit behind a large table with a number of plans and charts laid out on it.

'Yes, thank you,' replied Cuthbert.

'I have given careful thought to what task we may find for you here at our Abbey and I have decided that some work in the choir stalls is needed. Let us go and see.'

They made their way in silence back to the Abbey Church. Abbot Paslew was clearly not a man to talk unnecessarily.

They entered through the door used by the monks to attend services and made their way to the area where the monks sat for worship. Two rows of narrow wooden seats on opposite sides of the nave faced each other. Each was beautifully carved with a canopied back to the rearmost row on each side. The misericords, the narrow seats upon which the monks could rest during services, tipped up and the undersides would be richly carved with a variety of subjects. Cuthbert longed to look at them more closely as he knew from the Abbey Church in Chester that some of the woodcarver's finest work was often to be seen here. There was a wooden rest in front and the end of each row was carved as well. Abbot Paslew led the way to the far end then turned round to face them. He pointed down towards the floor.

'See, down there. The carving has been broken off or damaged by the passage of many feet. Can you make something to replace it?'

Cuthbert's dream of producing some wonderful piece for display immediately took a fall. He was being asked to do something right down in the furthest, darkest corner where few would ever see it. Hardly the great work he had expected. He knelt down on the tiled floor, careful not to bang his head on the narrow seat, and looked at the base of the wooden support. In the gloom he could just make out that there had been some sort of decorative carving round the base of the end post which had been worn away or broken off. He looked across at the other side but it was too dark to see what sort of thing had been worked there. Was he being tested in some way? If he could fulfil this task well perhaps he would be given something better to do. He must not show his disappointment. Remember what Jethro always said, 'Even the humblest part must be your best. If no one else sees it, God will know it is there.'

Slowly he scrambled to his feet and turned to face Abbot Paslew.

'Yes, I can repair that,' he said, smiling. 'Would you like to see a drawing of what I propose to do?'

'No, I will trust to your judgement. Brother John will show you where you may work and where our wood is stored.' With that, he turned and swept out of the Abbey.

'Not what you expected?' asked Brother John.

'Not really. I didn't expect to be creating some great work of art at first but repairing some minor damage in an obscure place where no one will ever see it is a surprise. Is he testing me?'

'Oh yes. He often does this to see what men are made of. We have had craftsmen who have been so insulted by being asked to do something they regard as beneath them that they have walked out and refused to do it. You have made the correct decision by agreeing to do it. He will see that as a very good point. Now all you need to do is make something well and that meets with his approval. Have you any ideas?'

'Yes, I have actually, but I will see what wood is available to match what is here before I make my final decision.'

'We had better go to the wood store then.'

The Abbey wood store was housed in a small building tucked away around the back of the other buildings. Cuthbert could see that a great deal of wood was stacked neatly along the walls, divided in to raw timber and discarded pieces which had been worked in some way and were the leftovers from other work. He walked slowly along the rows looking for exactly what he wanted, a small piece but one which would blend in with the stall he was repairing. He did not want a fresh piece of timber that would stand out from the original. At last he found two or three that may be suitable, all of which were clearly the remnants of something much bigger.

'May I take these back to see how they blend with the existing work?' he asked.

'Of course,' replied Brother John. 'Most of our craftsmen find working under the shelter by the Abbey gardens suits them. There are good strong benches to work on and it is in a good light and sheltered if the weather turns inclement. You have your own tools but if you require anything else speak to Silas, he is usually to be found in the herb garden.'

Cuthbert returned to the church and got down on his knees with his pieces of wood to compare the colour with that already there. It was rather dark in this corner but the first piece he had selected was definitely too light in colour. Both of the others were suitable and he turned them about, working out which was going to be best for what he had in mind. At last he made his selection and made various markings on it so that he could cut it to the exact size.

Back in the woodshed he returned the rejected pieces then set about marking out where he would make his first cuts. He fetched his tools from the dormitory and, settling onto the seat overlooking the Abbey gardens, he began his work.

He spent the whole morning cutting and shaping the wood, and after several visits back to the church he was satisfied that the piece was fitting perfectly and he was ready to begin his carving.

Whenever he was creating something new like this Cuthbert spent a great deal of time just looking at the wood, noting the direction of the grain and looking for any slight knots or blemishes which may affect the finished piece. Then, slowly, he would begin to work the wood, carefully chiselling out the outline of what he was depicting. When he was satisfied with that he would start to add the detail which would bring it to life. The work was slow and painstaking but this was the part he loved, putting life into a scrap of wood. Time did not matter, he was totally absorbed, so when Brother John came to find him, Cuthbert was amazed how many hours had passed.

'How is it coming along?' asked Brother John.

'Not too bad,' he replied, covering the work with his jerkin which he had removed to work in the warm sunshine. Brother John smiled.

'I see you guard your work well,' he remarked.

'I'm sorry. I like to complete a piece before I let anyone else see it,' said Cuthbert. 'It is a habit I have developed. Sometimes people make unhelpful and hurtful remarks when they see something part done so I prefer to keep it under cover until I am ready to show it. I hope you understand.'

'Completely. When I was a merchant in cloth there were many weavers who would not let me see a partly made piece for the very same reason and also to prevent rivals trying to copy it before the original had been finished. When do you think it will be finished?'

'Maybe tomorrow, then I want to put it in place before Abbot Paslew sees it. It would spoil it if he saw it out of context.'

'I am intrigued as to what it may be. This is really quite exciting but I will restrain my curiosity until you are ready. However, you must eat, so put your tools away and we will go to the evening meal.'

Cuthbert kept the piece of work with him, wrapped in a piece of cloth. It may only be small but it was important to him and to his future here at Whalley. He could not afford to let it be lost or discarded as rubbish if anyone else found it.

After the evening meal, taken in silence as usual, Cuthbert left the Abbey grounds and walked down to the river. He wanted to be alone, to think, and to plan. If the Abbot approved of his work what might he ask him to do next? The possibilities were endless. From what he had seen so far only the best craftsmen had ever worked here and he was humbled to think that he could well become one of them. He took his carving out of its cloth and looked at it, turning it over and over in his hands. It was good, not quite perfect yet but with a few more hours work on it tomorrow, it would be as good as anything he had ever produced before.

The quiet peacefulness of the riverside was calming and his thoughts turned to Chester. What would Mildred and Nell be doing? Were they managing without him? Of course, they would be. There were many among their friends who would help the widow, make sure they were all right, and Mildred was a resourceful woman. She would grieve for Jethro but she would not let her grief dominate her life. She would carry on as before, cooking, sewing and cleaning the house, shopping in the busy market, attending the church and doing good works in small ways among her friends and neighbours. She had Nell to share the evenings with and would be teaching the girl the skills she would need if she was to work in any household in the future. The girl had already proved herself a willing pupil and the two had a close relationship, like grandmother and granddaughter. Cuthbert smiled as he imagined the two of them, heads bent over some mending as they sat by the fire in the homely parlour of their home. Yes, they would manage without him and one day he would return to visit them.

As the light faded he got to his feet and made his way back to the Abbey. The brothers were processing into the church for Compline but Cuthbert made his way to the lay brothers dormitory. Some of his fellow workers were already preparing for bed and Cuthbert suddenly felt very tired. His work may not be as physically tiring as theirs but the mental concentration involved was equally wearing. He removed his outer clothing and with his precious carving safely tucked under his straw mattress he lay down and was soon asleep.

His work was complete by mid-afternoon next day and he spent some time between Nones at three in the afternoon and Vespers at sunset fitting it into place in the Church. As he stood back to look at it he realised he had been right in his first assumption; no one would ever see it down there unless it was pointed out to them. Father Abbot had better be satisfied with it and hopefully give him something a little more prominent to do next.

Cuthbert went in search of Brother John. He found him in the cloister quietly reading in the last of the days light.

'It is finished,' he said. 'Do you think Father Abbot would like to see it now? We would need light to find it down on the floor.'

Brother John laughed.

'I shall go and see and I will bring candles. We would not want Father Abbot to miss your masterpiece.'

It was quite gloomy when they entered the church, a little procession of Father Abbot, Brother John and Cuthbert as well as three other monks who were attached to the Abbot's household and were curious to see what this new, much acclaimed young man could do. They moved into the choir stalls and Father Abbot took the candle holder from Brother John and directed the light towards the floor. He gave a startled gasp and stepped back, then looked more closely. The others craned their necks to see what had alarmed their Father. Abbott Paslew got down on his knees and examined the new work closely. He stretched forth a finger and touched it, feeling around where the join should be between old and new, then all over the surface of the carving. With his face almost on the floor he stared at it intently for several seconds before he got to his feet and turned to find an anxious Cuthbert standing in the aisle.

'Young man, what you have done here is create something the like of which I have never seen before.'

Cuthbert stared back. Was this good or bad? Was he pleased or angry? He waited for the Abbot to continue.

'It is remarkable, quite remarkable. You have indeed a great gift, a God-given gift which you must use to the best of your ability here in our Abbey.' He smiled, a rare occurrence. 'I was testing you, as you may have guessed. Greater men than you have turned down the opportunity to work here after I have asked them to do work in such an obscure place, but you have produced something quite unique, knowing that only a very few will ever see it or even know that it is there. That is remarkable in itself.' He turned, taking in all the others with his gaze. 'Come, look upon this work and praise God that He has sent us Cuthbert to work to the glory of God in our Abbey.'

Father Abbot stepped into the aisle to allow the others to kneel to see what had caused such commendation from him. There were gasps of astonishment, hands tenderly touched the carving and exclamations burst from lips. Brother John spoke for them all.

'Wherever did you learn such skill?'

'From my father and from Jethro Milton, Master Carver of Chester who taught me all that I know.'

'And from your own ability,' added Father Paslew. 'I cannot wait to see what else you make for us during your many years here as part of our community. Welcome, Cuthbert Watts.' He seized Cuthbert's hand and shook it heartily before turning and walking out of the Abbey. The others gathered round Cuthbert exclaiming and congratulating and kneeling to take another look at the work. At last they all made their way outside, the three monks returning to the Abbot's lodging, Brother John and Cuthbert to a seat in the cloister.

'What gave you the idea?' asked Brother John.

'For the mice? The position so near to the floor, the ease of carving them, and the fact that even a humble mouse is one of God's creatures and deserves a place in such a magnificent building.'

'The ease of carving! Cuthbert I have seen mice carved before but a mere suggestion of shape and size. Yours is so detailed that there is a twinkle in their eyes, you can feel their fur, the stripes around their tails. No wonder Father Abbot exclaimed when he saw them. I thought they would run away, they are so realistic. I stand in awe of your ability.'

'Please, I am merely doing something I love.'

'Long may you live to produce many more such wonders. You are going to go far young man.'

For the next few days Cuthbert was praised and thanked for what he had done. At some point almost everyone made their way into the Abbey to gaze in wonder at Cuthbert's mice. Far from being an obscure position where they would never be seen it soon became a spot where everyone knelt down to see the wonder created. Even some of the visitors to the Abbey were shown them and Cuthbert became embarrassed at all the attention, but within a few days Abbot Paslew had set him his next task and his time was taken up with plans and ideas for its execution. This was going to be far more prominent than two little mice at the foot of the choir stalls.

CHAPTER EIGHT

The weeks and months flew by as Cuthbert worked on the tasks he was set. Not all were as decorative as his little mice but, nonetheless, he poured all his skill into everything he did. A small box in which spare pens and inks could be carried when one of the monks travelled to an outlying grange to record the harvest; a new chopping block for the kitchens, made from a hefty piece of an elm tree which had blown down two years previously and was nicely matured; shutters for the window in the infirmary; repairs to a screen in one of the chapels, damaged by water from a leak in the roof; new handles for some of the tools used on the farm and in the herb gardens. He soon grew used to the gentle life observed at the Abbey, fitting his work between services and meals. There were other craftsmen there with whom he became friends; Adam, a stonemason from York who was building an extension to one of the store barns; Michael, an elderly potter who made the beautiful tiles used in the floors of the principal buildings; John, the blacksmith whose work was never done, there being so many horses and mules to be shod, tools to be mended, latches to be created. All of them were able to call on the lay workers for help carrying things or holding pieces whilst they were fixed permanently into place and Cuthbert soon felt completely at home in the community.

He was working one day in the woodshed the spring after he had first come to Whalley when he heard a number of horses ride into the courtyard. Curious to see so large a group of men arrive he watched as they dismounted, their horses taken in charge by some of the Abbey's grooms, and the men taken towards Abbot Paslew's lodging.

'Looks like trouble,' murmured John who had just carried a new spade into the shed for Cuthbert to fit a handle to.

'Trouble? Why?' asked Cuthbert.

'There are rumours going about that the king wants a new wife.'

'What's that got to do with us?'

'Not absolutely sure. Summat to do with the Pope, I hear,' replied John as he walked out.

Cuthbert stared after him. New wife? What was wrong with the old one and why should it affect them here. Why should anything the king did affect them? They were just an Abbey. How could their life have anything to do with the king? In London? It was a mystery. A mystery he put to Brother John when he saw him in the cloisters later that evening.

'I'm not altogether sure,' was the unsatisfactory answer. 'They were talking to the Abbot for most of the afternoon. There were even raised voices, I hear, but nothing has been said to anyone else since they departed. No doubt we will be told at Chapter tomorrow.

If anything was said regarding the visitors Cuthbert never got to hear of it and the incident was soon forgotten, the life of the Abbey going on much as before. Cuthbert completed his latest commission, a Bible box to be sent as a gift to a neighbouring Abbey in gratitude for their help over some legal matter concerning land exchanges. Once again Cuthbert had used the motifs from nature he so enjoyed carving and the substantial box was richly decorated with leaves and flowers, insects and small animals. Even Father Abbot was seen to smile when he saw the finished box and he praised Cuthbert for his remarkable gift. For several days it was kept on a table in his lodging awaiting its transport to its recipient and it was here that it was seen by another very important visitor.

Once again a large group of men rode into the Abbey grounds and some of them were taken to the Abbot's lodging, the rest, mainly servants and a sizeable bodyguard, were taken to the kitchens for refreshment after their long ride. Cuthbert noticed the livery many were wearing and asked one of them to whom they were pledged.

'My Lord Derby,' the man replied.

That was a name Cuthbert had heard many times before. A great lord and landowner hereabouts, he had the ear of the king and was influential in the Royal Court. What could such an important personage be doing here? Or was this to be another unsolved mystery? Realising his curiosity was getting the better of him Cuthbert returned to polishing the chest he was working on, working the beeswax into the grain to give it a beautiful sheen. It was therefore unexpected to hear his name being called from the path outside the shed. When he went to the door he was surprised to see one of the Derby servants standing there.

'You are to come with me. My master wants to see you,' he said, turning to go.

'See me? Why?'

'I was sent to fetch you. Come now else my master will be displeased.' The man walked on, so Cuthbert quickly wiped his hands on the piece of sacking he had tied round his waist to protect his clothes from the wax, untied it and followed the man. They were headed for the Abbot's lodging.

'Wait there,' ordered the man, entering an inner room. Cuthbert stood by the window, wondering what warranted this summons. What could Lord Derby want with him? He did not have long to wait. The servant reappeared and beckoned peremptorily to Cuthbert. He went into the room where the Abbot received visitors. The man he took to be Lord Derby was standing by the table where Cuthbert's chest was sitting. A small group of other people were standing nearby, talking amongst themselves and drinking from goblets which only came out for the most important of visitors. They were looking at some papers and pointing out passages to each other.

'Young man,' said Lord Derby in a voice that was used to giving orders and being obeyed. 'I understand that this is your work,' he said, pointing to the chest.

'Yes my lord, it is,' replied Cuthbert.

The man turned back to the box and bent to examine it more closely, touching the surface and feeling the richness of the carving.

'It is quite remarkable,' he said, 'I don't think I have ever seen such incredible detail in a piece of wood. This is not the first such box you have made?'

'No, my lord. We were quite often asked to make such things when I lived in Chester.'

'We?'

'I was taken into the household of Jethro Milton, Master Carver, after the death of my parents. My father was a carver before me and I became apprenticed to Master Carter. He taught me all I know.'

'He was a good teacher,' said Lord Derby, 'and you were a willing and very able pupil. Skill like this cannot be taught, you have to have a special gift for work of such exceptional quality.'

Cuthbert wasn't sure how to respond to such effusive praise, so he kept silent. The distinguished guest continued to examine the chest from all sides. When he stood up he turned to Abbot Paslew.

'Is this young man bound in any way to the Abbey?' he asked.

'No, my lord. He came to us on the recommendation of one of the brothers who had seen his work in the Abbey Church of St Werburgh. He has served this Abbey diligently and with great skill. There are many examples of his work here.'

'Indeed? Let me see. Cuthbert, show me what you have done.'

Surprised, Cuthbert led a small entourage round the various parts of the Abbey complex, pointing out his work. Normally he would have been embarrassed to do so but he somehow felt that there was some unknown purpose behind this great lord's actions. Finally they reached the Abbey church and he led them to the choir stalls and the first of his creations.

'Father Abbot set me a test when I first came,' he said, 'to see whether my work was worthy of such a great place. This is what I did.'

He pointed to the floor and the worthy gentleman looked puzzled, but when Cuthbert knelt down, he followed and looked where he was pointing. It took a few seconds for his eyes to adjust but when they did, he gasped and called for candles. For several minutes he looked, felt and caressed the little mice before clambering to his feet and, without a word, he walked out of the church. Once outside he made his way to the cloister and sat on one of the stone seats against the wall, still without saying a word. Everyone else was standing nearby wondering what all this was leading to.

Eventually he got to his feet, beckoned to the Abbot and together they went back to the Abbot's house, leaving everyone else behind.

'Well,' said one of the Derby servants, 'it's not often my lord is speechless.'

'Is that good or bad?' asked Cuthbert.

'Depends,' said another man, and smiled.

Cuthbert wasn't sure what he should do. Stay, or return to the work he had been doing? He turned to go and was halfway across the cloister before a voice called him back. It was one of the men who had seemed closest to Lord Derby. Cuthbert followed him back to the Abbot's lodging. The Abbot was sitting in his usual place behind one of the big tables with Lord Derby next to him. A number of papers were scattered in front of them.

'Cuthbert, how would you feel about working on a new building?' asked Lord Derby.

Cuthbert was momentarily dumb. New building? Where? Here? Doing what?

'Er, well,' he managed. 'Does Father Abbot wish me to leave?' he asked.

'I do not *wish* you to leave but you are a young man with your future before you. You have many years and many fine works to create yet. Perhaps it is time for you to see new places, serve new masters, create more fine things. Your work here has been exemplary and my lord here sees many opportunities for you elsewhere. You would go with my blessing.'

'Where would I be going to?'

'Initially to one of my estates,' replied Lord Derby, 'and then I have an idea that your skills may be of great use to a young friend of mine who is building a new house and needs skilled craftsmen like you. There would be work there for many years. He has drawn up plans for his house, it is to be large and impressive and will need many men to complete it. Would you be willing to be part of this new venture?'

Why, yes, I would,' excitement growing within Cuthbert. 'When would you require me to go?'

'By the end of this year. That will give you time to complete whatever tasks you have in hand here. Initially you would come to my estate and when your skills are needed you would move to your new workplace.' He looked at Cuthbert. 'Men of your skill are rare. It will be a great opportunity for you to advance yourself and give great satisfaction to your new master.' He stood up and turned to Father Paslew. 'I will send a servant to fetch him when we are ready, shall we say December, before the Christmas Feast? I presume you can ride,' he asked over his shoulder.

'I have ridden a pony in the past, though I am not what you would call a good rider.'

'As long as you can stay in the saddle. It will be a faster journey on horseback than foot at that time of the year. I don't want you freezing to death on the wayside.' He turned back to Father Abbot. 'I presume the goods have been loaded. I will leave you now.' To Cuthbert he said, 'Until December,' then turned and left.

Outside his men had loaded several pack horses with heavy looking panniers and the body guard were assembled closely around them. They rode out with a clatter of hooves and squeak of leather. Then they were gone and peace descended on the Abbey.

Cuthbert returned to his polishing but his mind was in turmoil. New places. New work. New challenges. It was only later that he realised that he had not been told where this new beginning was to be.

CHAPTER NINE

As December approached Cuthbert had heard nothing further from either Abbot Paslew or Lord Derby and he was beginning to wonder whether they had made empty promises. He continued to work diligently at whatever tasks he was set and in free moments he explored the countryside around the Abbey. He liked particularly to walk along the banks of the river watching the birds and other wildlife that abounded in the fields and woods. He often made drawings of what he saw; a rabbit washing itself by the hedge, or a kingfisher sitting on a branch waiting for a fish to swim by, a fox stalking a bird through the long grass or a butterfly resting in the last rays of sunshine on a leaf. These were the source of his inspiration for his work and he was as capable of catching them on paper as he was in wood. Time sometimes caught up with him and he would have to hurry back to the Abbey so as not to miss a meal.

The days grew shorter and colder and he was glad of the warming room, the only place where the residents in the Abbey were allowed a fire. Otherwise he wrapped himself in the good woollen cloak he had brought from Chester and worked in a warm corner of the workshop. Sometimes the blacksmith gave him tasks to do and he was glad to enter the forge and sit near the blazing fire as the smith made a variety of metal implements. He was one of the busiest of the craftsmen, there was always something needing repair, horses to be shod, tools to be made, door hinges to fashion, as many people from the village and surrounding farms came to the Abbey blacksmith to make use of his skills. Cuthbert continued to learn and improve his skills when working with wood.

It was during these times that he often thought of his life in Chester and wondered what Mildred and Nell were doing now. Mildred was a sensible woman and would not have let her grief overshadow her life. She and Jethro had been married for many years and their life had been comfortable because Jethro worked hard to make it so. Their love was one of the abiding things he remembered about them. He had never heard a cross word pass between them, their minor disagreements were settled quietly and always before the day was over. The way they had quietly taken him into their home when his parents died was an example of their love of their fellow man. There was no argument, they just did it, opening their home and their hearts to a bewildered and grief stricken young boy. He had grown and developed in their love, quietly encouraging him with his lessons and later in his developing skill in working wood. It was Jethro who had apprenticed him and devoted seven years of his life to nurturing that skill until Cuthbert was recognised as having completed his apprenticeship and could move on as a journeyman. He could have moved away to pursue his life anywhere he wished but he had chosen to stay with these adoptive parents and continue to work alongside Jethro. What a precious time that had been.

***

One bitterly cold day a group of men rode into the Abbey grounds and Cuthbert recognised the badge they wore; it was that of the Derby family. Perhaps, at last, the promise made was to be fulfilled. The men disappeared towards the Abbot's lodging, their horses taken to the Abbey stables, out of the cold wind. Cuthbert felt a shiver of apprehension down his spine. They may have come on some other errand. They may have brought a message to the Abbot that he was not needed after all. They may ride away without him. It was almost more than he could bear.

At last a servant emerged from the house and spoke to a passing lay brother who pointed towards the workshop where

Cuthbert was trying to concentrate on smoothing a wooden handle he had just made for a farm rake. The servant turned towards him.

'Father Abbot wants to see you,' he said and turned back the way he had come. Cuthbert dropped the handle and followed. He was shown into Father Abbot's room where the group of men were sitting by a roaring fire with cups of warmed wine in their hands and the remains of refreshments on plates at their side. Of course, he thought, they would have been offered something to warm them after a long, cold journey.

'Cuthbert,' cried Abbot Paslew. 'Here is your escort to take you to my Lord Derby's residence, as promised some time ago. It is time for you to leave us. Can you be ready within the hour to accompany them?'

'Yes, Father,' replied Cuthbert. 'I have few belongings to gather.'

'Then go and prepare. These men have some goods to collect here and then you will be on your way. They wish to return in daylight and the days are so short.' He rose and came towards Cuthbert who knelt for his blessing. A gentle hand was laid on his bowed head. 'May God go with you and keep you safe on your journey, not just today but on all your days. You will be remembered in our prayers with grateful thanks for all you have done for our Abbey and this village. Go in peace.' He made the sign of the cross over Cuthbert's head then lifted him to his feet and gave him one of his rare smiles. 'Farewell, my son.'

Cuthbert emerged into the cold winter sunshine. When he had arisen that morning he had no idea that he was about to start on another stage of life's journey that very day. He looked up at the clear blue sky and then at the buildings around him. It had been his home for such a short time but one which he had come to love and would always remember. He hurried back to the workshop and gathered his tools into the stout leather satchel he had arrived with, then walked over to the lay brothers dormitory to collect his few belongings. Silas was there, as always, sweeping the floor between the narrow cots.

'So, you are going,' he remarked matter-of-factly. 'Time to move on, eh?'

'Yes, Silas. Time to move on. Thank you for your kindness to me ever since I arrived.'

''Tis nought but my job,' was the reply. 'Safe journey.'

Cuthbert went in search of Brother John. He had a special fondness for the monk who had recognised his skill in Chester and brought him here to work for the great Abbey. As expected he found him in the cloister, sitting in one of the sheltered bays, well wrapped in his thick woollen cloak that he used when travelling, reading a manuscript laid on the desk before him. Cuthbert recognised it as one of the Gospels, copied so beautifully by a monk many years ago and held in the Abbey library.

Brother John looked up and smiled his warm, welcoming face always a joy to see.

'I see you are ready to go,' he said.

'Yes, how did you know?'

'Oh, Cuthbert, my son, have you not yet realised that little goes on within these walls without it being known throughout the community within minutes? Brother James saw the men from the Earl of Derby arrive and go into the Abbot's house. They have come for the rest of the treasure and will be returning today so I assumed you would go with them.'

Cuthbert laughed.

'You wily fox! Yes, I have been summoned and depart with them. I came to say goodbye and to thank you.'

'Thank me for what? I have merely set you another step along your life's journey.'

'And what a step. Without that push from you I would still be carving boxes in Chester.'

'What a box, though, eh. You will go far and create many more wonderful things. Trust me.'

Cuthbert felt embarrassed by the praise and tried to change the subject.

'You mentioned treasure. What treasure is that?' he asked

'Treasure left here by some rich man for safekeeping. The

Abbey has had it in the Treasury for years, added to now and again until it has become a vast fortune, I'm told.'

'Does he want it back now?'

'Yes, it is to go to his son, to build a house. Some friend of Lord Derby, I believe. That's why they keep coming back, taking a bit at a time. Safer that way. The Treasurer tells me this is the last so you will have to go with them too.'

'Hence the pack ponies they brought with them.'

'Yes, though I hope they give you something better to ride, those ponies can be skittish at times.'

They clasped hands in farewell, looked into each other's eyes and nodded in agreement. No further words were needed. Two friends parting for who knew how long, maybe forever.

Cuthbert rode out on a decent horse surrounded by the escort and the pack ponies. As they passed under the gatehouse he looked back and there was Brother John standing by the inner gate. He raised a hand and Cuthbert waved back then set his face to the front, to another turn in his life and another step into the future.

CHAPTER TEN

'Where is that Cuthbert?' snapped the cross looking man in the dusty tunic and hose, brandishing a large saw in one hand and a piece of paper in the other.

'He went to find Ezekial to fetch the new wood,' replied Will. 'We'll need it soon, once they finish the roofbeams.'

'I'm well aware of that, my boy. That's why I sent him but he should have been back some time ago.'

'Perhaps there's a problem,' suggested Will. 'He may have got lost.'

'Lost? How can he get lost between here and the wood yard? He'll be talking to someone, that's what it'll be. He's always talking to someone. Only been here three weeks and he's made himself known to everyone. A timewaster, that's what he is, a timewaster. As if I didn't have enough trouble trying to get this job finished and the Master coming over here every few days and changing his mind about what he wants. That's the trouble with working with young Masters, always changing things. I've been building houses like this for thirty-five years, man and boy, and I knows what works and what don't. Now, when I worked over in Yorkshire, the Master told me what he wanted and left me to it and there was nothing wrong with the place when it was done. This one! I mean to say, whoever heard of a fireplace on the outside wall of a Great Hall? Great monstrosity of a thing it is, takes up half the wall. There's nothing wrong with a good fire in the middle, makes a central point for the room, but oh no! not this one. "It's the latest thing, Abel," he says. "All the great houses will have them soon," he says. Not if

I have anything to do with it. Why change what's worked for centuries, I say?'

'I think it's …'

'What you think is of no importance,' interrupted Abel. 'You are still my apprentice and you do as you're told, whether you like it or not. Now go and find Cuthbert and tell him I want him here immediately. Go on, boy, go.'

Will ran off, not wanting to get the sharp edge of Abel's tongue. He had been apprentice carpenter for six years, only one more year to go and he would be able to call himself a journeyman though he would still stay with Abel. The old man had no family, no sons to follow him and Will recognised when he was well off. When old Abel died he wanted to be ready to step into his shoes. He saw Cuthbert as a rival. Arriving here on the recommendation of Lord Derby, no less, he was heralded as a great carver of wood. Not that they had seen any of his carving yet. Abel had kept him on mundane tasks so far, sawing wood into lengths for the men constructing the building, making endless basketfuls of wooden pegs, holding things whilst others fastened them in place, fetching and carrying. Not that Cuthbert ever complained. He recognised that he was the newest man on the site and did anything he was asked to willingly. But Will was not going to let him take his place, Cuthbert was not going to worm his way into Abel's team.

Will smiled when he got outside. There was still no sign of Cuthbert with the new wood. Good. He wondered how long it had taken him to realise he'd been sent in the wrong direction. Looking round quickly, Will could see everyone was busy working. Plenty of time to sneak off and go and sit by the Mere for a little while whilst he waited for Cuthbert to return, then waylay him and berate him for taking so long. He knew of a place at the waterside, well hidden from anyone passing where he could rest whilst he planned his next move against Cuthbert.

Ezekial and Cuthbert were making their way back to the building site with a cartload of timber for the builders. It had taken Cuthbert a considerable time to find the wood yard and it was only after asking a passing farm labourer that he realised that Will had sent him the wrong way. He wasn't sure why the boy had taken such a dislike to him, he had barely spoken to him since arriving, but he was constantly doing things to annoy; 'accidentally' tipping over the basket of pegs Cuthbert had just filled, hiding the tools he was using, moving the pieces he had put in place ready for fastening together.

'How do you like working with Abel?' asked Ezekial, cutting into Cuthbert's thoughts as he steered the horse round a sharp corner.

'Fine,' he replied. 'I arrived unexpectedly with one of Lord Derby's men and I don't think Abel was too pleased to have a stranger thrust upon him and told to give me work. He has his gang of workers who he always uses, he didn't need any more and I feel he resents my presence.'

'Don't take no notice of that. Abel is, or was, a first class master builder but since his wife died he's become a crusty old devil. His tongue can be sharp and he doesn't like change, new ideas. His ways are tried and tested and he sees no need to alter them. I hear he put up a right stink about that chimney. I've heard it's the latest method and it works well but Abel won't have it. You just put your head down and get on with your job. It may take a while but Abel will come round. Eventually.'

They turned into the area where the new house was gradually taking shape. Great stone blocks marked the foundations of the building, stone brought on heavy carts pulled by six horses from quarries the family owned not far away. Cut and shaped by a team of stonemasons they were mostly in position and the carpenters had almost completed the walls. The good oak wood from family estates had been felled, cut to size then brought to the building site. Sections of wall were put together on the ground, all the mortice and tenon joints cut exactly to fit, then, when it was ready, each section was hauled upright by rope and tackle and fastened in place on the top of the stone foundations, propped up by great beams until the various sections were secured by cross ties. All the gaps between the timbers were filled with wattle made from willow from trees by the Mere and then covered with daub, a mixture of mud, and horse hair and straw. Most of that was now drying in the sun, great gaps still showing where windows would be inserted, and doors fitted. The foundations had looked big but now that there were walls arising from them it looked even bigger. The central block, the Great Hall, was a lofty building and the wings set at right angles across each end more than doubled the size of the house. Men were busy all over the site, dozens of them, like ants around an ant hill. It looked chaotic but Cuthbert knew that each and every one of them had a specific job to do and was fitting the whole place together. He gathered that many of the men had worked with Abel for years but there were also many local men, valuable because of their local knowledge of the land and the resources they needed. Although the ground was very flat and there was an extremely large Mere very close to the house, Cuthbert had been reassured that the actual site of the building was a few feet higher than its surroundings, a few feet that made all the difference to avoiding flooding.

They were passing close to the Mere when a figure suddenly emerged from the undergrowth, startling the horse. Ezekial pulled on the reins, bringing the animal under control again before cursing the boy soundly.

'Don't you ever learn? How many times have I told you, Will, not to jump out near the horses?' he shouted. 'He could have bolted or overturned the cart, you stupid idiot.'

'Well it didn't, did it?' replied Will cheekily. 'Besides I wanted to warn Cuthbert that Abel is angry with him for taking so long. Sends you on a simple task and you take all day. We're waiting for that wood.'

'I would have been a lot quicker if you had given me the right directions,' hissed Cuthbert through clenched teeth. He felt Ezekial's hand on his arm and refrained from saying anything else.

'We're here now and that's what matters. If you get out of the way we can deliver this load all the quicker,' said Ezekial.

'I'll jump on the back for the rest of the way,' said Will, moving towards the rear of the cart.

'No, you won't,' retorted Ezekial, shaking the reins to move the horse along. Will stepped back hurriedly as the cart almost ran over his foot and when Cuthbert glanced back the boy was making a very rude gesture in their direction.

'Didn't like that,' he murmured. 'He doesn't like you, does he?'

'The feeling is mutual. Will is an idle, lying, cheat, always trying to impress Abel, expecting to inherit his business when Abel dies. I've yet to see him put in a full day's work but whenever Abel needs him he's there, toadying up to him, his "Master", trying to keep in his favour. I've no time for lads like him.' He glanced across at Cuthbert. 'Don't let him annoy you. He's only trying to anger you so that Abel will think even less of you if you retaliate.'

'He's doing a good job at that. I've never worked with someone who constantly taunts me, tries to make me make mistakes, petty little things but irritating.'

'You keep on as you're doing. Abel knows he can't dismiss you, not when Lord Derby himself sent you over. Even Abel daren't go against his orders.' He smiled at Cuthbert. 'Your day will come. We are all waiting to see your work when the house gets to that stage. It's your carving that has brought you here.'

'How did you know that?' exclaimed Cuthbert.

Ezekial laughed.

'I know a man who knows a man who works for Lord Derby. He saw your work at Whalley Abbey and never stopped talking about it. We expect great things of you Cuthbert.'

Cuthbert was dumbfounded. Had they really been talking about him in such a way? He thought he had come as a general carpenter with the possibility of doing some special work maybe, but not that his carving was the main reason. He was silent the rest of the way.

Ezekial drew up close to the wood stack for the builders and jumped down to start unloading.

'About time too,' yelled Abel striding towards them. 'Glad you could make it today. Not interrupted anything important, I hope.' He marched right up to Cuthbert and glared into his face. 'When I send someone to do a simple job I expect them to do it, immediately, not when you feel like it. Now get this lot unloaded.' With a sneer of contempt he turned on his heels and marched away. Cuthbert saw Will sniggering by the wood saw and felt like punching him but he took a deep breath and turned to unload.

'Well done, lad. Ignore him,' muttered Ezekial, as they lifted the beams of wood off the back of the cart. 'Your time will come and you can put Master Will in his place.'

Cuthbert heeded the good advice but Will was like an annoying insect always buzzing around him, sneering at him, laughing behind his back, making comments to the other men on the site. Most of them ignored him, they knew Will for what he really was and he had few real friends though he liked to make out he was everyone's good friend. He was tolerated, that was all. Everyone was too busy to take much notice, until the day his pranks nearly caused a nasty accident.

A group of the carpenters were fixing some of the crossbeams for the roof of one of the wings of the house. The wood had been cut to size on the ground and several of them were manoeuvring the longest beam into position. They had rigged a pulley system to lift it and several of the men, including Cuthbert were up tall ladders waiting to catch the ends and get it into the right place atop the walls. It was a difficult job as both ends needed to be in the correct position and at the right angle across the space. A little bit out of line and the ends would not meet up with the holes already cut to receive them. All of them, including Cuthbert, had done this many times before on this and other buildings and knew it took patience to get it right. Once the roof was on it could not be changed if it was found to be wrong without dismantling a major part of their work.

As the beam was inched towards its place by the men on the pulley below and guided by those above, all eyes were directed upwards, with quiet instructions from those at each end to,

'Move it a bit this way,' or 'a bit more,' or 'up again'. There was a certain tension in the air. Cuthbert was at the top of the east wall, holding the ladder with one hand and reaching towards the beam as it was swung his way, ready to guide it into place. Suddenly he felt the ladder move, only slightly, but enough to unnerve him and he grabbed the top rung with his free hand to steady himself. The approaching beam swung towards him and caught his elbow a painful blow. Stifling a cry of pain, he reached out again and pulled the end of the wood towards the wall, just managing to connect it with the horizontal beam, pushing it into place and quickly inserting a wooden peg from the bag attached to his belt, then hammering it into place with the mallet dangling from his belt. He glanced across to the other side of the room and saw that the man over there had also secured his end. The rope fastened round the beam was pulled free and fell back to the ground. Cuthbert watched it fall and out of the corner of his eye saw Will moving away from the foot of the ladder Cuthbert was standing on. What was he doing there? He was supposed to be over in the other wing helping with hanging one of the big doors, at least, that was what Cuthbert had overheard Abel telling him to do, so why was he here, in the opposite wing?

He descended to the floor and, feeling slightly sick, sat down on a pile of wood by the wall.

'Only another six of them to put up today,' declared Thomas, the man who had fixed the opposite end of the beam to Cuthbert. 'Hey, are you all right? You are as white as a ghost? Not got a head for heights?'

'No, I'm fine,' Cuthbert assured him. 'Just took a knock on my elbow up there. Hurts a bit.'

'Let me look,' said Thomas, squatting down beside him. Cuthbert pulled his sleeve up. Blood was beginning to ooze from a cut right on the end of his elbow but not enough to warrant the severity of the pain he was feeling.

'Not too bad, you'll live but that's going to be a colourful show by tomorrow and a bit stiff for a while. Odd things, elbows, the slightest knock can hurt like hell. Feel a bit queasy?'

Cuthbert nodded.

'Best not go up the ladder for a bit. Don't worry, I can get someone else, plenty of us around,' he grinned. He called to Ezekial who had just come in to see what wood was needed for the next day. 'Ezekial! Liliath will be able to see to Cuthbert here, won't he? He's taken a bang on the elbow.'

'Yes, she will,' replied the woodman. 'Works wonders she does. Go and see her later.'

'Where will I find her?'

'Wife of the blacksmith, good with healing balms and such like. Her mother was a healer where she came from. She's good with cuts and bruises, she'll put something soothing on it, take the ache away and bring the bruise out. Seen her works wonders with injuries. Many of us here have had Liliath's cures for one thing and another. See her, at the forge, tonight.'

'Thanks,' said Cuthbert, as the two men stood up and walked away. He flexed his elbow and the pain shot up his arm, making him wince, and he hugged the arm to him, waiting for the sick feeling to go.

'What do you think you're doing?' Abel was standing in the doorway of the building, his eyes fixed on Cuthbert. 'No time for sitting about, there's work to do. Get up and help the men. I want all those roofbeams in place by nightfall.' With a disdainful sneer he walked away, shaking his head and muttering to himself.

Cuthbert got to his feet and went over to the ladder he had been up. He knew he had set it in place safely, both feet squarely on the ground, as he always did. It was not like that now. Marks in the earth showed that it had been moved sideways a couple of inches, not much, but enough to make it unstable. Whoever had done it would have had to give it a kick to move it. Was that what Will was doing in here? When everyone's attention was concentrated upwards? If that was the case, he was a complete idiot. If Cuthbert had fallen from the ladder he would have been seriously injured, if not killed. Goodness me, he only had to think back to that awful day in Chester when

Jethro had fallen from the ladder. He shuddered at the thought. Dare he accuse Will of what he suspected? If no one else had seen him, what proof did he have? In future he would be more careful. Rubbing his elbow he went back to work, using the arm gingerly but managing to complete his day's work.

CHAPTER ELEVEN

The men had finished their work for the day, all the beams had been put in place as Abel had ordered and they dispersed to the huts where they were living temporarily during the building. The smell of food cooking pervaded the air and Cuthbert's stomach rumbled. He hadn't realised how hungry he was until now and looked forward to eating. Some of the men had their wives with them and they managed to produce good food for their menfolk. It was understood that if the men were well fed they worked better so many owners made sure that there were adequate provisions for the workforce. It was usually a wholesome meal of vegetables with some meat and a rich gravy, served with hunks of fresh baked bread. Filling and satisfying after a hard day's work.

Afterwards many of the men went to their beds, tired out after their labours. Some sat outside in the late evening enjoying a drink and a talk. The village brewer provided some good ale for a price and Cuthbert usually joined them but tonight he wandered towards the village to see the blacksmith's wife.

The village of Rufford was small but it had its own blacksmith by the road to Ormskirk. Cuthbert had been past a number of times and the blacksmith always seemed to be busy about the forge. Since the start of the building of the hall his work had doubled, mending broken tools, sharpening blades, making the hinges for the doors and gates that would be needed as well as his task of shoeing the numerous horses used to transport all the building materials. He had even heard that Lord Derby himself had had to stop for him to attend to his fine horse which had cast a shoe on the road.

Although it was fairly late in the day Cuthbert could hear the ring of metal on metal as the smith worked on something beside the great fire burning in the forge. Another man was pumping the bellows, a smaller version of the smith and Cuthbert wondered whether they were related. He stood and watched as the sparks flew from the anvil as he worked a long piece of metal into shape. Only when he plunged it into a bucket full of water at his side, causing a cloud of steam to rise up around him did the smith look up.

'Looking for me?' he asked, wiping a brawny arm across his brow.

'No, I was looking for your wife,' replied Cuthbert. 'I've been told she has some healing knowledge.'

'Aye, that she has,' was the answer. 'Are you from the building? Got hurt have you?'

'Yes, just a bad knock on the elbow,' said Cuthbert. 'Ezekial said she could ease it for me.'

'Ezekial sent you, did he?' He's the wife's cousin. Sends everyone to her, does Ezekial.' He grinned, lifted his lump of metal from the bucket and examined it before plunging it back into the fire. 'Jacob, go and get Liliath. Tell her someone needs her.' The young man who had been pumping the bellows went off round the back of the building. 'My little brother,' explained the smith. 'I'm Jehan, Jacob helps me, especially with the horses. He's good with horses, is Jacob. They trust him.' He turned his metal bar over in the fire and turned back to Cuthbert. 'Building going all right? Haven't had time to walk up and look at it this week.'

'Yes, it's coming on well. Abel wants the roof on before it rains, then we can at least work under cover.'

'Very wise. Ah, here's Liliath. Liliath my dear, another injury for you. You go inside with her, she'll sort you out.' Jehan placed the glowing metal bar on the anvil and began hammering it again as Jacob resumed his position by the bellows.

Cuthbert followed Liliath to the little cottage behind the forge, bending low to enter the doorway. Inside was a basic but comfortable room, a fire burning in a brazier and a table and chairs set near the window. Shelves held various pots and pans and at the back another held an array of bottles and jars, evidently the tools of her healing. Bunches of herbs hung from the roofbeams, drying and there was a delicious smell coming from a large pot suspended over the fire. She gestured to a stool by the table and Cuthbert sat down.

Cuthbert had watched her as she walked in front of him to the cottage and noticed how slender she was, with a thick dark braid of hair hanging below her waist. Her simple dress emphasised her tiny waist. She looked quite a bit younger than her husband and when she finally turned towards him she gave him a beautiful smile that lit up her face.

'Jacob tells me you have been injured at the hall,' she said quietly, in an accent he couldn't quite place, but very different to her husband's, and he wondered where she came from.

'Oh, yes,' he said. 'I got hit on the elbow by a swinging beam. I don't think anything is broken but it's very sore and stiff.'

'Let me see,' she said, and took hold of his left arm as he held it out to her. Her hands were warm and surprisingly soft as she rolled his sleeve up above the elbow. The material had stuck to the wound and she peeled it gently away, causing the blood to start to flow again. She touched the area gently and felt Cuthbert tense. 'Is that where it hit you?'

Cuthbert nodded. Liliath went to the fire and poured some water out of a kettle hanging near it into a bowl. She placed this on the table and went to the shelf of bottles, taking down an earthenware jar stoppered with a wooden peg and a piece of cloth. She poured a small amount into the water, took a piece of cloth out of a basket and dipped it into the water. Holding Cuthbert's hand she turned his arm so that she could clearly see the cut and touched it with the cloth. Cuthbert winced as it stung and bit his lip. Liliath looked up at him.

'It will sting but this will stop it going bad.' She dabbed at the cut until she was satisfied it was clean, then dried it on the other end of the cloth. With gentle fingers she prodded round his elbow, finding the most tender spots whilst Cuthbert flinched at the pressure.

'This will be sore for a few days but I don't think there is too much damage. By tomorrow it will be every colour of the rainbow. I can give you some salve which will numb the pain but try not to knock it if you can.' From the shelf she took down another small jar and handed it to him. 'I'll put some on now, you do the same tonight and tomorrow morning. By the end of the week you will hardly know it's there.' Once again Cuthbert was struck by how incredibly gentle her touch was as she smeared his arm with the fragrant salve and pulled his sleeve back down.

'There. All done. Try not to bang it for a while, it'll be tender but it'll heal.'

'Thank you,' said Cuthbert, 'It feels easier already.'

As he walked back out to the lane he passed the forge where the smith was still working.

'Has she sorted you out?' he called. 'Good woman, is Liliath. The best wife a man could have.' He turned back to the forge and Cuthbert regained the track leading to his lodging near the site. He felt a lot more comfortable now and just hoped that Will wouldn't try any more of his tricks on him. A suspicion was not evidence Will was involved but Cuthbert would watch him more closely.

Passing the Mere on his way Cuthbert stopped to watch some birds on the water, dipping their heads to feed on the weed and small fish which grew there. He had heard some of the men who lived nearby say that there was good fishing to be had and that eels were particularly plentiful. Flocks of ducks and geese were hunted and the occasional swan provided a good meal, whilst on shore there were hordes rabbits for the pot, provided the landowner didn't catch you. Poaching was forbidden and the penalties, if caught, were harsh, but many of the men provided extra for their families with a bit of free food. If a big family was going to be living at the new hall there may be opportunities for some to legitimately provide food for the kitchens from the Mere and its surrounds. The land may be low lying and poorly drained in places but it could provide employment for many of the villagers when there was a big house to provide for. Cuthbert had always lived near a town and had never really thought about where people living in the country found food. He supposed there were village markets but there would not be shops and stalls every day as in Chester. It was a quieter yet harder way of life in the country.

As he turned towards the lodgings where he was staying he saw Will coming towards him with a girl beside him. She was giggling and looking at Will shyly. She looked young but Will was steering her towards a coppice by the water. Cuthbert thought his behaviour typical of the man he knew, nothing done openly, Will wouldn't want a courtship and marriage, just a quick liaison, soon done, soon forgotten, move on. He felt sorry for the girl. How long before she realised Will was only after one thing. The girl's giggles were smothered as the pair disappeared among the trees and Cuthbert hurried past. It was none of his business.

He was almost asleep when he heard someone come into the hut where several of the men slept. Whoever it was was trying to move about quietly but judging by the bumps and curses from the occupants of the beds the person was a little worse for wear and was stumbling his way to his bed in the far corner. It was Will, of course, who eventually reached his own bed and fell across it and within minutes was snoring. Whatever he had been doing in the copse, he was getting a good night's sleep now.

Next morning, after breaking his fast with a bowl of thick porridge cooked by one of the men in a great pot over the fire Cuthbert made his way to the Hall, ready to begin his day's work. There seemed to be more activity than usual as he drew nearer, men carrying wood and tools in and out of the place with purpose, but not actually doing much work yet.

'What's going on?' he asked one of the lads as he hurried by carrying a ladder.

'Abel's all of a fuss,' was the strange reply. 'He's had a message that the young Master is visiting today with his wife, wants to see how the building's coming along so Abel's in a foul mood.'

'Why should that be? Surely he would welcome an interest in the progress of the work.'

'Not Abel,' said another of the builders who had overheard the conversation. 'I've worked with Abel for over fifteen years and he likes to be left to get on with the job he's good at. That way he knows what he's doing, but this young Lord? He wants to be in on every stage, see what's being done, but worst of all, he keeps asking for changes and alterations to the original plans. Abel hates that. You'll have heard about the fuss over the fireplace? Well, if he'd had his way it would not have been built. Abel don't like new ideas.' He spat on the ground. 'Leave Abel to get on with the job and it will be a good 'un. Upset him and we'll all suffer his tongue. You'll see.'

It was just what Cuthbert had heard before and he wondered what would happen today if the young Lord started changing things again. He made his way over to the shelter where he had been cutting wood for the boards of the floors in the upper part of the west wing. Best to keep out of Abel's way he decided but it wasn't to be. He had only laid three boards when he heard someone coming up the ladder to the first floor. It was Abel and he was not pleased.

'Who told you to do this room?' he snapped.

'You did, yesterday. You said you wanted this one completed so that Alfric could start on the wainscot.'

'Well get on with it then and be quick about it.' Abel would not admit his mistake under any circumstances. He watched Cuthbert nail another board in place. 'Don't go wasting nails either. You don't need that many if you put them in properly.'

Cuthbert did not rise to this challenge. He knew Abel was trying to provoke him, make him argue back but Cuthbert ignored him. Abel turned to go then said,

'You stay up here until I tell you to come down. I don't want you wandering around the site today. Keep out of my way.'

With that he descended the ladder and left him. Cuthbert knew exactly what had been left unsaid. 'Keep away from the master. I don't want him to meet you.' By keeping Cuthbert occupied up here Abel would prevent any questions about his work, especially his carving, which Cuthbert knew he was being kept from on purpose. He was prepared to wait though. Enough of the other workers knew about his reason for being brought to Rufford, someone was bound to mention it sometime and Abel would have some explaining to do if there was none of his work to be seen.

Not long afterwards Cuthbert heard the sounds of several horses outside. He went to the window space and looked down on a busy scene. Several horses had arrived carrying not just the young master, but quite a party with him. There was a lady he presumed was his wife, a small boy, probably his son, a lady companion, and several other men, including, to his surprise, Lord Derby who he recognised from the Abbey. Well, this was really going to upset Abel, he thought. One visitor was bad enough but a whole party of inquisitive people would be unbearable to the Master carpenter. Cuthbert couldn't help smiling at what was probably going through Abel's mind. If they all started making comments and criticising the work so far, or offering suggestions for changes, Abel would be unable to hold his temper. There was trouble brewing. Well, he would keep out of it and see what happened. He had enough wood in the room to complete the floor without having to go back to the wood store.

It was nearly an hour later when Cuthbert sensed there was someone standing behind him. He turned and looked straight into the face of the small boy he had seen arriving earlier.

'What are you doing?' asked the child.

'I'm laying the floor,' replied Cuthbert, sitting back on his heels.

'Why?'

'We have to put a floor down or we couldn't walk about in the room, could we?'

'Are you making all the floors for the whole house?' asked the child.

Cuthbert laughed.

'No, there are lots of carpenters working here.'

'What's a car … carden … too?'

'Car … pen … ter.' repeated Cuthbert, slowly.

'Carpenter. What else does a car … pen … ter do?'

'We help to build the house, we make all the wooden parts. See, over there, the wooden parts make the walls and the gaps are filled in with a sort of plaster. And look up at the ceiling, that's lots of wood too, and the doors and the shutters on the windows. When the house is finished we will have to make all the furniture too, all the tables and chairs and stools and shelves and cupboards and beds and chests. They are all made of wood.'

The child looked at Cuthbert with his big eyes.

'What's your name?' he asked suddenly.

'Cuthbert. What's yours?'

'I'm Thomas. My father is building this house so that we can come and live here. Will you live here too?'

'No, Thomas. When the work is finished I will go somewhere else and build another house.'

The solemn little boy took all this in, then nodded.

'What are you doing up here, anyway?' asked Cuthbert. 'Won't your mother and father wonder where you are?'

'They were too busy talking to the man. I wanted to know who was banging up here.'

'I'd better take you down again before they miss you,' said Cuthbert. He ushered the child towards the doorway. 'How old are you, Thomas?'

'I'm five,' was the reply. 'How old are you?'

Cuthbert smiled at the candid question, typical of a child.

'Oh, I'm a bit older than that. Now, careful on these steps. They're not quite finished yet.'

To his surprise, Thomas put his hand in his as they went carefully down the steep stairway which was without a handrail on the side. At the bottom Thomas kept hold of his hand and they went through a doorway that led into the Great Hall.

'Thomas! Where have you been?' cried the lady standing by the young master. 'We've been looking for you everywhere. I told you to stay with Martha. You naughty boy.'

'I wanted to see who was banging,' explained Thomas, perfectly reasonably. 'This is Cuthbert. He's a car … pen … ter. He has been telling me how he is building the house. He's my friend.' The child beamed up at Cuthbert, still holding his hand.

'Well, you are back now and you must say thank you to Cuthbert for looking after you but you must stay with us now.'

'He was perfectly safe, my lady, I brought him down the stairs to make sure he didn't fall.' Cuthbert released his hand, touched his forelock to the party and was turning to go.

'Wait one moment,' called a voice from the other end of the room. 'Cuthbert, you say?'

The man Cuthbert had recognised as Lord Derby strode across the bare floor to join the group.

'Robert, my friend, this is the man I mentioned to you, from Whalley Abbey.'

'Whalley Abbey?' Lord Hesketh wrinkled his brow, trying to place him. 'You mean the woodcarver?'

'Yes, I sent him to you. Have you not met him before?'

'I don't remember, I may have done, there are a lot of carpenters and stonemasons and such like working here. I can't be expected to remember them all. Wasn't there something special about him?'

'Robert, really! He's is the most marvellous worker of wood, made a box for their library and figures in their choir.'

'Oh, him! Of course, yes, I do remember something about it. It had quite gone out of my head.'

'I hope that he is doing some wonderful work for you here. Cuthbert, have you anything you can show us now.'

Cuthbert shifted his feet uncomfortably.

'Well, I haven't actually done any carving yet. I have been doing regular carpentry work in the construction of the house so far, beams and floors and doors and so on.'

'What? A man of your talent is wasted on plain woodwork. Master Builder?'

He looked around for Abel who had been standing at the end of the Great Hall listening to the conversation and going redder and redder in the face, his fury barely under control. He stepped forward.

'Yes, my Lord?' he said.

'Why isn't Cuthbert employed in the decoration of this house? I sent him here expressly to use his considerable talent to the betterment of the property, not to waste it building walls and laying floors. He is far too good to be doing that. There are plenty of other excellent men to do the basic work. Cuthbert is different.'

'I … I'm sorry, my lord, but we have to build the house before we can decorate it.' Abel snapped and immediately regretted the tone of voice he used the moment the words were out of his mouth. He had not intended to sound churlish.

Lord Derby raised his eyebrows and stared at the man.

'May I remind you that you are *employed* to build this house using the plans approved by Sir Robert here. You have worked on many houses in the north of England that I know of and everyone says you are the best but I do expect you to listen to those who pay you and if a person of my standing sends you workmen of great talent specifically to do certain work I expect that order to be obeyed. I understand from Robert, here, that you quibbled about the building of the great fireplace and chimney? Is that correct?'

'Yes, sir, only, I don't hold with these new-fangled ideas, not when I have no proof that they work. I have never built one, never seen one. If it didn't work, and I doubt it will, then I would get the blame for it. Sir.' He stumbled to silence, knowing he had gone too far now in his temper.

'So, you do question your betters? I, also, have never seen such a fireplace but I have heard reports of them from among acquaintances and they assure me that they do work, and very well indeed. Are you telling me that you do not accept new ideas? Ideas which may be an improvement on the old?'

'Yes, my Lord, I mean, no.' Abel was letting his personal feelings cloud his judgement and was regretting having spoken so rashly. He did not want to be dismissed from the job but he wasn't used to being questioned and criticised and was not sure how to handle it. He took a deep breath.

'I am a master builder with thirty years behind me of building houses like this all over the north of England. Nobody has ever questioned my work or stated their dissatisfaction with it, and no one has ever told me to do things in any way different to what I've allus done. If a thing works I don't hold wi' change, never have. Young Master here keeps coming and telling me he wants this changed and that moved and the other done another way. It upsets my plans, upsets my workers, upsets me. If you ain't satisfied wi' my work, I'll go and leave it to them what knows better.' He looked defiantly at the two lords. He'd really burned his bridges now, and no mistake, he thought.

Lord Derby stared at him for a long moment, noting the abject look, the feet shuffling in the muddy floor, the dropped shoulders.

'I am not suggesting that Lord Robert should dismiss you. There is no doubting your experience and ability but all of us have to recognise that new ideas are sometimes better. Good God, man, if we didn't accept change we would all still be living in caves and hovels! All I am asking is that you follow your plans but learn to accept changes which are usually for the better. Robert is young, he has travelled a little and seen things you and I have not. If this fireplace,' he turned and indicated the enormous arch at the side, 'is as good as Robert believes it is you will be building them into all your future halls because everyone will want one, so accept what lord Robert says, he pays you after all. We are none of us too old to learn,'

Abel looked up at him. Was he telling him he was old? How dare he? It only served to stoke Abel's fury but there was nothing else he could do now if he wished to keep the job. Later he would give Cuthbert a piece of his mind, oh yes, that young upstart would know the wrath of Abel. For now he must appear to accept what had been said.

'Very well, sir,' he replied through gritted teeth. 'I will do as you say.' And not enjoy doing it, he added to himself.

'Very well. Next time I come I expect to see some of Cuthbert's work, and by that I mean, his carving. Now

Robert, you wanted to show me where you planned to build your stables.'

The group moved off, the difficulty settled, the peace restored as far as they were concerned. They went out through the big doorway at the far end of the Hall. Young Thomas turned and waved to Cuthbert as he went.

Abel glared round at all the workmen who had stopped to watch the drama, see their master being berated, humiliated.

'What are you looking at? Get on with your work.' He sought out Cuthbert who was still standing by the door to the west wing. 'I'll deal with you later,' he hissed and marched out into the sunshine, his fury boiling inside. He shouted at a young apprentice who had dropped his hammer as Abel passed. Another got a clip round the ear for tripping over a pile of wood shavings and a third was pushed aside for not moving quickly enough out of his way.

Everyone breathed a sigh of relief and immediately began talking about what had happened. It wasn't everyday you saw your master builder spoken to like that. They all knew they must watch their step for the next few days.

'It's Cuthbert I feel sorry for,' whispered one of the men to his neighbour as they continued measuring the doorway to the outside. 'We all knew why he has been sent here. Abel refuses to accept it but he's going to have to now and he won't like it.'

'What can he do though? They'll expect to see Cuthbert's work now.'

'Nothing, but he can make life very uncomfortable for the lad. Pity, I like him.'

Cuthbert returned to his floor. He had had no intention of causing any problem when he had taken young Thomas downstairs but the situation had been taken out of his hands. Now, he feared, Abel would have to accept him grudgingly and could no longer keep him occupied with mundane tasks. Cuthbert did not mind doing building work at all, but with Lord Derby's words ringing in his ears the following weeks and months were not going to be easy.

CHAPTER TWELVE

The storm broke within the hour, both within the house and in the countryside around. The day had been overcast, clouds rolling in from the west since dawn in great, grey sheets, obliterating the sun and dropping the temperature. Not long after the visitors had departed on their journey home it began to rain, gently at first but gradually coming heavier and heavier until the soft ground was churned to mud, people scurried for shelter and outside work on the house ceased. Cuthbert continued what he was doing, his part of the house being roofed and although few of the windows were in place, he did at least have a roof over his head and plenty of materials to hand to work with.

He could hear men shouting to each other across the site, asking whether they would be able to do any further work today. He heard a cart arrive, splashing through the water to come to a stop near the wood store. Ezekial must have got caught between the forest and Rufford with a fully laden cart and had little choice but to continue. Unloading in the rain would be a messy job even with extra hands helping but he would want to get it under cover before it got soaked. Cuthbert considered going to help but decided it would probably give Abel another excuse to shout at him and he had had enough from him for one day.

Abel, unfortunately, had other ideas and once he had seen the wood safely undercover he went in search of the person he thought was the source of his trouble today: Cuthbert.

Cuthbert heard him coming up the stairs, his wet boots squelching mud all the way up the new treads and into the room behind him. He got to his feet and turned to face his tormentor. Abel was standing in the doorway, water streaming off his leather jerkin and pooling on the floor around his filthy boots. His face was red, his fists clenched at his sides and he was clearly looking for trouble.

'There you are,' he roared, 'hiding away where you thought I wouldn't find you?'

'I was completing the job you set me,' replied Cuthbert, calmly.

'The job I set you, yes, but not the job you want to do, eh?'

'I will do whatever task you set me. I am a carpenter.'

'You are also a woodcarver, as everyone keeps telling me,' snapped Abel, advancing slowly, leaving a trail of mud across the newly laid floor. '*A wonderful* woodcarver, a *marvellous* woodcarver, a woodcarver of *great renown*. Everybody keeps telling me I won't see the like anywhere else. Well, master woodcarver, where is this marvellous work? What have you done since you got here? Tell me that. Where is it?'

'You have not, as yet, asked me to do any carving,' replied Cuthbert, reasonably.

'No, I haven't, have I, and shall I tell you why? Because I have woodcarvers already, men I have worked with for years, since before you were born. Why should I need another one when I have them? Tell me that.' He began to circle Cuthbert, his dark little eyes fixed on him, a pulse beating in his temple as he worked himself up into a fury. Suddenly he jabbed Cuthbert's arm, his sore elbow, though whether that was a coincidence or whether he knew of his injury he wasn't sure, but it made Cuthbert gasp with pain.

'Come, that didn't hurt, did it?' Abel taunted, and hit him again. Cuthbert grabbed his arm and held it away from Abel. He would not fight back. He felt a sharp dig in his ribs, then a kick behind his knees that sent him sprawling. He rolled away and tried to get up, but a shove in the back sent him down again. Abel moved closer and kicked him on the back of his thigh, then again in the small of his back. Cuthbert tried to roll away again, away from the onslaught but Abel followed, landing kicks on any part of his body he could reach. Kick after kick struck home until Abel ran out of breath and stood bent over him, panting. Slowly Cuthbert got to his feet and backed away against the wall hoping he wouldn't fall down again. Abel's face was distorted with rage, spittle gathered on his chin, as he glared at his victim.

'Don't you *ever* disobey me again, boy, do you hear?' he growled. 'Don't you ever go crawling to the gentry again, making friends with the child so that you could blatantly come to their notice by bringing him down to them, claiming he had made his own way up here and you had to see him safe downstairs again. How did you entice him up here in the first place? Tell me that.'

'He came up of his own accord,' gasped Cuthbert, holding aching ribs. 'He's a child, he was exploring. He heard me hammering and came to see what was happening.'

'A likely story,' sneered Abel. 'The lad's only five years old.'

'It's true.'

Abel sneered and straightened up.

'I told you to stay out of their way and you couldn't do a simple thing like that, could you? Well, now I have to find you some carving to do or your friend, Lord Derby, is going to want to know why not. He and the young master are going to come back in a couple of weeks to see what progress we've made and he expressly told me before he left that he expects to see *your* work too. I tell you, master carver, if I had my way you would be off this site by tonight, but my hands are tied, I'm stuck with you. So, I want to see some drawings of work you have done and work you think you could do and I'll let you know if it is good enough for *my* building. You are not touching a piece of wood here until I am satisfied you are as good as everyone keeps telling me. Is that clear?'

'Yes' said Cuthbert. 'I have several drawings with me. When do you want to see them?'

'Tomorrow morning, first thing. Now finish here and get out of my sight.'

He started to turn away then spun back and punched Cuthbert hard in the stomach, doubling him over, before walking away and down the stairs.

Cuthbert collapsed on the floor, fighting for breath, every bone in his body hurting from the attack. He gagged and vomited then lay panting in a heap by the wall.

Suddenly he heard a noise by the door and looked round in alarm, hoping it wasn't Abel coming back for another go at him. There stood Will, leaning nonchalantly on the door frame, grinning.

'How do you feel now?' he sneered. 'Not so high and mighty are you after all. Just another carpenter like the rest of us. Needed taking down a peg or two. Master carver indeed. Let's see you come back from that.' He walked over towards Cuthbert who scrambled to his feet and flinched expecting another kicking but Will just looked at him then spat in his face before turning on his heel and walking away.

Cuthbert slid down the wall and sat on the floor trying to gather his thoughts. Never before had he been subjected to such an unprovoked onslaught. He gingerly moved his arms and legs. Nothing appeared to be broken but he was going to be covered in bruises. He touched his jaw where one blow had landed and opened his mouth wide to ease it. Blood trickled down his cheek from a cut on his brow. His ribs were sore and he could feel where kicks had landed on his back and thighs. Thankfully his hands were untouched though whether by luck or deliberately on Abel's part he did not know for without his hands he would not have been able to do any carving for some time. He flexed his fingers and turned his wrists. It occurred to him suddenly that if he had not had the word of Lord Derby he could well have been more severely injured or even killed, a victim of an 'accident', not unheard of in building projects, but he could never let Lord Derby know what had happened here today.

He bowed his head on his knees. He had to lay the last couple of boards somehow then go back to his pallet and find the drawings he had done of some of his work at Whalley

Abbey, then spend some hours doing some more for new work here. He was not going to get much sleep tonight.

Outside the rain continued to pour. All work was suspended for the day and many of the men took advantage of the break and made their way to their shelters or to the village inn where it was, at least, dry. The tracks turned to liquid mud. Carts were stuck up to their axles and the horses were led away into their stables and rubbed down for the night. It was still light but the dim light of a dreary, dull day. Thunder could be heard rumbling in the distance over the far hills and occasional flashes of lightning split the sky and the rain poured down relentlessly, a continuous roar all around.

How long he sat there he wasn't sure, he may even have nodded off but a sound broke the stillness of the room.

'Cuthbert? Cuthbert? Are you all right?'

Cuthbert put his head up trying to work out where the voice came from.

'Cuthbert? It's me, Ezekial. Where are you?'

He gave a sigh of relief.

'Up here, in the saloon,' he called. 'First floor, top of the stairs.'

He heard footsteps coming up the stairs, more than one pair of them and hoped it was indeed friends. He was in no fit state to cope with another attack. A head appeared round the door. It was Ezekial followed by three of the other men, fellow carpenters Thomas, Alfric and Harry.

'Good God, man!' exclaimed Ezekial, hurrying over to crouch by Cuthbert. 'What happened to you?'

'Abel didn't like me talking to Lord Derby,' said Cuthbert.

'We heard the shouting,' said Thomas. 'Abel was fair mad wi' you but we didn't realise he'd laid into you.'

''E don't like being told what to do, don't Abel,' said Alfric, 'and we knew there'd be trouble as soon as we 'eard t'master was comin'.'

'That was no reason to beat the living daylights out of you,' said Ezekial, touching the bruise that was already appearing on Cuthbert's face. 'Where else has he got you?'

'Pretty well everywhere. He went berserk, knocked me down and kept kicking me over and over until he lost strength. I thought I was for it.'

'He'd have had some answering to do if he had. As it is the young master isn't going to be best pleased when he hears about this.'

'Don't tell him,' said Cuthbert, quickly. 'No, I'll be fine, no harm done in the long run. Bruises will fade. I don't want to get the reputation of being a troublemaker. Let it go.'

'Well, if you're sure,' said Ezekial, 'Best get you to Liliath. Let her see to you.'

'No, I can't, I've work to do.'

'What work?'

'I've to finish this floor then produce drawings of work I've done at Whalley and work I could do here.'

'There's time for that.'

'No, I have to do it by morning or there'll be trouble and I don't want to antagonise him any further.'

'Harry and I can finish here,' said Alfric. He looked round. 'There's only two boards to do. We'll soon do it, don't you worry.'

'Thanks, that would help.'

'Meanwhile, we'll get you to the forge. I'm afraid we're going to get wet, the rain hasn't eased at all. Thomas, give me a hand with him.'

Cuthbert accepted the help offered. He was too sore to argue anyway. The two men lifted him to his feet and he groaned.

'Sorry,' he said, 'I'm a nuisance, I know.'

'Nonsense. You lean on us and we'll get you there.'

Slowly they helped Cuthbert down the stairs. He didn't like to admit it but he doubted he would have been able to do it alone. The cold rain revived him a little and the three made their slow way towards the forge.

Jacob saw them coming through the doorway of the forge and ran out to meet them, calling to his brother over his shoulder.

'What in heaven's name happened to him?' he cried, taking Cuthbert's weight on his broad shoulder to let Ezekial stand upright.

'He's taken a beating,' said Ezekial. 'He needs Liliath's work.'

'Get him round the back, out of this rain,' said the blacksmith.

Liliath came to the door of the cottage and opened it wide as they approached.

'Put him down by the fire,' she said, and the men lowered him into the wooden rocking chair beside the roaring fire. 'Now go, I'll see to him,' she said, shooing them all out of the door again. They trudged back through the rain and into the warmth of the forge where they told the blacksmith what had happened.

Meanwhile, Liliath was examining Cuthbert. The walk had exhausted him more than he could have imagined and he wanted to crawl into his bed and sleep it off but Liliath was trying to get his clothes off him so that she could see the damage. Clad only in his breeches she examined every inch of him.

'Well, he's drawn very little blood apart from re-opening the wound on your elbow and the cut on your face, but there's not much of you that's not going to turn black and blue. Who did it?' she asked.

'Abel,' he said, and told her briefly what had occurred.

'He's always had a temper, has Abel,' she said, busying herself with warm water and cloths and potions. 'One day he's going to go too far. His wife used to be able to calm him but since she died there's no one who dares cross him for fear of what he'll do.'

'You know him from before?' asked Cuthbert and winced as she touched the spot where the kick to his back had landed.

'Yes, his reputation goes before him. He's a good builder, one of the best, but his temper gets the better of him if he's crossed. I take it you crossed him?'

'Not intentionally, no.'

'It doesn't need to be intentional. Sometimes you only need to look at him wrong and he flares up. Now hold still while I put some of this salve on the cuts.'

Cuthbert bore her ministrations stoically. He was sorer than he had first thought and her touch, though gentle was painful. He dreaded to think what he would be like in the morning, that is if he got any sleep at all.

Only when she was satisfied she had done all she could did she fetch a spare tunic of her husband's and held it out to him. 'Yours is soaked through' she said. 'I'll dry it by the fire, get it back to you tomorrow. I could give you a sleeping draught?' she suggested.

'No, I have work to do if I don't want to draw Abel's wrath again on the morrow,' he said.

'Surely not! You need rest.'

'I'll go to my bed when I've done what I have to do, not before.'

Liliath looked at him, hands on hips. There was no arguing with him, she could see that.

'Very well. In that case you are staying here tonight. There's a pallet in the storeroom at the back of the forge. That way I'll see you get a meal inside you as well. You can work in here but once you have finished you are having something to help you sleep. I tell you, you'll be too sore else.'

Cuthbert could see she was not going to back down. At least he wouldn't have to meet a gloating Will again tonight if he stayed.

'I need my bag with my things in,' he said.

'Jehan can fetch it if you tell him where. No one will question him.'

Jehan was despatched to the builders' shelters to collect Cuthbert's bag and explain where he was staying. Most of those he met asked about Cuthbert. By now everyone knew what had happened and most were concerned about Abel's behaviour yet Jehan got the impression they were too scared to do anything about it. Afraid they would lose their jobs probably.

He returned, carrying the leather satchel, soaked to the skin through the pouring rain which had not let up for hours now.

'Water will be high if this continues,' he reported. 'It's not rained this hard for years.'

'Will the Mere flood the building?' asked Cuthbert.

'I doubt it, it never has but it could come close. Let's hope it stops soon or we'll all suffer if the Hall goes under.'

After a good hot meal of rabbit stew Cuthbert set to work sorting out drawings he had done for Whalley. He had always kept any designs for future reference and frequently returned to those he found most successful. Among them were designs for the sort of decorative carvings Abel wanted. One in particular brought painful memories. It was the design he and Jethro had been working on when he had the fatal fall. He looked long and hard at it. Could he do that one again? No, it would remind him too much of that painful day and it was not something he would let Abel mock him over. He carefully returned it to the package of drawings.

There were, however, some others which would be good enough. With perhaps two or three new ones that would be enough surely to satisfy the most recalcitrant employer, so he settled down to produce some new ones. He never found it difficult to come up with new ideas, his mind was always buzzing with shapes and details and he loved to draw them, developing them as he worked, adding bits, removing other parts until he was satisfied. Working thus his physical aches seemed to melt into the background as he bent over his sketch book and it was no surprise when Liliath came to him and said it was nearly midnight and he must stop if he was to get any rest at all. He agreed and even let her give him some of her sleeping draught before settling down on the borrowed bed and in a short time fell into a deep sleep.

CHAPTER THIRTEEN

Dawn came with a freshly washed face, a delicately pale blue sky that looked as though the rain had washed all colour out of it. Small fluffy clouds drifted by and everything dripped. The thatch was darkened by the soaking it had had but was as watertight as ever. The trees dripped into puddles around their trunks, the vegetables in the little patch by the cottage were flattened. Jehan was looking ruefully at them.

'They'll come back as long as we don't get any more rain,' he said. 'Surprising what a bit of sunshine will do.'

Liliath set bowls of oat porridge before them, warm and filling. Cuthbert was surprised how hungry he felt but he was stiff from his beating and moved gingerly as he made ready to go to the site.

'The bed's there for as long as you want it,' she said as he went out of the door and Cuthbert turned to smile gratefully at her.

'I'll see how today goes,' he said.

The track to the Hall was full of puddles surrounded by mud, not a dry inch to be found and his boots were caked in mud before he was halfway. He wondered what sort of reception he would get but he had his drawings with him and hoped Abel would find something to assuage his anger.

As he neared the shore of the Mere he noticed that many of the bushes on the bank were standing in water, the level having risen during the night. The little jetty where a rowing boat was usually tied was almost underwater. It wouldn't have taken much more to flood over onto the track and he wondered how near it had been to flooding across the track and onto the building site. Surely they wouldn't have planned to build it where it was if there was the possibility of inundation.

Men were surveying the building from all angles, assessing whether there had been any damage during the storm. Everything was still standing though very wet. The parts already roofed were driest but the half built walls were surrounded by mud. It was going to be incredibly dirty work for a few days.

Thomas saw him coming and ran across to greet Cuthbert.

'My word, you've a face to behold!' he said. 'How many colours would you say, Alfric?'

'Oh, at least a dozen,' replied Alfric, then asked seriously, 'How are you? Did you get any sleep? We finished the floor without Abel knowing so we won't tell him. Best that way.'

'Thank you,' said Cuthbert. 'Liliath gave me a sleeping draught so, not too bad. Where is Abel? I'd better get these drawings to him as soon as I can.'

'He was over by the woodshed seeing if the wood Ezekial brought in is dry enough to use.' Thomas went on quietly. 'Don't mention last night, don't start him off again. We're all on tenterhooks today, not sure how he'll cover up what he did. He certainly won't mention it so don't you.'

Cuthbert made his way towards the large sturdy building where wood was stored in the dry and where the carpenters were able to work undercover. He could hear voices from within and stepped through the doorway to find Abel with Ezekial and a number of other men, including, he noticed, Will. Abel had spread out the plans of the building on a pile of wood and they were discussing progress. Nobody acknowledged Cuthbert's presence so he was able to hear what was said.

'We need to get the roof completed as soon as possible. If we get another storm like last night we may not suffer as little damage as we have. With winter approaching the weather could go against us.' Abel was intent over the plans and turned to a second sheet which Cuthbert could see showed the construction planned for the Great Hall roof. 'This is what I suggested to the young master and he agreed, thankfully. I hope he doesn't come up with any foolish alterations when we are halfway through it. It is a standard construction of oak. He wants as much ornamentation and decoration as we can do so I have drawn in moulded and carved beams with plaster quatrefoils between. Additional carvings could be added later if he so wishes but we need to get the basic structure in place first. He has some ideas for the ends of the hammer beams but will tell me what they are when he has decided. That should not make any difference to what we put up first. Whatever it is will be decorative rather than structural.'

Cuthbert was impressed with Abel's drawings. Every encounter with him so far had been acrimonious but he could see now what an excellent master builder Abel was. The drawings were clear and precise, as he would expect, and were probably adapted from a master plan that Abel could alter to suit whoever he was building for. Cuthbert had seen something similar many times in buildings he had worked on in Chester. Great Halls like this were always rectangular but the scale varied with the purse of the owner. He had seen much smaller versions for more modest houses. Rufford was large as befitted the purse of Sir Robert. The roof would be divided into five equal bays by four hammer beam roof principals. There would be a screens passage at the east end and access to the family wing at the west end, the area Cuthbert had been working in yesterday. Projecting to the north was a compass window, adjacent to the area where the family would sit. The amount of glass depicted in the drawing was astonishing. There was certainly money to be spent here. The only major difference to the plan was the vast stone fireplace and chimney which had caused so much controversy. The walls either side had had to be adapted to accommodate it but the structure of the roof was not altered. Cuthbert could understand why Abel had not wanted it as he was a man who did not like change, but it was looking as though it would be a good change, a modern part drafted onto a good solid plan without detriment to the overall design. At least, that was Cuthbert's view.

Abel had turned to Ezekial.

'We are ready for those speres you brought over from the old place,' he said. 'Once they are in place we can get the roof under construction. I took their measurements when you brought them. They are going to take a lot of work to get them in place but they are vital to the next stage. How many men will you need to get them in here and in place?'

'Many,' replied Ezekial. 'They are solid oak, whole tree trunks, so very heavy. They are slightly different in girth but that won't be noticed once they are in place. They are already carved and moulded but they may need some slight repairs once we get them up. Have you prepared the floor bases?'

'I have,' said Thomas, 'measured them precisely with Alfric here. Four feet in from the side walls with fourteen feet between.'

'That's correct,' affirmed Abel consulting the plans again. 'We'll need plenty of props to hold them in place until we get the tie beam in place.'

'They are cut already,' said Ezekial.

'Let's get started then. As many men as possible needed in here today.'

'I wonder if that includes you,' said a soft voice in Cuthbert's ear, and he turned to see Will standing directly behind him. Cuthbert said nothing. He wanted as little to do with him as possible, but Will had other ideas.

'You look as though you've had a rough time,' he sniggered, and dug Cuthbert in the ribs with a sharp finger. Cuthbert winced, knowing what Will was trying to do. He moved a step away.

'You will be needed in here,' Cuthbert said. 'They need all the strong men they can get today. Very heavy work. Are you up to it?'

'I'm strong enough,' replied Will, 'but are you?', and he gave Cuthbert another hard nudge.

Abel turned round and his manner changed instantly.

'There you are. I wanted to see you first thing. Have you got your drawings?'

'Here they are.' Cuthbert handed over the bundle of drawings and noticed Will's sudden interest in them. 'You will recognise some as fairly common designs but the others are of my own design.'

"Of my own design" mimicked Will and knew instantly that he had overstepped the mark. Abel looked at him with a steely eye. 'Go and help bring in the speres, Will,' he said curtly.

Will left sheepishly. How he would have liked to see what wonders the 'master carver' had produced. Never mind. He would get a chance later.

Abel unrolled the papers and laid them on top of the plans on the wood pile. He looked at each sheet carefully, giving no indication of what he thought of them. He lingered over Cuthbert's own ideas then rolled them up again.

'I'll say one thing,' he said, 'you know how to draw. Yes, I recognise some of these, the others are far too fancy for here. They are not what is wanted in this house. Good reliable designs always work best, not this stuff.' He rolled the papers together roughly and thrust them back at Cuthbert. 'You can do some of these in the upper floors of the house. You are to do nothing in this Hall. Only my designs will be used here. You know what I feel about you being here at all. Well, following that fiasco the other day you will confine your work to other parts of the building. I can't stop you working here, more's the pity, but I will not have you working in the main hall. Is that clear?'

'Yes, but Lord Derby will be expecting to see my work when he comes again.'

Abel ground his teeth.

'He may not return for many weeks if at all. He will have forgotten about you by then. If he does ask I will say you have nothing ready yet. He'll soon forget. He has more important things to see to than a jumped up carver from Chester.' He looked Cuthbert in the eye and repeated his warning. 'Not in the Hall. Ever. Now get back up to those floors you were doing.'

He pushed roughly past Cuthbert and left the building, striding through the mud towards the Great Hall.

Cuthbert sighed deeply. Was there no way he could make the man see what he was capable of? If it wasn't for Lord Derby's promise to see his work adorn Rufford Hall Cuthbert would have left there and then but he had faith in the noble Lord and was not going to be bullied by a man who refused to change his ideas. He stood alone in the shed wondering how to carry on when he came to a decision. During the day he would do whatever work Abel assigned him to but the evenings were his and he would work alone on ideas for the Hall. There were plenty of scraps of wood he could use, off cuts discarded from other work and of no use for anything else. He would work on those and when Lord Derby did return he would have work ready to show him. But how could he hide them in the meanwhile? Liliath's offer of a bed came to him and seemed the ideal solution. He dare not try to hide anything he did in the room he shared with Will and the others, but at the smith's cottage he would find somewhere safe.

He went outside just as several of the men staggered past carrying one of the great oak speres they had been talking about. Slipping and sliding in the mud they staggered towards the shell of the Great Hall. The wood was already decorated with moulding and panelling from top to bottom, each section headed by trefoils and embattled at the top. Cuthbert wondered what craftsman had originally done the work in the hall they came from. How old were they? They certainly didn't look new but work like that lasted for many years.

The men were turning the corner to carry their load inside the walls of the hall when one of them slipped in the treacherous mud and fell to his knees, pulling two other men down with him. A great cry went up as one of them was caught by the legs and pinned under the great weight. Alarm spread rapidly as the rest tried to lift the spere off the man but they could not get a foothold in the mud. Cuthbert ran over, seized a beam of wood from a pile by the doorway and thrust it under the fallen wood.

'Quick!' he cried, 'Get that log under here. That's it. Now, pull down on this piece and lever the spere up. Go on, press harder on this beam … harder … again.' Some of the others joined him as he levered the great load slowly off the man, their muscles straining under the weight but slowly it began to rise. 'Pull him out, gently,' groaned Cuthbert, and two others grasped the victim under his arms and dragged him clear. Once he was well away they lowered the spere onto the ground.

Abel came rushing over to see what was happening.

'What's this?' he cried. 'Why is that spere lying in the mud? It'll get too wet.'

'It fell on Japheth,' cried a man on his knees beside the injured man.

'I'm all right,' gasped Japheth. 'I slipped, that's all.' He tried to rise and fell back, groaning.'

'Is it broken?' asked Abel.

'Don't know.'

'I'll fetch Liliath,' said Thomas and ran off towards the forge.

'This is all we need,' cried Abel, showing remarkably little concern for the injured man. 'Get this spere inside, now. Come on, the rest of you. Liliath will see to him. We've got work to do.' He turned and saw Cuthbert. 'What are you doing here? I told you …'

'He saved him,' said Harry, 'Cuthbert levered the spere off him.'

'With help from several others,' added Cuthbert.

Abel looked at Cuthbert.

'Quite the hero, aren't you? Well, now get back to work.' He turned to take in all of them. 'All of you. We've a house to build.'

The men moved away, just leaving Harry with the injured man. Cuthbert turned towards the west wing and almost bumped into Will.

'You dropped these when you rushed to the rescue,' he said and handed Cuthbert's bundle of drawings to him, wet and muddy, crumpled and slightly torn. 'Bit of a mess, aren't they? Never mind, a master carver like you will soon be able to draw some more.' He sniggered as he walked away and when Cuthbert unrolled what was left of his drawings he saw that most of them were covered in mud, far worse than from merely being dropped. Will had probably taken great pleasure in trampling them in the mud before handing them back. Another example of his spiteful nature but with no proof that that was what had actually happened. Luckily Cuthbert carried many of the designs in his head and would soon be able to redraw them.

Cuthbert kept to the family wing for the rest of the day. He could hear the work going on in the Great Hall and when he left late in the afternoon he looked through the doorway and saw that preparations for lifting the great speres were almost complete. Tomorrow the tie beam would be attached across the top to form an impressive arch and give some idea of the roof which would tower above. From the plans he had seen there would be plenty of good oak up there, scope for numerous decorative pieces but done to Abel's designs of course.

On his way back to the forge Cuthbert had a look at the pile of waste pieces of wood near the wood store, selected a few odd bits and carried them down the track.

'No need to bring us firewood,' said Jehan as he carried a horseshoe out to the beast waiting patiently under the shelter.

'It's not for the fire. I would like to accept Liliath's offer of a bed and use my time trying out some new ideas while I'm here,' explained Cuthbert. 'If you don't mind.'

'Not at all,' replied Jehan, lifting the horse's foot and placing the new shoe on its hoof. 'This wouldn't have anything to do with Will by any chance?'

Cuthbert hesitated in answering.

'I hear things here at the forge when people are waiting for work to be done. They think I can't hear when I'm hammering away, but there's not much gets past me, and what I miss Jacob hears. Will's making your life … difficult, isn't he?'

Cuthbert nodded.

'He's taken a dislike to me. I've given him no cause but he has been goading me ever since I arrived.'

'He's jealous, that's what. He thinks you are going to take his place in Abel's eye and Will thinks he's going to be handed the business when Abel gives up. Aside from that you have the favour of Lord Derby and Will is jealous of anyone who is supported by gentry. There's something in his background that we can't fathom, something that makes him distrust landed people. You should hear him go on about them when he's had too much ale. One day he'll say too much.' Jehan lowered the horse's foot and patted it as he went back inside. 'You are welcome here,' he added and smiled.

That conversation had given Cuthbert much to think about. Why ever should Will think he was trying to take over his place in Abel's life? He had only just arrived, he may have come with a reputation for his carving but that was hardly a cause for such a vendetta against him. The way Abel was treating him could hardly give Will the idea that Abel favoured him over Will. Whatever the reason behind it Cuthbert felt he would be better keeping as much distance as he could from Will and staying at the forge would at least give him some peace each night.

CHAPTER FOURTEEN

Cuthbert spent the last light of the day whittling a piece of the wood he had salvaged. Among the tools he had brought with him was a set of fine chisels which had belonged to his father and which he used for the finer carved detail of his work. He loved to hold them as it brought him closer to the father he had adored. He remembered being shown how to use the razor sharp blades properly, how to hold them and place them on the wood he was working. He had been very young, maybe five or six years old when his father had taught him the basic skills and which he had developed over the years. After his father's death, Jethro had continued to teach him and the combined skills of the two men who had been his inspiration had made him the master carver he was. It never failed to move him whenever he used them, no matter how simple the piece he was making. Tonight it was a tiny figure of a rabbit that gradually emerged from the wood, hunkered down with its ears laid along its back, the hair of its back depicted in the fine strokes of the smallest chisel.

'What have you there?' asked Liliath , watching him work as she mended a tear in a tunic of Jacob's.

'Just a little figure,' replied Cuthbert, handing it over to her. She took it and held it on the palm of her hand.

'This is exquisite!' she exclaimed. 'Beautiful. A miniature of the real thing. Look, Jehan, see what Cuthbert has made from a scrap of wood.'

Jehan took the tiny figure in his huge hand. It looked lost on such a large palm but he held it as though it was something really delicate. He examined it in detail.

'No wonder they call you a master carver,' he said. 'Is this the sort of thing you have done at Whalley that got Lord Derby so excited?'

'Something like it,' said Cuthbert. 'I carved some little mice for the prior which started my work there. I like to use things from nature in my work though usually they are on a panel of some sort, a box or a plaque. I use leaves and flowers as well as animals and birds. There are so many wonderful things around us if we only look for them and as I have the gift, as Jethro used to say, I use it to make beautiful items.'

'It is truly a gift. I wonder whether Abel would change his mind if he actually saw the quality of your work.'

'I doubt it. He has set his mind against me from the start. He is allowing me to use some of my drawings in the upper reaches of the house, in obscure corners where no one will see them. He told me today that under no circumstances was I to do anything in the Great Hall. Only his designs are to be used there.'

'The man is a fool then. Did he see your drawings?'

'Yes, but they are not for him. He did acknowledge that I can draw,' said Cuthbert, ruefully.

Jehan snorted.

'Good of him! Well, the man is a fool, as I've said before. He does not know what he is missing.'

'Will you show him this piece?' asked Liliath.

'No, he'll probably throw it on the fire. He's not interested.'

'May I keep it?' asked Liliath.

'Of course, as small payment for letting me stay here.'

'I wonder what Will would do if he saw this,' mused Jehan.

'That is partly why I was glad to be able to stay here,' said Cuthbert. 'He is spiteful enough to try to destroy anything I made like that, and I dread to think what he would do to my precious tools. He damaged my drawings today, said I had dropped them in the mud, which I had, but I believe he 'accidentally' stood on them before he picked them up.'

'Are they ruined?'

'I can easily redraw them, it's no great loss.'

'If it has got that bad be sure to bring all your tools back here. At least we can keep those safe for you,' said Jehan. 'One of these days he will go too far.'

***

Next day Cuthbert headed for the west wing of the house to continue working on the internal structure of the building. There was much to do. Seven men were working in that part of the house and he enjoyed their company as they installed doors and door frames, window frames and shutters, some wainscoting in the more important rooms, a large overmantel in what was to be the solar, a large light room reserved for the ladies of the family. There was a noisy cheerfulness as they sawed and planed, hammered and banged, knocking wooden pegs in to mortice and tenon joints to keep them in place. Some of the junior apprentices were tasked with keeping the endless supply of wooden pegs coming as hundreds would be needed to complete a house of this size. Some of the boys were only sixteen or seventeen, still in their early apprenticeship and Cuthbert remembered his own time at that age when all the mundane tasks seem to be given to him, but he was grateful for the thorough grounding it gave him. He had learnt about the uses of different woods, their strengths and weaknesses, when to use them, and when not to. He could recognise different woods by their grain and, occasionally, their smell. Sometimes he learnt from his mistakes when he used the wrong wood but it was vital that mistakes were made at the early stage before much harm could be done. Using wrong or unseasoned wood could cause untold damage later in a building. Seven years apprenticeship sounded a long time but every minute was valuable.

It was mid-morning when one of the men went to collect some more wood from the store. When he returned he was smiling broadly.

'There's trouble brewing down there,' he said, dropping the planks on the floor. 'Abel's gone with Ezekial to select the wood for the roof timbers and left, guess who, to supervise the fixing of the tie beam to the speres?'

'Alfred?' suggested one.

'No, Harry,' said another.

'Neither. Will.'

'Will!' exclaimed several voices. 'He's not skilled enough.'

'They're saying Abel gave him strict instructions before he left, even laid the beams out on the floor for him, told him to have it in place by the time he returned his afternoon.'

'So what's happening?'

'It won't fit,' was the gleeful reply.

'What do you mean, it won't fit?' asked Cuthbert. 'It fitted in the last place. What's wrong with it here?'

'I don't know, but it won't fit onto the pegs cut for it, the ones used before. They can get one end to slot into place but the other won't reach.'

'How can that be? It will have been made to fit perfectly originally. Unless, of course, there's been some damage when it was taken apart.'

'So what are they doing about it?'

'Will is panicking. Doesn't know what to do. I think he's afraid of what Abel will say if the job's not finished.'

Cuthbert felt sure he wasn't the only one who would not be too concerned if Will did get into trouble. He was not popular, and not only because of his treatment of Cuthbert. However, they had a house to build and they would all suffer if things went wrong. They looked at each other.

'Do you think we should go and see if we can help?' someone suggested.

'There are plenty of them down there already. Won't we be in the way?'

'We've all done work like this before,' said Cuthbert. 'There may be a simple solution.'

'If it was simple even Will could have found it,' laughed another.

'Still, I don't see that having a look will be a problem.'

'You'd better not go, Cuthbert,' said Alfric. 'You know what Abel's said about you going in the Great Hall.'

'Abel isn't there, and besides he said I wasn't to *do* any work, not that I couldn't *look*.' It seemed reasonable, so they all went down to the ground floor and into the Great Hall.

All the other men were standing round the disassembled arch which was to be a major part of the structure of the eastern end of the hall. It was laid on the floor, the bases of the two speres in the correct position for when the whole arch would be hauled upright. The tie beam which would hold the two massive trunks together at the top was laid on the floor across the end but it was here that most of the men were standing, scratching their heads and looking puzzled.

'What is the problem?' asked Alfric.

'Can't get both ends on at once,' explained Thomas. 'We've had both ends on, but not at the same time.'

'Are the speres the right distance apart?' asked Cuthbert.

'Yes, Abel checked them himself, several times to be sure. They are exactly right.'

'So why won't they fit?' mused Cuthbert.

He walked round the pillars, looking closely at the tops. He stepped back and looked at them from a distance. They were dead straight. He borrowed a measure and checked the space between the two. Correct to an eighth of an inch.

'Could the wood have swollen getting it into here? It was pouring down earlier,' asked Alfric.

'It had stopped by the time we brought them in,' snapped Will, who had been observing all the attempts from a distance. 'Someone isn't doing their job properly.' He gestured at the men near the beam ends.

'You checked the pegs and the holes?' asked Cuthbert.

There was a slight pause before Will answered.

'Of course, I'm not stupid,' he replied in a voice that betrayed a note of doubt. 'Why are you in here anyway? I'll tell Abel you disobeyed his order.'

'Do you want this in place before he returns or not? You clearly can't solve the problem on your own so we thought we would help, but if you want to explain why you couldn't do the job you were asked to do, we'll leave you to it.' Cuthbert turned to leave and was halfway down the hall when Will called,

'Stop! Wait. As long as you don't tell Abel you did it, if you can that is, you can try. But I don't expect even you can solve this.' He was beginning to look smug as though he was planning to lay the blame on Cuthbert somehow if Abel returned and the beam was still not in place. 'Can our brilliant master carver save me?'

'Very well,' said Cuthbert, 'but I'll need to have a closer look.'

Will stood back and bowed as though condescending to the suggestion.

Cuthbert knelt down gingerly by the top of one spere and examined it minutely, feeling with his fingers where the mortice and tenon joint should fit. Then he crossed to the other end of the tie beam and did the same there. Getting to his feet he looked at the beam itself, a huge timber that would span the distance between the two uprights. On the inside of the arch there was a bracing piece already fixed in place at each end to give the arch added strength.

'So, what's your solution?' jeered Will. 'There isn't one is there. You can't work it out, can you, master carver?'

Cuthbert felt like hitting him but that wouldn't solve anything. Instead he stood back and looked at the timbers once more, then stepped over the arch and looked at it from the other side. His expression changed and he crossed back and looked at the other side of the beam. He smiled.

'Can we lever it up a little?' he asked and several willing hands came forward and lifted the tie beam slightly off the floor. 'That's enough,' said Cuthbert and knelt down, pushing his hands to the underside. A smile spread across his face. 'Put it down again,' he said, and got to his feet. 'Perhaps if you turned it round it might work,' he suggested.

'What!' exclaimed Will. 'What do you mean, turn it round?'

Cuthbert pointed. 'Try putting this end at that side and the other end over here. See if that fits.'

'It's an arch!' shouted Will. 'Either end will fit.'

'Just try it.' Cuthbert tried to keep his temper. He wasn't sure but it might work.

With the help of several of the men it was lifted and turned through a hundred and eighty degrees and laid on the ground again.

'Now try it,' said Cuthbert, and watched as the two ends were manoeuvred into position. Heaving and grunting the men eased the beam into position on the spere ends and it slotted into position easily. Men stepped forward to hammer the wooden pegs in place to make it secure. A cheer went up from those watching and Cuthbert was clapped on the back. He turned to look at Will who was standing at the far end. The smile on his face was gone to be replaced by a look of astonishment and then fury.

'I was going to suggest that,' he said, stiffly. Nobody believed him.

'Would you like a hand hauling it upright?' asked Cuthbert, an innocent expression on his face as he saw Will struggling to hold his temper, but it was several voices together that called out in agreement. Ropes had already been brought into the hall and these were quickly attached to the speres. Others were holding props of wood which they would use to support the heavy arch as it rose slowly aloft. With others guiding the bases into the holes dug for them in the ground there was a concerted effort as as many as possible, including Cuthbert, hauled on the ropes and the whole arch slowly rose. Props were pushed into place to stop it toppling back to the ground. Everyone was heaving with all their strength, and finally the bases slid into their holes and the arch came to rest. The tie beam fitted perfectly, extending beyond the speres to reach the wall plate at either side, the beam which rested along the top of the walls. Ladders were quickly put in place and men ran up to insert pegs in the beam to hold it in place. Only when it was secure were the ropes removed and everyone stood back to admire the massive arch created. The wooden props were left in place too for the time being.

'We'd better get back to work then,' said Cuthbert, and started towards the west wing, passing Will on the way. He received a furious glare and saw him clench his fists but with so many standing nearby Will dared not do anything more. Cuthbert could almost feel the hate in his expression.

Back at work on fitting a window shutter, Alfred came quietly up to him.

'He didn't like that,' he murmured, as he held the shutter in place whilst Cuthbert fixed the hinges. 'How did you work out the beam was wrong way round?'

'When I felt the mortice and tenon joints on the floor, one side was larger than the other. With it wrong way round they wouldn't match up, they would never have gone together. I also noticed the marks left by the original carpenter didn't match. They were only faint, you could barely see them but one end had marks with three stripes, the other end had two. When it was turned the marks matched, but the most obvious difference was the decoration. There is carving in the bracing pieces under the arch but only on one side. The way Will had got the arch the carving was on the back of it as you faced it from the hall. Who would decorate the back of a piece and not the front?' Cuthbert glanced at his companion who was smiling.

'Trust a master carver to notice the detail of the carving. I expect most of us just saw an arch and didn't compare back and front, especially Will. Should we tell him?'

'No, at least not yet. Let him stew for a while. He probably thinks we will tell Abel what we did. Let him suffer for a while.'

'He's going to be watching you even more closely. You've got the better of him again and he won't like that. Do be careful, Cuthbert.'

'I am already.' He looked round to make sure no one was near enough to listen to him. 'When we were putting the crossbeams in in the other wing I was up a ladder guiding a beam into place when the ladder moved and I would have fallen if I hadn't caught hold of the wall. Will was just walking away. I didn't see him move the ladder, but somebody had, and I saw the marks in the ground later. Everyone was watching us up above so nobody saw him.'

'You must be careful, Cuthbert. I wouldn't put it past him to do you some real harm. It is as well you are staying at the forge, nobody will get past Jehan and Jacob, especially a weakling like Will.'

'My thoughts exactly. I am being careful and I've moved all my tools there as well. They are very special to me, they belonged to my father.'

'It will be interesting to hear what he tells Abel when he returns.'

'I am saying nothing. It's not worth it. Abel has me in his bad books anyway so I'll not add fuel to that fire.'

'Still, the other lads and I will keep an eye out for you.'

'Thanks, but I don't expect he will try anything so soon, he's too devious to be trusted. Anyway, let's finish these shutters or Abel will be complaining about us.'

It was much later when Abel returned with Ezekial and went straight to the Great Hall.

'Well done!' he cried when he saw the arch completed. 'Any problems?'

'No,' said Will immediately. 'Just dropped into place.' The men nearby gaped at this blatant lie but said nothing.

'Well done, lad. I knew you would manage. Come let me buy you a drink at the ale house. We'll call it a day now, carry on tomorrow.'

The men were pleased to be finishing a little earlier than usual and there was much talk amongst themselves as they made their way back to lodgings, a meal and an early bed. It was going to be interesting to see what was said tomorrow.

Cuthbert, Alfred and Thomas walked along by the Mere in companionable silence. It was a still evening, not a breath of wind to ruffle the water. Cuthbert paused at the water's edge and gazed across it. There was a perfect reflection in the water of the scanty trees further along the shore. Thomas and Alfred had carried on a little way before they noticed Cuthbert wasn't with them. They returned and stood beside him.

'What is it?' they asked.

'Look at the reflection in the water. See, you can even see those birds roosting in the branches. It is rare that it is so clear.'

'I have never noticed before,' admitted Thomas. He looked at Cuthbert's intent gaze. 'What are you thinking?'

'I am trying to remember every detail. If I had my sketch pad with me I would try to draw it, so that I could use the image somewhere, sometime.'

'That's amazing!' said Thomas. 'You mean, you could carve what you are seeing?'

'Not as a complete picture but I would use certain elements of it. See how that branch dipping towards the water arches gracefully, the size of the leaves diminishing the nearer they are to the end of the branch. It would serve as a frame for some other part of a panel or something. I could place an animal or a bird below.' Cuthbert was framing the view with his hands as his imagination took over and he was lost in the composition in his mind. Thomas and Alfred looked askance at him.

'You really see a complete piece in your mind from looking at that?' whispered Alfred in wonder.

Cuthbert relaxed suddenly and blushed.

'Sorry, I get completely carried away when I am planning. My mind races ahead as I look and I see other bits that I could add to the overall piece.' He grinned at his friends. 'Don't mind me. When I see something to attract my attention I forget everything else, even that you were there.'

'That's amazing. I have to have something to copy, a drawing at the very least. I could never start from new on what you are describing. If you drew it for me first I could make a fair copy but what you are doing is ……. well, astonishing. Does Abel know how you do this?'

'No, he's not interested, not even in my drawings. He has a set of designs and he won't stray from those. A great pity in my opinion, but I don't think he looks at things around him for inspiration. A shame because there is so much if he would only look.'

The peace was broken by a peal of laughter from somewhere along the bank.

'It seems we have company,' murmured Thomas.

More laughter followed and three young girls appeared among the trees further along the bank. It was clear they were related, all had the same auburn hair which glistened with lighter highlights in the fading sunshine. One was slightly taller than the other two and all three were dressed in the simple linen dresses of country folk, belted with a colourful band of material around slender waists. The two younger ones had a garland of flowers in their hair and were carrying posies of flowers in their hands. They were listening to the older girl who was telling them something which they found hilarious and their laughter pealed out again, causing them to skip around her and beg for more of her tale. It was an enchanting picture as they moved between the slender trunks of the waterside trees.

Suddenly they spotted the three men and stopped in their tracks, standing close together as if for protection. They had probably been told not to talk to the workmen at the house.

'Hello,' called Thomas, and waved self-consciously. 'Are you enjoying your walk?' What a stupid thing to say, he thought as they clearly were. 'It's a lovely evening.'

The older girl took a wary step towards them.

'You are from the house, aren't you?' she said. 'I've seen you about.' She indicated the two girls. 'These are my sisters, Martha and Mary and I'm Jennet. Our father is the woodsman.'

'Ezekial is your father?' said Cuthbert, stepping forward. 'I know him. We have worked together. I am Cuthbert and this is Thomas and Alfred.'

'Cuthbert? The master carver. Father has told us about you. You have come to do great work on the house. He says you are famous.' Jennet moved towards them until they were just feet apart. 'Are you famous?'

'I was brought to Lord Hesketh's attention by Lord Derby, if that is what he meant, but I don't know about famous.'

'He said you did marvellous work at Whalley Abbey,' said one of the younger girls.

'I worked there, yes,' replied Cuthbert, but his eyes were on Jennet rather than the sister who had spoken.

'Do you often walk by the Mere?' asked Thomas.

'Yes, we love it,' said the second sister. 'Jennet tells us wonderful stories when we walk. She makes them up herself.'

'You sounded to be having a good time,' said Thomas. 'What was it about?'

'Oh, just some silly tale I made up,' said Jennet, quickly. 'It wouldn't interest you, and anyway, we must go back before father wonders where we are. Come along, I'll chase you.' The three girls turned abruptly and ran off through the trees the way they had come, their laughter fading away as they disappeared from view.

'Pretty girls,' commented Thomas. Cuthbert was still staring after them, apparently oblivious to Thomas's remark. 'I said, "pretty girls".' Thomas gave him a gentle push. 'Are you listening?'

'Sorry,' said Cuthbert. 'What did you say?'

Thomas burst out laughing.

'Well, I think Miss Jennet and her sisters have made a favourable impression on you, Cuthbert.' He smiled to himself. Was his friend truly smitten on this their first encounter? 'Come on, time we got back too before the light goes completely.' They returned in silence to the village, Cuthbert stopping at the forge whilst Thomas and Alfred continued on to their lodging. All three young men had a lot to think about that night and, for once, it wasn't just about the work they were doing.

CHAPTER FIFTEEN

Abel was pleased with the progress of the building. The two wings were roofed over and the internal work was going well. Some of the glass for the windows had arrived two days before and the men were creating frames to fit. Each little diamond pane then had to be enclosed in lead strips and inserted in the frame. It was time-consuming work but the result would be stunning, especially when they started on the vast windows of the Great Hall. Lord Hesketh wanted his main room to be flooded with light and his commission for the great compass window at the western end was one of the biggest Abel had constructed.

Inside, nearly thirty men were fitting all the internal walls and furnishing the dozens of rooms. Some were to be panelled, others left with the bare plaster which would be decorated later. There was little decoration in the east wing: this was the working part of the house but the buttery needed to be fitted out with racks to hold the barrels of ale, the dry goods storeroom needed shelves all round to hold the stores that would be needed to feed such a large household, the scullery needed lead lined sinks for cleaning the pots, pans and utensils used in the great kitchen. This latter building was away from the main house as fire was such a great danger in a wooden building. All day long there was the noise of hammering and sawing, planning and shaping. Ezekial was constantly replenishing the wood store with every kind of wood he was asked to find. The Hesketh estates included many acres of mixed woodland and his gang spent all their time felling whatever was required. Everyone, from the youngest apprentice to the Master Builder, was working long hours to finish the house.

As he stood outside watching great slabs of stone being stacked near to the Great Hall, ready for hauling up to the roof Abel was counting the days to when it would be complete. Since that early day Lord Hesketh had not visited more than half a dozen times and then only briefly. That was the way Abel liked it, being left to get on with it without what he called interference. No more wild suggestions and modern ideas of which he disapproved. The further on the work progressed the less likely that major alterations to the plans would be suggested. Soon he would be able to turn his attention to detail within the house especially the Great Hall. He himself planned to do some of the decorative carving as befitted his position as master builder, and he had asked one or two of his chosen men to do the rest, but not Cuthbert. He gritted his teeth as he thought of that man. At least he had done as he had been ordered and not worked on anything in the centrepiece of his creation. Abel had gone into the west wing one evening when he was alone. He had been pleased with what he had seen but had no way of knowing what any individual had done. He did not find any of the carving that Cuthbert had shown him as his own designs. All that he found was of the basic designs Abel favoured although he had to admit the carving was very fine. He did not look hard enough though and missed some beautiful floral designs Cuthbert had executed in a dim corner of the solar. Early in the morning the sunlight would catch the panel but late in the evening it was hidden in the shadows. Cuthbert was working his magic as he had done at Whalley but only those who were shown it knew where to look and they would not betray their good friend, Cuthbert.

Cuthbert was, in fact, creating many pieces of work which he hoped to use in other more prominent positions. One or two had already been used in the Great Hall, inserted by one or other of his friends so that Abel would think it was their work. It was rather a sneaky way to go about it but, at the moment,

Cuthbert could see no way to progress. His friends were rather enjoying the subterfuge and in no way felt it detracted from their own handiwork. Fixing a piece of delicate carving high up on the walls was part of their normal work, so who was to ask who had actually made it? One of the bracing pieces beneath one of the hammer beams was Cuthbert's work, put in place by Thomas under the watchful eye of Abel! Thomas had told Cuthbert later that he had found it hard to concentrate with his beady eye on him but he dared not betray any idea that it was not his own work. A carving of foliage over a doorway was also by Cuthbert, fixed in place by Alfric.

The most difficult person to deceive was Will. He was a man who could look very busy without actually getting anything done. He would bustle about carrying pieces of wood or tools but nobody saw him actually use either. If Abel happened to be near he would make an effort and start to take measurements or hold a piece of wood in place as though that was his purpose at that moment but as soon as Abel left, Will would move on somewhere else. He was very good at watching and Cuthbert frequently turned from doing a particular job to find him leaning in the doorway watching him. Cuthbert talked to the others about Will's lack of work.

'Does he ever do anything?' he asked one evening as they ate a late meal.

'Not if he can help it,' replied Alfric. 'He imagines himself in Abel's position, giving orders, supervising others, being the master. What he doesn't realise is that even masters have to learn the job from the very beginning. Abel worked for his grandfather for years before he got to the position he's in now. He may be stuck in his ways now but he knows what it is to work hard at every aspect of this job. He could turn his hand to making simple pegs as easily as any raw apprentice. I don't know why he hasn't realised that Will is just a lazy so-and-so, too keen on causing trouble to be trusted with any responsibility.'

'He would rather be chasing the village girls than putting in a full day's work,' said Harry through a mouthful of bread and cheese. 'He doesn't have much success there either, from what I've heard. They soon realise he's only after one thing and avoid him if they can. There are a few fathers who would like to catch him with their daughters and give him a beating, I can tell you.'

'If he's so lazy himself why does he resent anyone else working. It's not as though we were taking work away from him if he's not doing it anyway,' reasoned Cuthbert.

'That's just Will,' said Thomas. 'It doesn't surprise me in the least that he's taken a dislike to you, Cuthbert. You are the newest here and he is making sure that you know he can cause you problems if you cross him.'

'But I haven't crossed him. I'm only doing my job.'

'He recognises a fine craftsman and you came on the recommendation of a member of the landed gentry. Will would rather be in their position than working as a humble carpenter.'

'I heard there was some history to his life. What is it? Do you know?'

'Not really. When he first appeared he used to hint that he had come from a good family, that he had relatives in high places,' said Thomas. 'The only high place he's been is up a ladder.'

This caused much laughter but Cuthbert wondered whether there was a shred of truth behind the rumours. Will wouldn't be the only young man to be disowned by his family for some grave misdemeanour in his past and the truth would catch up with him one day.

The year was drawing from autumn to winter. The daylight was closing in and they worked shorter hours on the house. There was still plenty to do and despite the cold evenings Cuthbert was often to be found carving some piece by the light of a lantern.

'You'll ruin your eyes,' cried Liliath, catching him working, hunched over, by the fire.

'Almost finished,' replied Cuthbert, blowing the last shavings away, and he held up a piece of wood with the strange face of a man on it.

'Whatever is it?' asked Liliath. 'It's an ugly thing, whatever it is.' She turned it about, looking at it from different angles.

'It's an idea for one of the carvings in the Great Hall,' said Cuthbert. 'There was one on a misericord at Whalley Abbey which fascinated me. It is an ancient symbol going back centuries. The face of a man surrounded by leaves and vegetation, it looks like a mask. Some have shoots and other vegetation coming out of the mouth but this is just a face.'

'A face with its tongue hanging out,' laughed Liliath. 'Are you trying to say something, Cuthbert?'

'I wondered whether I dare put one up in the Great Hall.'

'I hate to think what Abel would say,' she cried. 'Would you dare?'

'I don't see why not. He likes decorative carvings and he must have seen something like this somewhere.'

'But is it in his range of carvings? He won't like it if he hasn't approved it. Dare you face his wrath?'

'He may not even notice it, but perhaps I should keep it here for the time being.'

'It may be safer to.'

So the Green Man's carving joined several other pieces which he had produced over the months and was saving until there came an opportunity to use them.

Another project Cuthbert was involved in was trying to meet, or just see, Ezekial's daughters again, especially the eldest, Jennet. He had never really taken much notice of young women before despite there being many on the periphery of his life in Chester. He had always been too busy working and those he did meet were sisters or nieces of people he knew. Mildred had once teased him that Nell was soft on him but she was a child as far as he was concerned. Jennet, however, was different. There was something about her that he found attractive, something he couldn't quite put his finger on. She was pretty but not of the pale simpering sort that many men liked. Hers was an attractiveness unlike any he had seen before. Her hair was of a lustrous shade that caught the sunlight in the strands and made it glow. Her flawless skin shone with health from the outdoor life she led. She was tall and slender with an enchanting, teasing smile that she had no idea had melted something in him. When he had seen her with her sisters he had noticed the way she was attentive to them but not over bearing. They clearly adored her as much as she did them. She was often in his thoughts as he went about his work and he wondered what colour her eyes were, what made her laugh, what she enjoyed doing when she wasn't helping her mother with the household tasks. Did she sew? Did she make baskets like Nell had sometimes? Did she feed the chickens or milk the cow? Did they even have chickens and a cow? He was ignorant of life in the countryside but would willingly learn if it meant he could see more of Jennet.

His chance came one late autumn Sunday afternoon. Like everyone else he had attended prayers that morning with the village priest and after a meal of bread and cheese had taken his drawing implements and wandered along by the Mere, looking for inspiration from nature around him. He was sitting on a fallen log drawing some of the ducks that were feeding in the water when he heard voices approaching along the bank. As they drew near he saw that it was Jennet and her sisters, ambling slowly through the trees, talking and laughing together. They clearly hadn't seen him and he remained still, watching. They made an enchanting group, three pretty girls, their hair the colour of the autumn leaves around them, a picture of loveliness, and he quickly began to sketch them. They had paused and one of the younger sisters was gathering some of the glorious golden leaves and entwining them to make a coronet which she placed on Jennet's head.

'Queen of the woods,' she pronounced, and all three giggled as Martha and Mary made mock bows to her. Jennet struck a regal pose, accepting their gestures with dignity.

Cuthbert was enchanted, but the scene was spoiled when Will stepped out from behind a clump of bushes a little farther along the bank.

'Well, well, well! What do we have here? A royal court, no less, and such enchanting ladies to attend their queen.'

He made a deep but mocking bow and drew nearer. The girls turned towards him and crept together as he approached, their faces clearly showing their shock at his presence. 'Come, let me pay homage to such beauty. A kiss at the very least.'

He stepped up to the youngest girl and would have put his arm around her waist if Jennet had not moved quickly to her side and moved her behind her.

'Leave us alone, Will. There is nothing for you here,' she said, defiantly.

'I only beg a kiss, a simple kiss from each of you,' he pleaded, smiling sweetly.

'There will be no kisses for you,' said Jennet. 'Go, leave us be.'

Will persisted, the smile on his face becoming a sneer as he tried to grab the younger girl by the arm.

'Think you are too high and mighty because your father is the woodman, do you? A mere woodman. I tell you, I come from better stock than a humble woodman. I could give you a far better life than you would have from some village yokel.'

'Leave us, I say. I know what your intentions are and you will find no easy conquest here. I know what you want, I have heard what you do with other poor girls and I tell you, you will have none of that from my sisters or from me. Go, before you regret it.' She stared at him fiercely, a wolf protecting her cubs.

'You will regret this,' hissed Will.

Cuthbert stepped forward.

'Leave them alone, Will,' he said, quietly. 'They do not want you near. Go now and we will hear no more of this.'

Will looked at Cuthbert, startled at his sudden appearance.

'You!' he cried. 'I should have known you would come to the rescue. The hero, saving the damsels in distress. Well you listen to me, master carver. Your day will come, you watch out, one of these days I will put a stop to you and your plans to show me up.'

'Why should I want to show you up?' replied Cuthbert. 'What have I done to attract your animosity? Why do you so resent my presence?'

Will had no answer but turned furious eyes on the girls.

'You'd better watch out,' he said, menacingly. 'One day, when you're out alone I will get you. He won't always be there to protect you. Be aware. I will find you and I will take what I want whether you like it or not. It is my right.'

He turned on his heel and ran off, back through the woods towards the village.

Cuthbert approached the girls.

'Are you sure you are all right?' he asked.

'Yes, he did us no harm,' replied Jennet, hugging her two sisters to her. 'He scares me though. I have heard what he has done to some of the village girls and father has told us to keep out of his way but how can we when he lives almost among us?' There was a note of panic in her voice and one of the other girls was crying quietly.

'Why does he do it?' she quavered. 'Why does he want to hurt us? What have we done?'

'I don't know,' replied Cuthbert. 'Have you any idea why he keeps saying he is better than us, that he could treat us as he wants if he so wished? Who is he? Where does he come from? Who is this family that he keeps alluding to? Do you know?'

'No, we don't. He came with Abel and his men but we don't know any more than that. Abel may know but he's not saying.' Jennet squared her shoulders. 'We have to be strong and try to keep out of his way.' She turned to face her sisters. 'Don't you ever go out alone, do you hear me? Always go together or with me.'

'We won't,' they nodded.

'I will walk home with you, if I may?' said Cuthbert. 'I want to ask your father about some extra wood.'

'Oh, what are you making? Something special? Liliath showed me the little rabbit you made. It is beautiful.' Jennet's face lit up as she spoke, and something turned over in Cuthbert's chest. There was a lump in his throat and he cleared it noisily before he spoke.

'Er, yes, I have an idea for something for the house but don't say anything to Abel. I want to try it out first. If it doesn't work, no one will know.'

'Will you show us first if it does work out?'

Cuthbert couldn't resist her plea.

'I may do,' he teased, 'but no more questions now. Let's walk back to the village.'

The walk was only about half a mile but to Cuthbert every inch of the way was precious. He longed to hold Jennet's hand, feel her touch on his skin, but he restrained himself, not least because of Mary and Martha. He walked on air through the wood, his heart thumping in his chest. Afterwards he had no idea what they had talked about but the time sped by and soon they were approaching the cottage where the girls lived with their father and mother. Ezekial was hoeing the weeds in the small garden at the side, clearing them from the rows of beans which were coming to the end of their growth. He paused when he saw them and leaned on his hoe as they approached.

'Now there's a glad sight!' he declared. 'Nice to have the time to stroll by the Mere and through the woods.' He smiled at Cuthbert. 'Enjoy your walk?' There was a twinkle in his eye which Cuthbert did not fail to notice and, to his horror, he felt himself blush.

'I happened upon your daughters not far from here and decided to walk back with them,' he said.

'He saved us from Will, too,' blurted out one of the twins. Ezekial's face instantly became serious.

'Him! What did he want? I hope he didn't touch any of you.'

'No, father,' replied Jennet, quickly. 'Luckily Cuthbert arrived and told him to leave us. Nothing happened.'

'I don't trust that young man with any female, young or old,' snarled Ezekial. 'He's a bad lot. You are sure you are all right?'

'Yes, father, don't fuss.' She took her shawl from her shoulders and headed for the house. 'Let's go and help mother with the meal.'

Ezekial watched them to the door then turned to Cuthbert.

'What was Will after?' he asked.

'The usual. He didn't see me at first but when he tried to grab one of the girls I thought I'd better intervene.'

'Thank the Lord you were near! The tales I hear about him are not good. I don't know why Abel doesn't get rid of him. He does next to no work anyway, from what I hear.'

'Do you know anything of his family, where he comes from?'

'Not really. He's been with Abel a while now, apprenticed to him for years but I don't think the lad's heart is in the work. He wants an easy life and hints that he would have one, if ...'

'If what?'

'Well, there's the question. Nobody knows the full story but he's always hinting things, implying he's better than we are, but we don't know any more and, believe me, people have asked often enough, but he always clams up. He's probably making it all up anyway, just in his nature to make up stories. Whatever it is, it is not good for the girls. Thank you for seeing them home.'

'I wanted to see you anyway. Do you have any pear wood , by any chance?'

'Pear wood? Now there's a fine wood for carving.' He looked sideways at Cuthbert. 'Something special planned?'

'Just an idea. I don't want to say more in case it doesn't work.'

'I'll look some out for you, let you have it tomorrow. How much do you want?'

'Only a small piece. An off-cut will do.' Cuthbert indicated with his hands the size he needed.

Ezekial smiled again, the same glorious smile that his eldest daughter had bestowed on Cuthbert earlier.

'Your secret is safe with me,' he said, solemnly, as Cuthbert turned and walked away. Nice young man, he thought as he watched him go. Nice young man.

It was a couple of days before Ezekial sought out Cuthbert, carrying a piece of wood in his hands. He was in the shelter where the carpenters were busy making furniture for the house, helping Alfric to fit together a meal ark to hold the precious oatmeal for the dry store. Alfric was screwing the lid in place whilst Cuthbert held the hinges at the required angle.

'No decoration needed on that then,' remarked Ezekial, watching quietly, not wanting to disturb their concentration until the job was done. Cuthbert lowered the lid and checked that it was closed firmly to keep out any insects or other pests. He looked over his shoulder at Ezekial.

'I may put the date on it, if asked,' he said, running his hands over the smoothly planed wood of the little chest. 'It is a workaday item which I scarcely think the cooks and kitchen scullions will notice that much, just another food store.'

'I've brought some pear wood for you,' said Ezekial, holding out the wood. Cuthbert took it and ran his hands over it lovingly. He sniffed it.

'Don't you love the scent of fruit woods?' he breathed. 'I love it when apple logs are burning on the fire, they give off such a fruity smell, and this,' he breathed in deeply, 'I can smell the fruit it has borne.'

Ezekial couldn't help smiling and cast a sideways glance at Alfric who was grinning at him.

'Don't worry,' he said. 'He won't actually eat it.' They laughed and Cuthbert gave them a quizzical look.

'What? Can't I enjoy the wood I work with?'

'Of course you can, lad,' laughed Ezekial. 'It's a joy to watch somebody who takes such a pride in his work and such pleasure in his tools. You sniff away all you wish, no one is going to stop you.' He clapped him on the shoulder. 'I'd be interested to see what you make of that though. It's not every day I'm asked for pear wood, such a fine grained piece too.'

'You will only see it if my idea works,' stated Cuthbert, firmly. 'Otherwise it will be going on the fire.'

CHAPTER SIXTEEN

Will was not content with his life or his work. Restless, unsettled and constantly seeking for something, he tried to work out what had changed to make him feel this way, why he was no longer prepared to wait until Abel retired and he could take over his work and his team. Was it because he was getting impatient, wanting more of the rewards without putting in the effort? No, for a long time now he had been prepared to wait but as he got older he saw other apprentices reach the end of their apprenticeship and move on whilst he felt as though he had come to a standstill. He never saw it as his fault that he hadn't progressed beyond a barely competent apprentice. He didn't know that Abel had been paid to take him on as a young boy and was not able to release him once his apprenticeship was complete. An agreement had been signed which could not be broken except by the death of Abel.

He pushed his way among the scrubby bushes along the edge of the Mere. This had become his own place, somewhere he could disappear when he didn't feel like working or wanted to avoid someone. Increasingly he was becoming disillusioned, dwelling on the might-have-been and not accepting what had become his lot. He found the spot where he had woven the branches into a sort of shelter and pushed his way inside. It was reasonably dry due to the dense foliage all around him and he had created a dry seat from dead branches where he now threw himself down and gave himself up to thinking of his past.

Why had he become an apprentice? The couple who had brought him up from birth were not his real parents but he hadn't discovered that until he was ten years old. An honest, hard-working yeoman farmer, he and his wife were childless and when they had been approached about taking an orphan boy they had accepted that his parents were dead and they were to be the only ones he knew. For some this would have been seen as cheap labour once the boy was old enough to work on the farm, but in Will's case he had been raised as the son of the household and to help on the farm when he was older. A tutor had been engaged to educate him in the basics needed for running the farm when he was older, how to keep account of what they sold at market, what they could afford to buy for the farm and the household, how to read. At quite an early age he had shown some talent for drawing but it wasn't until he overheard some of the village boys talking about him that he realised that he was different.

It was harvest time in his tenth year. Everyone was busy in the fields gathering in the crop and they had stopped to eat and drink in the middle of the day. Everyone gathered under the trees at the side of the field where it was shady, the younger members of the group tending to sit together. Having eaten his portion of bread and cheese Will had lain down against the bank and closed his eyes. He hadn't intended to sleep but the others must have thought he was dozing and were talking more freely than they would have normally. When he heard his name mentioned he pricked up his ears but did not open his eyes.

'Of course, they're not Will's real parents,' stated a voice he recognised as belonging to one of the older boys, Arnet. 'They were paid to take him in when he was a baby.'

'Who by?' asked another.

'Dunno, but it was all arranged secretly.'

'Does Will know?'

'Don't think so. He's never said anything, but would you, if it was you who had been palmed off on strangers?'

'How do you know then?'

'I overheard some of the men talking when I was ratting in the barn. They said it was something to do with a rich boy and a servant girl and it had to be hushed up. No one must ever know, so don't you go saying anything, especially to Will.'

'Right everyone, back to work,' called Will's father, getting to his feet further along the field and beckoning everyone to start again.

Will stood up and joined the others but his mind was no longer on the work. Not his real parents? A rich boy and a servant girl? Who were they? How could he find out? Who would know? Did his parents, or the couple he thought of as his parents, know where he came from, who his real parents were? Why had he been sent away? It was all too much for a ten-year-old to understand. Would his parents tell him anything? Should he ask?

Over the coming days he went over the conversation time and again trying to understand what it meant for him. Who was he really? Where did he come from? Why was it necessary to send him away? The more he thought about it the more he saw how different he was from his ma and dada. They were both blonde haired whilst he had jet black hair. They had blue eyes where his were dark brown. Although he was only ten he was already showing signs of being tall and lean whereas they were quite short and stocky.

Suddenly his whole world had been turned upside down. He started going off on his own, not completing the tasks he had been set, defying the tutor and being generally disobedient. After a third beating from his father for not feeding the chickens again, his father stormed at him in fury.

'What has got into you, lad? You've never been disobedient before. What has happened, 'cos it has got to stop. As long as you live here you work, pull your weight, do as I say. We can't run the farm without you doing your share.'

'Why should I?' yelled back Will, rubbing his stinging backside where the leather belt had beaten him. 'I'm not your son. I don't belong here. Why should I work for you?'

His father had stared at him, thunderstruck.

'What do you mean? Of course you're our son. Why wouldn't you be?'

'I heard some of the others talking. You were paid to bring me up as your son even though I'm not.'

'Why would we do that?'

'Because you were paid to,' yelled Will.

His father sat down suddenly on the bench behind him.

'Who has been telling you these lies?'

'They're not lies. My *real* father was a rich boy and my *real* mother was a servant girl. You were paid so that I could be got rid of. I was a bastard but you have made out I am a true son, a son of yours.'

'You are a true son,' said his father. 'Why else would we have given you a good education, fed you and clothed you for ten years? Have we not loved you?'

Will could not deny that until now they had done all that and more, but it still rankled with him that they had all been living a lie.

'When were you going to tell me the truth? Or was I going to live my whole life never knowing? Who were my real parents?'

The man put his head in his hands. What was he to do? He had promised to say nothing but what was he to do now the boy had found out? Would he be punished, the money taken back? He pushed himself upright and sighed deeply.

'I do not know who your real parents were, we were told they had died, you were an orphan.'

'Didn't they have any other family? Have I got grandparents, or do you mean they didn't want me either?'

'I don't know about that but I do know we were asked to adopt you and bring you up as our own. We couldn't have any children of our own.'

'So you were bought. Raise me, call me son and all would be well!' Will stamped his foot in frustration and unwanted tears welled in his eyes. 'A bastard and a bastard nobody wanted. That's what I am. Unwanted.'

He flung out of the room, slamming the door behind him and ran and ran and ran. He didn't know where to and cared even less. Unwanted, unwanted, unwanted. The word drilled into his brain, tears blinded his eyes, the pain of the beating paled in comparison to this. He didn't know who he was, where he came from. But worst of all nobody wanted him and that was what hurt most. That a new-born baby could be sold to strangers because nobody wanted him.

He ran until he could go no further. His legs gave way and he fell to the ground, lungs on fire for want of air, a stitch in his side like a knife thrust. He cried until no more tears would come then lay still, his head in a whirl. Eventually he fell asleep, exhausted.

When he woke the light was fading. Night must be approaching. He sat up. He was in a wood but he didn't recognise it. He was lost but nobody would care because nobody wanted him. Slowly he curled up in a ball on a bed of dead leaves and cried himself softly to sleep.

From that day he was a changed boy. The men searched for him all night and eventually found him as dawn was breaking, curled up under a tree in the woods many miles from home. They carried him home and his mother fussed over him, putting him to bed in his own room and sitting by his bedside until he woke again. She called for her husband and they talked to him but Will remained silent. For three days he lay on his bed, refusing all food and drink, staring at the wall. They called the village priest but Will wouldn't listen, putting his fingers in his ears and turning away.

When at last he came out of his room he sat silently at the table and ate a little bread.

'I want to find out who I am?' he said quietly.

'What good will that do?' said his mother. 'You can't turn back time. If you ask questions people will just clam up. If they didn't want you ten years ago they aren't going to welcome you back now, are they?'

Will thought about it. She was right. If these parents hadn't known where he was from all that time ago they weren't likely to find anything out now. He would have been forgotten, gone from the lives of those who fathered and bore him. A nobody.

'I want to go away from here,' he said.

'Where would you go, lad?' asked his father. 'You're only ten years old. What could you do? Where would you go?'

'I could work on a farm.'

'You can do that here.'

'I don't want to be here.'

The couple looked at each other. What was to be done? They cursed the person who had told Will about his background, but who else had known and talked? Who could they ask now? The man who had approached them ten years ago had been unknown to them but he had sounded so convincing and they were so desperate for a child that they had accepted whatever he said. And the money. What fools they had been.

They talked about it long into the night. Something must be done as Will was clearly never going to be happy with them now. Could they apprentice him to somebody as farming was not in his blood and he would never settle to it. They would talk to the village priest, he, at least, would be discreet.

So it was that next day they found themselves setting the problem before the priest who promised to think about what would be best for the boy. A few days later he called at the farm and said he had found a possible solution. Did they think Will would be willing to be apprenticed to a joiner and woodcarver?

'A woodcarver? Why?' asked the farmer.

'I understand Will has some talent in drawing and has shown some skill with tools around the farm. Could that not be used to give him a trade in a useful skill? People will always need good joiners.'

'It may work, but what do we tell his master? We have no information about his real parents or where he came from.'

'Ah, there is where my job may be useful. I may have an idea as to his origins which I cannot divulge to you but which I could use to persuade the man I have in mind to take him on. No names need be mentioned but perhaps a little money may be useful and we could draw up a legal paper stating that once he has completed his apprenticeship he has to stay with the same man for life.'

'Why?'

'To prevent the man dispensing with him later. It would give Will a job for his life with a master who would agree to pay him, feed him, clothe him, no questions asked.'

'It all sounds rather strange,' commented the farmer's wife. 'Why would anyone agree to this?'

'I cannot tell you that but the man I have in mind would rather do what I suggest than that I should reveal certain things about his own background which he has confessed to me.'

'You would be breaking the sanctity of the confessional!' cried the farmer, appalled.

'Then let me do this and I won't be. For a consideration.' He smiled. He named a figure which was nearly as much as they had been paid to take him as a baby.

'Let us think about it,' said the farmer, eventually.

The couple talked it all over late into the night. It seemed the only way to go. Will would never settle with them now but he was too young to set out on his own. At least if he was apprenticed he would learn a trade and be fed and clothed in the meanwhile. They did wonder what secret the priest had which would help him persuade the joiner to take a boy who was, after all, rather young to be an apprentice. Would Will accept this solution? If he was determined to find his real parents would he stay with a stranger, albeit one who would do so much for him? He must be made to understand that, for now, he needed to be with someone older and if not them, then some other adult. If he was really determined in his quest then he must leave it until he was older. Nobody would answer the questions of a child but when he was an adult he may have more chance even though more years would have passed.

Thus it was that he had gone to live with Abel Carter but not as an apprentice for the first three years but as a young helper to his new master. Abel had a wife in those days and she took to the boy immediately, let him help her with the work of the house and garden but most importantly, encouraging him with his drawing and number work. Abel never revealed, even to his wife, that he had been paid to take the boy or that he was not allowed to release him from his apprenticeship once he had completed it. He would deal with that when the time came. As it happened he never had to tell because his wife died just before Will was due to complete his time and Abel vowed never to say a word to a living soul about it.

Will had found that he settled to his new life and actually enjoyed it most of the time. He was prepared to wait. He would have the rest of his life to discover his roots and if nothing came of it he could carry on when Abel died and reap the rewards he saw his new master now had. After the death of his wife Abel had become forgetful although he was still capable of leading a team of men in the building of a house. It was his personal life that suffered. There was no one to wash his clothes or cook his food, clean the house or tend the garden where his wife had grown many of the vegetables and fruit they ate, no one to light the fire on cold nights or warm his bed. He became short-tempered, easily picking a fight over some trivial lapse. His men learnt to keep out of his way when he was in a black mood but still worked for him as his skills and reputation were still there if he concentrated. Will learnt how to calm the worst of his moods and keep him clear of the ale house when he was in a bad mood as drink caused more trouble. Without a wife to tell him when to stop he was likely to take too much.

When the request came for Abel to build the hall for the new Lord Hesketh at Rufford, Abel saw a last chance to shine as he knew his days were numbered. He was getting too old for this hard labour, let him finish with the best he had ever done. Will had watched him draw up the plans for the house using all his experience over many years. Left alone to build it, as he was used to doing, everything would have been fine but this new lord had his own ideas which didn't fit with Abel's and the two had clashed repeatedly, not only over the fireplace but the size and shape of internal rooms, the large number of windows and, most recently, over the decoration to be used to embellish the building. Will could see Abel getting more and more frustrated. He tried to see it from Abel's point of view.

He was the master builder, free to employ whoever he wanted and build in the way he always had done yet here was some young unknown upstart who was being foisted on him, forced to find work for him when he neither wanted or needed him, Cuthbert. Abel hadn't liked him from the beginning. He used his own men, who, in turn, used his ideas. Now not only was this Cuthbert putting forward ideas Abel disapproved of but he had the support of a lord who insisted Cuthbert's ideas were used and Cuthbert should produce them himself.

Will shifted his position on the mat of branches. Cuthbert. Everything had started to go wrong when he had appeared. Will wanted to do the carving for the Great Hall, but Lord Derby wanted Cuthbert to do it. Abel had done his best to keep him out of the way but somehow Cuthbert always managed to make his presence known. Will was sure he was sneaking around the site doing drawings, making carvings for the hall, but he had never actually seen him doing anything wrong. If only he could catch him out. Some of the other men were friendly with Cuthbert, men who had tolerated Will and his lazy ways because he was Abel's man. He must watch them too, see what it was they were planning for he was sure they were planning something.

Then there was the girl, Jennet, Ezekial's daughter. Pretty girl, he'd had his eye on her for a while but she was always with her two sisters. If he could only get her on her own he would show her what a real man could do. She wasn't good enough to be a wife to him for he was a rich man's son, he must never forget that. One day he would wed a girl worthy of his status, one day when he was rich. Meanwhile, Jennet would be worth a tumble or two in the hay. He'd show her why the village girls couldn't resist him. He was oblivious to the fact that the village girls were scared of him and only went with him because he forced them to. He closed his eyes and imagined what he would do with Jennet. Oh yes, one day he'd have her.

CHAPTER SEVENTEEN

The year was drawing to a close as the days shortened and the temperature dropped. The main structure of the house was complete but a tremendous amount of work was yet to do inside. Most of the internal walls were in place but making all the furniture would keep all the men busy throughout the winter. The hours they could work were shortened, dawn to dusk meant as little as six hours some days and they were glad of the shelter of the woodshed where work was mainly centred. Pieces of tables and stools, benches and chests were strewn about in a seemingly random fashion but each man knew exactly what was where and worked on whatever piece was current. Many worked alone, some in pairs as they constructed the larger and more complicated pieces. Cuthbert was engaged in cutting and planing long boards that would form the top of a long table in the Great Hall where the family would sit. Each had to be the same length and thickness and fit closely with the rest. Together with Alfred they had already constructed the base with its several legs and cross pieces for strength. A wood turner had fashioned the stout legs from solid oak, creating wonderful shapes up the length of each one. It had been fascinating watching his skill as he created the first one and once Abel had passed it as good he then had to reproduce it as closely as he could for the other seven legs to match. Cuthbert was always interested in watching other craftsmen work and had kept an eye on him as the lump of wood had been turned into a thing of beauty.

By the end of a week's hard work the table was ready and the top and base were carried into the Great Hall ready for assembly the following Monday. They placed the base exactly in the centre of the west wall where a stout, protruding length of wood was set into the wall between the stone base and the upper wall and would provide a long seat for those who sat at the top table. On Monday Cuthbert and Alfred would, with the help of several others, lift the top into place and fix it in position from underneath. It was awkward work, lying underneath and slotting pegs under the table into slots on the base, then securing them, and not work to be done on a tired Saturday afternoon. They needed to be fresh and ready.

That night it was particularly cold with a hard frost which transformed the morning scene. Every leaf of every tree was coated with a silvery white cover, each blade of grass glistened and in the bushes the spiders webs were picked out in delicate links of frost. Most people shivered and hurried about whatever they were doing, breaking the ice on the water troughs for the animals, picking their way delicately on the ice covered pathways and scurrying back indoors as soon as they could. Cuthbert welcomed the warmth of the house and sat close to the fire as he worked on a small carving again. Liliath watched him as she kneaded dough at the table.

'What is it this time?' she asked. 'Something for the house?'

'Maybe,' replied Cuthbert, deliberately avoiding a straight answer, and he smiled at her. 'It's a gift for someone.'

'Oh? Now who may that be I wonder?' She watched a pink tinge spread across Cuthbert's face. 'Feeling the warmth of the fire?' she asked, innocently, and the tinge became a blush. She laughed quietly. 'No need to keep it secret, we all know you have eyes only for one in this village. Jennet, is it?'

Cuthbert nearly sliced into his finger.

'Is it that obvious?' he asked.

'You mean, nobody notices you become tongue-tied whenever she's near, your eyes follow every move she makes and you spend long minutes gazing into the distance when she passes by on her innocent duties? No, Cuthbert, it's not at all obvious.'

Cuthbert bent his head over his work, his concentration gone now that it was out in the open.

'She's a lovely girl,' said Liliath, gently. 'She'll make someone a good wife.'

'Oh, it's not gone that far!' cried Cuthbert.

'But you would like it to?'

Cuthbert nodded. For someone who had never really thought about the future in that way he was finding it remarkably clear cut for him apart from one thing. Did Jennet feel the same way about him? She always smiled kindly at him and usually stopped if he was passing. He had rescued her from Will's attentions but her sisters had been there as well. Her father was always welcoming whenever he called for some special wood or other and her mother, a shy, quiet sort of woman, clearly did not object to his presence, busying herself about the house whenever he called. Her younger sisters giggled behind their hands a great deal, but that was girls, wasn't it? Oh dear, it was so difficult. He wasn't one for talking about his feelings so what could he do?

'Why don't you go for a walk?' suggested Liliath. 'It's cold but it's dry and it's lovely down by the Mere on a day like this, very still and quiet. You won't meet many people and, you never know, Jennet may have the same idea. You could do with some fresh air anyway. You can't sit by the fire all day. Go on.'

Cuthbert wrapped the piece of work he was carving in a cloth and stowed it in his tool bag. Perhaps a bit of exercise would clear his head. He pulled on his thicker leather boots, wrapped his warm woollen cloak about his shoulders and left the house. The cold hit him like a wall as soon as he stepped outside. He could see his breath in the air and icy fingers penetrated down his neck. He pulled his cloak closer and set off briskly towards the Mere, frosted grass crunching underfoot and icy puddles glistening in the weak sunlight which held no warmth in it at all. The sky was a beautiful pale clear blue with not a cloud to be seen. There wasn't a breath of wind. It was as though life had stopped and was holding its breath until the warmth returned.

On the track leading to the Mere he caught a glimpse of a fox trotting purposefully across the way, nose to the ground, following a scent it had caught. It was probably hungry, all the rabbits it usually preyed on were warm in their burrows below. The trees were golden with their falling leaves and had a special glow in the clear air. He could see further into the wood but there was no sign of anybody moving. Maybe he should walk to the water's edge and along the track in the direction of Ezekial's home and wood store on the off chance of seeing Jennet or her sisters.

At last he reached the shore and sat down on an old trunk to gaze across the water. A thin skimming of ice covered the surface but further out a pair of ducks were swimming across from one little promontory to another. Everything was so still and quiet, he could have been alone in the world. His hands caressed the log he was sitting on, feeling the wood as he always did and something in his mind registered that this was different. He looked down. This was no newly fallen log, it was old, worn but beautifully intact, no gaps in the bark, and blacker than any wood he had seen. He would guess it was oak but not like the oak he worked with every day. He had only seen wood like it once before in a hall in Chester where a great screen had been made of it, beautifully carved with intricate designs. Was this something he could work with? Ezekial would know, and there was his excuse to go to the house and ask and hopefully see Jennet as well. He got to his feet immediately, looked around to fix the place in his memory and turned towards the track leading to the woodshed.

Exekial emerged from the wood store as Cuthbert approached.

'Ah,' he said, 'here for something special, are you?' He smiled at Cuthbert. He liked the lad, he was a good worker and patient with it. He had watched him at work, always fully concentrated on whatever he was doing and only satisfied with the best. Somebody had trained him well and he would go far. He wouldn't just be a jobbing carpenter, taking whatever work he could find. Before long he would be able to choose where he worked and for whom as his skill was recognised more widely and the quality of his work became known.

The question had also had another meaning but Ezekial kept a straight face. He and his wife had noticed how often the girls, especially Jennet, dropped Cuthbert's name into the conversation. Cuthbert said this and Cuthbert did that. It was Cuthbert after all who had rescued Jennet from the unwelcome attentions of the slimy toad of a man, Will. They were not averse to the friendship, in fact, they welcomed it and Cuthbert would always be welcome in their house.

Cuthbert took the question as he interpreted it.

'Yes.' he said. 'I saw some wood down by the Mere, a huge log of oak but it looked different to the wood you cut, as though it was very old. Is it good to work with, do you know?'

'You mean the bog oak, as we call it? Yes, it is very good, very hard, very endurable but you have to work it before it dries out. When it's freshly out of the water it's soft and easily cut but once it dries it's as hard as iron and is very difficult, if not impossible, to work. Why? Are you thinking of using it for something?'

'Is there a lot of it? Do you have any?'

'No, I don't, because as I say, it goes too hard if it's stored. You need to work on it straight away. What have you in mind?'

'Has Abel said anything to you about a screen for the Great Hall? Most of the other halls I have worked on have had one.'

'He's not said anything to me yet but I presume he will. I know of others he has done.'

'Do you know whether he has used this bog oak before?'

'Now, that I don't know. Why don't you ask him?'

'I'm not sure he would take a suggestion from me. He's tried to keep me out of anything major so far.'

'That hasn't stopped you from what I hear.'

Cuthbert looked in alarm at the older man.

'What has he said?'

'He hasn't *said* anything, but from what I hear there are several pieces of your "special" work already in the house. Now, don't look so worried, remember, you have friends who would not betray you. I know most of the men there and they know I would never betray you either. Besides, Jennet also told me about some special carvings you have been doing.'

'How does she know?'

'She listens when she is about the site and the village. People don't always stop talking when she walks by, she is, after all, only a girl! But don't worry, your secret is safe with her. In fact, she would do a lot for you, Cuthbert.' He gave him a meaningful look and was not surprised to see him blush. 'Why don't you come inside where it's a bit warmer and we can think about this bog oak a bit more.'

Cuthbert followed him into the house and was immediately hit by the warmth. He took his cloak off and hung it on a peg by the door.

'Here, sit down near the fire. It smells as though someone has been baking. Is there any to spare?' he asked Hester, his wife.

'Of course, isn't there always,' she replied, and set a bowl of newly baked little loaves down on the table. 'Mary, fetch some cheese from the larder, and there are a few of the windfall apples left. There'll be some broth soon but it's not been on the fire long enough yet.'

Cuthbert immediately felt at home as Hester and the girls bustled about to gather the few essentials for their unexpected guest, but it was Jennet that Cuthbert followed with his eyes as she studiously avoided his gaze and sat down at the far end of the table. The reaction between the two of them did not go unnoticed by her parents though, and after he had left and later in the day when the family were settling down for the night, Ezekial and Hester whispered about him in the privacy of their bed chamber.

'He is unaware of how important he is to this build,' whispered Ezekial, pulling the blanket up around his ears.

'Whatever do you mean?' asked Hester, snuggling close and wrapping her arms around him.

'He was sent here by Lord Derby, no less, and Abel was told he must use his special skills here. Abel doesn't want him and has done his best to thwart any attempts by Cuthbert to work in the Great Hall. He can't send him away but he puts every obstacle in the lad's way, even gave him a beating a while go.'

'No!' cried Hester, sitting up in alarm. 'You never said. Why? Is he all right?'

'He's fine now but it has only made Cuthbert more determined to use his skill here, despite what Abel says. He has secretly been working on various carvings and his friends, and there are many among the men, who put it in place for him, sometimes even under the very nose of Abel. I think they are quite enjoying it.'

'What if Abel realises?'

'I doubt that he will because Cuthbert continues to do the tasks he sets him, out of the way, mundane but necessary work, and he thinks he has no time to do anything else, but Jehan tells me that every night he is working away at something or other until he goes to bed.'

Hester gave a girlish giggle.

'It reminds me of that time the girls made you that shirt for your birthday, hiding it away whenever you came in and always looking busy. You had no idea about it, did you?'

'No, and I didn't dare tell them later that it was too tight either. They'd have been so upset.'

They settled down again and were drifting off to sleep when Hester asked, 'Do you think he'll ask for her hand?'

After a long silence he answered,

'Yes, I do, and he'll be very welcome. Now, stop your dreaming and get to sleep. It's another day tomorrow and I need to talk to Abel.'

'What about?'

'Wood, of course. What else? Now go to sleep.'

CHAPTER EIGHTEEN

Monday morning was unusually cold for late October with a touch of frost still on the ground as the men walked to their work, hands stuffed in pockets or tucked into armpits for warmth.

'If it's as cold as this now, what's the winter going to be like?' asked Harry as he blew into his cupped hands.

'Cold, very cold,' replied Alfred. 'My grandfather used to say that if it started cold this early we were in for a long winter and he was rarely wrong.'

'Good thing we've plenty of work to keep us warm then,' said Cuthbert, looking round for the others and almost tripping over a tree root in the path.

'*You* don't need to work to keep warm when you've got someone to warm you,' remarked Alfric, grinning at Cuthbert who immediately blushed.

'Whatever do you mean?' cried Cuthbert, concentrating on where he put his feet.

'Ezekial's lass,' replied Alfric. 'Don't think we haven't noticed you whenever you see her.' He nudged his neighbour. 'Cuthbert's "falling in love",' he sighed, clutching both hands to his heart.

'No, I'm not,' denied Cuthbert, hotly, but he was fooling none of them and there was much banter as they approached the house.

Cuthbert stopped to look up at the fine building and couldn't help feeling a certain amount of pride in the fact that he was helping to build such a wonderful place. There were still a few sections of the wooden scaffolding up around the walls where gutters and some of the roof stones were being finished. One or two windows in the upper floors of the west wing were still open to the sky but the glass was coming in the next few days to finish those off, the inner wooden shutters already in place to keep the rooms dry. Over the main door to the Great Hall some carved woodwork was half finished, the missing piece being carried by Alfric. To the right the west wing projected forward towards them, a grand house for the family. To the left a smaller east wing held all the domestic part of the house with sculleries and storerooms aplenty to service a large household. The kitchens were housed in a separated wing out to the east, away from the main building. Nobody wanted a stray spark from the cooking fires to ignite the main wooden building. It was the largest house he had ever been involved with though he had helped with bigger Great Halls in Chester.

He passed through the main door and stood in the vast space of the Great Hall. The walls towered above with the span of the roof lifting high above him. He had always admired the use of hammer beams which removed the need for supporting pillars for a high ceiling. By transferring the weight of the lofty roof down the timbers of the walls to the ground they opened up the whole room giving a greater impression of space. There were still several ladders against the walls where carvings were being fixed at the tops of the walls. Otherwise there was little decoration in here as Abel preferred plain wood. Some of the furniture may well be painted later but that would very much depend on the owner once the building was completed.

'Are we fixing this table today or not?' called Alfred from the far end.

'Sorry,' called Cuthbert and hurried to the west end where the two parts of the table awaited them. They checked that the base was central along the wall then several of them lifted the great weight of oak onto it.

Alfric was standing at one end ready to position it correctly with Harry at the other.

'Bit more to me,' he said, bending to see that the top slotted onto the pegs on the base which had been cut to receive it.'

'Whoa!' cried Harry from the other end. 'Too far. Back this way a bit.'

The men shuffled sideways but Alfric cried,

'No, no, no. You've missed it.'

Harry got down on his knees and peered underneath.

'Can't see where the holes for this end are. Just a minute.' He felt underneath with his fingers then bent to look closer again.

'Hurry up,' said Cuthbert. 'It's heavy.'

Harry looked up a puzzled expression on his face.

'There aren't any holes cut,' he said.

'What! Of course there are, I cut them myself.' Cuthbert stared at Harry.

'Well, they aren't there now. Look for yourself.'

'Put it down, carefully, that's it, now tip it on its side.' The men laid the huge piece of wood down and tipped it so that it stood on one edge. Cuthbert bent to look at the places where he knew there had been slots ready to fit into the pegs on the base. There was nothing there. He stood back, totally bemused.

'They were there, I know they were,' he cried.

'I saw you do them,' affirmed another of the carpenters. 'You were right next to me when you shaped them.'

They all stood looking at the smooth underside of the table top. Suddenly, Cuthbert ran his fingers along the edge of the table, then bent down to look closely.

'I don't believe it! Someone has cut the end of the table off completely. Look. I sanded it to make it smooth and slightly rounded, but this is straight and sharp.'

'Why? Who would do such a thing? What for?' cried several voices at once, and those nearest felt with their own fingers, the sharp edge of the wood.

'When was it done?' asked Harry.

'I reckon on Saturday or Sunday night. No one would be around then. It was so cold that few would venture forth.'

Cuthbert looked at the table. It had taken ages to assemble the top to make it as smooth as possible and sturdy enough for its purpose.

'Who would do it though?' asked Alfric.

'I could think of one but what evidence have we?' said another of the men.

'Do you mean who I think you mean?' asked Harry.

'Will. He's mean and nasty enough to do it, though it would be the first time he's done anything as difficult without being caught. It will have taken a fair while if he was trying to be quiet,' reasoned Alfric.

'But why?' queried Cuthbert. 'What was he trying to achieve?'

'He knew that you had been working on it, Cuthbert. You're not his favourite carpenter, remember.'

'But to deliberately spoil such a vital piece of work is just … ridiculous. I know he doesn't like me but to deliberately do that.'

'See, over here,' cried Alfric. 'Sawdust. We haven't sawn anything in here for ages, we always do that work in the woodshed. This is fresh.' He bent and picked up some between his fingers and sniffed it. 'Yes, this is oak, and look, he's tried to sweep it up but he's left some.'

'Probably couldn't see properly in the dark with only a lanthorn candle to work by.' Cuthbert rubbed his hands through his hair. 'Well, there's nothing for it, we'll have to remake the whole end of the table. I can probably splice a piece in so that it's hardly noticeable. Lay it down and I'll measure what is needed.'

'Look out! Here comes Abel,' called Joshua, one of the apprentices by the door.

'Just what we need,' muttered Cuthbert as he bent down with his ruler.

'What's going on here?' cried Abel, striding the length of the hall. 'That table should be finished.' He stood, legs apart, hands on hips and glared at the group of men. 'Why isn't that top in place?'

'Because someone has cut at least eight inches off the end, maybe more. I'm just measuring it,' replied Cuthbert, from the floor.

'Cut the end off!' bellowed Abel. 'Don't be ridiculous! Why would anyone do that?'

'Perhaps you should ask Will,' replied Cuthbert, getting to his feet and standing to face the master builder, a glint in his eye that was rarely seen except when he was really angry, and Cuthbert was barely controlling the anger that was bubbling up inside him.

'Will? Why on earth would he do such a thing?'

'Because ever since I arrived here he has done his best to belittle me, sneering at me, moving work when I turn away for a moment, taking my tools, putting me down in front of you, destroying my work when it is half finished, ruining the plans I showed you. He is jealous of me though God knows why. I have never done anything to him except prove that I am the better worker. Who do you think sorted out the problem with that arch?' He pointed behind him to the great arch at the far end of the hall. 'You left him to erect it and he couldn't even do that. Trying to put it together the wrong way round, he was. No wonder it wouldn't fit. Who saved Bern's leg when that trunk trapped him in the mud? We did because I saw what happened and was able to help quickly.' Cuthbert moved a step nearer. 'It's about time you looked at what he does every day, really looked. Oh yes, he can look ever so busy but what does he actually do? Show me a piece of work he has actually completed. You won't find much, though to listen to him in the ale house you would think he was building this place single-handed. And where is he now? Oh surprise, he's not here. Probably sleeping off his night's work sawing the end of this table off.'

Cuthbert was shaking with fury as everyone stood round in stunned silence. They had never heard him talk like this. He had always shrugged off all the slights and comments from Will, all the derision he had heaped on him but this was too much. They had spent many hours creating this table only to have it spoilt by a jealous young man who knew he could never match up to their craftsmanship. He was breathing heavily as he stared into Abel's face, his hands clenched at his side to prevent him hitting him.

'How dare you?' hissed Abel. 'I knew from the moment you were foisted on me that you would be trouble. Master carver! Huh! I know a master carver when I see one and you are not one. I never wanted you here but because the great Lord Derby brought you I had to accept you. I have told you time and again to keep out of the way, to do as I say. Well, your days are numbered, my lad. Next time I see the owner of this building I shall tell him that I find you totally unsuitable and refuse to have you on site. Then what will you do, master carver? Who will you run to next with your cock-and-bull stories about your fellow workmen, because believe me, you will never work in this county again nor in any other once I spread the word about you. A trouble-maker, that's what you are, a trouble-maker.' He turned on his heel and pushed his way through the group of men who had gathered to hear the argument, their shouting having been heard all over the house.

Cuthbert was still shaking with fury, breathing hard, his heart pounding in his chest. He felt like smashing something but was stopped by a gentle hand on his arm and he turned to see Ezekial by his side.

'Well said, lad,' said the older man. 'It needed saying and you were the only one who had the courage to do it. Well done.'

A murmur went round the rest of the men.

'You don't deserve it,' said one.

''Bout time someone stood up to him,' said another.

'Aye, I've worked for him for nigh on twenty year and I've never heard him speak like that. He's getting past it.' said a third.

'He's had his troubles,' said Ezekial. 'He's never been the same since his wife died. He can't cope with it any more. He can still do the work but he can't cope with problems any more. One time this would never have happened. Still, he should never have taken it out on you, lad.'

'At least I didn't get a beating this time,' commented Cuthbert, calming down a little.

'What happens now?' asked Alfric.

'I say carry on,' advised Ezekial. 'The house still has to be finished.'

'Wait till I get my hands on that slimy snake, Will,' growled Harry.

'The best you can do is to completely ignore him,' said Ezekial, thoughtfully. 'He will probably turn up in here soon and expect there to be trouble over what he's done. Well, don't give him the satisfaction. Carry on as though nothing has happened. Just go about your work as though nothing has been said or done. See how that pleases him, eh?'

'He'll think he's got away with it!' exclaimed Alfric. 'We can't do that.'

'Ezekial is right,' said Harry, quietly. 'He wants to see a big fuss over this, Cuthbert blamed for bad workmanship and dismissed. If we replace the timbers and make no deal about it he'll wonder why. He can hardly go to Abel and say the table was damaged when he did it, can he?'

'But Abel already knows. Won't he speak to Will, see what he knows?' asked Japheth.

'Will can talk himself out of anything,' pointed out Cuthbert. 'What we need is proof that he and only he could have done it.'

'How?' asked several voices.

Cuthbert thought about this for a while then said,

'We probably can't prove it this time but he's not likely to give up, is he? Why don't we lay a trap for him?'

'What do you mean? Keep watch?'

'We know he's always going on about my carving. He hasn't seen much of my work yet because we've always kept it apart from everyone else's and you have put it in place for me. What if I make a show of creating something for, say, the solar in the west wing? Just a small piece but detailed enough to catch Will's attention. Make sure he knows what it is and where it is intended for. At the end of a day I leave it out in the room ready to put in place next morning, making sure Will knows about it, perhaps by showing it to him when none of you are around, as though I am sharing its importance with him alone. That will peak his interest. If it is damaged or even missing next morning you can all truthfully claim to know nothing about it while I can point the finger at Will as being the only person other than myself who knew where it was going.'

'What about Abel though? He always believes whatever Will tells him,' said Harry.

'He has said I may only work in the wing. I could tell him what I intend to do with the piece, maybe even show him a drawing of it for his approval. He can't deny me completely.'

'It might just work,' agreed Ezekial, rubbing his chin, thoughtfully. 'If you painted it before you fastened it in place and said you were leaving it to dry overnight, we could look for traces of paint on Will's hands or clothing next day. Paint it last thing so it will still be wet for most of the night.'

Several heads nodded. Whilst it was unusual to paint carved decorations, doing so before they were in place was not unknown.

'Let's do it then,' cried Alfred. 'How soon can you have something ready, Cuthbert?'

'I have just the piece,' grinned Cuthbert. 'A green man face I did a while ago but haven't used. I have the drawing too so I could show Abel today and in a few days produce the carving ready for painting. Make sure Will is around to overhear, then paint it and leave it out in the room upstairs. Even better if he happened to come up and see it.'

'Let's do it,' cried Alfric.

Later that day, when the table had been repaired and fixed to the base, Cuthbert sought out Abel with his drawing of the face. Abel was still grumbling about his carelessness but glanced at the drawing Cuthbert gave him.

'Hmm,' he muttered. 'Not bad. Where are you thinking of putting it?'

'In the solar, in the corner by the window. It will look down on the room. I have made several before now. The owners seem to like them, some sort of symbol of good luck, I believe.'

'You need plenty of that,' grumbled Abel. 'Get it made then but show me before you put it up. If it's not to my standard you won't be using it. I won't have poor craftsmanship even in dark corners.'

'It won't be,' agreed Cuthbert.

Work continued for the following week. Cuthbert kept mentioning in Will's hearing that he was working on a special carving in the evenings, something for the solar. Will pretended indifference at first but at the end of the week he actually asked, sneeringly, if his masterpiece was complete.

'Almost,' replied Cuthbert. 'I'm quite pleased with it. I should be able to put it in place in a couple of days.' Will nodded and walked away. We'll see about that, he thought.

Next day, Cuthbert showed the piece to Abel who grudgingly approved it, then told a few people that he was ready to put their plan in action. He made sure that Will saw him head for the solar and wasn't surprised when he suddenly appeared in the doorway. Cuthbert was kneeling on the floor and pretended surprise when he saw Will.

'I didn't think you were interested,' he remarked.

'Always like to see a *master carver* at work,' said Will. He peered over Cuthbert's shoulder. 'Nothing special, is it? Anyone could carve that.'

'Maybe, but not with as much detail. See, his hair is waved with tiny cuts along the length. Look at his eyes, I've detailed his pupils, and the mouth shows his teeth.'

'Huh! Detail? Waste of time when it's stuck up in a dark corner. Who'll ever see detail like that? Could have done two carvings in the time it's taken you to bother with detail.'

'I take pride in my work, Will. Do you? Besides, Abel has approved it.'

'Get the job done, I say' snapped Will, and turned to leave.

'I'll put it in place tomorrow when the light's a little better,' Cuthbert called after him and got to his feet. Crossing to the window he saw him walk away towards the village. Cuthbert got back down on the floor and took some small jars of paint and some brushes out of the bag he had carried up earlier. It didn't take him long to mix the paint and decorate the carving in green with piercing brown eyes, red lips and white teeth. When it was done he sat back and looked at it. Not bad, he thought. If only it could talk and tell him what happened during the night. He touched it carefully with one finger. With any luck it would still be wet in the morning. He shivered. A cold night was what was needed to prevent it drying completely.

The weather, however, turned slightly warmer overnight and by morning there was an inch or more of snow on the ground. It transformed the countryside, hiding all the ugly parts of the building site, making the light so much brighter and with more snow likely to fall from the heavy clouds. As the men gathered to start work, pulling thick capes about their shoulders and blowing on cold fingers, Cuthbert smiled to himself.

'What are you so pleased about?' asked Alfred, beating his sides with his hands to warm himself.

'Look,' said Cuthbert, pointing at the ground. 'Footprints! And see where they are coming from. The west wing.' He looked about and said softly, 'Has anyone been into the house yet?'

Nobody had.

'Don't walk on those prints,' he said. 'I'm going to look.'

He went inside and up the stairs. His carving lay in pieces on the floor of the solar, smashed by a sharp tool clean down the middle and flung aside like a piece of rubbish. The ruse had worked. Now they had to prove it was Will. He made his way down again, a big smile on his face.

'It worked?' asked Alfric.

'Someone has taken a blade to it, smashed it. Now we have to find Will, see what he has been up to. He must have done it before it started snowing, there are no wet footprints inside but we have these footsteps leading out. Let's see where they lead.'

The clear prints in the snow led them straight to Will's billet. He was just emerging, rubbing the sleep from his eyes and shivering. He looked in surprise at the group of men walking towards him.

'What's happened?' he asked.

'Perhaps you could tell us,' replied Cuthbert. 'What have you been up to in the night?'

'Me? Nothing. Slept like a log.'

'How come your shoes are wet then,' asked Alfred pointing at Will's feet.

Will looked down at the clear signs of moisture on the sides of his shoes.

'Let's see if your shoes fit these tracks, shall we?' suggested Cuthbert, and grabbed Will's arm, propelling him towards the footprints in the snow. He forced Will to put one foot in the mark. 'Perfect fit, I'd say.'

'It … it could be anyone,' blustered Will. 'Someone going to the privy or … somewhere.'

'On a freezing cold night like last night? I hardly think so.' Cuthbert felt the sleeve of his jerkin. 'Why are your clothes damp? Was it snowing when you went for a walk?'

'A walk? Why would anyone go for a walk in the snow?' Will tried to pull away but Cuthbert held him fast.

'Let's have a look at your hands.' He grabbed Will's arm and held it out. Will tried to pull away but Cuthbert was too strong. They all looked at smears of green paint on his fingers. 'How did you get paint on your hands?' he asked, sternly.

'I … I … must have got it on yesterday.'

'Did anyone see Will doing any painting yesterday?' asked Cuthbert of the gathering group of men. They all shook their heads. 'Let's have a look in your tool bag.' He pushed Will back into the room and threw him down on his bed. Bending down he pulled Will's tool bag from underneath and tipped it out on the floor. He picked up a small axe with the tip of his fingers and looked at it. 'If you haven't been out all night would you like to tell me how smears of green paint are on the blade of this, and on the handle too?' He touched one carefully. 'Still wet.' He glared at Will. 'Well? Can you explain?'

'I … I … Someone must have borrowed it,' he stuttered.

'Rubbish! You saw me take the carving up to the solar yesterday. Suddenly very friendly, weren't you? You knew I was going to put it up today so you decided to damage it, like you damaged the table in the Great Hall last week. If we take you and this axe to the solar now, what do you think we'll find? Eh?'

'How should I know? It wasn't me who smashed it.'

'How do you know it was smashed? I didn't say it was smashed, just that it was damaged. It was you, wasn't it, you worthless creature?'

'It could be anyone,' blustered Will. 'Lots of people use green paint.'

'Not this green paint. I mixed this specially last night. It's not the same as any other green paint around here. Shall we go and match it up?'

He hauled Will up from the bed and they marched him across the site and up the stairs into the solar. Cuthbert pulled out Will's hand and wiped some more of the green paint onto it from the broken carving. It matched perfectly.

'What do you have to say now?' he shouted.

'What's going on here? Why aren't you all at work?' demanded a furious Abel from the doorway. 'As if the days aren't short enough without you wasting time up here. Get about your work.'

'We have been discovering who has been wrecking Cuthbert's work.' Alfred spoke up and there was a murmur of agreement from everyone else.

'What are you talking about? What has been wrecked?'

'The table last week and now this.' Cuthbert held out the piece of broken wood. 'You agreed yesterday to me putting this up but Will, here, had other ideas. He smashed it with his axe during the night.'

'Why would he do that? What proof have you got that it was him?' Abel stood in front of Cuthbert and growled at him.

'Footprints in the snow. Green paint on his axe and his hands and probably on his clothes if we look.'

'Anyone can get hold of green paint,' replied Abel scathingly.

'Not this. I mixed it specially last night. You won't find an exact match anywhere on the place. He as good as admitted it when we confronted him.'

'He would admit to anything if you all ganged up on him.'

'He's guilty,' said Alfred. 'He's had it in for Cuthbert ever since he got here. You have no idea what he has been up to behind your back, Abel. He wants Cuthbert off the site but it's Will you should get rid of.'

'Don't you tell me who I can employ,' yelled Abel. 'I've known Will for years, I trained him. It's this mad man who has been causing all the trouble.' He jabbed a finger at Cuthbert. 'He's the one who should be going but I can't get rid, can I? He's the favourite round here.' He glared round all the faces. 'Now get back to work, all of you.' Grabbing hold of Will's arm he hauled him out of the room and down the stairs.

'Will's for it now,' said Alfric. 'What do you think he'll do to him? He's not going to get rid of him.'

'That's for him to sort out.' Cuthbert sighed. 'The best we can do is get back to work.'

'What about your carving? Will you do another?'

'Yes, and I'll put it up myself.'

It was only to be expected that there would be repercussions from the night's events. As everyone went back to their work it was soon clear to all that Will was getting a severe telling off from Abel. The two could be heard shouting all over the site and when Will emerged from the woodshed he was sporting a black eye and a bloody nose. He got no sympathy from any of them and slunk off towards the Mere. Nobody was sorry to see him go. Good riddance was the general opinion.

Cuthbert didn't expect to be let off however and before long he heard heavy footsteps ascending the stairs in the west wing. He had been gathering up the mess Will had left, trying to rub out the paint marks he had left on the floor boards. He turned as Abel launched himself at him, taking his full weight on his left side as Abel hit him at full speed. Cuthbert went down hard, knocking the breath out of him but Abel was on him straight away, kicking and punching in fury, swearing at him, threatening to maim him, kill him, anything to get rid of him. Abel was beside himself with fury, taking out his anger on the one person he saw was to blame, calling him every name he could think of as blow after blow landed. Cuthbert curled into a ball, trying to protect himself.

Suddenly the room was full of people as the men tried to pull Abel away but he was strong and it was several minutes before they managed and dragged a yelling and kicking Abel out and down the stairs. Alfred knelt down beside Cuthbert.

'Are you all right, lad?' he asked, as Cuthbert uncurled and looked with relief into his face. 'We saw Abel come in and feared the worst after what he did to Will. Gave him a beating too, not that he didn't deserve it.'

Cuthbert spat out a tooth and sat up, wincing at the pain in his side and on his thighs where Abel had kicked him. He had a deep cut on his forehead which was bleeding heavily, and another on his ear which was still ringing from the blow.

'I'll survive,' he gasped. 'It's not the first time after all,' He struggled to stand and had to lean on Alfred's shoulder.

'We'll get you to Liliath,' said Harry, taking his other arm and between them they half carried Cuthbert down the stairs.

'Best get back to work' said Alfred to the others. 'We'll see to him.'

The men drifted back to work, discussing what had happened and wondering whatever would happen now.

Liliath was shocked to see the state of Cuthbert and set to work to clean his wounds. Jehan and Jacob immediately set out to find Will, not so much to give aid as make sure he wasn't creating trouble anywhere else. They searched his billet but no one had seen him, so they made their way towards the Mere where they knew he spent a lot of his time but despite a thorough search could find no trace of him.

'Let's hope he's gone and drowned himself,' muttered Jacob. 'Best thing for him, and us.'

'Probably couldn't even do that properly,' answered Jehan. 'He'll get a beating from me if he causes any more trouble.'

They worked their way back towards the house, stopping at Ezekial's home on the way to tell them what had happened. They were horrified and Jennet wanted to go to Cuthbert straight away. Her mother advised strongly against it.

'Your mother's right, lass,' said Alfred. 'The lad's in no fit state to see anyone. Maybe tomorrow. Liliath will look after him but knowing Cuthbert he will be back tomorrow. Meanwhile, you take care. If you see any sign of Will, keep well clear and tell one of the men.'

'He's right, love,' said Hester. 'You and you sisters must stay close. I don't trust that Will. Until he's found or turns up of his own accord you are not to set foot out of this house, any of you.'

The twins looked scared stiff and Jennet reluctantly agreed though she longed to go to Cuthbert. Her parents exchanged glances over her head. He clearly meant a lot to her.

Will was hiding in his lair among the reeds, certain that he would not be found there. He heard Jehan and Jacob searching for him and kept still and quiet until they had passed. He tore a strip off his tunic and bathed his swollen eye with cold water from the Mere, wiped away the blood from his nose, which he was certain was broken, and nurtured the hatred in his heart. He would kill Cuthbert for this. He would kill Abel for turning on him. He would find and kill the parents who had abandoned him at birth. His fury knew no bounds. He would find out who he really was and he would make everyone sorry they had ever crossed him. Yes, he would, every last one of them. He was not going to let this go. Never, Never. Never.

CHAPTER NINETEEN

Abel walked off in a fury, heading he knew not where. His anger frightened him. It was so unlike him. If Dora had still been alive he would never have behaved as he had been doing lately. Things had never upset him to this degree before so why should it happen now? Why was he lashing out so violently? Was he just getting old? He walked on along the track heading north until he calmed down then turned and retraced his steps, wondering what he was going to do now.

Ezekial, worried about the younger man, had gone in search of him. He had worked with him for many years, supplying the wood he needed for whatever he was building. It was so unlike him to behave in this way and he wanted to make sure he was all right.

He met him coming along the path from the north. He looked calmer now than when he had stormed off though still not his usual self. Something was troubling him.

'How about we stop by the ale house?' he suggested as he came abreast. 'You look as though you could do with getting some things off your chest.'

At first, he thought Abel was going to ignore him and walk past, but he stopped, looked Ezekial in the eye and said, quietly,

'Aye, I've got to talk to someone. I've got mesel' in a mess, haven't I?'

'You could say that,' said Ezekial with a gentle smile. 'Come on, let's set the world to rights over a jar or two.'

It was only a short distance to the ale house. Few people were there so early so they took their drinks into a quiet corner and sat on a bench against the wall. For a while nothing was said then Abel spoke quietly.

'I dunno what's matter wi' me. Can't settle to nowt. I'm all … all a muddle in me 'ead. I can do me work but I can't cope wi' anything else, not Will and his laziness nor Cuthbert being pushed onto me when I don't need him. Any upset gets me mad and I lash out.' He looked sideways at Ezekial. 'You've known me nigh on twenty year. What's t' matter wi' me, eh? Why am I like this? I know Will has his faults but I can't stand him anymore. And I know yon Cuthbert's a fine craftsman but I resent him. Why?'

Ezekial took a long swig of his ale before answering.

'I reckon you're missing Dora more than you'll admit. You allus had her to talk to at the end of the day, to sort out your problems with. She was taken so sudden that you can't accept that she's gone. Now you've no one to settle those things in your head anymore. She was a grand woman, was Dora, allus had an answer to a problem and you're missing that.'

'Aye, mebbe you're right.' Abel peered in to the depths of his drink. 'We allus talked did me and Dora. She had that gift of seeing the way out of a problem when I couldn't. Tek Will, for example. When I took him on we knew he had problems but they didn't seem so bad at first, we saw him as a lost young lad who needed somewhere he could grow and become a young man, somewhere where he could have a settled life. He were fine at first but he would never make a master joiner, passable one mebbe, but not a great one. Too lazy for one thing, soon bored by a job if it were takin' too long.'

'I gather the others get annoyed with him for not doing what he's supposed to. You know he had no idea how to put that arch together, don't you? It was Cuthbert who put it right, then Will took the credit.' Ezekial drank deeply, then got to his feet. 'Another?'

'Aye, go on,' said Abel, handing his mug over. Ezekial went for a refill, carrying their drinks back to the corner.

'I know Cuthbert's a good worker,' Abel said, taking the drink from Ezekial. 'It's the way he was dropped on me that I object to. I was caught on a bad day. I'd dreamt of Dora and couldn't get her out of me head. It allus makes me upset when that happens, as though she's there, trying to tell me summat. What with being ordered about by Lord Hesketh, wanting this and that changed, new ideas I can't be doing with, then Lord Derby ordering me to take on Cuthbert to do special carving when we hadn't even built the place, it was too much. Left to meself I can get on wi' job. Heaven's above! I've built more houses like this than they've ever seen and there's never been anything wrong with any of 'em. I were building 'ouses afore the young lord were born! And there he is changing things what I know work. It were all too much, too much to cope wi' alone.'

'I can understand that,' said Ezekial. 'I dunno what I would do wi'out my Hester. It took me long enough to find her but I dunno how I coped afore.' He leaned back against the wall and stared in to the distance. 'We all of us need someone special, someone to rely on, to complain to, to … love, I suppose. You were lucky wi' Dora and I'm lucky wi' my Hester, I reckon I'd go to pieces wi'out 'er and that's what's happened to you. You're lost.'

'Aye, you're right there. That's what it is. I'm lost, but what do I do about it? I can't go around using my fists to sort out problems, can I?' He looked at Ezekial. 'Have I hurt t'lad badly?'

'Which one? You gave them both a pasting from what I hear. Cuthbert's gone to Liliath, no one knows where Will is. He allus goes off on his own. What is it with that lad? Where does he come from? Do you know?'

There was a long silence. Abel drank deeply, wiped his sleeve across his mouth and sat forward, staring at the floor between his feet.

'It's not easy,' he said at last. 'I know about him but I don't want to talk on it. He's got some big ideas in his head, that's what he's on about.'

'I've heard as much but is he right?'

'Some of it is, yes, but not all. He's woven a tale about it that he has grown to believe and the more he thinks on it, the more he imagines it's true, and it ain't. Every time I hear what he's been saying he's added a bit more but he believes every word he says is the truth. It's all a muddle now and I don't know how to stop him' He groaned. 'My Dora would have known what to do, set him straight she would, make no mistake but I don't have the words to do it.' He glanced up at Ezekial. 'So what do I do?'

'Tell him the truth. Stop him making it worse before he does himself or someone else any harm. You are the only one who can set him straight.'

'You may be right but I'll have to do it at the right time. If I choose wrong he'll fly off the handle.'

'Where will he have gone now? Any idea?'

'Not really. He's a loner, is Will. People don't like him so he hasn't anyone he would go to. Keeps his own company. I don't know where he is when he's not working, certainly doesn't tell me. I sometimes think he despises me too even though I've tried to teach him all he knows.'

'Why did you keep him on when you realised he wasn't any good?'

Abel shifted uneasily on his seat.

'It's complicated,' he muttered. Suddenly he sat up. 'Best be getting back. Work to do.'

He was up and away in a trice and Ezekial looked after him in surprise. Whatever it was there were deep secrets somewhere in the relationship between Abel and Will that he wasn't prepared to divulge. It only added to the mystery. Had his talk been of any good? He couldn't tell. Perhaps he had caused more problems than he'd solved.

He drained his mug, shivered in the failing light of the day and went outside. He looked about but could see no sign of either Abel or Will. Where had the lad gone? To lick his wounds no doubt. Well, there was no point trying to find him when he had no idea where to look. He turned towards home. There was a lot to think about but at least he and his family were safe, secure and, as far as he knew, happy, at least Jennet was. He smiled as he thought of his eldest daughter who was clearly falling in love with the young carpenter. She wouldn't do any better than choose Cuthbert. Ezekial liked the lad for his straightforward honesty and decency. He was a hard worker, talented beyond any of the others. He would go far if he could just survive the wrath of Abel and the jealousy of Will. He turned towards the forge, eager to see how he was, how badly he had been injured and see if there was anything he could do.

***

Will shivered in his lair and pulled his short cloak around him. His face hurt and he could hardly see out of his eye. He didn't deserve the beating Abel had given him. He may have spoiled the table but it had been put right, hadn't it? *Master carver* Cuthbert had mended it, of course. Done it to spite him probably, show he wasn't going to take notice of him. Well, he'd take notice when he did something that couldn't be mended. He smiled, winced as his sore face stretched, then huddled closer and began to make his plans to show them all that he deserved better, that he *was* better than any of them. He'd show them.

***

Liliath dealt with Cuthbert's injuries as she had before though there was nothing she could do about his missing tooth except staunch the bleeding.

'Good thing you've got some to spare,' she said, wiping the blood off his chin, and drew a small smile from Cuthbert. 'As for this cut on your head, you're going to have a scar, I'm afraid, but it won't spoil your handsome features.' She salved his other cuts and applied a lotion to his bruises. 'You're in for another uncomfortable night,' she said, standing back and looking at the mass of bruises on his body, 'and this time I am going to insist you have a sleeping draught. No, no objection! Your body needs sleep to recover from this.'

Cuthbert was too sore to resist and after a dish of her soup he was only too glad to curl up on his bed and surrender to the draught.

Jehan, Jacob and Liliath sat down and were discussing what they could do when Ezekial arrived.

'How is Cuthbert?' he asked.

'Asleep,' said Liliath. 'Not quite as bad as last time but this can't carry on. Why did Abel do it?'

'I've just been talking to him,' said Ezekial, and sat down to tell them what had occurred.

'Poor man,' she said. 'He's suffered in silence so far. He and Dora were devoted to each other but he always thought he would go before she did and when that didn't happen his world was overturned. We should have seen this coming, we should have helped.'

'How? He's always been a private man, not one to share troubles. He just buried himself in his work and tried to carry on. When all's going well he's just like the old Abel. It's all this other business that's upset him, all this to-do with the house, Will's laziness and Cuthbert's arrival. I should have seen it coming.'

'How could you? You just find and cut his wood, you don't see him every day and you certainly don't know what he does at night.'

'Still I should have done something.'

Suddenly the door was flung open and Jennet ran in, her hair loose about her shoulders, her shawl clutched at her throat.

'Where is he? Is he all right? Is he badly hurt? Can I see him?'

She looked from face to face. Her father stood up and took her in his arms.

'He's all right,' he reassured her. 'A bit knocked about but he'll be fine. Now, what were you thinking coming out like this? Haven't I told you not to come abroad on your own? It's not safe.'

'I had to see if he was all right, father.' Her eyes filled with tears. 'I can't bear for him to be hurt. Can I see him, please?' She looked round at Liliath, pleading to be allowed.

'I'll come with you,' she said, 'but don't wake him if he's asleep, do you understand?'

Jennet nodded and followed Liliath through to the little room at the back of the forge where Cuthbert slept. The door creaked open and they went in. A candle was burning on a stool by the bed, enough for them to see that he was indeed asleep. Jennet gasped when she saw his face, the bandage round his head, the bruises and the blood stains on his tunic and in his hair. Liliath squeezed her arm.

'It looks worse than it is. Nothing that won't heal in time.'

Jennet looked into his face, the face of the one she loved and felt a surge in her heart as though she too was hurt.

'Can I sit with him for a little while, please? I won't wake him. Please, just a little while.'

Liliath understood the girl's pain and relented.

'For a few minutes only. Don't wake him and I'll come back for you.'

'Thank you,' breathed Jennet , and moving the candle to a shelf, sat down on the little stool. Liliath slipped out of the room.

Jennet looked at Cuthbert's face. The bruising was beginning to show and there was a slight cut on his lip where the tooth had caught it when he was hit. His lips were slightly parted and she could see the gap. One ear was swollen. The bandage around his head made his hair stick up like a crown and she gently stroked it flat. Dried blood made it stiff and she longed to wash it clean.

'Oh, Cuthbert,' she breathed. 'Why is Abel treating you so? What have you done to deserve this?' She held the hand that was lying on top of the rough blanket, feeling callouses on the palm from hard work, noting the broken nail on one finger, the grime down several of the others, healing cuts from small nicks picked up from his work. A workman's hand, hard and strong, yet gentle. It was the hand which had held her when he had rescued her from Will, the hand he had stroked her hair with when he saw she was upset, the hand she wanted to hold again. A tear slid down her cheek and she laid her head on his arm, willing him to get better so that they could be together.

When Liliath came back a few minutes later she was touched to see the tenderness with which Jennet held his hand, and smiled. It was clear to see that the girl was in love and hurting for him. Gently she touched her shoulder and Jennet rose and followed her out of the room.

CHAPTER TWENTY

The following day calm was restored. Abel said nothing to Cuthbert beyond telling him what work to do. Will slunk around doing as little as possible as usual but looking at Abel from his one open eye. Everyone else got on with their work and did their best not to do anything to antagonise Abel. There was an atmosphere across the site that was almost tangible, as though everyone was waiting for something to happen though what that could be no one could tell. The house had to be built and the sooner the better, then they could all move on.

Cuthbert continued constructing furniture, anything from simple benches for the Great Hall, supports for the trestle tables, to chests for storing food in the kitchens. He was grateful to be able to fill his days with good honest work and go to his bed tired at the end of the day. It was several days after the argument with Abel before he realised that wherever he was working, in the house or in the woodshed, he was never alone, there was always at least one of the other men with him. At first he thought nothing of it but when he was doing tasks which didn't need more than one, or just walking between buildings, he began to suspect they were doing it deliberately. It was when Thomas followed him to the privies that he confronted his friend with his suspicions.

'Are you following me?' he asked, turning to face him.

'Sort of,' replied Thomas. 'We want to make sure you aren't the victim of any further attacks, that's all.'

'Attacks from Abel?'

'And Will. It's for your safety and for the rest of the men. There are undercurrents of unrest from those two and as you seem to be the victim of more than your fair share of, shall we say, bad temper from them, we are keeping an eye on you.'

Cuthbert didn't know what to say.

'I don't want to appear to be ungrateful but I thought I could take pretty good care of myself.'

'Not when you are alone. Every time it has happened it's when you were alone somewhere, did you not realise? They don't do anything if there are others around.'

'I suppose you're right.' A cold shiver ran down his spine. 'Thanks.' It was a sobering thought that he needed to be protected and not a very pleasant one. 'I'll be more careful.'

Later that day, as he ate his meal with Jehan and his family his thoughts turned to Jennet. What if she was to be hurt? He didn't think Abel would do anything to a young girl but he wouldn't put it past Will. What would he do if anything happened to her because of him?

When the meal was finished he took the piece of carving from his bag that he had been working on for a while now. It was something that he wanted to give to Jennet when it was complete. He held it in his hands, turning it over and over.

'What's that you have there?' asked Liliath. 'Something new?'

'Yes. It is something I saw once in Chester and I thought it would make a little gift for Jennet sometime. Do you like it?'

'What is it? Let me see.' She held out her hand and took the carving that Cuthbert had spent so many hours working on. It fitted neatly into the palm of her hand. 'It's wonderful!' she exclaimed. 'Beautiful! It looks like some sort of flower but I can't quite place it. What is it?'

'It's a Tudor rose,' he explained, 'the badge of the House of Tudor. When the houses of York and Lancaster finally came together with the marriage of Henry VII and Elizabeth of York, the red rose of Lancaster and the white rose of York were combined to form the Tudor rose you see there. It became the badge of the Tudors which I have seen on banners at celebrations in Chester. It is usually painted in red and white but I like the plain wooden version as much. Do you think Jennet will like it?'

'Oh, Cuthbert, she will love it, especially as you have made it for her. When are you going to give it to her?'

'I don't know. It is difficult to see her on her own, her sisters are usually around and neither of us dare go anywhere alone to meet, especially now that Will seems bent on doing us harm. It is very difficult.'

Liliath looked at his forlorn face, the face of a man in love but thwarted in his desires. She handed the carving back.

'Leave it with me. I'll think of something,' she said, smiling at him.

***

Early one morning in late November Abel called everyone together in the Great Hall before they started work. It was unusual for this to happen, he would normally have spoken to various groups of men about their particular area of the building or tasks they were involved in, and would see what everyone was doing during the course of the day. He was a good overseer and always knew exactly what was being done at any time. He carried a copy of the plans with him wherever he went, to check that everything was as it should be. Today the plans were laid out on the big table for all to see.

When everyone was assembled he spoke to them all.

'We can see the end of this building now, it should be finished within six months. The main structure is largely complete and the internal work is proceeding well. As you can see there have been a few changes to the original plans but those have been at the instigation of the owner, not me. I had hoped that he would allow us to finish the task without further interruptions. Much of the work yet to do is concerned with detail, particularly decorative detail. A lot of carving has been completed but there are still some areas where additional decoration is yet to be done. I put on my original plans the detail of work I expect to be done, patterns and designs I have used for years and which have always given satisfaction to the owner. I would expect those ideas to be used here without complaint or alteration. I know what works, what adds to the building's finish, what people like. Look at these drawings and you will see what I mean. There's nothing too fancy, nothing that spoils the overall look of the building. That is in my opinion. Left to complete it my way this will be a fine building which any other owner would be pleased with and accept.

'However, I have received a message from Lord Hesketh saying that he will be visiting in the next few days to see the progress and *bringing with him his own plans and drawings for the decoration of the house, particularly of this Great Hall, which he expects us to execute forthwith*.' Abel paused and it was plain to see that he was not pleased with this idea at all. He glared round at the company. '*His plans. His decorations.* Once again he is going to interfere with the building of a perfectly good building with his own ideas of what is right and fitting for it. I shudder to think what those plans will be but if they are anything like that monstrosity of a fireplace then I will say so and in plain terms. I was employed to build this house, he approved the plans, but if he is not satisfied with my work I will go and leave him to it. I will, I really will. I have never been treated in this way before in all my years. He employed me because he had seen many examples of my work and liked them, so why is he changing everything and at this late stage?'

Abel's voice had risen as he delivered this diatribe and ended on a shout. His whole body was shaking with fury, his hands clenched, his face red as he glared round at the astonished men and there was a stunned silence.

'I will not stand for this,' continued Abel. 'What does he know of building? He's probably seen some fancy rubbish that would detract from the plain beauty of this Hall. It would be desecration to change what *I* have created, to ignore *my* experience on a whim.' He turned and thumped the table with his fist. '*This is what I designed and this is what will ..... be ..... done.*'

He glared round at the shocked faces gathered about him.

'*My designs, my house.*' Then to the astonishment of all, he seemed to crumple and all but fell to the ground had not those nearest caught him and sat him down on a bench. He bowed his head, covered his face with his hands and wept, his shoulders shaking with the violence of his emotion. The men looked at each other in shock, unsure what to do until Thomas hissed at those nearest,

'Fetch Liliath. Quickly.' Two of the men left at a run. Thomas knelt down beside Abel and tried to pull his hands away from his face but Abel just rocked back and forth moaning, 'My designs, my house,' over and over again.

'What should we do?' somebody asked. Thomas looked up.

'I think it best if we all get on with what we were doing. Liliath will know what to do with him. I'll stay until she comes. Go on, back to work.'

Slowly the men drifted away, talking quietly to each other about this unexpected turn of events. They had never seen Abel so angry, so upset but many recalled how he had changed over the last weeks getting ever more morose and angry over little things, remembering how he had beaten Cuthbert, twice, how he had argued repeatedly with Will. Had his will broken, was he getting too old? Was it time he gave up?

Thomas stayed with Abel until Liliath came running in with the two messengers. Abel had hardly moved and was still rocking slowly back and forth, moaning and weeping. She was shocked to see him so and knelt down beside him.

'Abel?' she said, quietly. 'What ails thee? What has happened? Tell me. It's me, Liliath. Tell me what has happened.'

There seemed to be no response for a while but Abel suddenly sat up, his face tear streaked and pale and looked at her.

'I can't take it any longer, I can't. I've always done my best but I can't do it anymore.'

Liliath tried to soothe him but he just got more agitated and fell to weeping again. She had brought a draught with her after hearing what had happened and she eventually persuaded Abel to drink it, after which he became calmer. With Thomas's help they helped him to his cottage and to bed.

'Rest is what he needs,' she said. 'I'll see to him. You'd better get back.'

Thomas was relieved to be able to leave him in her care. He had never seen Abel in such a state and he was greatly worried about what would happen now. Who was going to oversee the work with Abel unable to? As long as Will didn't expect to. He feared what would happen if he took over so it was with a heavy heart that he returned to the building.

The rest of the men gathered around him, eager to hear what had happened but he could tell them little other than Liliath was looking after him.

'Who is going to take charge if Abel doesn't recover?' asked Alfric. 'We need him to direct the work, He has the plans, after all.'

'We'll be all right for a while,' replied Alfred. 'We all know what work we are doing for the next couple of weeks and we could manage up to Christmas. Ezekial will help with wood as we need it and there is a long list of pieces of furniture we need to make, carving to do in the west wing, window shutters, doors, all that sort of work. Until he has had a rest we will still be able to carry on.'

'But what happens if he doesn't get better?' persisted Alfric.

'Then I will take over,' said Will, coming into the room. He had been listening outside the door and saw that it was the time to reveal himself. 'I am his favoured apprentice, all the work will be mine when the time comes anyway and as far as I am concerned, it has come.' He smiled round at their shocked faces as he made his way to the centre of the room. 'Abel is old. He's a broken man. His day is over. It is my turn now.'

'Do you honestly think that we will take your orders?' sneered Harry. 'You? Who can't complete a simple task without help? Can you even read those plans of Abel's? Can you actually read?'

Will reddened. Reading was not easy for him, he had hated trying to learn but he could get by.

'Of course I can read the plans,' he cried. 'Abel showed them to me many times whilst he was creating them. I know every detail as well as he does. They are no mystery to me.'

'You are a mystery to us,' said Alfred. 'Why are you so sure that Abel will hand everything over to you?'

'Because there is no one else, is there? He has no son, no heir whereas I am the heir to a great family.'

A groan went up from the assembly.

'Oh yes, so you keep saying,' jeered Harry. 'If that is true, why are you a humble carpenter? Why aren't you revelling in your good fortune? Where is *your* great house? You must be very rich so why do you wear the simple clothes of a workman? *Why are you here?*'

Will took a step back whilst he thought of an answer.

'I am awaiting the call to take up my inheritance,' he declared loftily, and jumped as a howl of derisory laughter came from the men. 'It is true. I am the son of a great lord.' The laughter increased. Turning furiously about he glared at them all. 'You will live to regret this,' he yelled. 'One day I will make you suffer. You will rue the day you laughed at me. Then it will be my turn to laugh in your faces as you face poverty and degradation because you won't be able to find work when I tell people how you treated me. I will have money. I will have power and you will have nothing.' With a lofty expression on his face he pushed through the gathered men and stalked out of the room, followed by the jeers and laughter of the men.

'Well,' cried Alfric, 'He really has made an ass of himself this time. Great lord, my foot. He's no more a lord than I am.'

'I'd love to know the truth about his background,' mused Alfred. 'It's not the first time he has made such claims but he said more this time than ever before.'

'He has made it all up,' cried Harry. 'Why would Abel employ him if he was as rich and well-connected as he claims. He's invented a story and now he believes it is true. There's no truth in it, I'd wager on it.'

'There must be some shred of truth there or where has he got the idea from?' asked Cuthbert.

'He has probably heard a snippet of information and built a story around it to make him feel important because he's a nobody. The story has grown and now he believes it. I reckon the story is about somebody else and he wants to be that person so he pretends he is.' Everybody turned to look at Japheth. A quiet man he rarely said anything or stated his opinion. Such a speech was unheard of.

'Well, you've certainly been thinking about it!' exclaimed Alfred, and Japheth reddened.

'It's just an idea,' he murmured.

'He could be right though,' commented Cuthbert. 'I don't think Will's clever enough to make it up but he is capable of making it fit himself. The only person who knows the truth is Abel and he's not going to say anything.'

'How do you know that?' asked Alfred.

'Something Ezekial said.'

'Ezekial? Well they have known each other a long time. It could be true.'

'Whatever the truth is,' said Harry, 'I am not being told what to do by him.'

There was a rumble of agreement from them all.

'I reckon it should be Alfred,' called one.

'I agree,' said another.

'Wait a minute,' said Alfred. 'Abel hasn't gone yet. He may recover, he just needs some rest. Meanwhile, we have all got work aplenty to be doing so let's get on with it.'

With nods of agreement the group dispersed to continue the work they had been assigned.

Three days later, to everyone's surprise, Abel appeared mid-morning looking pale and tired. He didn't speak to anyone until he had walked round the entire building and examined what everyone was doing. Nobody knew what to say or do for fear he would descend into the depths he had reached before but it was noticeable that he paid particular attention to all the carvings that had been completed, even climbing a ladder to examine some in the Great Hall.

'What's he up to?' hissed Harry, as Abel made his way into the west wing.

'No idea,' answered Alfric.' 'It's as though he's looking for something but I can't imagine what it may be.'

Abel reached the top floor where Alfred and Cuthbert were fitting window shutters on a small room that would be a bedroom eventually.

'Leave us,' he ordered Alfred, who looked puzzled at the command. 'Did you hear me? I said leave us. I want to talk to Cuthbert. Alone.' Glancing at Cuthbert Alfred left but paused outside the door. 'Don't linger out there, go downstairs and stand outside where I can see you,' called Abel and Alfred had little choice but to obey. Once outside he went to stand on the frozen ground below the window and looked up. Abel was watching for him and nodded when he saw him. 'Stay there,' shouted Abel from above. Out of Abel's sight Harry and Alfric were standing round the corner of the building.

'What are you doing?' asked Alfric. Out of the corner of his mouth Arthur whispered,

'He's got Cuthbert alone up there. He's told me to stay here where he can see me. One of you creep up and make sure he's not beating Cuthbert again, but don't let him know you're there. Go quietly, be careful.' He glanced up and he could see Abel standing with his back to the window and as he watched he turned and looked down again, checking that he had not moved. Harry ascended to the top floor as quietly as he could and entered the room adjacent to the one where Abel and Cuthbert were. He could hear their voices but not what they were saying but he dare not go any nearer. At least he wasn't beating Cuthbert. He decided to stay there in case of trouble.

Abel leaned back against the wall, occasionally looking down to where Alfred was standing shivering in the cold air.

'Well, it appears you have your guardians,' he began. 'Very diligent they have been these last few weeks. Are they expecting me to harm you in some way?'

'We all look out for each other,' said Cuthbert, not sure where this was leading. He was uncomfortable being alone with Abel but would not be caught unawares as long as he kept his distance.

Abel stared at him for a long minute, as though deciding what to say. It made Cuthbert feel uncomfortable. Where was the belligerent Abel, the argumentative man who used his fists to get answers, and would stand for no lies? When Abel did speak it was not what he had expected to hear.

'I want to explain what has happened, to say sorry for the way I have treated you since you came here. I have not … been well. I have not treated you in the way you deserve. I have not accepted you as one of my men.' He glanced out of the window at Alfred who was beating his arms to try and keep warm. 'You came here expecting to be given special work, on the recommendation of Lord Derby and Abbot Paslew from Whalley. Am I correct?'

Cuthbert nodded.

Abel bowed his head and said,

'The other day everything got on top of me. I lashed out at you in an unforgiveable way. There are circumstances in my life about which you know nothing. I thought I was managing to suppress certain feelings, jealousy, anger, frustration … a deep longing and sadness, but I couldn't.' He glanced up at Cuthbert who was surprised to see that there were tears in the older man's eyes. He continued. 'I had a wonderful life working in a job I loved with a wife I adored and a team of men around me who trusted me to provide work for them and their families. I knew exactly what I was doing, where I was going but then my wife died and it all fell apart.' He wiped his sleeve across his eyes. 'We shared everything, she was always there to smooth things over when I had a bad day and when she … died, it was as though part of me died too. Suddenly I was alone with only my work to occupy me and for a while I have carried on but things changed. Will, who we had adopted and brought up as our own, has become lazy, spouting ideas above his station and I didn't do anything to stop him. I knew he wasn't working as he should but I ignored it. Then you came along, a stranger with a glowing reputation and I was told, no, ordered, to give you special work on a building I had designed down to the last detail. I had no one to talk to, to set things straight and, well, you know what has happened.'

He turned to look out of the window at Alfred, stamping his feet.

'Liliath gave me something to make me sleep the other day, the first proper sleep I have had for weeks, and afterwards Ezekial came and talked to me for a long while. He has known me for years and knew my Dora too. He saw what was happening to me and realised that until I recognised what was going on I was not going to get any better. He told me how unreasonable I was being with you and that I must tell Will the truth about his background before he lets his dreams get out of hand. I will do that soon and I am not looking forward to it one bit. He won't like it and I don't know what he will do.' He looked up at Cuthbert again. 'You are a fine worker, I can see that. Despite what I have done to you, you have continued to work as hard as anyone. That shows character. I also understand, that despite my telling you that you were to do no work in the Great Hall, you have managed to carve a number of pieces and persuade others to install them. I have seen them and they are of the highest quality, what I would expect from your glowing recommendation.' He looked Cuthbert full in the face. 'Can you ever forgive me for what I have done?'

Cuthbert was stunned at these revelations and was lost for words for a moment. He realised how difficult it must have been for Abel to reveal all this. He was a very private man, not given to showing his emotions. It must have cost him a great deal to say this.

'Of course,' he said eventually.

'You are a very lucky man. You have faithful friends around you, like Alfred out there. Perhaps you had better go and release him before he freezes to death. But Cuthbert, I would prefer it if you say nothing of what I have told you to anyone, except Ezekial perhaps, who knows it all anyway.'

'You can trust me.'

'I know that now and I would be interested to see more of your work when you are ready.'

Cuthbert was surprised at this sudden change in opinion but before he could speak Abel walked out and down the stairs.

Remembering Alfred out in the cold he hurried after him and found Alfred shivering with cold.

'Come to the woodshed,' said Cuthbert. 'At least it is warm in there.'

'Are you all right? What happened up there?'

'We talked, that's all. He explained a few things but I don't want to talk about it now. Come on, let's get warm.'

Cuthbert never did tell the others what had passed between him and Abel in that room. He knew how hard it must have been for him to speak so openly and he respected his desire for it not to be spread abroad. Their work carried on though Cuthbert wondered what Will's reaction would be to the truth about his family.

CHAPTER TWENTY-ONE

Despite Abel's revelations and promise to speak to Will as soon as possible it soon became apparent that he had not done so. Abel returned to work, even helping the men with hanging doors, carrying pieces and holding ladders, something he had not done for a long while. He was very quiet, not speaking unless absolutely necessary and certainly not to Will. But when Cuthbert showed him some drawings of a screen he had seen constructed in Chester, the two men had a long discussion about it. Both had certain suggestions for the design which would make it unique to Rufford and Abel liked the idea of using locally found bog oak to make it. They drew detailed plans together, a task Cuthbert found particularly pleasing as it reminded him of the days when he and Jethro had pored over plans a few years ago. This was how he had imagined his work would be when he was sent to Rufford.

'We could all help to make this together,' suggested Abel. 'There are many skills among my men. I know who would produce the best for each part and together we will make it as the final piece for the Hall. What do you think?'

What a change from the broken man of a few weeks ago, thought Cuthbert. This could be the saving of them all.

'What about Will?' he asked, and a shadow came over Abel's face.

'No,' he said, emphatically. 'No, I do not want him working on this, he will only spoil it somehow.'

'Have you spoken to him yet, about his family?'

Abel looked up sharply.

'No. I told you, I need to choose the time.' He rolled the plans up. 'I might leave it until after the Christmas festivities.' He walked away, leaving Cuthbert unsure whether he was angry with him for mentioning Will at all. There may be an understanding between them but he still needed to be wary where Will was concerned. He turned his thoughts instead to ideas for the great screen, the final masterpiece of the construction.

In the week before Christmas Alfred's grandfather's weather prediction proved to be true as the temperatures plummeted. The ground froze rock hard, the bare trees stood stark against an icy blue clear sky as though fixed in position without a breath of wind to move them. Even the edges of the Mere were coated with a thin layer of ice, and every branch and twig was coated with it. Cuthbert gasped at the beauty of it even as he hurried between buildings and longed to sketch what he saw, but it was far too cold to sit outside. As the men emerged from their various billets and made their way to the house their breath plumed in the air and they huddled closer into their warmest clothes, noses red and fingers frozen. At least vigorous work would warm them and there was still plenty of that to do.

In the largest woodshed where furniture was created a small group of men were studying the drawings for a large bed which was to go in the main bedroom. The canopy, headboard and pillars were very ornate and Cuthbert was one of those selected to carve the intricate decorative panels. Abel had approved his preliminary drawings and Cuthbert was eager to start the work, having selected the wood he would need the day before. Laying out his tools on the bench where he would work he lifted the panel of wood into place and started to mark out the design on the surface.

He had not got very far when there was the sound of an argument outside and, laying down his tools, he went outside to see what was happening. Abel was remonstrating with a tall young man on a horse.

'Today? They are coming today?' he was saying, forcefully. 'Why? How many are coming?'

'My Lord Hesketh wishes to see the progress before the winter feast,' replied the young man. 'He has guests staying with him and is bringing them to show them his new house. They will be arriving shortly after noon. As to the number in their party, there will be about a dozen. Lady Hesketh is coming too, and bringing their eldest son. I am not too sure how many of the other guests will join them.'

'But we are very busy,' cried Abel. 'If Lord Hesketh wishes the house to be completed in the spring we need to work as many hours as we can on these short winter days. We could lose vital time if we have to have visitors.'

'May I remind you that Lord Hesketh is paying you to build this house and if he wishes to view progress he has every right to do so,' said the young man, tartly.

'Of course, of course,' replied Abel. 'I meant no disrespect. Of course he may come to see the building.'

'Very well. Expect him after noon.'

With a sharp look at Abel he turned his horse and galloped away.

'He'll be coming with his wonderful plans for the decorations again,' grumbled Abel.

'Don't let him annoy you,' counselled Alfred. 'He is young, he will have his own ideas. As long as he doesn't want any major alterations to the structure we will have to accommodate his ideas, if they are workable. He may want something that can't be done. He's not a builder and what he wants may not be possible.'

Abel looked gratefully at one of his senior workmen.

'You are right. I must not let him rouse my anger.' He gave a weak smile and took a deep breath. 'I will bite my tongue if I have to this time but don't be surprised if I refuse some of his ideas if they are as wild as his last suggestions.' He gave a deep sigh. 'I am beginning to think that this may be my last big work.'

'Never!' cried Alfred. 'There are other masters and other houses for you to build yet. Don't let a few mishaps on this house deny you further work.'

Abel looked sideways at him.

'Would you still be willing to work for this old man then?' he asked.

'Of course, and you're not that old.'

It was about an hour after noon when they heard horses riding towards them and looked out to see the party approaching. About a dozen was an underestimation as there were nearer twenty in the party. Lord Hesketh led the group, drawing his horse to a standstill while still a little way off. The riders were clearly taking advantage of their position to survey the house as a whole and when they approached there was a lot of chatter among them. As well as Lord Hesketh they recognised his wife, Lady Hesketh, a groom with the young heir, Thomas, riding pillion, another groom with Martha, Lady Hesketh's maid, riding behind him, several young men and three ladies riding side-saddle and, bringing up the rear, Lord Derby with two young men who looked so like him that they must be his sons, and a lady they correctly presumed was Lady Derby. As they drew close they stopped to dismount, handing reins to the grooms and walked slowly towards the house, clearly discussing it as they pointed to features and exclaiming favourably on what they saw.

Lord Hesketh came forward and Abel went to meet him, doffing his cap and bowing respectfully.

'Greetings, my Lord,' he said, bowing slightly.

'Master builder, I see you are making fine progress. The house looks splendid, though I have been receiving reports from various people who have passed this way.'

'Indeed, my Lord. I trust they were favourable.'

'Oh yes, most favourable. We are eager to see how far you have progressed within. Shall we ...?'

'Cuthbert!' cried a young voice and a small boy hurtled towards them and stopped in front of Cuthbert, then remembered his status and said, eagerly, 'Do you remember me? I am Thomas. You showed me how to lay a floor last time I was here and we …'

'Thomas!' cried a firm voice. 'Remember who you are.' Lord Hesketh looked around. 'Where is your nursemaid?'

'I am here, my Lord. I am sorry, my Lord, I will take charge of him now. Master Thomas, come and stand by me. Remember what we said? You must behave if you are with your father.'

'But I was only saying hello to my friend, Cuthbert.'

'Thomas. Do as Betsy says.' Lady Hesketh stepped forward and took the child's hand. 'You promised to be good if we let you come.'

'Yes, mamma,' replied Thomas, meekly, and took his nursemaid's hand, but not before turning and giving Cuthbert a gap-toothed smile.

'Let us go inside,' said Lord Hesketh, and swept past Abel to enter the west wing. Dressed in a rich blue velvet cloak lined with fur and wearing thick gauntlets, stout boots and a fur trimmed hat he looked every inch the wealthy landowner. Lady Hesketh was similarly dressed with a deep red velvet cloak also lined with fur and with the fur-edged hood pulled over her head. The skirts of her dress were thick and richly embroidered and revealed a pair of elegant but serviceable boots beneath. She wore thick gloves with fur linings visible at the cuff. No expense was spared to keep out the cold and most of the rest of the party were similarly warmly dressed, even young Master Thomas who was a smaller version of his father with a shorter woollen cloak and a fur trimmed hat. On his feet he wore little leather boots which he shuffled through the frosty grass leading to the door, taking a childlike pleasure in the rustling noise it created. The nursemaid, warmly but more simply dressed, chided him and took his hand as they began a tour of the house. Abel showed them into every room and they exclaimed at the panelling, the carved wooden shutters, the over mantels and the few items of furniture already completed.

'This will be my bedchamber,' declared Lady Hesketh, entering a large chamber on the first floor, 'with the solar next door where it will catch the sun.' She hurried to the window and looked down. 'I will create a garden there so that I can look out upon it from here. It will be full of flowers and over there we shall have a herb garden. See, Martha, we can grow all the herbs we needed for the cooking and for our medicines.'

'My dear, are you already preparing for illness to befall the household?' cried Lord Hesketh.

'Not at all, but we should be prepared. I understand it can be cold and damp hereabouts so we must be ready for the aches and pains of winter.'

'My Lady,' laughed Lord Derby, who had been attending to this conversation, 'would that *my* Lady prepared in such a manner. I am afraid she relies on the servants to do such things and they do not always attend as carefully as they should to such matters.'

'I was raised to pay attention to such things by my mother and I take great pleasure in so doing. I will show your dear lady, if you wish.'

Lord Derby bowed his assent and they turned back into the room. Lady Hesketh suddenly exclaimed,

'Look! A Green Man!' and pointed to the carving in the corner by the window. 'I have always wanted one of those. How delightful,' and they all craned to see.

'That is the work of Cuthbert,' declared Abel, 'the man you sent from Whalley Abbey, my Lord.'

'Ah, finally he has carved a piece for us.'

'There are several examples of his work around the house now. He is indeed a fine craftsman as you said.'

'I told you he would be an asset,' said Lord Derby, 'but come let us see the rest of the house.'

The party went into every room in the wing then crossed outside to view the east wing where the domestic working of the house would be carried out, and into the great kitchen beyond where the hearths and bread ovens were still under construction. Outside once more, they entered the Great Hall by the big double doors on the north side. Everybody's eyes immediately rose to the vault of the roof and exclaimed in wonder at the size of it.

'So much light!' exclaimed one.

'Look at the size of those windows!' cried another, and the whole party walked round, pointing and exclaiming at everything they saw. Young Thomas broke free from his nursemaid and ran into the great fireplace, craned his neck and looked upwards.

'I can see the sky,' he shouted. 'Come and see, father.' To the child's delight, his father joined him below the great arch and peered upwards.

'Whatever made you put the fireplace here?' asked one of the other young men, joining them in the hearth to look up to the sky.

'It was an idea I saw on my travels,' replied Lord Hesketh. 'It makes much more space in the body of the hall.' He emerged from the fireplace and crossed to the doors which led into the west wing, his eyes going to the carving over them. He nodded his approval. 'Is this Cuthbert's work?' he asked.

'No, but some of the carvings at the top of the walls are,' said Abel, and gave a sideways glance to Cuthbert who was watching from the main door. He couldn't refrain from smiling. Abel was finally recognising his work.

The group continued to walk around the hall as the family spoke of tapestries to hang on the walls, tables and benches to provide seating, great candlesticks to provide light during the darker months.

'There is still a lot of work to do in here,' explained Abel.

'Yes, indeed,' interrupted Lord Hesketh. 'I have brought some plans with me for the decorations. Jasper, where are those papers?' A young squire stepped forward and handed his master a roll of papers. Lord Hesketh took the roll and opened it out on the long table at the western end. 'Now, you have already carved above the doors as we agreed but I would like more carvings in the roof. See those square panels bounded by the crossbeams, I want a decorative piece in the centre of each, like this,' and he pointed to a drawing on the paper. 'On the bracing pieces below the hammer beams I want carvings similar to those over the doors. I have drawn a few ideas but I am sure that you, or indeed Cuthbert, could design some more.' He turned to look up at the highest points above where the arches met in the centre. 'Ah, I see you have already put some roof bosses in place, but they are so plain, like round cushions, nothing more. There are four? Five? No matter. I want some of our family crests there, to remember from whence we came. I have had drawn some of the more important ones. Perhaps you could select the most suitable. Some are very complex and may be difficult to reproduce but we can use those elsewhere in the house.' He looked at Abel who was trying not to show his discomfiture at these latest alterations to his perfect building. 'I trust this work is not beyond the capabilities of your men? I want only the best.'

'Of course, my Lord,' muttered Abel, and gave him a weak smile. 'I will set my best carvers to the task immediately.' He took a deep breath to calm himself and went on,

'Have you given any thought to a screen for the east end of the room, to screen the domestic side of the house from the guests?'

'Ah, yes a screen. It will have to be very large to be effective, will it not? I don't want a paltry little thing that is no real use.' He walked to the east end and surveyed the two external doors to the north and south. In the eastern wall were three doorways giving access to the buttery and other domestic rooms. 'Yes, I see what you mean. There will be a lot of movement through here, won't there?'

'With two external doors it may also be used as a passage from one side of the house to the other,' suggested Lord Derby, who had been following the conversation. 'A screen's passage, in fact. People could wait here to be received by you. That will be the main entrance, I take it,' he said pointing to the northern door, 'unless, of course they arrive from the south, as we have done.'

'Quite so,' agreed Lord Hesketh. 'Have you had some ideas on this?' he asked Abel.

'We have, my Lord. Cuthbert and I have been looking at some ideas and we were hoping to make something worthy of so fine a house, created by my best men from some of the best oak in the region, bog oak straight from the Mere.'

The company looked surprised and there was a murmur of approval. Abel produced the simple plans he had drawn and the men moved back to the long table at the far end to see them.

'My Lady?' whispered Betsy. 'May I take Master Thomas for a walk? He is becoming very restive with all this talk.'

'Of course,' replied Lady Hesketh, 'but not too far and don't let him get cold. Thomas, do as Betsy tells you. Now, put your hat on, it is still very cold out there even though the sun is shining.'

'Thank you, mama,' cried Thomas and almost dragged Betsy from the room.

The men were busy surveying the plans for the screen, whilst the ladies were deciding which of the tapestries Grace, Lady Hesketh, had brought with her on her marriage, would be suitable for this great room. Lady Derby said that the ones of hunting scenes would be appropriate whilst Grace wanted to display some of the floral subjects instead.

'Those would be more suitable in your solar,' suggested Lady Derby, and, on reflection, Grace agreed.

'I trust there is a good blacksmith in the village? I want two great candle stands for either side of the fireplace, each holding about twelve candles. We had such at home and they were much admired.' Lady Hesketh tuned about in the room, imagining it filled with people. She could not help but be excited at the prospect of welcoming her guests to such a beautiful room.

The plans for the screen had been of great interest to Lord Hesketh. He had not envisaged anything quite as elaborate as he saw drawn here but as Abel explained it he grew more enthusiastic.

'It will indeed be a wonder, if you can create such a thing. The wood is available locally, you say? … Whatever is that?'

A piercing scream rent the air and for an instant everyone froze.

CHAPTER TWENTY-TWO

'What is it? What has happened?' repeated Lord Derby. The scream came again and they all surged towards the northern doorway. The screams intensified and in the confusion everyone tried to discover where it was coming from.

'This way!' cried Jasper, the young squire, and set off at a run towards the Mere. Men who had been working in the house and woodsheds emerged to see what was happening and rushed towards the shore where the screams were becoming more and more hysterical. Cuthbert, who had been on his way between house and woodshed, was the first to reach the water. A short distance further north there was a wooden jetty sticking out into the Mere where the fishing boats of the villagers were often moored. Standing at the furthest end was Betsy, the nursemaid, screaming for all she was worth, bent over as though in agony, her hands to her face.

'What is it? What's happened?' cried Cuthbert, running carefully along the ice-slicked boards towards her. Several others followed. He reached Betsy and took her hands in his, trying to stop the hysteria. 'What has happened?'

As though suddenly realising he was there she clutched at him, pointed down into the water and managed to get out the words,

'There … down there … he fell … into the … water.'

'Who fell?' asked Cuthbert.

'The young master … Master Thomas … he was running … and he … slipped … and he … fell in.' She gulped, trying to catch her breath, and fell to sobbing again.

'Oh, my God!' cried Lord Hesketh, who had heard as he came up behind Cuthbert. 'My boy! No, no, not Thomas!'

Lady Hesketh heard the words and fell to her knees on the shore crying 'No, no, no, no, no, no.' Martha knelt on the ground beside her and tried to hold her up.

'What can we do?' asked Lord Hesketh.

Cuthbert was already pulling off his cloak and boots.

'I'll go in and see if I can find him,' he cried, and peered into the murky water.

'You'll freeze!' exclaimed one of the Hesketh party.

'It's madness!' cried another.

'Not if I'm quick.'

Cuthbert sat down on the edge of the jetty and peered into the water. A thin layer of ice covered all but a small area where the child must have fallen through. He could see no sign of him in the murky water. He gently eased himself over the side and into the freezing water. It made him catch his breath but he lowered himself down until he had to let go and drop. The water was not very deep here, he knew, but it would be over his head before he touched bottom. He pulled in a deep breath and let go, sinking fast until he touched the bottom. It was soft and muddy and his feet sank up to his ankles. Even with his eyes open he could see nothing underwater and felt around with his hands until he felt something, a piece of clothing, then, as he worked his way along it, he found a hand, then an arm, then the small body of the child. Grasping it in his arms he tried to pull it upwards but the feet were stuck in the mud. His lungs were bursting and he was beginning to feel dizzy from cold and lack of breath but he heaved on it until suddenly, the mud yielded and the body came free. Hoping he too wasn't stuck, Cuthbert kicked viciously and began to rise through the murky water until, at last, his head broke the surface. Eager hands reached out to take his burden from him and lift it onto the jetty, then helped Cuthbert out of the water. Lord Hesketh was kneeling over his son, sobbing but unable to do anything. Cuthbert quickly crawled to him and looked at the white face of the little boy, the blue lips and closed eyes.

'We must make him breathe,' he whispered, and wiped strands of weed from the child's face. He opened Thomas's mouth and gently scooped mud from it with his fingers then laid him flat on his back. He began to press on the little chest, trying to get the water out of his lungs without hurting him. Two, three times he pressed down with no effect, but on the fourth attempt, Thomas jerked, coughed and spewed a gush of water out. Cuthbert turned him gently onto his side and rubbed his back until he coughed another flood of water, then a third. Thomas opened his eyes, looked about him, and began to cry. It was the loveliest sound imaginable and a sigh rose from those clustered about them.

'Quickly, cover him up,' said Cuthbert. 'You must get him warm.'

'Bring him to our cottage,' said a young female voice and Cuthbert looked up to see Jennet bending over him. 'It's the nearest and there's a fire.' Lord Hesketh pulled off his warm cloak, wrapped his son in it and lifted him into his arms. 'Show me,' he said, and followed Jennet off the jetty and along the path to the cottage, followed by a weeping Lady Hesketh, Martha and Betsy.

'That was well done, lad,' said a quiet voice close to Cuthbert, and a warm cloak was laid around his shaking shoulders. 'Come, you also must get out of those wet things and get dry and warm.'

Cuthbert looked up and was astonished to see Lord Derby himself helping him to his feet. He couldn't reply with words, his teeth were chattering so much with cold and he felt as though his body was full of ice, but he nodded and staggered off the jetty onto dry land. Suddenly he was surrounded by the men from the site, exclaiming what a fool he had been to jump into the water, but what a hero, he could have drowned himself, he could have died.

'Take good care of him,' said Lord Derby. 'He risked his life to save the child.'

'We will, my Lord,' said Abel. 'We'll get him somewhere warm, don't you fret. And thank you for the loan of your cloak. One of us'll get it back to you afore ye go.' Lord Derby turned to go but Abel spoke again.

'I've been blind, my lord. You sent me the best workman I've ever had and I spurned him. Yet despite that he has worked as hard as anyone ever has and done extra at night as well, or so I'm told. Somehow I am going to make it up to him and hope he will forgive me for what I've done.'

Lord Derby looked at the master builder and smiled.

'It was understandable in the circumstances. You lost your wife, you had problems with Lord Hesketh changing your excellent plans, then I go and push an unknown man onto you as well. I'm surprised you didn't send him away as soon as my back was turned. I am glad you have changed your mind about him. He will be a credit to you.'

Abel watched him walk away, recognising a true gentleman. What a long way from the gentleman Will thought he was; as different as chalk and cheese they were. He determined that he would sort Will out for once and all. But first he hurried after his workmen as they took Cuthbert to the forge.

Cuthbert barely heard them as he staggered along, not even sure where he was going. He felt as though he would never ever be warm again. He was numb all over and didn't even notice that he was barefoot on the frozen ground. They guided him towards the forge where Liliath and Jehan were waiting for him.

Cuthbert's fingers refused to function so Jehan quickly stripped him of his clothes, wrapped him in a thick blanket and sat him down near the fire. Liliath wrapped some warm stones from the hearth in a cloth and set them at his feet, then spooned a bowl of broth from the pot on the fire and tried to feed him but Cuthbert's teeth were chattering so much he could barely open his mouth.

'You must get some warmth into you, you silly man,' she chided. 'Going into the water at this time of year is dangerous. Men have died from less.'

'He saved the boy though,' said Jehan, throwing more wood on the fire.

'Nearly killed himself in the doing of it,' replied Liliath.

'Is … he … all … right?' Cuthbert was shaking so much it was difficult to speak.

'He's alive, thanks to you,' replied Jacob.

'Try to get some of this down you,' said Liliath, holding the spoon to his lips and this time Cuthbert managed to swallow a little of the broth. He could feel it go all the way down into his stomach. 'That's better. Now, a little more.'

By the time Cuthbert had finished the bowl he had stopped shaking and was able to look around him.

'Whatever possessed you to get into the water?' chided Liliath.

'I knew we had to get him out as quickly as possible or he would die of cold if not of drowning.'

'But how did you know what to do?' asked Jehan.

'When I was a boy in Chester we used to play by the river. One winter there was ice on it and one of my friends dared his brother to walk on it. Of course, he fell through but luckily there was a man nearby who waded in and hauled him out. He pressed on his chest like I did today until the water came out of him, then wrapped him in his cloak and carried him home. It's funny what you remember.'

'I doubt anyone else would have done it,' said Liliath. 'From what I hear they all stood around doing nothing. Trust you to do it.'

'I didn't really think. If I'd stopped to wait and see if he came up again, I'd never have gone in. Anybody could have done it.'

'The thing is, nobody did.' Liliath put the bowl and spoon down. 'You, my lad, are going to bed. Rest is what you need now.'

'But …'

'No buts, you must rest and if you don't go I'll give you a sleeping draught to make you, so what is it to be?'

Jehan and Jacob were laughing quietly as Cuthbert accepted defeat and went to his bed in the room behind the forge. The broth, the warmth and the physical exhaustion soon claimed him.

It was two hours later when he woke up and realised he was not alone in his room. Jennet was sitting on the stool again.

'I'm making a habit of sitting by your bed,' she said, smiling. 'But then, if you will go and do daft things like taking a swim in a freezing lake in winter, what can you expect?'

'How is young Thomas?' asked Cuthbert, sitting up.

'None the worse for his dip. He's more upset at losing his fine boots in the mud.'

'Well, I'm not going back to look for them.'

'I think Lord Hesketh would like to see you before they go home,'

'I'd better put some dry clothes on then,' said Cuthbert, and looked meaningfully towards the door.

'I'll go and tell them you will be out in a moment then.'

As soon as she had gone Cuthbert quickly dressed in his best clothes, the only dry ones available and went out in to the forge. Jehan was forming a horseshoe on the anvil, closely watched by young Thomas but as soon as he saw Cuthbert, the child got up and ran to him, apparently none the worse for his ordeal. Dressed in somebody's tunic which was far too big for him he looked comical, almost tripping over the hem in his haste. This time there was no formal greeting, he flung himself at Cuthbert and wrapped his arms tightly round his legs.

'Thomas!' admonished his mother.

'It's all right, my dear,' said Lord Hesketh. 'I think on this occasion we can overlook an otherwise unseemly display. Thomas is hailing his hero in the only way he knows at his age.'

Cuthbert looked down into the adoring eyes of the child. He was more moved than he could say to see him safe and happy. He knelt down on the floor and looked the boy in the eye.

'Will you promise me something?' he asked.

Thomas solemnly nodded.

'Don't go swimming in the lake in the middle of winter.'

Thomas shook his head, then broke into broad smiles again and flung his arms round Cuthbert's neck.

'I'm sorry,' he whispered into Cuthbert's ear, then stood back and looked at him for a long moment before saying,

'Jehan is showing me how he makes horse shoes. He says that when I have my own pony he will make shoes for it too. Can you do that?'

'No,' laughed Cuthbert. 'I would have to make them out of wood and I don't think they would last very long. I could make you a toy sword though, a wooden one. Would you like that?'

Thomas's face lit up.

'Yes please.' He turned to his father. 'Is that all right, father? May I have a toy sword?'

'If you wish but we must be going now if we are to get home before dark. Say goodbye to everyone.'

Whilst Thomas solemnly thanked everyone there, Lord Hesketh took Cuthbert aside.

'I can never thank you for what you did today. You saved my son's life when the rest of us stood by helplessly. If there is ever anything I can do for you, you have only to ask and it is yours.' He shook Cuthbert's hand firmly. 'Anything, remember that.'

Cuthbert was overwhelmed by the gesture and hardly knew what to say. Together they all went outside and watched the party mount up and ride away, Thomas was now wrapped in someone's cloak but this time riding in front of his father on his fine horse. He waved as they turned away and Cuthbert felt a lump in his throat at the gesture. A warm hand slipped into his and he turned to look at Jennet.

'You have made a friend there,' she said.

'Lord Hesketh?'

'Yes, him too, but I was thinking of the boy.'

'A childhood fancy, that's all, he'll soon forget me.'

'I don't think so. Come, mother said I was to take you back with me. I don't think she believes you are unharmed so we'd better go and show her, hadn't we?'

So, hand in hand in the gathering twilight, they walked back to the home of Ezekial.

Cuthbert enjoyed eating at the table of the woodsman and his family and this was not the first time he had joined them after a hard day's work. Jennet no longer sat at the far end of the table but sat next to him whilst her sisters sat opposite and treated him as they would an elder brother. The food was plain but wholesome and there was always plenty of it. Hester was a good cook and was able to make tasty meals from the simplest ingredients. They had killed a pig at the beginning of the winter and they were still enjoying flavoursome stews from it along with plenty of her crusty bread to mop up the gravy. With a wedge of cheese and some of the last of the pears from the tree in their garden, it was a satisfying meal.

Afterwards they sat in the warmth and talked. It was lovely to be part of a family again. Cuthbert hadn't realised how much he missed the evenings in the home of Jethro and Martha and he wondered what Martha would be doing now, and Nell, the young maid. Perhaps, one day, he would visit them back in Chester.

Next morning Abel sought Cuthbert out but hardly mentioned the previous day other than to say it was a good thing he had been around when the accident had happened, before he brought out the drawings of the screen on which they had been working. After spending some time discussing it Abel rolled the plans up and stood back to look at Cuthbert.

'There are times,' he said, 'when I wish I had had a son, but it never happened. It is not good to look at old age and realise you will be alone.'

Cuthbert was surprised at the remark. Abel was not one to discuss personal things and he hoped he wasn't going to become morose and angry again.

'You have Will,' he said. 'He must be like a son to you. You have taught him all you would have taught a son.'

'He's no son!' sneered Abel. 'I wouldn't have him as close kin if he was the last man on this earth. There's many a time I wish we had never taken him in. He thinks only of himself and who he thinks he is. He hasn't got a shred of gratitude in his body.'

'Why did you take him in, then?'

There was a very long pause before Abel said.

'One day I might tell you but not yet, not until I've told him the truth about where he comes from. He won't like it and

I can't find the courage to tell him, yet. Ezekial counsels me to do it but I'm afraid of what he'll do or say.' He shook his head miserably. 'The longer I leave it the worse it gets. I know, it's me own stupid fault. If only ….'

'If only?'

'Never you mind. Suffice it to say that I'd give anything to have me time over again and do things differently. You don't know what a difference you have made. Now let's get some work done.'

With that he walked off leaving Cuthbert staring after him and wondering what he had meant. What difference had he made other than to annoy him by his very presence ever since the day he had arrived? Was that remark meant as some sort of apology?

He went outside to cross to the woodshed where he had a job to complete on a small table for the solar and almost ran into Will who was carrying a short ladder towards the east wing. At first he thought Will was going to ignore him but then Will turned, hawked in his throat and spat at him, leaving a gobbet of phlegm on his sleeve.

'What was that for?' cried Cuthbert, looking with disgust at the mess.

'As if you didn't know?' sneered Will. 'Who's the favourite around here?

'What do you mean?'

'Playing the saviour of the heir, risking his life to save a little brat from certain death. You make me sick. Turning up here with a cock-and-bull story about being sent by a lord to do special work and before we know it you are bowing and scraping to your betters, showing yourself in a good light for doing what? Let me tell you, when I come into my rightful place I will have you hanged for telling such scandalous lies.'

'None of it is lies, as you well know, Will. You are eaten up with jealousy because someone can do better than you. You are the one who is lying, trying to make us all believe you are from a rich family and will have land and property one day. It is you who is a nobody, Will. At least I can hold my head up for doing the best I can in whatever I do. Can you?'

Cuthbert turned on his heel and began to walk away but Will spun round and the end of the ladder caught Cuthbert on his shoulder, knocking him sideways. He slipped on some ice and went down heavily. Will dropped the ladder and would have jumped on him if several of the men hadn't come running out of the woodshed to see what all the fuss was about. Alfric and Ben grabbed hold of Will while Thomas helped Cuthbert to his feet.

'Are you all right, lad?' he asked.

'I'm fine,' snapped Cuthbert and immediately looked contrite. 'It's Will who needs looking after. He should be locked up. He's a danger to any right-minded man.' He rubbed his shoulder where the ladder had hit him. Just another bruise to add the collection.

'What's going on here?' demanded Abel, striding into view.

'Nothing,' replied Will, struggling against his captors. 'Cuthbert and I were just talking, weren't we?'

'Talking with his fists and feet, more like,' growled Thomas. 'Knocked him flying with the ladder and was about to set on him in earnest when we appeared.'

'Did anyone see this?' asked Abel.

'I did,' replied Ben, 'through the open door. That's why we came out.'

'Right,' declared Abel, grabbing hold of Will by his arm, 'You and me are going to have a talk.'

Will tried to pull away but Abel was stronger despite the difference in their age and found himself being dragged forcefully towards the lodging where Abel lived.

Thomas looked at Cuthbert.

'Are you sure you are all right?' he asked.

'I'm fine, really. He caught me unawares,' and he told them what had happened.

'You're right, he needs locking up,' said Alfric, 'and the key throwing away.'

'Let's all calm down and get back to work. Abel will deal with him.'

Slowly, the men drifted back to their places, wondering what would happen next.

CHAPTER TWENTY-THREE

Abel dragged a protesting Will all the way to the small cottage where he was lodging, flung the door open and threw the boy onto the floor before slamming the door closed behind him. Will scrambled to his feet and made an attempt to brush himself down.

'What was that for?' he whined. 'He's the one who should be …'

He got no further as Abel grabbed him round the throat and pushed him backwards until he fell onto the bed set against the far wall, banging his head hard and momentarily stunning him. Abel pulled up a stool and sat down facing him. He took a deep breath to calm the rage that was boiling inside him. Losing his temper was no way to divulge the information he must give to Will, information he should have told him years ago but had always shied away from. It was not going to be easy.

'That hurt,' protested Will, rubbing the back of his head.

'Good,' said Abel, menacingly. 'It seems to be the only way to knock some sense into you.'

'What do you mean? What have I done?'

'Where shall I start? It is time I told you a few facts that I should have told you years ago. You, Will, are a nobody. Do you hear me? A nobody.'

'What do you mean? I am the son …'

'You are someone's son, but not of the man you think you are. You have picked up a few bits of a story and woven your own fantasy around it and you've come to believe it is true, but believe me it is not.'

Will stared at him.

'Don't tell me you are my real father?' he cried, horrified at the thought.

'Thank the Lord, no! If you were born of my union with my dear Dora I would be ashamed of you. You are a lazy, good-for-nothing, selfish, mean, cruel child. We took you in out of the kindness of our hearts, thinking we could change you through our love for you, but the seed of hate was already sown within you. You were a hard baby to rear, always having temper tantrums, breaking things as you got older out of sheer spite. You enjoyed hurting us. Oh yes, we fed you and clothed you, even taught you the rudiments of arithmetic and reading, but what good has it done you? I offered to train you as a joiner, at least give you a trade to live by, but you were too lazy to work at it. Never once have you shown any gratitude for what we did for you. My Dora was worn out because of your cruel and lazy ways and that's why she died, tired of trying to do right by you, tired of constantly being taunted and sneered at, there was never a kind word or gesture from you. She tried so hard to love you but in the end she didn't even like you or have the strength to take any more. My Dora died because of you.'

Abel spat the words at Will, leaning closer until he was only inches away from him. For several seconds Will stared back at him but couldn't break that look on Abel's face. Eventually he said, 'If I was so bad why didn't you throw me out, or better still, send me back to where I came from. Surely my *real* parents would have taken me back.'

Abel let out a huge guffaw at the very idea, rocking back on the stool.

'You have no idea, boy, no idea at all. Your *real* parents? Your mother died giving birth to you. Your *supposed* father disowned you, as did your grandparents. You had no one but us.'

'Disowned me? Why? Tell me.'

He pushed himself away from the wall and faced Abel.

'Tell me,' he shouted.

'You will listen to me, Will, and what I tell you is the truth, not some made-up fantasy to appease you.' He took another deep breath and began. 'Your mother was a loving, decent young girl who worked as a serving maid in a large household. She was betrothed to one of the grooms and when they were a little older they were going to marry, perhaps when she was eighteen and he was twenty. However, there was someone else in that household who saw her and wanted to have his way with her. This was the youngest of the seven sons of the family, a spoilt, lazy boy of eighteen. He knew he had nothing to inherit. With six older brothers he would be expected to enter the church or join the army which he didn't want to do. He would need to make a good marriage if he was going to continue to live in the manner in which he had grown up, but he had other ideas. He had always got what he wanted but nobody seemed to have noticed how unpleasant he was becoming. He starting mixing with the village youths and joining them on poaching trips, stealing fish and game from his own father. He loved the adventure, the risk, the thrill of it. He began to drink far too much and to meet the village girls. The others goaded him on to molest them and many a village father would complain to his father when their daughters became with child. His father refused to believe it was his fault and blamed the company he was keeping. If the fathers continued to object they would find themselves faced with eviction from their farms. The boy thought it was all highly amusing and continued to sow his wild oats further and further afield.

'Then he noticed the little serving maid in his own family's kitchens. She was undoubtedly very pretty and he decided she would be his next conquest. He knew she was betrothed to the groom but that did not deter him. One day he sent the groom to another village to collect a horse he had just purchased. Knowing that he would be away for most of the day he waited for her to go to the kitchen garden to fetch fresh vegetables for the household, as she usually did. He waylaid her on her way back and dragged her into a farm building nearby where he had his way with her. He kept her there until his appetites were satisfied, then threatened to have her and her groom dismissed if she said anything. He left her sobbing on the floor.

'When the poor girl returned to the house in such a desperate state it was clear what had happened to her. She refused to say who was to blame for fear of losing their jobs but she told her young groom. He wanted to confront the young man but she begged him not to. Where could they go, who would employ a girl who was carrying a child?

'The months passed and her time came. The birth was long and difficult, she was so young and slender, and when the boy was born she bled too much and the day after, she died. The young groom was distraught and confronted his master with the truth. At first his claims were dismissed but when the young man as good as admitted it with a shrug and said, 'so what, she's only a slut from the kitchens,' his father remembered all those other claims from fathers in the village. Confronted with this the lad was very flippant,

'They were asking for it,' he laughed. 'Who could resist such tempting fruit? I say they enjoyed it, why wouldn't they, I certainly did.' His enraged father immediately disinherited him for bringing such shame on the family but also refused to have anything to do with the child. His son went out and got drunk then sought out the groom to punish him for exposing him to his father. The two young men fought in the stables, a bitter fight with damage on both sides but a slip on the wet straw of a stall led to the young man falling heavily onto the tines of a pitchfork left there by someone after mucking out the horses. It pierced him through the body and because of the dirt on the fork his wound became bad and within a week he died a painful lingering death. Despite it being an accident the groom was blamed and he was hanged for murder.

'So, you see lad, your mother was a humble serving girl, and although your father may have been born into a rich family he was disowned by them, not that he would have inherited anything anyway. All these years your dream of being a rich heir has been just that, a dream and you are nobody important.'

Will stared at Abel with hate on his face. His dream was shattered. He couldn't believe it, didn't want to believe it. He sneered at Abel. 'I don't believe you,' he spat. 'You're only saying this to shut me up. You don't want me to be better than you. All the time I was growing up I knew I was destined for something better. Anyway, how come you know so much about it? Why should your story be true and mine a lie?'

Abel got to his feet and walked away from Will. When he reached the door he turned, and said, 'Because your mother was my niece. A dearer, sweeter girl you could not have known. The eldest of the four daughters of my brother, she was a beautiful child who became a beautiful young woman, yet she never expected more of life than to hold a good job in a big household. She worked hard and loved her work, her mistress thought highly of her and would give her little tasks to do, mending some of the finer linen of the house because she was a fine needlewoman, but she never shied from hard work in the kitchen or the Great Hall. When she was betrothed to the groom everyone was so happy for her and so valued was she that she would not lose her job in the house because she was married, as happened in many households. She had her whole life before her and they had such plans together. But then the young lad found her and, well, I've told you what he did. He enjoyed it even more because she was promised to someone else, that was his idea of fun, spoiling things for others. He boasted about what he'd done, was proud of himself. It is a testament to her betrothed that he did not immediately reject her though what would have happened after the child was born is anybody's guess.'

He moved back towards Will and leaned down towards him.

'Because of the selfish actions of one man, a decent young girl died, and a decent, innocent young man was hanged. If the perpetrator had not died he too would have been punished for what he did to her. My brother could not bear to have the child in his house, despite being his grandchild, so Dora and I took you in. It was not easy but your birth was not your fault. There were conditions put upon us, however. You were never to be told the truth and once you reached manhood you were to be tied to me as apprentice and joiner. There was too great a risk that you would do exactly what you have done, try to find out your beginnings and nobody wanted that. If you were under my roof there was less chance of you returning to where you were born and raking up all the trouble.'

'What's to stop me now?' cried Will, peevishly.

'If you try you will get no help from anyone. As far as your other grandparents are concerned you do not exist, their son was disinherited before your birth, you have no claim on anything he may have had. You are stuck with me for life.'

'Why are you telling me this now? Why have you broken your promise?'

'Because you were making such a fool of yourself with your boasting and lording it over the others. Better you heard it from me than from someone who didn't know the full story.'

Will sat with his head in his hands. All his great dreams had come clattering down around him yet still he persisted.

'One day I will find them,' he said, quietly, 'and I will pay them back for all they have done to me. 'I will hurt them as they have hurt me. I will kill them if necessary. I will, I will kill every one of them.'

He stood up, glared furiously at Abel, and shouted, 'Don't expect me to do a minute's more work on this house. I'm finished with it and with you. I'll find work elsewhere and I will get my revenge.'

He flung out of the house, slamming the door behind him. As he ran down the track he almost knocked Ezekial over, never even seeing him as he tore along, not knowing or caring where he was headed.

Ezekial approached the door of the cottage and knocked before opening the door.

'Hello,' he called, and bent to enter under the low lintel. Abel was sitting on the bed, elbows on his knees, shaking his head. He didn't notice Ezekial until he was standing right in front of him.

'I take it you told him,' said Ezekial. Abel nodded and sat up. Looking Ezekial in the eye, he said,

'He didn't like it. I knew he wouldn't. I'm beginning to wonder whether I've made things worse. He's sworn revenge on everyone involved.'

'How can he? He doesn't know exactly where he came from, does he?'

'No, but I wouldn't put it past him to find out eventually. He's bad through and through, just like his father. Someone's going to get hurt, I can feel it in my bones and it could all be my fault. Why didn't I tell him years ago?'

'He would still have been angry,' said Ezekial, reasonably. 'At least he knows the truth now, whether he likes it or not. Where has he gone?'

'Away. He said he's finished with me and this house. He is eaten up by anger and hatred. I don't know where he'll go, and do you know, I don't really care anymore.' He rubbed his big hands over his head as if he was trying to calm his mind. 'I'm going to finish this house then I'm going to go far away from here, somewhere where I'm not known, maybe somewhere I've never been before, and try to put all this behind me. It's been over twenty years of my life I've spent on him, but he's not having any more of me, no more, ever.'

'Maybe that's for the best,' said Ezekial, laying a hand on his friend's shoulder. 'Why not come back with me and eat with us tonight?'

'I'm not very good company,' warned Abel, 'but I'll come.'

***

Will went where he always went when he wanted to be alone, his hideaway by the Mere. Buried deep in the undergrowth it was a place of shelter, if rather cold on a December day. He crawled inside and flung himself down on the thick bed of bracken and heather he had built up over the months. He had woven more branches above and covered them with sods so that only the heaviest rain penetrated. There was a moth-eaten blanket he had stolen from one of the better cottages, a cracked cup and a jug for water or mead when he could get it. Today it was full of the latter, taken from the ale house when the landlord had turned his back and he drank it down angrily. Furious thoughts of revenge and punishment raced through his mind, who he would find and what he would do to them. Plan after plan came to him but there was always a big problem: he had no idea where to start looking. Feeding on his thoughts he drained the jug and curled up under the blanket to try to make some sort of plan but the mead on an empty stomach soon sent him to sleep in a drunken haze.

The news of Will's departure soon spread but nobody showed any sympathy for him and most agreed they would do perfectly well without his laziness and bad work.

'Let's hope that's the last we ever see of him,' said Alfric as they began their day's work.

'I feel sorry for Abel,' said Ben, but most of the others felt Abel should have spoken out long ago. Nobody knew exactly what had passed between the two in the cottage but it was bad enough to send Will scurrying off into the dark.

'Perhaps he'll drown himself in the Mere and that'll be the end of him,' grunted another.

Whatever happened to Will, the Christmas feast was fast approaching and there was much discussion about what would happen this year. Last year Lord Hesketh had sent hampers of food for the men and they recalled the goose, the minced meat pies, the sweet cakes and the ale. On the eve of Christmas many of them went to the nearest church for a midnight mass, returning for a few hours' sleep before the festivities began. It was a rest day from work and there was the anticipated feast. Liliath and Hester and the few other women in the village had been busy for days making pies and pastries, bringing out fruits and nuts they had gathered in the autumn. A goose had been killed, some of the men had been fishing and there was meat and game to be cooked. There was plenty for everyone, and washed down with copious amounts of ale and mead there was soon a merry atmosphere with all problems forgotten for the day.

Several people exchanged small gifts they had made, a new wooden spoon for Hester, a little casket for Liliath, a new jerkin for Jehan, and a new leather apron for Jacob to use in the forge. The girls had made little leather purses for their friends which they could tie to their belts and Cuthbert had his little Tudor rose carving for Jennet. It was after the feast that he contrived to catch her alone when she had gone to fetch more of the sugar cakes from the larder that he caught her in the passage way and presented her with it. She was entranced with it, the best gift she had ever received and immediately went to show it to everyone. It was passed from hand to hand until it reached Abel who had been sitting quietly at the side watching the gathering. He took it in his big hands and looked at it closely, turning it round and round.

'Exquisite!' he declared at last. When he looked up at Cuthbert, there were tears in his eyes. 'Can you ever forgive me?' he said, quietly. 'I got you wrong. I have never seen the like of this in all my life.' He turned it about then looked Cuthbert in the face. 'Do you think you could make a bigger one?'

'A bigger one? What for?'

'Would it make a roof boss for the Great Hall? Lord Hesketh wanted family crests but what could be better than the crest of the Royal house? It would appeal to his pride, don't you think? How about it?'

Cuthbert beamed.

'Aye, that it would. I'll take some measurements tomorrow.'

'Do you mean that my little rose is going to adorn the house of a great lord?' asked Jennet, who had been listening to the conversation.

'Aye, I do lass,' said Abel. 'The Rufford rose for a Rufford lass, and for a great house too. How about that then?'

The festivities continued around them with music and dancing, clowning and laughter. For the day all problems were forgotten, all disputes set aside. Tomorrow the work would begin again, if a little later for some people who over indulged in the bounty of the season.

***

There were several sore heads and green faces next morning but Abel expected everyone to be ready to work from dawn to dusk on these short winter days. He was feeling a strange sort of freedom as he walked to the house. With Will gone he had no need to worry about him, no secret to hide. He was out of his life for good, he hoped.

As he neared the building he could see that something was not right. Doors were open that had been closed, neat piles of wood, ready for use, were scattered about and, when he entered the Great Hall, the wooden scaffolding they had erected to work on the new decorations in the roof, had been pulled down. A few panes of glass in the windows had been broken and there was a mess of mud everywhere, daubed on the walls and the newly completed furniture. He stood with his hands on his hips and surveyed the damage. As he was joined by the rest of the men they all stood and looked at the mess.

'Who would do this?' asked one.

'Do you need to ask?' shouted Alfric. 'Who would *want* to do this, destroy our work, set us back days?'

'Will.' They all agreed it was just the sort of spiteful act he would do.

'Well, it proves one thing,' said Cuthbert, picking up a fallen stool. 'He's still around somewhere.'

'Unless this was his parting gift,' suggested Ben.

'Wherever he is, it's going to take us the best part of today to clear up the mess,' sighed Abel, checking round the building to make sure there was no major damage. 'We'd better check in the rest of the building.'

The men split up, some going to the east wing and looking in all the many rooms there, and some entering the west wing and going into every room there. They eventually congregated in the Great Hall again.

'Well?' asked Abel.

'He's been in the scullery and pulled all the washing troughs away from the wall,' reported Ben. 'He's also gouged great holes in the main table in the kitchen. Can't see anything else anywhere.'

'What about the west wing?' asked Abel.

'There are muddy footprints throughout so he's obviously walked into every single room,' said Cuthbert. 'Doors are open and a few of the window shutters but the only damage I can find is this.' He held up the Green Man carving he had made for the solar. It was in two pieces, neatly chopped with an axe or a chisel. 'Broken the wall fixing too.'

'Nothing that can't be mended,' sighed Abel. 'Let's get on with it.'

He split the men into groups and gave each a specific job to do. It wasn't what he had planned for the day but it had to be done. He just hoped that this was a parting gift and that Will had now gone and wasn't going to stay somewhere near and return another night. The same thought occurred to Cuthbert and he voiced it when everyone came together as the light was fading.

'Should we have someone keeping watch through the night,' asked Harry. 'I don't mind doing one night.'

'We should be in pairs,' said Alfred. 'We could cover more areas that way.'

'I agree,' said Abel. 'We can lock or barricade some doors to prevent entry but not all. Let's do that whilst we can still see.'

'I'll stay with Harry,' volunteered Ben.

'Right. Keep moving around and don't make any noise, so he won't know you're there. If you see anything, one of you rouse the rest of us and we'll surround the place. He has got to be stopped.' Abel sighed deeply. Just when he'd thought Will was out of his life he had to come back and do this.

Unseen by any of them, Will was watching from fairly close by. He had seen the activity going on all day as his former workmates had spent the day clearing up the mess he had created whilst they were celebrating the Christmas Feast. He laughed to himself. There was plenty more disruption he had planned for the coming weeks but he would do nothing for a while, let them think he had gone.

For nearly three weeks nothing happened and they were beginning to think that the first wrecking spree had been a final farewell from Will. Nothing had been seen of him despite their patrols each night. During the day the two men who had kept watch, slept whilst the rest continued the work. All repairs were made and the new work in the roof of the Great Hall was going well. All the additional decoration meant plenty of work for all the skilled men, whether erecting ever more scaffolding, carving the pieces necessary or installing them at great height. Even Abel had to admit that the new designs did add to the splendour of the Hall. Decorative diamond shapes were created in each of the large panels with central decoration in the form of great lozenge shaped pieces with elongated rounded corners. They looked as though they should revolve for some reason but they were purely decorative. Along the top of the walls, above the windows each small panel was decorated with a decorative arched design, not unlike the fancy arches Cuthbert had seen at Whalley Abbey. They had been his idea and once he had drawn it out on paper, other carvers were busy cutting the pieces to fit.

The new designs for the roof bosses were being worked on in the woodshed. Using the designs suggested by Lord Hesketh, four were being created. Some of his ideas had been too complex to reproduce in wood and would be reserved for use elsewhere, possibly painted instead of carved. Cuthbert was busy producing an enlarged Tudor rose from a large lump of oak he had selected from the store. It was no easier doing it in a larger version than it had been in miniature but he was a perfectionist and would not be satisfied until it was to his standard.

Abel was concentrating on creating the screen. He had chosen a small group of men and they were creating the various panels which would come together to make the whole. Ezekial had found him two tree trunks of bog oak of almost the same length and diameter which would form the two supporting sides and be joined by crosspieces holding the panels in place. Such was the size that they would only be able to see it complete after it was erected inside the hall. As they worked new ideas presented themselves to him. To compliment Cuthbert's Tudor rose he suggested that a head of the king and queen could adorn each side, in the centre at the top of the main panels. This was agreed and the work to carve them began. They had to work quickly before the wood dried out and became too hard to carve.

All this activity at least kept the men warm through the bitterly cold days of January. A cold east wind created an icy surface on the Mere and froze the muddy roads as hard as iron. Ezekial was pleased as he didn't waste time digging mud-locked wagons out of the deep ruts. Jehan and Jacob were busy in the forge creating heavier chains for the same wagons. The heavy horses strained to pull their loads, their breath steaming in the frosty air. Anybody going to the forge to leave orders or collect completed work tended to linger in the warmth until chased out by Jacob. The days were so short and the nights so long that the time seemed to go slowly and everyone looked forward to spring bringing warmth and longer hours of daylight to work by.

Will had moved away from Rufford for a while finding a very accommodating widow woman in the next village. She at least provided a warm bed and a roof over his head and he couldn't help smiling when he thought of those keeping a vigil at the hall for him. He had returned one night and seen two of his former colleagues huddle in a doorway before walking off round the building and he guessed they were looking out for him. Let them freeze outside in vain whilst his widow kept a very warm bed for him and filled his belly with good warming food. His time would come.

CHAPTER TWENTY-FOUR

The last week in January proved particularly trying for everyone. Not only was the temperature close to freezing day and night but there was a cold mist overlaying everything. Clothes felt cold and damp within minutes of going outside, it was impossible to see more than a few yards. On some days it was so thick they couldn't even see the roof of the building, so low-lying was the mist. People emerged from the gloom when only a few yards away and anyone straying from a well-worn track easily became lost. Burning torches barely penetrated more than a few yards and at night it was even more difficult to move about. Ezekial was unable to cut trees down when he couldn't even see their tops and concentrated on bringing in wood he had left to season in the woods.

'I'll be glad when this mist lifts,' grumbled Abel one day as he tripped over a tree root on the path to the woodshed.

'There is still plenty of work to keep us warm,' said Cuthbert, holding the door open for him. 'In here at least we can see what we are doing. How are the panels for the screen looking?'

'Good,' said Abel. 'Alfric is particularly good at that sort of work and he doesn't mind repeating the same design several times. He has even reversed the design for one of them. Ezekial has found me some particularly thick logs to carve the supports from. They are going to have to be quite substantial to keep the whole thing upright.'

'Are these the side supports?' asked Cuthbert, looking at two whole tree trunks laid side by side across trestles.

'Yes, I want them to match so we are doing both at once to the same measurements. There is a lot of work to do yet on just these, measurements have to be accurate for the pegs and holes or the whole thing won't fit together properly.' He walked over to the bench where Cuthbert's work lay, the rose for the roof boss. Already he could see the design emerging from the wood and even at this stage it was a thing of beauty. Next to it Ben was working on another of the crests for the roof. Abel felt pleased with how it was all proceeding. There was still the shadow of Will in the background though.

'Still no sight of Will?' he asked.

'No, though it is difficult to see anything in this mist. We aren't even sure if he is still anywhere near. There was a rumour he had been seen in a village to the south, but the man who saw him couldn't be sure. We won't stop being vigilant though.'

Abel nodded in agreement and went over to the Great Hall to see how work was progressing there. It was only slightly warmer in here than outside but it was a hive of activity. Wooden scaffolding had been re-erected down the centre of the hall ready to install the roof bosses. The carvings at the tops of the walls were almost complete and the decorative pieces in the sloping parts of the roof were finished. Abel stood, hands on hips and looked at the wall at the western end. The two doorways into the west wing were complete but he wasn't satisfied with the wall as a whole. For the principal end of the room, where the family would sit for their meals at the table running along its length, it was very plain. Tapestries had been mentioned for hanging on the side walls but he couldn't recall any being allotted to this one and it was a huge expanse. Light would flood in from the side through the compass window and there was a large window opposite, but it needed something to make it special. He scratched his chin in thought and let his eyes drift upwards into the gable end. On the other side of the wall was the west wing, the family wing so this was an internal wall. How could it be made more important, more prominent? He thought about other houses he had designed. Was there something he could use here to make it different? An idea began to form in his head and he stepped backwards to get a better view, backing into one of the scaffolding supports.

'Watch it!' cried the man at the top who was fixing the final pieces, then apologised when he saw who it was.

'I'm coming up there,' called Abel, and began to clamber up the structure. At one time he would have swung his way aloft easily but he was feeling his age and took greater care where he put his feet as he ascended. He was surprised when he reached the top to find he was out of breath.

'Is something wrong?' asked Thomas, the man who had shouted down.

'No, no, I just wanted to see this wall closer up.'

Thomas followed his gaze.

'There's nothing wrong, is there?'

'No, far from it. I've had an idea. Thomas, you worked on that Hall over in Yorkshire five or six years ago. Do you remember the canopy we built that protruded over the principle table? Do you think it would work here?'

Thomas surveyed the wall.

'It would but I'm not sure how we could marry it with the side walls which are complete. It could look a bit, well, unplanned, if it doesn't match up properly.'

'Mmm,' mused Abel, 'I see what you mean. Let me get the plans out and see whether it's possible. We could maybe adapt the corners somehow, add some decoration to hide the join. I'll have a look later.' He looked along the length of the hall from his vantage point. 'Not bad, is it?' he commented. 'Get a whole different perspective from up here.' He looked down. 'Funny how it feels a lot higher from up here than when you look up at it from the floor.'

'It's still a long way to fall,' said Thomas, drily. 'Men have died from less of a fall than from here. We've been lucky with this one. Apart from a few cuts and bruises there have been remarkably few injuries and no broken bones.'

'Yet,' said Abel, then smiled at Thomas's face. 'Don't worry, I'm not planning to push you off. I'd better get down, let you finish.'

Climbing down was a lot easier than the climb up had been but he was glad to get his feet back on firm ground. He went through one of the doors into the west wing and up the staircase to the first floor. In one of the bedrooms he found himself at the other side of the wall he had been looking at from the Great Hall. The wall was panelled in fine oak, fairly plain at this stage, the beautiful natural grain of the wood clearly visible. He ran his fingers over it. He loved the feel and smell of beautifully worked timber, the perfection of joints and corners when worked by a master craftsman, no gaps or rough edges to catch. He was immensely proud of the workmanship throughout the house. He always insisted on the best. That was the way to keep good customers. If Lord Hesketh ever wanted any further work done here he would ask for him to do it, relying on a craftsman he knew. He in turn would recommend him to friends who might need a master carpenter. It was the way it worked, how one job led to another, on recommendation.

He tapped the panels. They sounded solid enough for his purpose and they should be strong enough to support the weight of a false wall, which would be needed to carry the hanging canopy on the other side. He would need to attach some horizontal beams from the upper part of the wall on the hall side then curve panels down to the top of the wall below. It was tricky work but not impossible. He would look carefully at the original plans to see whether it could be done and he must put his suggestion to Lord Hesketh next time he visited them. His lordship had made alterations already so he may be agreeable to something his master builder suggested. It made Abel smile that he was actually thinking this way when he had been so opposed to new ideas a few months ago. But then, he had had the weight of responsibility and guilt associated with Will, and that was all changed. He actually found himself smiling, something he had rarely done since Dora's death. Yes, he was well rid of him.

***

Will rolled out of the bed, sat on the edge and rubbed his face with rough, none too clean hands. He blinked tired eyes and yawned. Squinting towards the grimy window he rubbed his eyes, wondering why everything was blurry then realised it wasn't his eyes or the dirty window but thick mist outside. Even though it was daylight it was gloomy and he had no idea what time of day it was. How long had he been here? What day was it? The last thing he could remember was staggering along the track from the inn on the road south of the village of Ormskirk. He had drunk far too much and the road seemed to undulate beneath his feet. He couldn't walk in a straight line but he must try to get back to the cottage he was sharing with his very obliging widow woman, a very obliging woman indeed who had fallen for his hard luck story and agreed to let him stay until he sorted himself out. His hard luck tale of a lost job as a master carpenter had been convincing enough for the gullible woman to be taken in. She saw a young man, down on his luck through no fault of his own who needed somewhere to stay. Perhaps she was lonely too and fancied the company of a not bad looking young man.

The walk back had been longer than he remembered but as he tripped several times it was hardly surprising it seemed further. Picking himself up for the fourth time he had tried to stand upright only to roll over again and ended up in the ditch at the side of the road which fortunately was dry. It was such an effort to get up that he had curled up and may have dozed off for a while. Sometime later he had woken with an unsettling feeling in his stomach, got to his knees and heaved a stomach full of ale out of him before crawling back onto the track. This time he managed to get onto his feet and stay on them as he completed the journey back to the cottage. The widow woman had commiserated with him and tucked him up in bed to sleep it off. Poor boy, she thought, drowning his sorrows in alcohol. Best to let him sleep.

Will went into the other room but she was nowhere to be seen. There was a pot of something hanging over the fire and he spooned a bowl full of it onto a dish. It was a tasty broth of some sort, full of vegetables and settled his stomach. He went to the door and looked out, surprised that he could barely see across the road. Well, he would stay here, no point wandering about in this weather. Perhaps tomorrow, when it had cleared he would make another visit to Rufford and see what mischief he could do there. He went and sat in a wooden chair by the fire as he planned his next move.

It was time that he did some more damage to their precious house he decided, damage that could not be repaired as easily as a few broken windows and carvings. Fire would be good. A wooden building would burn beautifully. There was plenty of material to use as tinder, heaps of sawdust, small off cuts from the work. If he piled it around the main door to the Great Hall it would spread quickly before anyone could stop it. Yes, a fire would be his next move.

***

'Will this fog never lift?' complained Alfric. 'I'm tired of never being dry.'

'Even a fire doesn't seem to warm anything,' said Ben, moving his stool closer to the fire in the lodgings they shared. Work had finished early today as the cold and damp had seeped into everyone's bones and they had dispersed to their various lodgings for the night. Only Abel and Cuthbert were still working in the woodshed, Abel constructing the base of the screen and Cuthbert carving his rose. Both were near to completion and, although the room was cold they were warm with their work.

'How much longer do you think we'll be?' asked Ben.

'Before the house is finished? Not long, though Abel has some idea of building a canopy over the table at the west end of the Hall, or so Thomas tells me,.' said Alfric.

'A canopy? How will that fit. We've already finished the walls.'

'Thomas and Abel built one at another house a few years ago. They think it will work.'

'I thought Abel didn't like changes to his plans.'

'He's changed, ever since Will left. He's changed his attitude to Cuthbert too.'

'About time he did. Cuthbert's a fine lad. I can't help liking him and I've never seen carving like it. I wish mine was half as good. He seems to put life into every piece he does. I can carve but not like that. He not only had a good master to teach him but he has a rare talent. I'm sure he sees what he wants to do in the wood before he's even started to work it.'

'My grandfather could do that but he didn't pass it down to my father or to me,' said Alfric, ruefully, reaching for another hunk of the bread they had had with their meal. He chewed on it thoughtfully for a while. 'Some would say it is God-given to have a talent like that.'

'He worked at Whalley Abbey before he came here so perhaps that's true.' Ben stretched and yawned. 'I'm going to bed. Perhaps we'll get an earlier start tomorrow if this mist clears overnight.'

Next morning was a good deal better. A light wind had blown up during the night, clearing the mist and allowing a little watery sunshine to come through the scudding clouds. There was still no warmth in the sun but at least they could see once again. Despite the cold there was a much lighter atmosphere as work began and after the several gloomy days it was nice to be able to see clearly. Abel and Thomas pored over the plans and decided they could make a canopy in the Great Hall after all.

'Perhaps we could decorate the squares on it with paintings of those family crests which were too complex to carve,' suggested Thomas. 'There will be plenty of room for more as well if Lord Hesketh wishes.'

'Good idea,' said Abel and noted it down on the plan. 'Must finish the screen as well. Next time we have a visit I want to be able to show how much more we have done since they last came.' All this planning had reinvigorated everyone and someone was even whistling as they worked. What a difference a little winter sunshine could make.

***

Will watched from the shelter of the trees by the Mere. Everyone looked very busy and no one saw him as he moved towards his den amongst the undergrowth where he planned to wait until nightfall before putting an end to all their good work. He had to stifle a laugh as he thought of what tomorrow would be like with the whole building lying in ashes. He crawled inside the den and was pleased to see it was still largely intact. He would have a cold wait but he had brought some cold meat and bread and had his warm cloak to wrap himself in. Now all he needed was darkness to put his plan into action.

The short day passed quickly and soon everyone was going back to their lodgings for a meal and a rest. It would still be some hours before they slept but Will crept out to explore his old work place. He knew every track and building, where everyone lived, where wood was stored, where the tools were kept. He got into the woodshed through a loosely shuttered window and felt his way around until he found a lanthorn which he lit and shaded just in case anyone went by. He saw the panels for the screen, the mighty side posts and the hefty base. On a table he found the carvings for the roof bosses and guessed which one was Cuthbert's work. He was tempted to destroy it but he didn't want to risk someone hearing him break it up if they passed too close. After all, it wouldn't be needed at all if the Hall was burned to the ground.

A pile of wood shavings had been swept into a corner and he filled an empty sack with as much as he could manage. There were plenty of bits of waste lying around and he gathered a bundle ready to carry to the Hall. There was so much that he wondered whether he should set several fires all around the hall to be sure. There would be plenty of time, all night in fact. He was finding this all rather exciting and had to suppress his eagerness to start straight away. No, he must wait until at least midnight. With several bundles prepared he went out again to look round the building and decide where to set each fire.

The patrolling of the building still continued with Ben and Tom preparing to do it tonight. Wrapped in their warmest clothes they crept out and began to walk round the building, looking out for Will who had still not been seen anywhere near Rufford. Neither of them noticed him as he lay along the ground in the darkest shadow of the east wing but he saw them and realised that he must be very careful where he set the fires. He did not want them to see the piles before he had time to light them. As far as he was concerned it added a further risk but one in which he revelled. To cheat them even when they were clearly looking for him added to the victory he confidently expected. So sure was he that he could not see any possibility of failure. It was going to be a game of whether the cat could catch the mouse before the mouse caught the cat out and a thrill ran through his body as he crept round the corner of the building to build his first pile.

Ben and Tom separated and began to walk in opposite directions around the whole building. They confidently thought that it was the house that would be attacked and did not therefore include the woodshed and other separate buildings in their patrol. A watching Will realised their mistake and timed his return to the woodshed for more fuel very carefully. There were only minutes when neither Ben nor Tom could see the shed but it was time enough for Will to enter, take another load of wood chippings and get out again. There were many dark corners and deep shadows to hide in whilst they passed and he had to stifle the desire to laugh at their stupidity. Perhaps they had become lax because he had not been seen for so long but it only boosted his confidence.

Soon he had piles ready to light in six places around the house. Ideally he would like to light them all at once but knew that was impossible. He decided to light two round the east wing and whilst they were dealing with those he could light the four he had placed round the Great Hall and west wing. He crept back to the east wing and waited. He let both the guards pass him twice so that he could judge the time he had when they were away from him, then, approached the first pile near the door to the scullery. His tinderbox struck a spark at the first attempt and he carefully nurtured it in the wood shavings until it was blazing beautifully. He fed it with some bigger pieces until it took hold properly then went to the pile on the other side of the building. This took a little longer as a breeze kept blowing his flame out but at last it caught and he fanned it into a blaze and crept into the shadows of the trees to watch.

Tom first realised something was wrong when he caught a whiff of smoke as he rounded the corner and immediately saw the small fire developing against the wall.

'Fire!' he yelled as loudly as he could. 'Fire! Fire! Fire!' He rushed to the blaze and tried to stamp it out, still yelling fire at the top of his voice. Ben came rushing round the corner and spotted the second smaller blaze near the scullery door. He joined voices with Tom as the two of them stamped and kicked at the fire, trying to get it away from the building. It felt like ages but was only a matter of minutes before sleepy men came running, half-dressed, roused from their beds.

'Get the buckets!' yelled one.

'Form a chain from the Mere,' cried another. Rushing for buckets from the kitchen area they ran back and forth with water, dousing the flames and the walls which were threatened.

Will watched all the activity with glee then, keeping to the shadows, he worked his way round to the Great Hall and began his trail of destruction there too. By this time virtually the whole workforce were rushing around dealing with the other fires and Cuthbert came running with Jehan and Jacob from the forge. Quickly they joined the other men and it was out of the corner of his eye that Cuthbert saw a movement near the Great Hall as a fresh fire blazed up there too.

'Quickly, to the Hall' he yelled, racing across with more buckets. To his horror as he turned the corner there were two more fires just getting going. 'Here, round here,' he cried as he was joined by half a dozen men, some with buckets, others trying to drag the burning timbers away from the building. Cuthbert dashed across to the Mere, which was only yards away, with two buckets and as he turned he saw a figure run from the far side of the Hall, a figure he recognised immediately.

'He's there, over there,' he shouted, pointing, and several men clearly saw Will outlined by the flames, running away down the track towards the woods.

'After him,' shouted Jacob, and set off in pursuit but Will was too far ahead and he knew the woods like the back of his hand having spent so many hours hiding there to avoid work. They soon realised they had lost him and turned back to help. At least they had proof of his presence this time.

The fires were soon out but some damage had been done. As the men stood around panting from the exertion, Abel and Thomas made a quick inspection of the buildings.

'Can't do much until daylight,' said Abel, 'but we were lucky. It could have gone up like a torch and been lost. Thank you, every one of you. Now get back to your beds. You will need all your strength in the morning to make repairs. Some of us will stay to keep watch till morning. Now go.'

Slowly the men drifted away leaving Abel with Cuthbert, Jehan, Jacob, Thomas, Ben and Tom. The latter two were devastated.

'We never saw him,' said Tom. 'Never heard a thing.'

'He must have laid these fires whilst we were out of sight,' said Ben. 'But where's he got the stuff from?'

'There's a window shutter open in the woodshed,' said Jehan. 'I've just checked. He must have got tinder and shavings from there.'

'He's not done any damage inside, has he?' asked Abel anxiously, thinking of the carvings laid out on tables.

'Not as far as I could see. He's concentrated on destroying the house.'

'At least one good thing has come of this,' said Thomas.

'Good? What's good about trying to burn the place down?' exclaimed Abel.

'Some of us saw him and it was definitely Will so we know he is still around and our guarding the place isn't a waste of time. I guess he's been letting us think he had gone away and therefore we weren't as vigilant as we were.'

'Wait till I get my hands on him,' growled Abel. 'I'll …'

'You'll what? Kill him? Let the law deal with him. Let us catch him and hand him over to the local magistrate to deal with and we all know who that is.'

'Lord Derby! Of course. But how do we catch him?'

'He won't stay away. He will want to see how bad the fire was. He meant to burn it down. He won't be able to resist coming to see but he will be disappointed and we will be ready for him this time.'

The men moved into the relative warmth of the woodshed to make their plans.

Next morning daylight revealed the extent of the damage. Two doors were badly charred and would need at least their bottom halves replacing. Some timbers in the lower walls would need new wood splicing in once charred pieces were removed. There was smoke damage almost to roof height on the west wing.

'Thank goodness everything was so damp after all that mist,' commented Cuthbert. 'If it had been midsummer and the timbers bone dry, it would have burned much more quickly and Will may well have destroyed everything.'

'I never thought I would have been thankful for such awful weather,' laughed Ben. 'But we must increase the guard around the place. You're right. He won't give up.'

Abel assigned men to carry out the repairs. Everyone was to be extra vigilant and at night at least six men would keep guard. There was no shortage of volunteers. No one wanted to see over a year's work destroyed by a madman.

Will returned to the widow woman's cottage. She didn't ask him where he had been but she did wonder why he smelt so strongly of smoke. Perhaps he had been sitting round a bonfire somewhere, trying to keep warm. He seemed excited about something but when she asked him about it he just said,

'Something I had to deal with,' which was no answer at

all. Whilst he slept she tried to wash his clothes but the smoky smell lingered and it took ages to dry them over her little fire. She had learned from her late husband not to question the nocturnal activities of men. Best you don't know, he used to tell her, then give her a big hug, and all was well again.

CHAPTER TWENTY FIVE

Within a few days all signs of the fire had been removed. Everyone was more determined than ever to finish the job. There was much talk about what had happened and people were constantly on watch. Any stranger who passed was observed with caution. Was Will working alone or would he have asked someone to check for him as he dared not show his face so soon after the fire?

Away from the building though there was still time to try and relax. Cuthbert particularly enjoyed sharing a meal in the evenings with Jehan, Jacob and Liliath or going to Ezekial's family. Both accepted him as a family member, particularly the latter. Jennet always sat beside him and her sisters had stopped teasing them. Her parents sometimes left them alone together, accepting the growing closeness between them. Cuthbert appreciated this time with Jennet as they got to know each other better. It was unusual for this to happen, a girl was usually closely chaperoned when a young man was present. Cuthbert may not have mentioned marriage yet but everyone else was expecting it. Her mother and Liliath had been talking about it when they met in the village.

'I see Cuthbert prefers your cooking to mine,' said Liliath with a twinkle in her eye.

Hester laughed.

'I don't think it's my cooking that's the attraction,' she said. 'I have a daughter who enjoys his company.'

'Has he said anything to her?' asked Liliath. 'It's been clear for a while that he is more than attracted to her.'

'Not as far as I know but we give them the chance to be alone occasionally. I rather think he is trying to find the words sometimes but doesn't quite make it.'

'Do you think that marriage is in his mind?'

'I do, but his mind is as far as it gets. He gave her a little carving at Christmas, a miniature of that roof boss he's been working on. It is beautiful and she carries it in her pocket all the time. It is a sort of love token, I suppose.'

'He never struck me as being shy.'

'I've never known a lad who can blush so easily. We like him very much and would be happy for Jennet to marry him. It is up to him to ask though.'

'He'd better hurry up then. Once this build is complete he may well move away to his next work.'

'I wonder if he realises that. Well, we can only hope.'

Jennet was growing closer to Cuthbert every time they met. She wanted to know all about his life before coming to Rufford and he was willing to share it with her, the sad and the happy times. She was wonderfully kind when he spoke of his parents and he wished he had been able to take her to meet them, they would have liked her. It was when he was returning to the forge one night after one of their long conversations that he realised the obvious: he wanted to spend the rest of his life with her. There was then the knotty problem of how to go about asking her. He had never even thought of marriage and all it implied before and he stopped in his tracks as the seriousness of it all hit him.

'You look as though you've seen a ghost,' said a voice just behind him.

Cuthbert nearly jumped out of his skin and leapt round to find Thomas coming along the path on his regular patrol round the building.

'Oh, Thomas! I didn't hear you.'

'Clearly. You'll have to be more careful. I could have attacked you. So what's the solemn face for?'

'Thomas, have you ever been married?'

'What! Married? Me? No, I'm not the marrying sort. Are you?'

'Yes, I think that's what I want but how do I ask her?'

'Her being …?'

'Jennet, of course. I think she's wonderful, beautiful, such fun to be with, I enjoy every second I'm with her, I want to spend the rest of my life with her, share a home together, have children together …'

'Whoa! Hang on a minute. There's one word you haven't mentioned yet. Do you love her?'

'Of course I do, didn't I say?

'How does she feel about you?'

'She likes me, I think.'

'There you go again. Does she love you?'

'I expect so.'

'Expect so? Oh, Cuthbert. You have to tell her, you can't just expect her to know. I take it she is the first girl you have been close to?'

'Oh yes, there was never anyone in Chester, it was all work, work, work, and there weren't any females of any age at the Abbey.'

'Well, my advice is *show* her how much you love her and *tell* her so. Now, it's time I turned back. I have a patrol to do, not sort out your future wife for you.' He clapped Cuthbert on the shoulder and turned back towards the Hall.

Cuthbert covered the short distance back to the forge trying to compose the words he wanted to say next time he saw Jennet and as he lay in bed that night it was thoughts of Jennet that lulled him to sleep.

***

Will was furious. He had confidently expected to hear news about the disastrous fire at Rufford Hall during the following days but there was nothing at all. What had gone wrong? A major fire at a massive new building should have been the talk of the area. He had set enough fires and though he expected the first couple would have been put out, the bigger ones around the main Hall should have taken their toll. He couldn't openly ask anyone as then he would reveal that he knew something about them but despite drinking in several inns nearby there was no word at all. The only thing left to do was to pay a visit and see for himself, but he would have to be extra vigilant as they would be looking out for him.

One moonless night he returned, keeping well within the trees until he was as close as he dared go. He heard stealthy footsteps rustling through the leaves and a shadow crossed an open space. He stepped silently along the edge of the Mere until he was opposite the Hall and was horrified to see the outline of the undamaged building, large as ever, against the lighter sky. It was difficult to see any detail but there were no tell-tale gaps in the roofline, no walls missing, no empty windows. He had failed. His great plan had been for nothing. Now what was he going to do?

He stealthily retreated and returned to his hideaway, evil plans forming in his mind. He would not be defeated.

***

It was another week before Cuthbert joined Ezekial's family for a meal again, a week in which he completed his rose roof boss, helped Abel with the carving of the side supports of the great screen and took his turn on the night patrols. It gave him plenty of time to contemplate his future. If he did marry Jennet, where would they live, where would he work once this house was completed and would he earn enough to feed and clothe them? He could probably find work on any building in the north especially as his reputation spread. Perhaps Lord Hesketh could help, or Lord Derby, after all it was on Lord Derby's recommendation that he was here. But would Jennet want to move around from one place to another? Once children came along she would want a settled home, wouldn't she? Children!

He hadn't even asked her to marry him yet and here he was already thinking of children. He took a deep breath. He would go for a walk with her on Sunday and ask her. Definitely. Yes. Sunday. That's when he would do it.

The following day, however, an unexpected visitor brought something for Cuthbert, wrapped in fine linen and with the simple message, 'For Cuthbert Watts' written on a piece of paper attached to it. It was left at the forge and the messenger rode away before Jehan could ask from whom he came. When Cuthbert came back as dark fell Jehan gave him the bundle.

'Who is it from?' asked Cuthbert.

'I didn't have chance to ask before he rode off,' replied Jehan.

'Did you recognise him?'

'No.'

Intrigued Cuthbert took the bundle into the cottage and sat down at the table. Perhaps there would be something inside to help. Peeling back the layers of cloth he revealed a stout leather belt, beautifully worked and with a fine silver clasp attached.

'This can't be for me!' exclaimed Cuthbert. 'It's far too fine a piece.' Liliath looked at it, turning it over in her hands.

'This is a gentry piece,' she said. 'I've never seen such workmanship on a belt for a workman. This buckle is silver. There must be a year's wages gone into that alone.'

They looked at each other in astonishment then Cuthbert noticed the corner of a piece of paper among the folds of the cloth and pulled out a sheet with a short message written on it. He read it, read it again, then said,

'Listen to this. 'Cuthbert Watts, Thank you for restoring our son to us. We are forever indebted to you. Thomas and Grace Hesketh.'

'Well I never!' exclaimed Liliath, and dropped onto a stool beside the table. 'Read it again.' A second reading confirmed there had been no mistake.' Oh, Cuthbert! How marvellous! I must tell Jehan,' and she ran out to the forge. Cuthbert was still sitting, stunned, when they returned and the message was read again and again.

'I never heard of anything like it,' said Jehan. 'My goodness, lad, you've made an impression right enough. A gift from his lordship!'

By the next morning everybody had heard of Cuthbert's good fortune.

'It's well deserved,' said Abel. 'No one else would have done what you did.'

'If I jump into the Mere in the depths of winter can I have one too?' asked Alfric, laughing.

'Why aren't you wearing it?' asked Ben.

'It's far too good for working in,' said Cuthbert. 'It's for very best and special occasions. I've never had anything as valuable as that.'

'Special occasions such as weddings?' asked Alfred, keeping a straight face as Cuthbert blushed scarlet.

'Maybe,' he replied.

A special occasion was looming on Sunday, he thought, if asking Jennet counted. How to go about it though.

Cuthbert wrestled with the problem for the rest of the week but on the Sunday it was partly solved when Ezekial suggested the two young people go for a walk by the Mere as it was a beautiful winter's day. Jennet's two sisters immediately said they would come too but their mother overheard them and suddenly found things that needed doing which they must help her with. So, Cuthbert and Jennet set out, alone at last. They wandered down to the shore of the Mere, chatting together and enjoying each other's company. Cuthbert wanted to choose the right moment and several times was about to speak when a patch of ice needed to be negotiated or a fallen tree, climbed over. They had gone some distance when a cool breeze blew up across the water and Cuthbert led her into the lee of a thicker clump of bushes.

'Oh, that's better,' said Jennet, and turned to look at Cuthbert as he pulled his cloak tighter around his neck. How handsome he looked today. What had he done? He was wearing his better clothes as befitted the Sabbath, with the new belt fastened about his slim waist. The weak winter sun raised a glint from the buckle and she put her hand over it to feel the cold smooth surface. 'I am so proud of you,' she murmured. 'A real silver belt buckle. And to think, if you hadn't saved little Thomas you would never had had it.'

Cuthbert was looking at her with a surge of love in his heart. He put a hand up and tucked a stray strand of her hair behind her ear, feeling the silky softness of it. Something moved deep within him and he put a finger under her chin and lifted her face towards him.

'Oh Jennet, I think I am falling in love with you,' he whispered, and gave her a tentative smile. 'May I ask, do you feel the same about me?' He held his breath as he waited for her answer. Jennet looked into his eyes and, not trusting her voice, she nodded gently. He exhaled sharply, his heart doing somersaults in his chest and a broad smile spread across his face. They gazed at each other for a long moment then fell into each other's arms and held on tightly for several minutes, revelling in the confession they had just made to each other.

When they broke apart Cuthbert felt close to tears as he asked her,

'Jennet, will you marry me, be my wife and bear our children?' Again she nodded but this time she found her voice.

'I have longed for you to ask since the first time we met. I love you with all my heart, Cuthbert Watts.'

They came together again and this time they kissed, gently at first then more fervently as their love grew, pressing closer together as though they would never be parted again. At last they drew apart and looked at each other.

'You have made me so happy,' said Cuthbert. 'I have been trying to find the right time to ask but there was always somebody else around.'

Jennet giggled.

'I think mother and father noticed. Don't you think this winter walk was planned on purpose? Even keeping Mary and Martha back was contrived. Mother hasn't got anything special she needs doing today.'

Really? I have a lot to learn about the deviousness of women.' He shivered suddenly. 'Come on. Let's go back and tell them they can stop trying to throw us together.' He took her hand and together they wandered back along the shore, no longer noticing the cold wind, warm in their love for each other.

Deep in the clump of trees where they had been sheltering somebody else had heard every word they had uttered. Will had come to his den to be alone and wait for darkness before he began another damaging visit to the hall. When he had realised who was on the other side of the screen of bushes he had frozen, taking in all that passed between the lovers. At first jealousy had coursed through his veins as he heard of the silver buckle and its significance but when they declared their love for each other he had yearned to burst out upon them and attack them. How could they be so smug in their love while he was an outcast, unloved, unwanted and alone? This put a whole new perspective on his actions. Not only was there a house to destroy but a young couple upon whom he now concentrated every fibre of hatred in his body. This was to be a sad day for Master Carver Cuthbert, the beginning of the end for him and his girl. New plans must be made to end the reign of Cuthbert forever. He came out of hiding and as darkness fell he made his way secretly back to his widow woman to plan the final revenge.

CHAPTER TWENTY-SIX

'About time too!' exclaimed Alfred when the news spread. 'Perhaps now we can get on and finish this house without you being distracted.'

'But I …' protested Cuthbert.

'We could all see this coming. We wondered how long it was going to take you, that's all,' laughed Ben.

Cuthbert took all the light-hearted banter from his colleagues. Nothing now could spoil his happiness. He was going to be married to the girl he loved and he wouldn't let anyone or anything stop or spoil that. Her parents were thrilled, her sisters immediately wanted to know what they would wear, and it was going to be an occasion for everyone to look forward to in the spring. He felt as though the smile on his face was going to be a permanent fixture for months to come and it gave him a warm glow inside. Even the weather was being kind as the temperatures rose and the sun came out for several days. Work continued but there was a joyful atmosphere and somehow that helped everyone to work harder and faster.

Abel was pleased to see the improvement as he continued his work on the screen along with a number of the men and was looking forward to seeing the structure when it was assembled. Translating a drawing into an actual object was exciting but demanded precision at every stage. The eight panels of the main part were complete, the faces of the royal personages were emerging from the wood, the base supports were ready and the cross pieces which would hold it all together were in production. The tops of the end pieces were proving a little difficult to carve as he had drawn a complicated twisted pattern to rise to a pinnacle at each side, a design he had seen elsewhere, but only once. There were times when he wondered whether he had dreamt it because it was so complicated but he persevered. The work could not be delayed as the wood would soon dry out and become impossible to carve.

Lord Hesketh sent his land agent to assess the progress. The man was an unsmiling, dour person who clearly took his errand seriously, checking every room, every piece of furniture, every fitting meticulously. He made copious notes on a desk slung round his neck and compiled a list of work still to do. After his third circuit of the outside of the building he nodded sagely and appeared to be satisfied, though he gave little away.

Abel offered him food and wine before he returned to make his report but it was declined.

'His lordship requires me to make a full written report of my findings to be sent to him in London,' he intoned in a grave voice, putting his desk and all the papers into a stout leather satchel which he hung from his horse's saddle.

'Oh, he's in London, is he?' replied Abel.

'Of course. He is an important personage and must appear at Court. He will, however, expect the house to be ready for him and his family to take up occupation in the summer of this year. I shall inform him of your agreement on this point?'

'Er, yes, I expect it will be ready,' said Abel, wondering when he had agreed to any date during the course of this visit.

'It *will* be ready,' stated the man, firmly, and swung into his saddle. Looking down on Abel he continued, 'I was not making a suggestion, I was stating a fact.' He kicked his horse and rode away down the track.

'He was a bundle of fun,' commented Alfric, who had overheard most of the conversation.

'Do not criticise your betters,' said Abel. 'He has a job to do, but he could be a bit more relaxed. A smile or two wouldn't go amiss either.'

'So, we have to finish by the summer then?'

'I expected to be done by then anyway,' answered Abel, 'but a finish date has never been mentioned yet. Still, let's make sure we complete it for Lord Hesketh and not for that stiff-necked clerk of his.'

The lengthening days lifted everyone's spirits. Night guards still kept watch but there had been no sighting of Will for some time now. They dare not withdraw their vigilance though as a fire or any other damage at this late stage would be devastating.

Cuthbert spent as much time as he could with Jennet without neglecting his work at all. His carving reached a perfection even he had not achieved before and his work throughout the house, particularly in the west wing, was outstanding. His earlier banishment there by Abel was serving him well even though Abel's attitude towards him had changed completely and the two men frequently spent time together either working on the screen or deciding on work to be done. Unlike Will, Alfred and Thomas, the two most senior men after Abel, bore no grudge towards Cuthbert. There was no jealousy between them, instead they learnt from him, particularly when he carved intricate pieces inspired by using drawings he made from the wildlife around him. They remembered the first time Cuthbert had shown them how to frame a scene down by the Mere which he later used to create a panel for one of the principal rooms in the family part of the house and they began to look at their surroundings differently. They were all capable of drawing detailed plans for buildings, some better than others but decorative pieces were different and then interpreting from paper to wood took a very special skill.

As the year moved towards March, the days lengthened and the weather was warmer, more detail was added to the outside of the building. Jehan fashioned the metalwork for the spits and pot hangers over the great fire in the kitchen. A stone floor was laid and a water supply for the building dug with a well in the yard outside. Stables for the horses were built away from the main building with a hayloft above. It had not been decided whether further barns would be built nearby or use would be made of those already existing on other parts of the estate. The stiff-necked clerk made a second visit of inspection, made more copious notes, barely spoke a word and left with the same dour expression he wore during his last visit.

'He's happy in his work,' quipped Alfric sarcastically when he had gone.

'Some people take their work very seriously,' said Abel.

'I can't imagine going all day without a smile,' replied Alfric.

'That's because you don't have a strict master breathing down your neck.' Abel cuffed him lightly as he passed by. 'Now, let's get this finished.'

Cuthbert couldn't help smiling. Everything seemed to be going so well now that he couldn't imagine anything unforeseen happening.

***

Will was obsessed with his hatred. He spent more and more time sitting in dark corners in an ale house, muttering to himself and growling at anyone who attempted to engage him in conversation. At times he imagined himself in his grand house somewhere where he was lord and master of all. He would be strict, nobody would be allowed to treat him badly ever again. He would have a rich young wife who would give him heirs, she would do everything he demanded of her, he would have servants at his beck and call, a stable full of horses, a kennel full of hounds and he would spend his hours hunting and fishing. Anyone who crossed him would feel the weight of his hand in law. Oh yes, he would rule his kingdom.

The widow woman was becoming frightened of him but dare not tell him to go. He had lashed out at her a few times when he was drunk and sometimes spent whole days in bed. He rarely washed or changed his clothes, demanded food whenever he came in and complained if it was cold or wasn't to his taste. She considered leaving but had nowhere else to go.

Her sympathy for him had long since waned and she saw him for what he was, a cruel, spiteful and drunken boor.

In his sober moments Will remembered his time at Rufford and vowed revenge but it wasn't until April that he did anything about it. He overheard a conversation in the marketplace in the village. Two grooms were watering their horses at the horse trough. He gathered that they worked for Lord Derby and had been with their master to Rufford. The house was almost finished but what made Will prick up his ears was mention of a wedding to be celebrated in early May between the daughter of the village woodsman and a handsome young carpenter. He moved nearer with a pretence of looking for something he had dropped on the ground.

'She's a pretty wench,' said one.

'Aye, and the bridegroom is something of a hero they were saying. Saved Lord Hesketh's boy from drowning in the Mere. He's not bad looking though he's not from around here. Something of a carver too.'

The two men moved off and Will heard no more but it had peaked his curiosity. They could only be talking about Cuthbert and that haughty lass from the woodcarver's family. So that secret tryst of theirs that he had overheard that cold day in the woods was going to end up with a wedding, was it? Well, he'd see about that. He all but rubbed his hands together as he imagined all sorts of things he could do to ruin their day. How he would love to deflower the slut before her big day. That would be a slap in the face for master carver Cuthbert. This was going to take serious thought and he went off to the nearest ale house to think, with the aid of a jar or two, of course.

Somehow he managed to stay fairly sober that day as his mind whirled with plots and plans to spoil the couple's special day. Ideas of murder were soon dismissed. A quick death would not be very satisfying to him although it would put an end to the marriage if one or both were dead. He wanted to make them suffer and he wanted them to know who was causing their pain. His imagination conjured up many ways of fulfilling his wishes but, being sober, he realised many were no more than fancies. He went outside to clear his head and walked up and down the lanes of the village muttering to himself and occasionally laughing out loud as some delicious moment came to him. People passed him warily as he chuckled, a foolish grin on his face and with staring eyes. He pictured what he would do so vividly that he occasionally stopped and acted out the little scene he saw in his head.

'He's gone mad,' declared a farmer, herding a flock of geese through the village.

'Not right in the head, he ain't,' agreed another.

'Someat ought to be done wi' 'im,' said an old woman who Will had swept out of his way as he passed, oblivious to her presence.

'He'll murder us all in our beds, he will,' stated another. 'I'm telling you, lock your doors of a night.'

Will's fantasies became dreams and he shouted out and laughed so often in the following nights that the widow woman left her house and sought sanctuary in the church. The village priest found her curled up in a corner in the morning and did his best to comfort her as she gabbled her strange story out to him.

'He's possessed, father,' she cried. 'He talks to himself, stares into space as though he can see people there. He does things with his hands all the time. I'm sure he thinks he's holding something.'

'What does he say? Can you tell?'

'A lot of it is just mumbling then he'll say things like 'I'll show you who is master here,' and, 'You won't say that to me again.' I'm afraid, father, of what he will do. And then he goes quiet and looks as though he's stroking a cat or something, all gentle like, and murmuring sweet words to it, then just as suddenly his face changes and he wrings his hands, like he's twisting something round and round.'

The priest was indeed alarmed.

'I must go and try to ease a troubled soul,' he said. 'Perhaps if he came to confession?'

'I doubt it. I've never seen him enter the church.'

'Oh dear, he is deeply troubled but fear not, I will see what I can do.'

The elderly priest hurried away and headed for the widow's cottage. There was no sign of life and when he knocked on the door there was no reply. He tried to peer through the tiny window but all was dark inside. He walked round to the back to see if there was another door and bumped into Will who was emerging from the privy.

'My son,' he exclaimed. It was the worst thing he could have said to him. Will, dirty and unkempt, stopped and stared at him and the look made the priest turn cold.

'You're not my father,' shouted Will. 'My father is a lord, a real lord, not your Lord, a figment of your imagination.'

The priest crossed himself at these blasphemous words, again the wrong thing to do for Will grabbed him round the neck and pushed him back against the wall of the cottage.

'I'll have none of your God stuff,' he snarled. 'God has never done anything for me.' He squeezed tighter and the priest tried to pull his hands away as he fought for breath, soundless words on his lips. 'Go back to your church and your God and keep away from me. Do you understand? Keep away. Leave me alone. I don't need you.' With a final tighter squeeze he released the poor man and turned to go back in the cottage, slamming the door behind him. The priest slid down the wall, holding his throat and gasping for breath. It was some time before he was able to get to his feet and stagger back to his own house where he fell to his knees in prayer for the lost soul. Later he would inform the village elders and let them deal with the mad man living among them.

Inside the cottage Will continued his raving against the priest, against God, against all who had denied him his birth right as he saw it. As his fury grew and reached new heights he smashed everything he could lay his hands on, pots, furniture, windows even the fire basket in the hearth, stamping everything to pieces until, exhausted he stood and surveyed the damage, and he began to laugh. He laughed until his sides ached. People passing outside stopped to listen to the noise then hurried away, fearful that the mad man would come out and attack them. Finally, exhausted and panting for breath he gathered up his own few belongings, tied them in a bundle and ran out into the road and away, not caring where he went or who saw him. He ran and ran until he had no strength left and crawled into a hut at the edge of the woods and fell exhausted in the straw that was stored there and finally slept.

***

'It's time we put this monster together,' announced Abel one morning in early April, standing back to look at all the various parts of the screen. Even in pieces it looked enormous but assembled it was going to look magnificent. 'Is the floor complete, because once this is in place we're not moving it again?'

'Yes, at least the part where this is going is smoothed and flat,' said Ben who had spent much of the previous day preparing the beaten earth floor. Later rushes would be spread on it and with wear it would provide a hard, firm surface.

A group of men gathered to carry all the parts into the Great Hall and Abel collected the tools needed for fastening the screen together, then one by one each part was carried from the woodshed across to the Hall. Bog oak was particularly dense and hence incredibly heavy so there was much puffing and panting as they manoeuvred the larger pieces through the big double doors and laid them out on the floor. Then, one by one they were put in place, pegged together and the creation grew. The hardest parts to handle were the immense side structures and ropes and pulleys were employed to hoist them upright then held in place whilst the panelled part between was fitted into place. Across the top, between the uprights, the heavy beam slotted onto its appointed pegs and fixed, the head of their sovereign gazing along the length of the Hall to the top table where the family would sit, whilst that of his queen stared at the domestic wing. Not perhaps the most prominent position, but appropriate for a lady, thought Cuthbert, wryly.

It took them most of the day to complete the work, a day of heaving muscles and straining backs but at last they were able to stand back and see it as a complete piece for the first time.

'Quite something, eh?' said Alfric.

'You were right, it is a monster,' commented Thomas. 'Lord Hesketh did approve your drawings for it, didn't he?'

'Of course, I wouldn't have embarked on it without showing him what I proposed. I appealed to his vanity remember, told him it would be bigger than any other.'

'Is it?'

'I hope so. I haven't actually measured any others, but it's big,' replied Abel and laughed. 'If he doesn't like it I'm not moving it.'

The general opinion was that they had created something momentous, fitting for the Great Hall and for a wealthy landowner. Cuthbert went to stand at the opposite end of the hall and looked back at it.

'Impressive,' he said, 'decorative and useful. It hides all those doors from this end. Perhaps a curtain either side would make the part behind separate from this side. It's got all the things Lord Hesketh likes: size, ornate carving, a tribute to his sovereign in those masks at the top, it's unique and it shows his wealth to all visitors. I will be most surprised if he doesn't like it.' He turned round and looked up at the canopy which hung above the top table, recently completed by several of the other men. 'It's a great contrast to this which is relatively plain but if, as you say, the coats of arms which we haven't carved are painted in the squares up here it will be a contrast to the dark wood of the screen.' His eyes moved to look at the outer ends of the canopy. As a later addition it had been difficult to match it with the side walls, leaving an odd look to the join which offended Cuthbert's eye for neatness. As he thought about it and wondered if there was anything he could do to neaten it an idea began to form in his head. He would think about it, develop it a bit more and put his idea to Abel when he had something to show him on paper.

By the time they had cleared away all the tools and props they had used it was time to finish for the day. Abel was very pleased as it had been his idea to create something worthy in what he still expected to be the last and largest house he had been involved in and it was with that thought in his head he went to Ezekial's home for his evening meal.

Following Abel's difficult time with Will, Ezekial and his wife had tried to take care of Abel by sharing meals with him, or Ezekial would meet him in the ale house and gradually Abel had opened up to them, talking more about his wife and the problems they had had with Will. It soon became apparent that they had soon realised that the boy was going to have all sorts of questions about his family and when they failed to answer them to his satisfaction he had become challenging.

'I've never known a child who could ask so many questions and never be satisfied with the answers,' he had said on one occasion. 'Whatever we told him he never believed us, said we were telling him lies. He would get angry, disobedient, he hit me once but I soon stopped that so he tried it with Dora. She used to get so upset. She saw it as her Christian duty to love him but it became harder and harder and it wore her down. He could be so cruel, not physically, but with words, spreading rumours and stories about us. It wore her down and I'm sure it led to an early grave for her and do you know what he did when I told him she had died, he laughed and said he was glad. That day was the nearest I ever came to killing someone. I was so hurt and angry.'

That admission had shocked Ezekial as he had always seen Abel as the mildest of men, very hard working but gentle and tolerant, but certainly not of Will.

'It was the beginning of the end between us. I would have sent him away but for the promise I'd made to keep him as my apprentice and journeyman. He was like a millstone around my neck and I thank the Lord that he has chosen to leave.'

'We have all seen a difference since he did go,' said Ezekial as they sat outside their cottage, enjoying the warmth of the April sun. 'Everyone has noticed, and you have finally accepted Cuthbert.'

Abel shifted uncomfortably on the bench.

'Aye, I feel bad about that. I treated him wrong from the start but what a mistake I made. He is truly one of the finest craftsmen I have ever seen. When he arrived I thought he was just Lord Derby's favourite and I wanted nothing to do with him. It shows his strength of character that he stayed despite what I said and did.'

'It would take more than a few harsh words to stop Cuthbert doing what he does best.'

'He had more than harsh words. I could have injured him seriously when I was mad with him. I refused to see that it was all Will's doing, dripping poison into my ear at every opportunity. Now we work together closely and he has some wonderful ideas. If only I'd listened to him earlier we may have produced even more work that has never been seen before. His ideas seem to pour out of him. But he is modest about his talent, he never boasts about what he does, never pushes himself forward despite what I have said about him in the past. He will make a fine husband for your Jennet.'

'That's what we think,' agreed Ezekial. 'and she is walking on air she is so happy. We welcome him to our family wholeheartedly.'

The couple under discussion were outside, leaning on the wall of the small garden where Hester tended the vegetables and herbs for the family.

'Only three days to go and we will be married,' smiled an excited Jennet, squeezing his arm. He pulled her to him, putting his arm around her slender waist and burying his nose in her abundant hair, breathing in the clean scent of it. He ached with his love for her so intense was it. He wanted to hold and touch every part of her, caress her, kiss her, love her forever. She pulled back from him and looked up into his face.

'What are you thinking about?' she asked.

'My love for you, my longing for those three days to pass so that we can be together. I don't think I have ever been so happy. Thank you for agreeing to marry me.' He bent to kiss her on the lips, a gentle peck at first then, as she responded, he held her tighter and pressed his lips more firmly until, breathless they pulled apart and gazed into each other's eyes.

'I love you, Jennet Henthorne.'

'And I love you too, Cuthbert Watts.'

Not many yards away someone was watching them from the shelter of a bush, loathing the very sight of the young lovers in each other's arms and vowing to end their dreams, but it would have to be soon if their wedding day was to be stopped.

CHAPTER TWENTY-SEVEN

Thursday morning dawned bright and clear and unusually warm for early May. As Cuthbert and the other men gathered for their day's work there was a lot of laughter and jollity, mostly at Cuthbert's expense, but he took the ribbing with a glad heart and went into the Great Hall to start building a scaffolding tower to install the last two of the roof bosses in the high arch of the roof. Working so high was difficult and great care was taken to provide a firm base for the temporary structure. Cuthbert was particularly careful as the fatal fall of Jethro a few years previously was always on his mind. One slip was all it took and with the end of building so near they did not want any accidents to happen.

The women of the village were busy cooking and baking, creating a feast for the wedding breakfast for the happy couple. Pies and pastries, sweetmeats and jellies, meats and fish all had to be prepared. Everybody contributed, even the innkeeper had brewed extra casks of ale and mead for the festivities. The big barn behind Ezekial's woodshed was cleaned and swept and trestle tables set out with benches and stools around them. The children gathered wildflowers to decorate it and scattered fresh rushes and fragrant herbs on the floor so that, as they danced, the air would be filled with the scent of lavender and camomile, rosemary and sweet marjoram. They made a note of where there were wild roses growing so that, on the morning of the wedding they could pick them early and weave them into garlands for their hair and for Jennet to carry. She and her mother had spent many hours sewing a new dress for her, palest green with a narrow belt of finest leather, a present from her grandmother who had worn it at her wedding many years ago. The excitement throughout the village was tangible with smiles from everyone. This wedding would mark not only a new beginning for Cuthbert and Jennet but the end of a marvellous building's construction and a worthy celebration.

By the end of the day the penultimate boss had been installed and admired. It was the eagle and child emblem, the symbol of the earls of Derby and a fitting tribute by Lord Hesketh to the family who had supported his ancestors for so long and who had been instrumental in the construction of this Hall. Alfric had carved it using a drawing done by Cuthbert and it recalled the legend from the Derby history when an early Lady Derby had been unable to produce an heir but Lord Derby had a son by a maid in the village. He arranged for the babe to be left in the forest and when he walked by with his Lady they happened to find the child which they took into their care and adopted as their own. In the meantime the child was protected from harm by an eagle. A romantic story but retold by the family until it passed into history.

That evening Cuthbert and Jennet walked together by the Mere, watching the sun set over the water, hand in hand.

'Tomorrow,' whispered Jennet. 'Our last day apart for the rest of our lives.' She smiled up at him and he took her in his arms and kissed her, holding her to him, feeling her slender figure mould so perfectly with his tall, strong body.

'You … are … so … beautiful,' he murmured into her hair. 'I promise that I will never let any harm come to you. I will never leave you, never hurt you, I will protect you always.' He hugged her closer and felt he would burst with his love for her.

They sat on a fallen tree by the water and watched the sun sink lower, his arm around her shoulder, hers about his waist, close, safe, together. Only when the sun kissed the water did they rise and return to the village to their separate beds. Just two more nights apart and they would be married.

The following morning everyone was up early as the finishing touches were to be put to the building with the installation of the final roof boss, Cuthbert's Tudor Rose. First the scaffolding had to be partly dismantled, moved along the Hall and rebuilt below the final arch. It was afternoon before it was ready and the boss was carried into the Hall. It was a hefty lump of wood to be lifted aloft and would take three of them to hold it in position whilst Cuthbert fixed it in place with wooden pegs, not an easy job at ground level but even harder at the top of a scaffold. A net had been fashioned from one of the fishermen's nets and the boss was laid in it on the floor. Ropes were attached to the sides of the net and their ends carried aloft by the four who would place it in position, Cuthbert, Alfric, Harry and Thomas. Guided by those on the floor they then hauled it slowly upwards, avoiding catching the net on the structure itself until they lifted it over the top bar and laid it on the platform between their feet. There was little room to manoeuvre but they grasped it between them and lifted it above their heads, kicking the net out of their way, and slotted it into the space Cuthbert had fashioned for it at the junction of the two arching timbers. He had cut holes to receive the pegs which would secure it to the roof and, struggling to get round the three straining men, he hammered home pegs in various positions around it until he felt it was secure and they could relax. As they stood back and lowered their arms a cheer went up from below.

'Not quite in the middle,' shouted Ben, and was quickly silenced by his colleagues, with slaps around his ears.

'Ignore him,' called Abel. 'It looks fine. Absolutely dead centre.' He turned to Ben. 'No ale for you tomorrow, my lad,' and he added a thump on his shoulder for good measure. 'Come on down. We have a wedding to prepare for tomorrow.'

Although it was early to finish Abel let everyone go and stayed to secure the building. He walked round every room in the west wing, admiring the workmanship of every part from the main structure to the doors and windows, the furniture and decoration. It was a job well done and he was proud of what they had achieved. Closing doors behind him as he went and securing all external ones, he passed into the Great Hall and sat for a moment on the bench behind the long table, looking all about him, at the mighty windows, the towering walls, the tables and benches they had made, even the great fireplace which had been such a bone of contention when it had been suggested. Soon this room would be alive with people, eating, sleeping, dancing, laughing at the actors and entertainers who would come, listening to musicians in the great compass window at his side, the walls covered by colourful tapestries, great iron candelabras filled with candles lighting it on dark winter evenings. His eye was drawn upwards to the carvings and decorations all around him. After the weekend they would remove the scaffolding, the discarded net and a few tools left nearby and the Hall would be ready for Lord Hesketh and his family to move in.

Finally he looked at the great screen he had designed and helped to make. What a masterpiece, a statement, a legacy. To see his ideas on paper translated to such a piece gave him a huge amount of pride. There were times when he had thought he had been too ambitious but it had worked and even now he was imagining a third central spire, matching the other two but broader, and set in the middle to tower above the rest. He would make drawings and show them to Lord Hesketh for his approval but he felt it would be the crowning glory of his creation.

He walked out of the Great Hall with a smile on his face. It had had its difficulties but it was a job well done, a job to be proud of.

Cuthbert paused at the trough by the forge and swilled his head and face with cold water to sluice away the dirt of the day. Jehan looked out of the doorway where he was making links for a chain to guide a plough.

'Finished for the day, have you?' he called. 'Well, I suppose the bridegroom has to prepare for the big day. Jennet said she'd meet you by the church when you're ready.'

'What for?' asked Cuthbert. 'We've made all the arrangements with the priest. What else is there to do?'

'I don't know, she didn't say. She passed by here, oh a good half hour since, and looking very excited about something. Perhaps you'd better go and see.'

'Aye, I will.' Cuthbert rubbed his face dry on a cloth and turned towards the church at the end of the village. Whatever could there be to do tonight? All was in place, they'd arranged everything earlier in the week. Perhaps she wanted him to see the flowers she and her sisters had decorated the church with during the day. Yes, that would be it, and he hurried on.

There was no sign of her outside so he pushed the heavy door open and went inside. The scent of flowers immediately assailed his nostrils and he paused to look in wonder at the array of flowers on every window ledge and surface available. They were beautiful, but there was no sign of Jennet. He saw a movement at the far end and the priest came out of his little vestry carrying new candles for the altar. Cuthbert went down the central aisle towards him. The priest turned when he heard him approach and smiled.

'They have made this simple little church beautiful, haven't they?' He breathed in the scent. 'This is so much nicer than the smell of wax candles, don't you agree?'

'I do,' agreed Cuthbert, and the priest burst out laughing.

'Are you practising your responses already?'

Cuthbert frowned in puzzlement then grinned when he realised what he'd said.

'I don't need to practise, I've been saying it for days in my head.' He looked about. 'Have you seen Jennet?'

'Not since they finished the flowers earlier on. Why?'

'I got a message she wanted to meet me here.'

'Is she outside? She hasn't been in here.'

'I'll go and look.'

He walked right round the building but there was no sign of Jennet. Strange. Jehan wouldn't have got the message wrong. He decided to return the way he'd come, see if she had stopped somewhere on the way.

As he passed one of the cottages he saw Old Bartholomew, the gravedigger, enjoying a mug of ale on the bench outside his front door. Nobody knew how old he was, some said near a hundred, which was probably wrong but he was a little, wrinkled old man who still insisted he could dig a grave better than anyone else and would probably dig his own if he could get his way. Cuthbert stopped and asked,

'Did you see Jennet pass this way?'

Bartholomew took a long drink before answering.

'Aye, lad, I did. 'Bout an 'alf 'our sin'. All smiles she were, as though she were goin' to meet 'er young man.' He grinned toothlessly. 'That'd be you, wouldn' it? Reet 'appy she looked too.'

'Did you see where she went?'

'Down towards the church.'

'That's where she told me to meet her.'

'Aye, mebbe she did, but she didna get that far.'

'What do you mean?'

'T'other fella came out from them trees and took her off that-a-way.' He pointed towards the Mere.

'What other fellow?'

'That lazy so-and-so from the 'all. 'Im as never does no work if 'e can 'elp it.'

Cuthbert went cold.

'Are you sure?'

'I told you so didna I?'

'How long ago?

'Jus' arter she passed t'other way.'

Cuthbert turned and ran back towards the village. He passed the forge first and shouted to Jehan, who was standing outside,

'Will's got Jennet.'

'What?'

'Will's got Jennet. He's taken her down to the Mere.'

'Oh my God! I'll get the others.' He turned into the forge and called for Jacob. The two men ran after Cuthbert.

A group of men were playing a game of skittles on a patch of ground by the track and Cuthbert yelled at them as he passed.

'Will's taken Jennet to the Mere. Help me find her.'

The game was immediately abandoned as every one of them ran after the others, calling to anyone they saw to come and help the search.

They reached the shore but there was no sign of either Will or Jennet.

'Spread out. You go that way, we'll go this,' shouted Cuthbert, splitting the group into two and running in opposite directions along the shore. They searched every bush and thicket they passed but there was no sign of them. When Cuthbert and his group stopped well north of the village they had seen no one.

'Where can they be?' he cried, running his hands through his hair in despair. 'If he harms her, I'll …'

'They can't have gone far,' panted Ben. 'We'll find her.'

'Let's go back, more slowly and spread out a bit more,' suggested Alfric. 'Shout her name. She may be able to answer.'

They spread out through the trees, calling Jennet's name, but all they disturbed was birds in the trees. When they met up with the other group they were puzzled that nobody had found them.

'Could they have slipped back into the village?' suggested Cuthbert, white with fear.

'Somebody would have seen them and raised the alarm,' said Ben. 'Listen.'

They turned as someone came running through the trees towards them. It was Ezekial and Abel with several more men from the village.

'Have you found her? Have you found my daughter?' cried Ezekial.

'Not a sign of them. They've just disappeared.'

'They can't have. They must be hiding somewhere.'

'Where, though? We've been right up to the north end and they've been beyond the village the other way. We've got to find her. Will can only mean harm. He's been waiting for this, ever since he left. Oh, Jennet, my love, where are you?' Cuthbert was almost in tears and it was Abel who said,

'Now lad, we've got to think. They've got to be about here somewhere, we'll find them, though nobody knows these woods better than Will. I believe he has a den somewhere nearby where he used to go when he wanted to be alone. I wish I'd followed him one day and found it. Let's think. It can't be far because sometimes he wasn't gone all that long. So let's comb these woods thoroughly, look behind every bush and up every tree that's big enough to climb. He may be up above us where we haven't looked yet. Look inside every dense bush or clump of reeds. Leave nothing to chance. And listen. He may have gagged her to stop her crying out but she could still make a noise.' He saw the terror in Cuthbert's face. 'Don't imagine the worst, lad. We'll find her if we have to tear down every tree.' The others nodded in agreement and split into pairs, agreeing on which areas to search and to meet back at the village when they'd combed their patch.

CHAPTER TWENTY-EIGHT

The woods had never been searched as thoroughly before. Looking up and behind and under everything took time but it was the only way they were going to find the two of them. Cuthbert was desperate, imagining all sorts of things. Will was capable of real cruelty and the thought of Jennet in his clutches was beyond bearing. He must find her, he must, before Will did anything to her.

They were down near the shore and standing close to a thick clump of reeds and undergrowth with young willow growing through it. Cuthbert groaned as he recognised that it was the spot where he and Jennet had sat to watch the sunset the evening before. Alfric looked at him and Cuthbert explained what had happened here. He was close to tears at the thought he might lose her and Alfric gripped his arm.

'We'll find her. We will, I promise. That rat of a human is not going to win this time.' He looked round. 'Let's see what's on the other side of this clump,' and he turned to the right. Cuthbert went round the other way but in a few seconds there was a cry from Alfric and he turned back. Alfric was holding something in his hands. 'I trod on it, in the mud just there.'

Cuthbert took the muddy piece of wood from him. It was the little Tudor rose he had carved for Jennet and his heart gave a lurch.

'She always carried it in her pocket,' he whispered.

'Perhaps she dropped it last night,' suggested Alfric.

'No, we didn't come to this side. We came from over there and went back the same way. She must be somewhere nearby.' He looked round desperately then yelled at the top of his voice,

'Jennet. Jennet. Where are you? I'm here. I'm coming for you.'

Startled birds flew up from the reed bed, and he called again.

'Jennet. Make a noise if you can't speak. We'll find you. Jennet. Jennet.'

For perhaps half a minute there was nothing and he was about to call again when something burst from the centre of the thicket they were standing by and Will appeared, dirty and dishevelled with his arm round a terrified Jennet.

'Here she is, master carver, Here's your precious Jennet. She's mine now. I've got her. No, don't come any nearer or this'll put an end to her.' He was holding a blade to Jennet's neck, a long thin chisel with a wooden handle. 'I can carve too, you know, though I never got the credit you did, master carver. Perhaps if I carve in flesh instead of wood you'll take notice of me,' and he nicked Jennet's neck just below her ear. She squealed and he tightened his grip on her. 'I can do better than that and I will if you come any nearer.' Cuthbert daren't move.

'Let her go, Will. What harm has she done to you? Let her go.'

'Never,' he replied. 'She's mine now.' He stroked her breast with the hand holding her to him. 'Lovely soft flesh. I'll have such sport with her,' and he held her tighter his eyes gleaming with lust. 'She will be married to a lord, not a woodcarver. I will take her to my manor and she will be my wife and you will have to let her go because if you don't I'll kill you.'

'That is all in your head, Will,' cried Cuthbert. 'Abel told you. You have no manor, no estate, no wealth. You have no rich family, no inheritance.'

'That's a lie,' Will shouted back, and turned sharply as Alfric suddenly ran towards him and tried to grab the hand holding the weapon. Will lashed out and cut deeply into Alfric's arm. As Alfric recoiled, Will plunged the chisel into his side, pulled it out and stabbed again. Alfric collapsed to the ground. Cuthbert went to his aid and Will sneered,

'I told you I'd kill. Now do you believe me?'

'Let Jennet go,' pleaded Cuthbert.

'Never.'

He turned, grabbed Jennet by the arm and ran off into the wood, dragging her after him.

Cuthbert knelt by Alfric, trying to staunch the blood which was pouring from the wounds.

'Go after her,' gasped Alfric, 'or you'll lose her. I'll be all right. The others will find me. Go and rescue Jennet. Go on, go.'

Cuthbert was torn but if he didn't follow now he wouldn't know where to look. With a last despairing look at his friend he got to his feet and tore after Will. He could hear Jennet's cries ahead and followed them. Thomas came running from the side.

'What's happening? Have you found her?'

'Will's got her. He's stabbed Alfric, back there, by the shore. Help him. I mustn't lose Jennet,' and he raced away.

Thomas was joined by Ben and Abel.

'Ben, with me, Alfric's hurt. Abel follow Cuthbert and get any of the others to join you. That way.' He pointed towards the Hall then turned and ran to the shore with Ben.

Cuthbert tore along the path, leaping over tree roots and dodging overhanging branches. He was joined by several men from the building site and they raced after the fugitive who seemed to know every twist and turn of the path and was slowly gaining on them, despite being hampered by Jennet. Cuthbert's lungs were bursting, his heart pounding in his chest. 'I'm coming, I'm coming my darling,' he said over and over in his head. 'God keep her safe. Don't let him harm her.' As they burst out of the trees onto the track that led past the Hall they lost them for a moment then someone spotted them by the Great Hall.

'There they are. Quick.'

Will had reached the main door of the Great Hall, flung himself at it and it burst open, it had been left unlocked. He went in, throwing Jennet to the floor whilst he closed the door and dragged a table across it. They wouldn't get him that easily. He looked around. It was the first time he had been inside since the day he had walked away from it. Abel and his men had finished it, even built a great monstrosity of a screen. He looked around. Where could he hide? In the west wing? The east wing? Then he saw the scaffolding still standing at the far end, waiting to be removed and a plan began to form in his mind. He dragged Jennet over to it.

'Get up there,' he said, pointing.

'I can't,' she cried.

'I said get up there', and he threw her against the structure. She began to climb, hampered by her skirts but pulling herself up higher and higher. Will turned to the discarded net still lying in a tangled heap on the floor where it had fallen from the top when they had kicked it out of the way. He untied one of the ropes which they had used to haul the Tudor rose boss to the top, loosely coiled it and slung it around his shoulders then began to climb after Jennet.

Outside the men were pushing on the door but it would only open a few inches.

'He's pushed something against it,' cried Cuthbert, despairingly.

Abel turned to the gathered men.

'Some of you try to get in through the other doors in the wings. Smash the lock if you have to. You two, fetch a ladder and put it up to a window so we can see what's happening inside. If you find a way in be careful, he's got a weapon and he's shown he will use it.' The men scattered but Cuthbert pushed the door open as far as it would go and tried to reach the table inside.

'If I could push it over we may be able to get this wide enough to get in,' he said, heaving his shoulder against it. A gap appeared that was big enough to get an arm through and he pushed against the table edge. Abel leaned over and worked his arm through and together they heaved on the table, trying to tip it away from the door. Jehan and Jacob appeared with a ladder and set it up against one of the high windows. Jehan climbed swiftly and peered through the glass. The view was distorted by the glass but he could see movement near the scaffolding tower.

'He's making her climb the scaffolding!' he cried in alarm.

'Why would he do that?' asked Jacob.

'I don't know but I don't like it.'

'Keep watching,' said Abel from below.

One of the men ran from the woodshed carrying a long piece of wood.

'Try this. See if it will go through the gap so we can push the table away from the door.'

They guided the pole into the gap then threw their weight behind it. Slowly they felt the table move and the gap in the door widened until it was possible to squeeze through and into the Hall.

The sight that met them was terrifying. Will and Jennet were at the top of the tower. Jennet was on her knees, clinging to one of the supports. Will was tying the rope round another. He saw them come in and stopped what he was doing.

'Glad you could join me,' he said, a note of triumph in his voice. 'You can watch your bride-to-be submit to me and then she will die. You will watch her humiliation and her death and you won't be able to stop it because if you try to stop me I will throw her over the rail.'

'Will!' shouted Ezekial. 'Don't do this. Don't hurt my daughter. Give yourself up before anyone gets hurt.'

'She is the only one who will get hurt. I am going to walk out of here a free man.'

'He's gone completely mad,' muttered Jehan. 'He thinks he's untouchable.'

'He's certainly mad enough to do what he says,' agreed Abel.

'Look what he's doing with the rope,' cried Jacob. 'He's making a noose. He's going to hang her!'

'We've got to stop him,' Cuthbert shouted desperately. Abel looked beyond the tower as Alfred, Harry and Japheth entered silently through one of the doors from the West wing. 'Keep Will's attention towards us,' he said quietly.

'Will, what will you gain from hurting Jennet?' asked Cuthbert.

'I will have taken her from you, master carver. That will give me the greatest satisfaction. I want her for my wife and I will take her.'

Abel moved behind the group, out of Will's sight and gestured to the three men by the west wing. They nodded and silently moved towards him until they were directly under the tower where Will could not see them. As carefully as possible, Alfred began to climb the structure on the inside, trying to make neither noise nor movement that would alert Will to their presence. Cuthbert kept talking to Will, whilst trying to reassure Jennet with glances in her direction.

'You will never walk away from here,' said Cuthbert. 'There are too many of us. You will hang for what you are doing. If you really love Jennet, as you say you do, you won't harm her.'

'Who said anything about love? Nobody ever loved me. I don't know what love is nor do I care.' He looked down at Jennet, cringing on her knees. He stretched out a hand and caressed her hair but she shrank away from him. 'I know what lust is though and I have lusted after her since the day I saw her but she was always with those darned sisters of hers.' He looked down at Cuthbert. 'You have been a pest, keeping me away from her but now I have her I intend to show her what a real man can do.' He smiled lasciviously at her then turned suddenly away as, out of the corner of his eye, he saw a hand appear on the edge of the platform and a head came into view.

Alfred had reached the top without being seen or heard but he ducked down as Will lurched towards him, the chisel in his hand. He peered over the side to see where Alfred had gone and saw the other two below. With a shout of rage he leaned over the opposite side to see whether there were any more, tripped on the coiled rope and clutched at the rail to stop himself from falling, the chisel dropping from his hand and spinning down to land in the discarded net below. Alfred quickly climbed onto the platform and reached for Will who turned and swung his fist at him. Alfred ducked and grabbed at Will's legs. They struggled, the platform shaking with their bodies thrashing back and forth. Somehow Will got to his feet but he had no weapon and no room to fight properly. He lunged at his attacker again but tripped on the rope and fell against the top rail which split apart and he fell, turning over as he dropped to land heavily on his back on the pile of netting on the floor.

For a split-second nobody moved then Abel, Jehan and Jacob rushed to Will's side intent on preventing him getting up and escaping, but they stopped and looked in horror. Will was moving feebly, his legs kicking, his body jerking. A trickle of blood appeared on his lips, became a gush and his eyes looked wildly at them for a moment, then clouded over and his head rolled to one side. Abel bent and held a hand to his mouth, feeling for a breath.

'He's dead,' he said, disbelievingly. 'But ...'

'Turn him over,' said Jehan, and the three of them heaved him onto his side. Buried to the handle in his back was the chisel he had used as a weapon. It had landed handle first in the mesh of the net, sticking straight up, ready to receive the man who had used it so wickedly, and administer rough justice.

'He got what he deserved,' observed Jehan, 'and saves a trial though I would have liked to see him hang.'

A noise from the top of the scaffold brought all their heads up. Jennet was sobbing in Alfred's arms. Immediately Cuthbert climbed up to her and gathered her into his arms and onto his heart, holding her as though he would never let her go.

'I've got you, my darling, I've got you. I'll never let you go. You're safe now, you're safe.' He rocked her as she wept, holding her tenderly until the first wave of tears eased. 'Help me get her down,' he said to Alfred, and together they lowered her to the waiting arms below. Her father held her close until Cuthbert was able to take her again, lift her into his arms and carry her away from the blood stained scene and back to her home where her mother and sisters were waiting anxiously. Only when she was settled and calm did he leave her to go and find out how Alfric was.

As he approached the forge he saw a group of the workmen standing in a huddle, talking quietly and a feeling of dread came over him.'

'What is it? What has happened? Is Alfric badly hurt?'

Thomas came towards him.

'He's dead. The bastard killed him,' he ground out between clenched teeth. 'There was nothing we could do. He bled to death where he fell. Liliath came but it was too late. He's dead, Alfric, one of the best of men, killed by a madman.'

'He's dead too and I'm not sorry but Alfric? No, not Alfric!' Cuthbert turned away, overcome by sorrow. 'He was one of the best and a good friend. If it hadn't been for him I would be dead. He tried to stop Will taking Jennet and he has paid for that with his life. Oh, Alfric, what have I done to you?' He fought to stop the tears but they flowed readily and he covered his face with his hands.'

'You're not to think like that,' said Thomas, sharply. 'Will was deranged, mad, out of control. He would have killed anyone who got in the way of his wild dreams. Alfric was just unlucky to be the one in his way at the wrong time.' He touched Cuthbert's shoulder and turned him to face him. 'You must never blame yourself. Nobody here does and Alfric certainly wouldn't. We will grieve for him but we will lay him to rest and remember his sacrifice as well as his love of life and of his work, the fun he brought to it with his funny sayings and laughter. He may have lost his life but he saved yours.' He squeezed Cuthbert's arm. 'Come, you have somebody who needs you now. Go to her.'

Cuthbert rubbed his face with his sleeve, nodded and turned back to go to Ezekial's house.

'He's taking it hard,' said Ben. 'He was there when Alfric was stabbed, he saw what happened and could do nothing to prevent it. It will torture him for a long while, no matter what we say to him. Will is the one to blame and no one else, but he has escaped his punishment. If he hadn't died by his own weapon he would have been hanged for murder.'

'Yes, we know and good riddance to him. Nobody will mourn him. If he hadn't killed himself I'd have done for Will with my bare hands.'

'So would any of us,' Ben said.

'Alfric will be laid to rest here, where he did some of his greatest work and he won't be forgotten,' said Abel, calmly. 'But now, let us go to the church and pray for his soul.'

With nods of agreement a small procession gathered and made their silent way to the village church where Alfric's body had already been laid before the altar, surrounded by his friends in peace and sorrow. On the morrow he would be washed and made ready for his burial but for tonight he was safe in the church surrounded by his friends.

CHAPTER TWENTY-NINE

The night was long. Few slept but they did gather in groups in their lodgings and homes as they talked about the events of the last few hours. How could everything have changed in such a short time? Instead of celebrating a marriage they would be mourning one of their own. How could the wedding go ahead in the light of this? Will's death was a relief but Alfric was mourned by all who had known him. Several had gathered at Ezekial's cottage, talking and remembering far into the night. Cuthbert sat beside Jennet as she slept, unable to let her out of his sight. Liliath had given her a sleeping draught as the girl was terrified of closing her eyes. Liliath and Hester had questioned her as much as they dared and had been able to assure themselves that Will had not harmed her beyond clumsily caressing and kissing her though what he would have done to her had her rescuers not managed to break into the Hall was unbearable to think about.

Abel blamed himself for all that had happened.

'How can you possibly be to blame?' asked Ezekial, as they sat in his cottage, huddled together in their grief. 'It's not your fault he was mad.'

'I should have told him years ago, when he started asking where he came from. I should have made it plain then but I thought he would grow out of it. I never dreamt he would really believe his stories.'

'I doubt anything would have stopped his wild ideas,' said Hester, handing Abel a refilled mug of ale. 'Once he got the idea in his head there was no way he would stop. It was what he wanted.'

'I could have done something.' He peered into the depths of his mug and suddenly jerked upright. 'My God! I left the Great Hall door open too. This afternoon, I locked up after you all left but I never locked that door. I wondered how he managed to get in. It's my fault.'

'That could be a blessing. At least we knew where he was. If he'd run off anywhere we may never have found them and God knows what he would have done to Jennet.' Jehan rubbed his eyes with his hands.

'Now stop that!' cried Hester. 'We must all stop these wild imaginings. The important thing is that she is safe and her tormentor is dead. She knows she is safe and has a man who will defend her with his life.'

'What about their wedding? It's set for a few hours' time.' They all looked at Ezekial, the wedding having been forgotten for the moment by every one of them.

'We can't have it tomorrow,' said Ezekial. 'What about Alfric? He is lying in the church as we speak. What about him?'

'I don't think Jennet would want it until he has been decently buried. We must speak to the priest first thing in the morning, see what he suggests.' Hester got to her feet and went to see if Jennet needed anything. Cuthbert was seated on a low stool by her bed, holding her hand, his head on his arm. He stirred when Hester entered but did not get up.

'She woke a while ago but when she saw me she went back to sleep,' he whispered. 'I'll stay until morning.'

Hester nodded but asked quietly,

'What about the wedding? We don't think it can go ahead as planned. Alfric must be buried first. Perhaps in a week or so you may feel ready.'

'Yes, I agree but I will talk to Jennet when she wakes.'

Hester crept quietly from the room. Cuthbert laid his head back down on the bed and silent tears leaked from his closed lids. How could one man cause such grief and unhappiness, he wondered. A cancelled wedding to be replaced by a funeral. A wonderful girl terrified. A good friend killed cruelly and so unnecessarily. A glorious spring day transformed into the darkest of nights. How would they ever come back from this? As the night passed he wept silently for all that was gone.

Dawn light was creeping over the window sill when Jennet woke and looked about her. As she moved she felt her hand held in a warm clasp and saw Cuthbert's head on the bedside beside her, fast asleep. Briefly she wondered why, then it all came back to her and a cold shiver ran through her. Gently she tried to release her hand but the movement woke Cuthbert and he sat up.

'My dear one,' he whispered, and enfolded her in his arms, holding her tightly to him. 'You're safe now. I will never allow such harm to come to you again.'

'I know,' she replied. 'All the time Will was holding me captive I knew you would find me and come to rescue me, I never doubted it, but how did you find us in the woods?'

'We knew Will had a hideout somewhere and we were looking for it when Alfric stepped on the little rose carving I gave you and we knew you must be somewhere nearby. Oh,' he groaned, 'if he hadn't he wouldn't have been … killed.' Cuthbert put his head in his hands in despair.

'Hush, my love,' soothed Jennet. 'If he hadn't, you wouldn't have found us at all. Perhaps it is a lucky charm, look at it that way. When Will heard you so close he wanted to show you what he'd done, he craved attention and bursting through the bushes that way certainly got it. If he hadn't stabbed Alfric he would have stabbed you. Alfric was unlucky to get in the way. Please don't blame yourself.'

Hester, on hearing voices, tapped gently on the door and came in.

'Ah, you are awake.' She looked fondly at her daughter. 'I have prepared some food for you both when you are ready.'

Nobody particularly felt like eating but they made the effort as Hester had prepared something. When they were almost finished the village priest knocked gently on the door and entered. Expecting to enter a joyous house of forthcoming nuptials he had had to prepare himself for the exact opposite.

He found a much subdued gathering and prepared to give whatever help he could.

He prayed with them in their time of trouble and offered comfort to the grieving but more practical matters needed to be discussed. The marriage would be postponed for a week, Alfric's funeral would take place on the morrow and he would be buried in the churchyard. Hester suggested that all the food prepared for the wedding breakfast had better be eaten after that as it would not keep for a week. This seemed a good solution as there would be many at the funeral. Abel said that he and his men would make a coffin today and they would carry him to his last resting place. The flowers could remain in the church as Alfric had only recently, since Cuthbert arrived, begun to notice the wild flowers around them and had started to learn from Cuthbert how to use them in his carving.

Cuthbert laughed quietly.

'I remember when he first saw the Tudor rose I made for Jennet, he thought it was a dandelion, but after that he began to notice the differences in flowers and was beginning to experiment with carving them. I showed him how to do simple ones and he was progressing well. Who knows what delights he may have created in the future.'

'He was a fine craftsman for all his lively humour and wry comments,' said Abel. 'I will miss his ready smile as he worked.'

They talked of the work he had done in the Great Hall and the Derby coat of arms roof boss which had only been installed two days before.

'A fitting memorial for him, I think,' commented Abel. There was silence for a while as they each recalled their own memories but eventually there was one subject which had to be discussed but which all were unwilling to broach. It was the priest who spoke first.

'What are we going to do about the other young man?' he asked.

'Let him rot where he lies,' spat Ezekial, an unusually bitter remark from a gentle man. 'I could never forgive him for what he did to my daughter and if he had lived I would have killed him with my own hands.'

'Ezekial!' gasped Hester who had never expected to hear such a thing from her husband.

'He's a murderer,' pointed out Cuthbert, bitterly, 'not to mention a liar, a thief, a vagabond, and a would-be rapist. Yes, I know the word hasn't been said but that is what he intended, isn't it, when he had Jennet at his mercy at the top of that tower with a ready audience below? That's what he would have done. It would have satisfied his vanity that he could do something as awful as that and we couldn't do anything to stop him.'

He felt a gentle hand on his arm and turned to see Jennet looking at him from tear-filled eyes.

'Yes, maybe, but he didn't because you and Alfred rescued me so he did me no physical harm.'

'I can never forgive him for what he did to you and to Alfric,' said Cuthbert, bitterly. 'I will have nothing to do with his burial and please don't ask me to.' He got to his feet and stumbled out of the cottage, blinded by tears and made his way to the woodshed where he could be alone, for the time being at least,

'I agree' said Ezekial, 'but we can't just leave him. What do we do, father?'

'I understand that nobody will mourn his passing but he can be buried in a quiet corner of the churchyard in an unmarked grave and we can do it at night with no more than a few prayers, no celebration of his life, no sermon over him.'

'How will we get his body there for I can't imagine anyone wanting to help you?' asked Alfred.

'I will,' said Abel quietly. 'I am the nearest thing he's got to family. I will wrap him in his shroud and take him to the churchyard in a wheeled cart. Don't think that I do it out of charity, I don't. He tormented us beyond endurance and I firmly belief that Dora died as a result of his behaviour. For that alone I have as great a grievance against him as any here. I will do it because I want to be sure that he's buried deep for he will burn in Hell for eternity for his wickedness.' He looked around the group. 'I will do it.'

The matter was settled then and the priest departed to make the preparations for Alfric's funeral. Ezekial went with Alfred to select the wood they would use to fashion a coffin for Alfric, collecting any who wanted to help on their way.

'What should I do?' asked Jennet. Her mother embraced her closely.

'My darling daughter, you have been so brave through all of this dreadful ordeal but there is someone who needs you now, just as you needed him yesterday. Go and find him, comfort him, love him as only you can do.' She kissed her on her forehead and gave her a motherly embrace. 'Go, go and find him.'

Cuthbert was in the woodshed when she found him, angrily chopping at a log of wood with an axe, venting his feelings in the only way he knew. Jennet watched him from the doorway as he hacked at the wood, putting all his strength into reducing the log to splinters, hitting it again and again. She knew why he was doing it. He could not punish the man responsible for all the hurt, grief and damage done to them all. Cuthbert had lost a good friend who had probably saved his own life by his actions and that was something unforgiveable. The wood would have to take the punishment instead.

When his strength was exhausted, he threw the axe onto the floor and stood panting from the effort, unaware of her presence. She watched his broad shoulders slump, his head droop and he slowly dropped to his knees among the chopped wood and put his head in his hands. Quietly she moved to his side, knelt beside him and put her arms around him. He turned to her and buried his face in her hair.

'Why?' he moaned. 'Why did he do it? Why did he have to kill?'

'He was sick in his mind,' soothed Jennet. 'He wanted revenge, he wanted his dream to become reality. Right to the end he believed he would marry me, carry me off to his manor and we would live happily ever after. Anything that was in the way of that dream had to be removed, destroyed.'

'Do you forgive him?'

'No, not forgive. I could never forgive him for killing Alfric, but I am not sorry that he is dead, either. He would have killed somebody eventually, he was so angry with the world, really, obsessed with a dream that would never come true and he would never accept that. He would have come to a bad end eventually.'

Cuthbert took her face in both his hands and looked deeply into her eyes. His insides did a somersault and he bent to kiss her.

'I don't deserve you,' he murmured. 'When I discovered he had taken you I thought my world had come to an end. I can't imagine life without you. If he had touched a hair …'

'Shhh. He didn't and we are still here and we can still get married. We will forget all of this in time. Let's get these few days over and then start our life together.' They embraced, their love a physical being within them both, shared in a way only true love can reveal itself.

Abel and his men spent the day making a coffin for Alfric from elm wood. They worked silently, missing his banter and humour with every passing minute. Only a perfect creation would satisfy the longing they all had to send him to his early grave in the best way they could. It was planed and sanded to a smooth finish, the lid fitting perfectly, the handles, made by Jehan, strong and simple. Cuthbert joined them to rub beeswax into the wood until it shone. It was a coffin fit for a lord, never mind a simple craftsman but he was special to them all and nothing but the best would do for him. Alfric's body had been washed and wrapped in a linen shroud and as they all gathered in the church, it was lifted into the coffin as the priest prayed for his soul. They would take it in turns through the night to stand vigil and there was no lack of volunteers to be with him.

Long after the sun had set a silent duo moved into the churchyard, pushing a low wooden cart with a shrouded body lying on it. By the light of a lantern carried by the priest they made their way to the furthest corner of the churchyard where a pile of earth showed them a newly dug grave. Between them they lifted the body and lowered it into the pit, then the cart was wheeled away whilst the priest murmured brief prayers before shovelling the earth back over the body until it was smooth again with only a slight hump to show where it was. An unpleasant task had been fulfilled. There would be no marker and in time the spot would grow over and be forgotten. No one would lay flowers or visit that corner. It would be as though the man below had never been.

It was a sombre congregation who gathered in the village church next morning, and many tears were shed for their friend and fellow worker. It was only when a person like Alfric was gone that it was realised how special he had been and as the funeral sentences were pronounced, the prayers offered and the sermon delivered each and every one of them had their own special memories of him. Six of the men shouldered his coffin, Abel, Cuthbert, Alfred, Ben, Japheth and Harry, to carry him to his last resting place, close by the church wall and as far away from that other grave as possible. His body was lowered into the ground and the priest said the final prayers before all gathered threw flowers or a handful of soil before leaving the old gravedigger to complete the burial. A simple wooden marker with his name on would be made and put in place in due course.

The village inn welcomed the mourners. All the food prepared for the wedding had been taken to a larger back room, an unexpected addition to the funeral ceremony but greatly enjoyed by all as they gathered to reminisce.

Gradually they dispersed, some to their homes but others who felt the need to keep busy and occupied, went to the Great Hall to dismantle the scaffolding which had been the centre of the drama. Abel could barely bring himself to touch it and ordered that it be chopped up and used for firewood. Jehan was among those who carried a cartful away, never refusing a gift of wood for his forge. When all had been cleared they found the spread of the bloodstain where Will had bled to death on his own weapon, seeped into the hardened earth of the floor. Abel had already left so Alfred suggested that they dig it out until there was no trace of blood in the ground, replace it with new earth, and spread rushes over the spot. At last everything was in order and they left, making sure this time that the door was secured.

What was to happen next? Everyone felt as though they had paused for a brief time and now didn't know how to carry on. The building, apart from minor details was complete, so what to do now? Some wanted to leave as soon as possible, some felt as though they should stay with Abel as he was waiting to hear from Lord Hesketh to make sure there was nothing else to do, no sudden alterations or additions. Meanwhile they started to sort out the woodshed, put aside any wood that could be used in the future, pack away their tools and sweep away all the sawdust which had accumulated. It would probably be used as a storage building, part of the estate yard once the household was working and busy.

In the afternoon a rider appeared on the road from the south seeking Will Topping, a young man who had suddenly disappeared from the house where he had been lodging and who they thought had, at one time, worked at Rufford. Abel asked who sought him and was told he was wanted by the law for assault and theft. Abel took the man aside and told him what had happened, that he would not be able to answer for his crimes as he was already dead and buried. The messenger was surprised and said he would have to report to his master, and rode back the way he had come.

'Will there be trouble?' asked Jehan, who had overheard the conversation from his forge.

'I can't see how there can be,' replied Abel. 'We didn't kill him, he managed that himself. He can't be tried and punished so there's no point pursuing the matter. I doubt we'll hear any more.'

But there he was wrong for next day Lord Hesketh, Lord Derby and certain men of their households arrived and asked to see Abel and anyone else involved in the death of Will Topping. Abel, Cuthbert, Ezekial, Alfred and Ben went into the Great

Hall with the party and closed the door. It was an anxious wait for everyone outside.

'They won't take them away, will they?' asked Hester, worried for her husband.

'Why would they?' answered Liliath, and turned as the Great Hall door opened, Ben emerging into the sunshine.

'They want to speak to you,' he said to Liliath.

'Me? Why?'

'You'd better come.'

Liliath followed him back into the Hall and speculation was rife about why they needed to speak to her. It was a long time before the doors opened again and to their relief everyone emerged apparently unscathed. A few words were exchanged and the gentlemen rode away.

'What did they want?' asked Harry. 'Is there trouble?'

'Not at all,' said Cuthbert. 'Will had apparently been acting violently in the village where he has been hiding and was last seen heading this way. Knowing his history with this place, albeit brief, they were anxious to find him and make him pay for what he has done. Abel was able to tell them his history and they weren't surprised that he had appeared to be deranged, it was becoming more obvious over the last few weeks. We gave them a full account of what happened here and they weren't surprised that he had turned so violent here too. He had destroyed everything in the house of the widow where he had been staying before he left. They wanted to find him to make him pay for all the damage, but there's no chance of that. I doubt he had much money anyway.'

'They can't hang him either,' said Ben, 'more's the pity.'

'So what happens now?' asked Alfred.

'They are coming back in a few days' time to look over the house. Lord Hesketh asked us to stay until he's been and is satisfied with our work.'

'And if he's not?'

'He will be,' said Abel firmly. 'We've done exactly what he wanted including his alterations. There will be no difficulties.'

'What happens to us then?' asked Ben.

'I have been asked to go to a house in Yorkshire which I had a hand in building ten years ago. They want to extend as they have such a large family now. Working at the Royal Court has brought the family huge wealth and they want to show it, just like here.'

'Will you be building stone fireplaces on outside walls?' asked Cuthbert with a straight face.

'I will do whatever I am asked but I won't suggest it in the first place.' He wagged a finger at Cuthbert. 'I can see I am going to have to watch you, Mr Watts. As many of you as want to can come with me as I will need men I can rely on and trust. We will put this behind us and look forward to our future.' At last they could see the way forward. New place, new work, new challenges, it was just what they all needed. But first there was a wedding to rearrange.

CHAPTER THIRTY

It was three days before the Hall's owner arrived together with a party of friends who wanted to see his new residence. They dismounted outside the Great Hall, leaving their horses in the care of numerous grooms before entering through the main entrance into the Hall and excitedly inspecting every room throughout the building. Voices could be heard exclaiming as they discovered bedrooms and the solar, Lord Hesketh's office from which the estate would be administered, a grand hall for the family in the west wing, smaller rooms for servants, storerooms and the guest rooms where numerous expected visitors would stay. There was a small chapel with a side room for the visiting priest to sleep in. In the east wing they inspected the buttery where racks awaited the barrels of beer, the scullery, the dry storerooms and the pantries, the game larder on the cooler north side of the house and, in a separate building, the kitchen where food for all of the household would be cooked. They peered up the great chimneys and stuck their heads in to the bread oven built into one wall. There was a hand pump bringing the water up from a deep well as well as another well outside in the stable yard. Drainage channels took away waste water. A vast table had been erected in the centre of the kitchen where most of the food preparation would take place and shelves along the walls waiting for the pots, pans and utensils which would be needed. Inside the chimney there were great iron hooks where sides of meat would be hung to smoke over the fire. Alongside the kitchen was a dairy where milk would be churned to make butter and shallow dishes stood ready for the making of cheese. A short distance away were the stables to house the numerous horses they would require with a hayloft above and a room where all the tack and harnesses would be stored and cleaned.

Most of the party then walked round the outside of the building, looking up at the stone-covered roof, the numerous windows and the vast chimney for the Great Hall. The men wandered over to the Mere to discuss fishing, eels and the possibility of duck shooting. The three ladies in the party gathered on the south side to see where the herb garden and rose garden would be, all on the sunny side of the house. It was clear that Lady Hesketh had already had plans drawn up for both of these and discussed them with the others.

Eventually everyone gathered in the Great Hall once more and settled on benches and seats to admire the heart of the house. A very well-behaved young Thomas dragged one of the young men of the party over to the great fireplace and showed him the chimney and the sky visible at the top. It was the first time many of them had seen the newly installed roof bosses and they craned their necks to admire them, identifying those they recognised and asking about the others. The crispness of the carving was amazing, making the designs stand out so clearly. Lord Hesketh explained the significance of the arms of the Derby family and proclaimed the Tudor rose to be the work of a master craftsman sent from Whalley Abbey. He did not, however, tell them of the drama which had so recently taken place directly underneath it. That was something which would be better forgotten. He did not want the taint of death to spoil his masterpiece.

The great screen came under intense scrutiny and all declared that they had never seen its like anywhere else. They touched the crisp carvings, peered up at the unusual speres and agreed that the masks of their sovereign and his queen was a splendid idea, just what Lord Hesketh had expected.

Abel and his workmen had been watching all this activity from a distance, amused at the comments they overheard and pleased that everything seemed to meet with approval.

'Too late now if they don't like it,' murmured Alfred.

'Hush, someone's coming over,' hissed Cuthbert, as a young squire approached.

'His lordship asks that all involved in the construction of the hall come before him in the Great Hall,' he pronounced, turned and led the way back, clearly expecting them to follow.

'Best obey his lordship, then,' said Abel, and took his men up the steps and in through the main door. Lord Hesketh beckoned them forward and they stood before him where he sat on the bench behind the table at the western end.

'Abel Carter I commend you for the fine work you have done here in building my marvellous new home. I have never seen such craftsmanship.' He gestured around the Hall, a beaming smile upon his face. 'This will be a fitting home for my family for many generations.'

'Thank you, my lord,' replied Abel, touching his forelock in respect. 'We are pleased that it is to your satisfaction.'

'It is most definitely. The funds I put at your disposal were sufficient for the work?'

'Yes, certainly, and I was able to take on some extra men when we needed to complete the roof before winter. Is there anything else you require us to do?'

'Ah, now there is a question.' He looked towards his wife. 'I believe my good lady has some small requests to make, for additional furniture mainly, but it would not require all your men to complete the work so I have a proposal to put to you. I wish to retain the services of a small number of men, maybe three or four to work for me and for the estate. Initially there will be these extra commissions from my wife but thereafter I intend to keep a small permanent number to handle maintenance of this and all my tenants properties hereabouts. There are several farms and cottages which require work. They will be paid from my estate and a cottage will be made available for their use. The woodman, Ezekial, is already employed by the estate so he will be your source of timber for any work undertaken. Would you be prepared to let such men remain here for the foreseeable future?'

Abel looked surprised. It was an unusual request but, on second thoughts, not impossible. Some of his men were bound to him as they were still working their apprenticeship, but the others were free to go where they chose.

'I would be willing to agree to your request,' he said, after a few moments, 'but I would like to consult them first.'

'There is one other request I make, in fact, I insist upon.' He looked across to Cuthbert. 'There is one man I would insist stays here and that is Cuthbert Watts.'

Cuthbert gasped. Why would he want him particularly? Abel looked as surprised but before he could speak, Lord Hesketh went on.

'Cuthbert came to you on the recommendation of Lord Derby after he had seen his work at Whalley Abbey. Whilst he has been here he has produced some exceptional carvings, I have seen them all over the house and there is nothing to compare with them in any other property which I have had the pleasure of visiting. Both Lord Derby and I would like Cuthbert to make some special commissions for both of us, for our homes and for various religious houses which we support. There are gifts we wish to be made for prominent people with whom we are acquainted, gifts which we feel only Cuthbert can produce. Both Lord Derby and I attend the Royal Court when we are summoned and work from the hand of Cuthbert would be most acceptable to such people. I will name no names but do I make myself clear?' He raised an eyebrow as he asked the question and all understood exactly what he meant. Royal gifts, no less.

Abel gaped at the request, opening and closing his mouth as he tried to think of a suitable reply. Lord Hesketh laughed and slapped his thigh in mirth.

'I see I have surprised you,' he cried. 'That is probably the last thing you expected me to say, eh? Come now, what do you say?'

'It would be a great honour for Cuthbert to do such work,' he managed at last. 'I always knew he was an exceptional craftsman and that he would go far, but the Royal Court?'

'Hush, hush. We don't spread abroad such things, some would say we were trying to buy Royal favours but a gift here and there would be appreciated. So, what does Cuthbert say?'

'I would be honoured, my lord,' replied Cuthbert.

'Very good. I leave my steward to agree the arrangements and enter the names on the estate workers roll. Now, I would like to have a private word with Cuthbert. Young man, come with me to the room I have chosen to be my place of business.'

He made his way out from behind the table and left by one of the doors into the west wing, Cuthbert following. They mounted the stairs to the first floor and went into a moderately sized room with a south facing window where a large table and two benches had been placed. Lord Hesketh closed the door and sat on one of the benches, gesturing to Cuthbert to sit opposite to him.

'It has come to my notice that there has been some trouble here during the last week. A young woman, the woman you were about to marry, was abducted, a man was murdered and the murderer cornered and died by his own hand. Is that so?'

'Yes, my lord. That is so.'

'Is the young woman in question all right? Was she harmed? In any way?'

Cuthbert knew exactly what he was being asked; had Jennet been raped by the man?

'She is well, apart from a few cuts and scratches. She was greatly shocked but is glad to be free once more and back with her family.'

'That is good. Now I want to hear the precise circumstances from your lips. I have been fed rumours and gossip but I want to hear the truth.'

So, for the next half an hour Cuthbert related exactly what had happened from the day that Will had left Rufford including all the attempts to damage and even burn down the hall. Lord Hesketh was a good listener and did not interrupt until the tale was told. Cuthbert left nothing out as he did not want his new master to fill any gaps with the false rumours he had heard.

Lord Hesketh betrayed nothing in his face until the tale was finished when he sat back and contemplated Cuthbert.'

'You are an honest man. I believe every word you have said and I am truly sorry for the trials that man brought upon you and all here. Your conduct throughout has been exactly what I would expect from what Lord Derby told me of you. I had already decided I wanted you to work for the estate before I heard all this and I am only confirmed in the wisdom of my choice. It is seldom that I have come to owe so much to a humble craftsman but not only did you save the life of my son and heir but my house as well. I know what it is to struggle as a young man, my father's family rejected me from birth, but I have triumphed over adversity and so will you. From this day forward I will be watching your progress with great interest and I believe you will go far.' He stood up and came round the table. 'Come we will return to the hall and this conversation will remain privately between us.' He looked at Cuthbert for confirmation of this and at his nod, he turned to the door, saying with a twinkle in his eye, 'Let us go and see what my Lady has decided she needs for her comfort in her new home. Be ready when you marry your girl for her to always find something else she needs. It is the way of women, I find.'

Cuthbert followed him down the stairs and into the Great Hall. Abel and his men had left, some of the gentlemen also, but the ladies were walking about the Hall imagining it furnished and lit by candles and the firelight.

'Grace, my dear, Cuthbert would like to know what items you have decided you need for your greater comfort.' He gave Cuthbert a look that warned him to be prepared to indulge his wife.

Cuthbert stood before the ladies and listened as she ticked off on her fingers numerous pieces she had decided were needed, mostly additional chests for clothes or comfortable seats in her solar, a decorated box for her to store her embroidery silks, another box for the family bible and some furnishings for the little chapel. There was going to be plenty of work for him in the coming months and most of it involved his beloved carving. At last he was to be able to spend most of his time on doing the carving he loved above all else. It was turning out to be an exciting day.

As Lady Hesketh came to the end of her requirements Cuthbert felt a tug on his sleeve and looked down to see young Thomas standing patiently at his side.

'Have you made the sword you promised?' he asked in his high, piping voice.

'Thomas! What did I tell you before we came?' admonished his mother.

'Not to interrupt, not to run about and …' His brow furrowed as he tried to remember. 'not to go near the water,' he finished triumphantly, and grinned up at Cuthbert. 'You didn't say I couldn't talk to my friend Cuthbert though.'

His mother made a tut of annoyance but she was smiling at the same time.

Cuthbert crouched down by the boy and looked him in the face.

'I made you a promise, didn't I? Well, I try to keep my promises, so, if her ladyship permits,' he asked looking up at her, 'I will take you to the forge where I live and show you something.'

'Very well,' agreed Lady Hesketh, 'but stay with Cuthbert and don't run off.'

'Thank you, my lady.'

Cuthbert and the excited child left the Hall and took the short path to the forge at the end of the village. Cuthbert noticed that one of the young squires was following them at a distance, probably on her orders. Thomas chattered away as they walked.

'We are going to come and live here very soon. I will be able to watch you make all those things for my mother. Father says I will have my own pony soon and he will teach me to ride. Can you ride? I want a little brown pony like father's big horse and when I am bigger I will have a proper horse as well. I will be able to bring it here to have its shoes put on and then I can watch the smith working as well. I like horses, don't you?'

Cuthbert let the child prattle on. To think that this vibrant little life could so easily have been snuffed out that day in the Mere. What a joy he was.

On reaching the forge Cuthbert left Thomas watching Jehan at work whilst he slipped into his room at the back and returned carrying something behind his back. As soon as Thomas saw him he ran to him and jumped up and down.

'Is that it, behind your back?' he cried.

'Close your eyes,' said Cuthbert and Thomas squeezed them shut and held out his hands. Cuthbert laid the wooden sword across his arms and looped the strap of a shield over his shoulder. Thomas opened his eyes in wonder.

'A sword *and* a shield,' he cried, and waved the sword around his head.

'A soldier can't go into battle with only a sword, can he?' said Cuthbert.

'Oh, thank you, thank you, thank you' and he ran off back to the Hall with the squire in close pursuit.

Jehan laughed.

'He's a lively one, isn't he? When they finally arrive to live here I can see I am going to have to watch out for him. Have they said when they are coming?'

'Not exactly, but I do have some good news. He wants four of us to stay and work for the estate and we are to have one of the cottages to live in. We are to look after all the buildings which he owns. There will be work for years to come and there will also be work for us on Lord Derby's property.'

'That is good news!' declared Jehan. 'Just wait till I tell Liliath.'

'Can you not tell her until I've seen Jennet? She was worried that we would have to go with Abel and she would miss her sisters so much.'

'I think I can manage that.' He clapped Cuthbert on the back. 'Remember when you first arrived, Abel couldn't stand the sight of you, Will was jealous and you got all the awful, boring jobs? You didn't let any of that stop you doing your best and finally that has been recognised. Well done! What do you think Martha will think over in Chester?'

'I must try to get a message to her next time someone is going that way. She doesn't know I'm getting married yet either. I'll go and find Jennet and tell her now.'

He walked away with a smile on his face and a wonderful feeling deep inside. He was about to get married to a wonderful girl, he had work for as long as he wanted it, a home here among people he had come to love and respect and the opportunity to produce carvings that may be seen by members of the Royal Court. No wonder his footsteps were light as he headed for Ezekial's house.

Jennet and her sisters were in the garden of their house raking the soil ready for the planting of the vegetables. He stopped to watch them. What a pretty trio they were with their light auburn hair, glowing skin and soft brown eyes. Dressed in their simple dresses, tied about their waists with a fine cord, chattering away, laughing and tossing their hair he couldn't help but smile. Mary looked up and saw him, nudged Jennet and gave Cuthbert a huge grin as she and Martha went indoors, leaving Jennet and Cuthbert alone.

'Shall we walk down to the Mere?' asked Cuthbert, putting his arm about her waist and hugging her close to his side. 'I've got lots of things to tell you.'

She looked up into his face.

'Nothing bad, I hope.'

'No, why should there be anything bad?'

'After all that has happened this week I wondered, that's all, and I believe Lord Hesketh has been to see the house, too. Is everything all right?'

'Yes, fine, but let's walk.'

Arm in arm they wandered down to the shore, deliberately turning away from the scene of her abduction, and, with the water on their right, strolled along the shoreline until they came to a tree stump and sat on it, close together.

'Well, what's all this news?' she asked eagerly.

'Lord Hesketh is very pleased with the building. He and his friends looked at everything and showed their approval of all we have done. The family will be coming to live here very soon.'

'That's wonderful but I feel there is something more.'

'Abel is going to work on a house in Yorkshire which he built a few years ago and the owner wants extending.'

'Yorkshire? Does that mean we will have to go there too? 'I'll miss …'

'Slow down,' he laughed. 'Let me finish. I am not going with them.'

'What? Why? I thought Abel had accepted you.'

'He has and most of the men are going with him but a few of us aren't.'

'Where are you going then? Back to Chester?'

'No, Lord Hesketh wants four of us to stay and work for the estate. He owns lots of cottages and farms around here and they all need repairs and other work on them so we will be employed by the estate and will have work for years to come.'

'So we won't have to move away? Oh, Cuthbert, that will be marvellous! I was going to miss my mother and father, and my sisters, of course, so much if we had to go away. Now I will be able to see them every day. But where will we live? I suppose we could stay with mother and father though it will be a bit crowded.'

'There is a cottage he will let us all have for as long as we stay. It means we will have to share with the others but at least we will be together.'

'Who else is staying?'

'Probably Harry, Ben and either Alfred or Japheth. Alfred may want to stay with Abel as he's worked with him longer than the others. Could you bear to share a house with three men as well as your husband?'

'As long as you are there I am happy wherever we are.' She squeezed him tight against her. 'You have made me so happy. Oh, what's this?' She put her hand in the pocket which was squeezed between them and pulled out the little carving of the rose which he had made for her. 'My rose! This will be my lucky charm.'

'Why?'

'Because it was the first thing you made for me, and because if it hadn't fallen out of my pocket when Will took me away and Alfric hadn't stepped on it, we might not have been sitting here like this, and who knows …'

Cuthbert pulled her to him and silenced her with a kiss on the lips which she leaned into for a long moment. They parted and she gazed up into his face.

'What are you thinking about?' she asked.

'I never imagined when I left Chester that I would end up with someone like you, somewhere like this. The Abbey was as far as I expected to go. There was still so much work to do there.'

'Do you miss it?'

'Not really. I could never be a monk. Their life is so ordered and restricted and getting up during the night to go into a freezing cold church was not good. I enjoyed the work I was able to do there but this is much better, oh, and lady Hesketh has all sorts of things she wants me to make for the house which mean I will be doing far more of the carving. I can't wait to get started. I have so many ideas.' He looked out over the water. 'I have enough drawings of the animals and birds, the trees and the butterflies around here that I will have work for years.' He looked into her eyes. 'You have made me so happy. We will raise our children in a beautiful, peaceful place.'

'Children?' she asked.

'You do want children, don't you?' he asked in alarm and she laughed.

'Of course I do, lots of them.'

'Well,' he said, pulling her to her feet. 'We'd better go and get this wedding organised and tell everyone the good news.'

'What good news?'

'That we are finally getting married and we are staying here amongst our friends.'

They walked back to the village hand in hand, into their new life, happy, contented and very much in love.

Lightning Source UK Ltd.
Milton Keynes UK
UKHW040656061022
410034UK00004B/488